About the Author

Rose began her writing career relatively late in life, but she always knew that she had a book inside her. She lives in a village in the south-east of England with her two Labradors and two cats. She has experienced much in her fifty years of being, reaching the conclusion that life with all of its ups and downs is truly wonderful. Each and every day should be embraced and nurtured whilst true friends and family should be cherished.

The Oak Tree A Tale of Intertwining Lives

Rose Warren

The Oak Tree A Tale of Intertwining Lives

Olympia Publishers
London

www.olympiapublishers.com
OLYMPIA PAPERBACK EDITION

A CIP catalogue record for this title is
available from the British Library.

ISBN: 978-1-78830-956-1

This is a work of fiction.
Names, characters, places and incidents originate from the writer's
imagination. Any resemblance to actual persons, living or dead, is
purely coincidental.

First Published in 2021

Olympia Publishers
Tallis House
2 Tallis Street
London
EC4Y 0AB

Printed in Great Britain

Dedication

I would like to dedicate this book to my brilliant friend, Maria
and to my beloved pal, Mandy, who passed away too soon

Acknowledgements

My profound and sincere acknowledgements go to Sarah and Jo for being my first proof readers, to my mum who is my stalwart, my carers and to those who have supported me through, not only this process but my own trials and tribulations — you know who you are.

Prologue

Humankind, the art of being "human(e)", is measured on so many scales.

It can be said that humanity evolved from the higher apes. It can also be said that humanity came from God:

"On the sixth day...God said 'let us make man in our image, after our likeness, and let them have dominion over the fish of the sea and over the fowl of the air and over the cattle and over the earth and over every creeping thing that creepeth upon the earth.' And God created man in His own image, in the image of God He created him; both male and female He created them." (Genesis 1:26-27)

If the latter is the case, maybe the mistake was giving dominion of mankind overall. If the former is truer, maybe the problem was that the higher ape ceased to evolve over a given time, which prevented man from becoming truly human — truly humane.

Therefore, was man denied the possession of the true qualities of absolute humanness, humanity, humaneness? But that is not for me to say.

From my experience the homo sapiens has many traits, facets — indeed personalities. One single human bears so many of these yet in one living being. Each individual has qualities and deficiencies; from being, for example truly benevolent to being truly malevolent depending on the circumstance. From being utterly depressed, to totally joyous. Likewise, a single human being can, although some may refute this with some ferocity, possess both genders — male and female inside them. Not hermaphrodite but a mix of both masculine and feminine thoughts and actions, perhaps.

Homo sapiens can indeed be identified with the oak tree, as farfetched as that may sound! One individual human being has multiple facets, which some may describe as personalities or part of. This does not mean that such a person has multiple personality disorder — it simply means that individuals are capable, quite sub-consciously, of dipping in and out of these facets/parts/personalities as the occasion arises. They can indeed be "itemised" into categories which, in turn, can seem to make a whole new person.

So, to the oak tree. This tree has many uses; its wood can be used for: fuel, timber, cork and the like. It is used to build furniture, ships such as Viking longboats, barrels in which some alcohols are left to ferment, such as wines, whiskies and sherries. Its wood is also used to build magnificent buildings — indeed the House of Commons in London.

The oak's boughs are used for shade from the hot sun and shelter from the rain, for both humans and animals alike. Its fruits are a source of food for creatures, like squirrels and birds.

Another such practical use of the oak tree concerns its thick, sturdy trunk which serves as its foundation. The trunk's sturdiness raises branches and leaves high above the ground enabling the tree to overtop other plants to outcompete for sunlight. Could this be that the oak tree is a thief, at worst, or at best selfish?

The trunk also serves as a vessel, transporting nutrients and water from its roots around all the tree's parts and distributes food produced by the leaves to other parts of its form, including back way down inside the earth to its roots.

The bark, covering the trunk, is the tree's protective layer which extracts moisture and nutrients from the soil and spreads them to other parts. At the innermost core of the bark, sap, containing sugars vital to the health of the whole tree, can be found. This sap is transported to the tree's extremities. These big branches divide into smaller ones which grow shoots growing into leaves. These are arranged in spiral formations. Amongst them and the branches, fruit called acorns are born. So, here it can be said that the Oak Tree is particular about caring for itself yet the fruit it bears is food for the animals that shelter in its boughs. The moss that grows on its bark is also a source of food and water to insects.

Oak trees are monoecious, meaning that each individual tree has both male and female flowers growing upon it. The male flower consists of drooping tassels, like catkins. The female flowers are tiny catkins which contain several million grains of pollen which are distributed by the wind and when pollination is successful, adhere to the receptive stigma of female flowers. The fertilised flowers develop into acorns. Back to one human housing both genders.

The oak tree is a symbol of strength and endurance as they can live for over 1,000 years.

The oak tree is the sacred tree of Zeus as his priests made divine pronouncements of the God by interpreting the rustling of the Oak's leaves. Likewise, the Celtic God Taranis the Giant was associated with these great and giant trees.

In Biblical times, Jacob buried all the foreign gods his people had, their pagan idols and earrings, under an oak tree (Genesis 35:4). Joshua erected a stone under an oak tree as the first covenant of the Lord (Joshua 24:25–27). Isaiah 61 refers to the

Israelites as *"the Oak of righteousness"*.

Moving forward in history, the English King, Charles I, and his fellow royalists fled from Cromwell's forces and hid in an oak tree. Elizabeth I, of England, was told that it was time for her to take the English Crown under an oak tree in the grounds of Hampton court — this tree still stands tall and proud.

Mythical or historical — Robin Hood and his Band of Merry Men used oak trees as shelter in Sherwood Forest.

So, one such "simple" oak tree serves multiple purposes, and it could be said to possess multiple facets and personalities — like an individual human being. It is practical, it is strong, it is selfish, it is kind, it is a protector, it reproduces, it knows loss and death as its leaves, flowers and even individual branches may die. It knows hardships, such as cold winters and the heat of the summer sun. It endures all weathers. It must know hunger and thirst in times of drought. It knows pain, when lightning strikes or the pain of the penknife when a heart and initials are etched into its "skin". It has seen so much history in its lifetime — so much social history. I am sure it hears and keeps to itself the secrets and confessions of many. It can be said to be humane and represent justice and integrity but can also be said to be selfish and criminal. Does this remind you of some facets of yourself, of individual human beings? So many different "personalities" in one.

So, now to my story.

Book 1
Saplings

Chapter 1
The Acorns — (in a nutshell)

It could be considered strange, bordering on the transcendental, how the lives of Bodhi (meaning awakening or enlightenment), Evanna (meaning young and brave fighter) and Petra (meaning The Rock) appeared to act in complete synchronicity.

These lives may be described as having some form of "tri" aspect theory, in that each individual shared the same experiences both mentally and physically yet had somewhat different perspectives on these events and therefore acted and thought accordingly[1].

Each was born at home, on the same day, in the same month of 1970 — yet they were not triplets! Each was taken seriously ill shortly after their otherwise uneventful births and taken into hospital where they underwent numerous blood transfusions and were placed inside incubators until they were well enough to return home. The doctors told their parents that if their fragile little bodies managed to survive the jaundice, they would sadly be brain damaged.

Throughout his life, Bodhi always held the belief that whilst he lay in his incubator, smothered in his own excrement, as he enjoyed sliding down to the bottom of his glass coup which was lined with his waste, he felt the warmth of some beautiful eschatological being enveloping his tiny wrinkled body, with its

---

[1] Take on of Dual Aspect Theory: In the philosophy of the mind, dual aspect theory is that the mental and the physical material, are two aspects or perspectives of the same substance.

feathery arms, lifting him up and guiding him towards bright rays of light which would have taken him beyond this plane into the next world. Thus, Bodhi was always on a spiritual quest of finding some kind of incorporeal awakening and enlightenment. He held a romantic view of what lay beyond this life, or realm, which he called "Ataraxia" (or tranquillity)[2].

So, the three began to grow up surrounded by their parents and older siblings. There was nothing remarkable about this as it was the same as most families of that time — single-parent families were rare.

Each of their families belonged to the working-middle-class social grouping if that was an actual stratum amongst the classes. They were not affluent enough to be middle class, yet nor were they strictly blue-collar workers.

In 1974 they all moved from the home in which they were born into more sizeable ones as their maternal grandparents moved in with them. See what is meant about their mirroring lives — as if they coexist inside one body.

The joy and love they shared with their grandparents, was abundant. All children should experience this. It also proved to teach them valuable lessons in the vagaries of old age and loss.

Evanna's grandmother passed away when she was four years old. Two years later her grandfather suddenly followed suit in his sleep. These deaths hit the young Evanna hard, although she was still too much of an infant to truly understand the concept of mortality in its entirety. As she grew up into adulthood, however,

---

[2] "Unperturbness" or tranquillity, is a Greek term first used in Ancient Greek philosophy by Pyrro and subsequently by Epicurus and the Stoics, for a lucid state of robust equanimity, psychological stability and composure which is undisturbed by experience of or exposure to emotions, pain or other phenomena, that may cause others to lose the balance of their mind. So one experiences ongoing freedom from distress and worry.

this topic often took hold of her mind.

As opposed to Bodhi, Evanna had no romantic ideal of the afterlife. To her death meant death: oblivion, silence, termination, darkness, nothingness — curtains. She spent many an hour meditating on this idea as she so desperately tried to imagine this nothingness where one simply ceased to exist. Frustratingly, no matter how hard she attempted to imagine this, Evanna found it impossible to do so. She tried to visualise life before she came into being in her mother's womb, at times when she did not exist and had never done so. Sadly, she was unable to experience this lifelessness.

Evanna was a historian at heart, so as she tried to visualise and touch the blackness she was only surrounded by history, historical times and events that she had studied at school or in books — right back to the Jurassic. These events and times were compounded in her mind by her imagination as she pictured and "lived" these times, sharing such experiences with the people of that particular moment in history. She hunted mammoth and sabre-toothed tiger with cavemen; she was friends with Brutus and then one of the 5,000; she was present for the signing of the Magna Carta; she witnessed the beheading of poor Anne Boleyn. Evanna formed part of the Royalist army who fought Cromwell — the cohort who found shelter hiding in oak trees. She discovered the Americas with Columbus. She was in Sarajevo on the 28th of June 1914 and then went on to fight in the rat-ridden trenches during The Somme Offensive. She saw the rise of the Nazi Party, Italian Fascism and Japanese Militarism. She was lucky to survive the armour-piercing bomb that hit the *Arizona* in Pearl Harbour. She experienced life immediately after World War Two in all corners of the world and then how life changed, particularly in the west, when the 1960s hit. This was the decade during which she discovered music: The Rolling Stones to Pink Floyd. The year prior to her birth she attended: "an Aquarian Exposition: 3 Days of Peace and Music" in a dairy farm near White Lake in Bethel, New York — 43 miles south-west from Woodstock. Here she watched and danced to Creedence Clearwater Revival and Hendrix in a drug-induced haze.

Therefore, it became apparent to Evanna that despite this knowledge and imagination of hers she was just not able to imagine or "remember" not existing — blackness. To Evanna death was simply death, like turning off a light switch — no heaven, no afterlife — no nothing. So contrary to Bodhi's ideal.

Despite being from multi-faith and basically non-religious backgrounds Bodhi, Evanna and Petra received Catholic school education.

It could not be claimed that Bodhi was not a trier because he certainly was. He did not excel at any particular subject but enjoyed the humanities, especially English, history and religious education. Science and mathematics proved to be his nemesis. Every Sunday night he dreaded the school week ahead as he feared his French and German teachers. The butterflies in his stomach made him feel so sick. When in bed he sometimes cried himself to sleep.

Evanna was more of a sportswoman albeit of schoolgirl standard but nevertheless may have climbed to higher heights in the sporting arena as she never gave up and was determined, especially in swimming and long-distance running, if the all-girl convent school had been in any way sports minded. Taking part appeared to be the all-important agenda of any match — the winning was incidental. Needless to say, winning was a rare occurrence and 10–0 was a "*good loss*" on the netball court! Evanna, though, was fiercely competitive, becoming team captain for all of the school's sports, namely netball and hockey in the winter and rounders and tennis in the summer. In the sixth form she became the school's overall sports captain.

Petra, excepting maths, was a good all-rounder. She, like Bodhi, preferred the humanities type subjects. She was also a keen sportswoman. Every year, it seemed, she would be awarded the Best Effort Cup at the annual prizegiving — never the Academic Cup. However, she was proud of her prize as she considered that effort and endeavour were better attributes than simply being clever as when that was the case you did not need to try. Petra had got to work for her successes!

As the years wore on, Bodhi had no particular ambition to "*become*" anything. He disliked the question: "*What do you want to become when you leave school?*" He considered that he already "*was*" something, so therefore he did not need to "*become*" anyone or anything else which others considered more substantial. Furthermore, Bodhi feared leaving the confines of school. He always disliked change, no matter how small. It filled him with the utmost dread. Given the choice, he would have chosen to be a hermit surrounded by his books: poetry books, history books — each having a history of its own and such books would be old and would have "lived".

Evanna had set her sights on becoming an actress in her younger years. As a young child, she was a tomboy. She always recalled the time when she stood in her parents' bedroom, her top half naked. Her mother was sitting at her dressing table brushing her very long blonde hair. Evanna posed a question to her mother: "*Can I change my sex when I get older? Can I change into a boy?*" Her mother simply laughingly replied: "*No, darling, you are stuck as you are.*" For a few years after this, Evanna would only answer to the name "Peter" whilst at home. As time went by, she revised her acting ambitions to becoming an Olympian. She still considered that to become a boy would be the "*best thing*". She hated wearing dresses and would often develop a migraine when it came to attending her friends' birthday parties as it would mean she would have to don a party dress, possibly pink and frilly! Trousers, but preferably shorts, and a football T-shirt, were never options available to her.

Petra, on the other hand, had always been a "helper" of others: an advisor, a listener and confidante. She wanted to help people so considered going into social work, the police or even the fire or ambulance services. She even considered the armed forces.

All three were popular at school with their teachers and peers, even the reclusive Bodhi. They never struggled for friendship groups, nor were they bullied or bullies. They were all kind, polite and well-liked children but had mischievous streaks — especially the more extrovert Evanna!

At the age of 14, Petra experienced the loss of a friend. This friend did not die but emigrated to Spain with her family. However, Petra mourned this loss as though her friend had died, which pushed her into thinking about death and dying. Her view lay somewhere between the spectrum of Bodhi and Evanna's visions of death. Petra did not think about death and what that may or may not entail. Instead, she was highly pragmatic about it. She had no particular beliefs about an afterlife, being open to pretty much anything. If there was life after death, in whatever form, "*that would be good*". However, if death meant exactly that — cessation, termination, lights out — then "*that would be okay too, and so be it*".

From this brief outline — the beginnings of their lives, "*in a nutshell*" — the similarities and differences of our three protagonists can be discerned through the multiple layers of facets that each possess. However, there is one similarity — as children they were each introduced to a particular tree, The Oak Tree, which came to represent to each of them a place of safety, a retreat, a romantic spot, a confidante, a peaceful spot to shelter from the rain or the sun. The Oak Tree came to somehow represent the lives of each individual as they grew in somewhat metaphysical, abstract and profound ways. It is therefore time to explore the seeds inside the acorn; begin to strip away the many layers of bark from the trunk and investigate the roots of our respective people in greater depth before their lives reached their fruition.

Chapter 2
Saplings, Roots, Branches and Trunks

Petra's personality lay somewhere halfway between that of Bodhi and Evanna.

Petra had a difficult childhood; well, they all did, but to those on the outside it appeared to be as perfect as perfect could possibly be. From this skewed outlook, of these outsiders, those who did not share Petra's body and soul, she had two loving parents who did everything within their power to provide everything she needed and a large proportion of what she wanted (although she was never spoilt). Her sister was three years older. Like most siblings growing up together theirs was a love/hate relationship but Petra could never claim that she was not loved or came from a loving home, as strange as that may come to see, but that was not the issue.

Her parents worked so hard to provide and pay for the best education they could. Petra's mother was a good cook and every evening they would sit down as a family and enjoy their supper. Every fourth Friday evening was "Foreign Food Night" whereby one member of the family chose a country's cuisine for their mother, or wife, to cook. As she grew into adulthood, Petra could count on five fingers how often family dinners were not on the menu or indeed how often her parents argued. Every summer her father would take himself away from his gift shop, which was a place he hated with a passion; the shop, its location and its very patrons — everything he loathed, for the family's two-week summer holiday in Dorset. It often rained but that never deterred them from playing cricket on the beach, rock pooling and having their sand-encrusted ham sandwiches and barbecues whilst huddled together sheltering from the wind and rain. They did not mind. Memories were made and fun was being had.

Christmas and birthdays were always a big deal within the household. Every year her mother would organise a birthday party for Petra and her friends. As she grew older these parties, full of games, balloons and goodie bags, were changed into more grown-up dinner parties. Petra would be showered with presents at both birthdays and Christmas. Christmas was always a family affair, hosted by Petra and her nuclear family. The turkey was consistently perfect as were the roast potatoes, the pigs in blankets, the Brussel sprouts, the roasted carrots and parsnips — oh, everything. The Christmas pudding was heavily laced with brandy, whose spectacular "blue aurora" dance was oohed and aahed over as it was taken to the table in darkness, apart from the festive candles. Only once did someone choke on the sixpenny bit that had been hidden in the pudding for good luck. Next came the lavish cheeseboard, always containing a full round ripe Stilton which was Petra's favourite and then a basket full of fresh lychees to cleanse the palate. The only downside was the Christmas Cake — mixed and baked by Great-Auntie Gwen whilst being iced by Petra's mother. This cake was nicknamed, far from the ears of Auntie Gwen, as Ash Cake. On mixing she would chain smoke leaving the long ash at the end to fall into the mixture, thus becoming one with the cake. The icing, however, would be perfect! Laughter was loud and happy; wine flowed throughout. Petra and her sister were both allowed a little wine to taste from a very tender age which grew into bigger and yet bigger tastes over the years. So, a perfect family.

Throughout her earlier years, Petra attended various clubs

after school: ballet (definitely not for her!), brownies (again a big no!) and gymnastics.

Petra hated ballet and gymnastics. She did not like the leotards or tutus. The leotard, as with the pink ballet tutu, was not for her as she felt so conspicuous, embarrassed and awkward in them because of to the way they seemed to hug the outline of her body — they felt uncomfortable both physically and mentally. She felt as if naked and just not right.

Evanna hated the leotards too, and those "sports". She wanted to be able to wear her faithful T shirt and shorts like the boys but was never allowed as she was a girl — but she did not like being a girl and did not necessarily feel like one. Bodhi was so fearful that he would make a fool of himself, at such clubs and activities, that he dreaded going and cried each and every time.

As stated, Petra was not spoilt. She understood the value of hard work and of money. Her parents were not wealthy, and she saw how they struggled. The shop was never a success and she was only too aware of her father's worried and drawn face that he continually wore. The family skimmed the edges of bankruptcy although Petra was never made aware of these financial worries and struggles.

ii

Petra was a good student: polite, well behaved and popular with both staff and peers. She viewed her school as a place of safety as it was quite small both in structure and number. Plus, there was no bullying, or at least none that she saw. In short, she felt safe whilst within its grounds.

It was an all-girls convent school, run by nuns, although they were short in googol. So, her teachers were mainly of the secular variety. The school was not particularly strict as the rules were basically obeyed, although the "no sitting up the hill" rule, when the builders were in situ, was flouted and legs were parted wider than they would have been if the rule had not been put into place!

Sexual education was non-existent, unless one could count the study of the sexual life of a broad bean! Petra, therefore, was highly naïve as to sex or anything related to it.

She was popular, having a very good circle of friends. However, she always felt somewhat "different and out of place" — odd even, but she could not pinpoint as to why. She was never treated differently from anyone else but inside she knew she was. She did not understand what the butterflies in her tummy were or what the nervous excitement she felt meant when Alison Moore went over to her house, or she to hers. Petra did not get why her friends raved about Simon Le Bon, Tony Hadley, Nik Kershaw and other such "hunks" having their posters stuck to their bedroom walls. Inside, Petra could not wait to watch Cagney and Lacey all because of the very beautiful Christine Cagney who summed up what Petra admired: a strong female cop but one who struggled with personal issues such as her relationships, alcoholism and rape. Somehow, though, Cagney always managed to pull through and she always caught the "bad guy". Petra chose not to put any posters on her bedroom walls as deep inside knew that her choice of pin up: Annie Lennox, Bananarma, Rachel Ward et al would be considered weird by her friends but she did not understand why — she just knew it would be so. She did not know the words: "homosexual", "gay", "queer" or "lesbian" but looking back she realised that her friends may have had a better knowledge and understanding, albeit minimal. She knew, even back then, that she would be the butt of jokes and even bullied if she ever admitted to her preferences, so she subconsciously, and probably wisely, chose to keep this secret. At the time, she would not have been able to explain exactly why she had chosen to do so as she had no concept as to her reasoning.

Nor did she understand what she was actually doing in bed when she rubbed herself — her sexual parts. She did not know what the wonderful shuddering feeling was or what caused the wetness between her legs or that tingly sensation followed by that blissful moment of ecstasy and release. She did not know what the clitoris was but recognised that some part of her body loved to be flicked, rubbed and played with. She also knew that this part of her was not exclusive to her; someone else had access to it, but it felt so much better when she did this to herself.

Yes, she was not the only person to "play" with her sex or to even give her that feeling of utter euphoria, for which, as she grew, she was deeply ashamed. From a very early age, five in fact, she was visited at night, in her bedroom, by an adult male who at first would caress her in a very tender way; starting with massaging her head, then lightly touching her neck with his tobacco-stained fingers. He would trace these same fingers along the contours of her small body above her pyjamas. He then would tenderly kiss her on the forehead moving to her lips after which he whispered in her ear: *"Night, night, my very special little one."* Over time the touching and caressing ceased to be over her nightwear as his fingers slipped underneath. Now he would trace the shape of her naked flesh, his fingers softly moving over her yet undeveloped breasts, her stomach, then the outside and inside of her legs. Again, before he left the room, he kissed her lips gently and whispered: *"Night, night, my very special little one."*

This touching eventually progressed to the wetness that lay in between her legs, which was when she was introduced to the feeling of something — a finger entering inside her followed by the wonderful excitement she felt when her wetness was being rubbed as that "button thing" was also being toyed with. Deep down she was aware that she should not be enjoying this and that what was happening was wrong, but she trusted this man who "*loved*" her and who told her she was his "*very special little one*". As time advanced, he would couple this phrase with: "*You are so special, too special to share what we are doing with anyone.*" He warned her that he would know if she had mentioned it to anyone and would immediately have to stop even talking to her as it would mean she had betrayed his trust, his love and their special bond. To her, at this still tender age, this meant so much — to be favoured above her sister and to be considered so utterly special. "*Too special,*" he had said. So, Petra kept this secret gladly.

As the years advanced, these biweekly visits became not quite so pleasant. She found she no longer enjoyed being persuaded to reciprocate his touches. Petra did not like the feel of his hardness being pressed against her body or having to rub it up and down. Nor did she like having to lick his now throbbing hard shaft, then having to put its end into her small mouth making it go deeper and deeper as she sucked and rubbed it whilst ensuring to lick its tip when she could. She found repulsive its "explosion" of, how she described, "*the horrible tasting salty, slimy stuff*" which to her eyes was gloopy and "frogspawn-like" in texture with a whiteish colour. She despised the way it felt when it slithered down the back of her throat making her gag. Nor did she like being made to kneel down in front of him in order to perform this act or the strong clasp of his hands around the sides of her head which forced her to go deeper and deeper as she sucked and fondled his member bobbing up and down as she went until he "exploded". She did not like to hear his groans of pleasure or the shuddering of his body or how he pulled away when it had apparently finished. She was still his "*very special little one*" but now she was also something called a "*whore*" and that now she was growing up if she told a soul she would be thought "*very badly of and be hated by everyone*". He, though, so he said: "*loved*" her like "*no one else could*", so she continued to harbour this secret, albeit now reluctantly.

Bedtimes became a time of fear now as the "intimacy" began to increase in intensity and pain as he penetrated her small vagina from different angles. Petra was growing now and developing, slowly but surely. Her breasts were small yet pert and he loved biting upon and squeezing her erect nipples. To her eventual shame she found she enjoyed her wetness being licked by his knowing tongue and fondled by his fingers. She did not mind her "button" (which she now knew to be called a "clit") being flicked and pinched. Oh, how she craved his tongue licking her wet sex and her clit making her shudder and want to cry out with pure rapture and intoxication, but she was silenced by his hand over her mouth. She did not like it when he lay on top of her with his thing inside her. It hurt, especially at first, and she would cry. She often lay there crying not knowing what was expected of her. She did not feel any rapture or intoxication here. She hated the smell of his breath tainted with stale whiskey, coffee and tobacco. She abhorred the sound of his breathing becoming heavier and heavier. She despised the quivering of his hot sweaty body as he finished and withdrew. Petra found the "balloon thing" difficult to put on him despite his lessons. She wanted to scream when he took her by surprise, turned her over, entering her from behind or worse being licked around her hole, her anus, and when he forced his penis deep inside that tiny space. How that hurt — how that bled.

However, she was still his "*very special little one*" but now she was older and knew this was not normal. She was informed that no one would believe her if she should tell. She would be considered a "*liar*" and would never be believed about anything ever again. Her mother would abandon her for "*spreading such lies*" and she would be "*alone forever*". Despite now being 14 years old she continued to believe and trust this man with his "predictions". She trusted his words but now hated and feared him.

Petra could not understand why her mother allowed this to happen. She "*must know*", Petra screamed in her head — she "*MUST*". Her mother went out in the evenings, after the family supper, twice a week, which coincided with these visits, but Petra still believed that her mother simply must know. However, she had promised not to tell so continued to bear this secret — but now no longer in loving collusion but out of fear. Somehow Petra decided that she had no choice but to "go with" this process whilst wishing she wasn't but bearing it and feeling it, without passion but with stifled screams and tears. Being aware of his every thrust, every breath — her pain, everything — whilst being too fearful to do anything about it but now being fully aware, comprehending its meaning and feeling.

All those years took an immensely heavy toll on Petra. She bore them steadfastly and bravely. No one would have known the horrific secret that she hid deep inside her. Nor did they recognise the fear or the mental and physical pain that she endured yet covered up so very well.

Petra tried to tell her mother, in a brave moment, on one occasion. This was after the first time he thrust his penis hard into her anus which bled a great deal and continued to bleed and hurt the following morning. Her mother perused the site saying that everything was "*fine*" and that she had obviously started her period. Her mother gave her some sanitary towels and duly packed her off horse riding, with a friend, as planned. However, Petra did not know what a period was but years later, when she started them for real, the realisation hit her that her mother had been mistaken — or then again had she been......? Whatever had happened — whatever her mother had done, whether her mother had purposefully denied something, mistaken something or lied, proved to have a huge impact upon Petra for the rest of her life.

She failed to comprehend why her mother had failed to ask her any questions; or explained menstruation to her or even consoled her in some way. Her mother obviously had also failed to confront the perpetrator or even speak to him as he still visited — nothing changed. It was plain that he knew nothing. Petra blamed her mother far more than her abuser and always would because she should have protected her — saved her.

By the time Petra reached the sixth form at school she began to drown in pain. Finally, she realised that she could bear this no more and somehow needed to make this secret an "unsecret". Oh, but how afraid she was. Her mother and the man were highly respected within her school community. Furthermore, she had no words for what torture and terror she had endured for all these years. Two of her schoolteachers, who appeared to be friends with each other, seemed to be the best place to start. She liked them both. In hindsight, Petra's way of "outing" her secret was not the best! However, she hoped that because of what she would say she was doing was so awful and out of character these two teachers would ask her questions which would then enable her to confess the secret. Confess is the right word, as Petra felt guilty — such deeply rooted guilt about allowing what was happening in her bedroom and such guilt for betraying this man and their secret which they had shared for most of her life. So, in order to acquire this help, Petra went into her mother's kitchen one Sunday afternoon, when she was alone in the house, took some pepper, baking powder and flour from a kitchen cupboard and some silver foil from a drawer. She mixed the ingredients together to form a brownish powder and then wrapped it in the foil. Petra had no idea what heroin looked like or knew anyone that did. Nor did she know anything much about drugs. She only thought, from watching TV and films, that heroin was a brownish powdery substance that was wrapped in silver foil. She arrived at school early the next morning walking straight into the classroom where the two teachers were having their predictable morning chat over a coffee. After a great deal of stuttering and tears Petra declared that she was on heroin. She showed the teachers the wrap who then asked her for it — she duly yet unwillingly handed it over. The teachers both looked horrified, possibly out of their depth, and were silenced. Petra waited all day in anticipation. Praying that she would be sent to the headteacher's office — but nothing. Even when she arrived home — nothing. So, she went through this process several more times. Eventually, upon her arrival at home one day her mother was there waiting for her with a face of thunder. All that Petra was told was that her mother had been called into school that day to speak to Sister Josephine, the Headmistress. The nun handed Petra's mother the wraps, advising her what Petra had declared they contained and that she was an addict. Her mum was then recommended to take the wraps to the police station. She did this and was promptly given the news as to the correct ingredients. Petra's mother was beyond furious — but still no one — no one — not one single soul asked Petra why. What's more, no one ever did. In fact, it was never mentioned again, swept under the carpet as attention seeking and seemingly forgotten.

Petra's place of safety, her school, swiftly became one in which she felt vulnerable, isolated — one where she could no longer retreat or ask for help.

iii

Strangely, Bodhi went through the exact same ordeal throughout his childhood, but he did not bear things quite as well as Petra. He retreated deep inside himself preferring to consider himself invisible to the whole world. When this man entered his bedroom and forced Bodhi to perform these horrific acts, Bodhi simply closed his eyes and "vanished" from his body and mind. He went numb — blank, feeling nothing whatsoever. He too held this secret which weighed so heavily on his little shoulders. He could not find the words, any words or signs for "help".

He often wondered why no one asked him why he chose to be alone but in actual fact when he chose to do so he was crying deep inside. In order to isolate and protect himself from the outside world he built an invisible barrier between it and himself. To rid himself of the terrible images and thoughts that went through his head he made up magnificent stories of adventure, heroic white knights on white steeds who went into battle, with their gleaming swords, against their foes who had kidnapped his beautiful maiden. These were pictures he preferred to view in his mind's eye.

Evanna too had a secret of the same ilk. She, however, exhibited its effects on the outside. Her use of self-harm escalated over the years, beginning with putting toothpaste in her eyes making them red and sore but when no one questioned this she began to make small scratches on her arms. Still, no one asked her why so she kept harming herself more and more severely —

never to a life-threatening extent but enough so that people would undoubtedly see but no one actually asked her why she was doing this to herself; instead, she would just get told off.

On one occasion, she did something very different but brave. She was lying on her back in bed when this man was there. One of his hands was inside her pyjama bottoms whilst the other one was moving slowly up into the air. The feisty Evanna took immediate and opportunistic advantage of this hand in the air managing to kick it hard with her foot. When the hand hit the wall, she heard a small crack coming from it. The man was in obvious pain, but he did not utter a sound. He simply left the bedroom. A short while later her mother came into the bedroom with a red and angry face. Evanna thought: "*At last, she knows, at last it's over!*" She even felt a wave of relief and happiness in the certainty of being asked why she had acted in this way but instead she was hit by a tirade of furious words by her mother. Apparently, she had purposefully kicked this man for no apparent reason apart from "*utter nastiness*" and now her mother had to take him to hospital. When they returned two of his fingers were bound together so that they couldn't move as they were broken. Even after this, she was never asked why she had kicked out. This was not something Evanna would ever do. She was and never had been a violent child in any shape or form yet despite this no one asked her why. Instead, she was in a great deal of trouble. Evanna never regretted her actions. She always felt secretly proud and pleased with her bravery — her secret victory.

When she reached her final years of school, Evanna felt that she had no other option but to begin bunking off lessons — which was also out of character and had risks of its own. There were only three students in some of her lessons, so she would easily have been missed — but still no one asked her why. No one called home, no mention of this at parents evening or in school reports. Not even the fact that she hadn't handed in an assignment for months! The question, once again, was why did no one ask her why? Did they not care? Did they not notice? Why did she not receive any help at all?

iv

Each of them, Petra, Bodhi and Evanna, however, took comfort of sorts in a particular tree — an oak that each had known since birth.

Petra's tree stood in the middle of a copse on the outskirts of a common. Her family enjoyed many walks here alongside another family. She knew "her" tree as "The Lollipop Tree" because on such walks its branches would be adorned with the most brightly coloured sweets on sticks which the children of the group would be allowed to pick and eat on the spot. They were always in easy reach of their short arms and always their favourites. She viewed this tall, sturdy tree as her life force in a way. It held some form of continuity for her as it was always there in the exact same spot as if waiting for her. It waited for her in the rain, in the wind, in the snow, in the hot sun. It waited for her when she was in tears and needed a hug, when she needed shelter from both mankind and weather and even when she felt joy and wanted to share her news. She admired how "her" tree coped with the extremities of weather — its strength and endurance as it battled storms and said goodbye to its leaves and its inhabitants of the winged variety in the winter months. How bravely it withstood the snow. It always stood tall and proud — never seeking to complain, never a tear, but simply waited for her visit even if they were months apart as she grew into adulthood. Petra gained her strength from this tree and saw it in her mind's eye in times of need.

Like the oak tree, Petra had the ability to use the tools around her which she considered useful to her plight. Thus, she used some of the contents of her mother's kitchen cupboards which she hoped would aid her. Sadly, despite her efforts and risks taken, she was not as successful as the oak tree who uses the sunlight to keep alive. It manages to reach far higher heights than other trees and plants in order to soak up the best of that sunlight to survive. It also uses its own parts to reach its best potential: like those tall boughs, such as its strong sturdy trunk to hold those boughs aloft. It uses its own roots to transport nutrients up through its trunk into its extremities. The oak tree also makes it possible to reproduce all by itself. Maybe Petra should have taken notice of this and used her own attributes to seek the help she needed to protect herself.

Through his reading of history and myths, Bodhi discovered such marvels about oak trees in general; how they sheltered outlaws and others fleeing for their lives in times of battle. He pretended that he too was being sheltered and protected by these mighty trees and their big sturdy branches. He conjured up some remarkable tales of his own in which he starred as the protagonist who needed a night's shelter or a hiding place where he knew he would be safe and kept warm and fed.

Bodhi withstood his pain deep inside never mentioning it to anyone. The oak tree, too, withheld its pain. The pain of sharp knives etching hearts into its flesh, the cold, the heat, the wind and the rain. Like Bodhi, the oak never made a sound or a complaint, not even when its own leaves were being wrenched from its branches or when the branches themselves were ripped from its mainframe.

Like Petra, who felt different because of the confusion as to her sexuality, Bodhi also felt different. He was always anxious, insecure and afraid. He saw that his friends were carefree. Given a choice he would isolate himself but he just felt too guilty if he did so. Bodhi felt, needless to say, guilt about everything he said and everything he did.

Evanna also took courage from an oak tree which was in view of her bedroom window as if it stood there only for her. She watched how it changed in appearance according to the season and admired its high branches, its thick trunk and how it proudly stationed itself towering over smaller trees and plants to get more than its fair share of sunlight. She admired how it was able to protect itself, something she was not able to do for herself but desperately endeavoured to do. She also saw, on the contrary, how this tree fed and willingly gave up its boughs as homes to other creatures.

As an oak tree, in effect, possessed two genders within it through having both male and female flowers, Evanna felt an affinity with such a tree. She felt that she also possessed these two sexes within her body, but the male gender screamed out to be the more dominant of the two if not the only one. Evanna identified so much more with boys: their bodies, their hobbies, their toys, their thoughts. The way they argued made so much more sense to her than that of the scorned female friend. She did not make a "good" girl. She felt awkward in feminine clothing even as she got older. She wanted a more "male" career — she wanted, in essence, to be a boy. She felt "wrong" inside her own body and often wondered whether she was inside the right one according to the gender she was assigned at birth. Nowadays she would, perhaps, be considered transgender but perhaps that is too big a diagnosis for Evanna.

So, all three children felt different from their peers but in differing ways. But they all looked to "their" oaks as some form of ballast. They anchored these three individuals, as they indeed had anchors of their own — in their roots.

Chapter 3
Dispersing the Acorn's Seeds

Despite all that was going on in the lives of our three now seventeen-year-olds, it was time for them to consider their future.

Each was keen to leave home, for obvious reasons, but each was nervous for reasons individual to them. This rationality may sound curious but nevertheless it was so. Each may have been fully capable of becoming students at university, but they rejected this form of higher education.

i Bodhi

Bodhi was the one who found any form of change almost impossible to cope with.

He was a quiet believer in justice. Quiet because he was not a "shouter", but he firmly believed in integrity and justness. He also believed in forgiveness. He hoped that people would receive their rightful redemptive justice at the Gates of God, whichever god that individual believed in.

As a very young child he sat on the driveway and cried such bitterly sad tears as the removal men had finished loading up the contents of his family home awaiting instructions to drive it to their new one. Bodhi did not want to get into the car. He did not want to leave his home of four years where he had literally been born and had then later made friends with his neighbours. He was so scared but was not exactly certain why. He just felt such a huge loss. Similarly, he felt the same loss when, now established in his new home aged about ten, on the day the old faithful cooker was about to be taken away and replaced with a new and more modern one. For some reason, he considered this old cooker to be almost like a friend and he again cried bitter tears as he just could not bear for it to be dumped, to be all by itself and lonely. To Bodhi, this piece of kitchen equipment had real feelings and would feel the same sense of loss as Bodhi felt. In order to appease her son, and in an effort to stop the noise of his tears, Bodhi's mother removed a small black cooker knob and gave it to him to keep. *"This way,"* she told him, *"the cooker will always be with you!"* Bodhi felt a bit better after that and kept that knob with him, in his pocket, for years ahead.

Now, in his eighteenth year, Bodhi had been told by his teachers and his parents that he had important decisions to make that would shape his future, his entire life it seemed. His career, his life's financial future which encompassed earning enough money to make huge purchases: a house, furniture, a car. Enough money to keep a family; to pay bills; enough money to be respectable and respected. Enough for his retirement and old age. Enough money for his funeral! This would inevitably lead to a happy life!

His friends were busy attending university open days but although Bodhi was very capable of obtaining an excellent degree, Bodhi did not wish to do so.

In short, he felt completely overwhelmed. He wanted to remain cocooned in his own self-made bubble which he felt was about to burst. In his mind's desire Bodhi wanted to hide away in a hut halfway up a mountainside or in a hideout inside an oak tree where he could dream of fighting dragons; dream of saving the world against dark forces.

Bodhi loved animals more than people, whom he actually loathed. Maybe, he thought, he could befriend the forest creatures who could teach him "the ways of the forest"; what was safe to eat; how to make fire; how to survive the weather...

Or perhaps he could dive into the clearest, bluest ocean, filling up his lungs with oxygen until they were fit to burst and live on the ocean's bottom. He imagined himself swimming in the water's depths, amongst its wondrous inhabitants, forever. Riding on the backs of dolphin and whale; playing castanets with crab and lobster; serenading mermaids alongside seahorses — he on the violin, they on the piccolo. But this was not meant to be either.

He thought about becoming a nomad in the desert where he believed he would learn the art of alchemy and see each and every individual molecule of sand in the greatest of detail. A place where he could gaze up and talk with the stars and the man in the moon. A place where he would tame arachnids and rattlesnakes; where it would be possible to learn how to survive the extreme polarities of weather — from the scorching heat and sunlight of the day to the freezing moonlit nights. A place where he would, undoubtedly, become lost but never be scared as his senses would inevitably lead him to an oasis housing a Bedouin tribe where he would be welcomed, at first with suspicion but then with glee, as he was an Englishman, and he would fall in love with a beautiful girl who would gladly follow him back into the desert. No, that wasn't open to him either.

He considered pilgrimages to Machu Picchu, Santiago De Compostela, Mecca, Jerusalem, Lourdes. On these travels he believed he would learn all that there was to learn about life, philosophy, God, death, the secrets of the world, the universe, of the meaning of life and existence. How could he begin to tell his parents of this dream?

He considered going to Rwanda or maybe Ethiopia to help

their victims of war and of famine. Those who had witnessed the most horrendous atrocities that had been inflicted on their friends and their families: their grandparents, their parents, their siblings…He was not brave enough to go ahead with this.

Basically, Bodhi wanted to disappear far away — to disperse from his family and from life altogether. He wanted to experience spirituality in all of its forms, meanings and depths. He wanted an awakening, to be enlightened as his name suggested. He did not believe in money, material possessions or wealth. He did not believe in settling down in the conventional sense with all of its trappings. He feared the responsibility of a family in case he failed them. Bodhi was scared of failure but mostly of failing others. He was scared of letting his parents and teachers down, which he knew he would, if he did not adhere to the decisions they made for him.

Bodhi was also scared of himself, of his abilities, of being rejected, disliked, of making the wrong choices. His mother had often called him "*stupid*" especially when his opinions, thoughts, beliefs and preferences differed from hers. He sometimes wondered if they were stupid and as a result was never confident about those, he professed out loud, so he kept them to himself mostly. This was sad as Bodhi possessed exceptional intelligence and formed brilliant opinions and thoughts about a wide range of topics, which needed to be heard.

He was desperate to find the meaning of life, that not only of his own existence but of all existence. He considered that the "secret" could be discovered "in the ancients" but lacked the courage to go out and find it. He was scared that he would probably go to his grave without ever attaining this wish. He hoped he would find it on the "other side" which made him feel safe and secure but also saddened him as he wanted to be able to have the ability to pass on this knowledge to others with a similar desire. He did not want any glory. He did not wish to do this in a messianic/prophetic way. He simply wished to share his knowledge with others as a nameless passer-by — as a "no one". Would he ever find the solutions or answers to life's ultimate questions whilst he was alive?

Bodhi considered himself asexual. He had never been sexually attracted to anyone and did not desire any form of sexual activity. Yet, he was a hopeless romantic. He believed in monogamy, in love and love at first sight. He wished to fall in love and settle down with a "best friend". He was not at all confused by this. He felt comfortable. He did, however, desire a family. He desired family unity and love. Not the kind of love he had experienced but real unconditional love. He wished he had had that as a child in the form that "outsiders" thought he had.

He especially loved a clear night's sky. He used to sneak outside in the dead of night in order to look in awe and wonder at the vastness of the skies overhead; its infinity, its limitless number of stars. He would stare up and higher still, beyond these stars, losing himself in the ethereal heavens above.

He often considered taking himself off to an open countryside clearing, with a stash of tablets and whiskey which he would slowly swallow. Then laying himself down on the dewy night-time grass he would feel totally at one with what sparkled and shone above him in the sky. He would then gently slip away and rise upwards — his perfect death, or one of them. Despite accepting that perfection was unattainable he was able to fantasise about it.

His other "perfect death" would be walking into the depths of the night-time sea or maybe a freshwater lake until he could no longer reach the sandy, or stony, floor with his feet. Here he would float, on his back stargazing, until he was ready to give himself up to the waters' depths. Slowly, he would sink — now it would be daybreak — the sun just rising. He would view the beauty, tranquillity and silence of these depths; the reflection of the sunlight and shadows on the surface up above and the colours underneath. He would be as naked as he was born underneath these warm waters where he would feel safe, secure — at home finally. It would be like a beautiful cathedral where he could not breathe. He would remain there anticipating the moment that would shortly come, when he would be reunited with those whom he had loved but who had gone: his grandparents, his Auntie Ruby, his dog. All stars, in the sky, were to Bodhi the bright souls of the dear departed. He believed he would be with these beloved beings for all eternity in a place where he would want for nothing as he would have found love, kindness, warmth and peace. Where his questions would be answered, and he would finally be fulfilled.

If these two scenarios were ever to occur or if he should die by his own hand in some other form, Bodhi did not consider that he would be giving up. He would merely be giving in. He knew the immense difference between the two but acknowledged that no one else would.

All this, he had thought and had even planned in his head, but as to his practical and actual reality concerning his future, he had no clue.

ii <u>Evanna</u>

Evanna also felt some form of trepidation about leaving the confines of her school environment but refused to wear this on her sleeve. She was one of life's brave fighters. Evanna was far from a dreamer.

She had begun to feel more secure with her sexuality and gender identity. She wished to be strong in both her body and her mind. Thus, she aimed to have the physical strength of a male, although she recognised, she would never be the strongest male! She wanted to be able to protect herself physically should the need arise and to be reassured that she had that strength and knowledge. She never wished to have to ask a man for his physical strength if she was too weak to lift something, for example. She had no hatred for men; indeed, she preferred male company to that of females. For her mind she desired the strength of a woman. She believed that the female gender possessed greater practical common sense, knowledge and the strength of mind to combat and overcome difficulties rather than use brute force.

Evanna was ambivalent when it came to relationships and settling down. She was too young to really think about this but when she did, she saw herself having a female partner, probably, but did not think she was ever meant to actually live with anyone.

It was time for her to plan for her next stage on life's journey but what would that be?

As a realistic and a pragmatic one at that she did not "waste" time, by thinking about higher realms or unrealistic lives, when she was ploughing through the numerous careers' booklets. The nearest she came to asking any of the ultimate questions of life was: "*Is there anything better than existence?*" Evanna hesitated, when she found this answer forming word by word in her mind: "*Is there?*" Her immediate answer to herself was: "*Yes, there has to be — anything has to better than THIS. Even lying dead in a wooden box far underneath the cemetery's soil whilst worms eat you. Or being cast into a burning oven in the crematorium's fires. Both of these things meant you were dead — that had to be better, right?*" However, after a few brief seconds, she decided that actually the answer was: "*No, for the moment there is nothing better than existence*" as this meant she could fight for some form of justice for herself but definitely for others. Not only that; life was full of possibilities.

As she perused the many careers brochures that had been given to all the pupils in her class by Sister Emmanuelle, she realised that all of the so-called "careers" advertised were purely for what she considered to be "jobs for girls". She did not want to become a secretary, a beautician or a seamstress. Not that there was anything wrong with those choices, but they were simply not designed for her. She wanted to get her hands dirty, to wrestle with justice and to be someone who not only had the ability to change lives but to actually do so. She wanted to be an inspiration to others, both male and female, and to right wrongs.

Evanna noted down her qualities. At the very top lay her athleticism. She had begun cross-country running and weight training discovering she was good at both. She had always been fascinated by the human form, primarily the muscular, athletic, well-formed male and female body. She understood the effort and dedication it took to sculpt these bodies to perfection and to excel at one's sport. This was not about body builders per se but about track and field athletes, triathletes, swimmers, judo players. She admired the strength of mind and body, the courage and drive, the will to be the best — to achieve greatness. Evanna had studied *Twelfth Night* for her English Literature O Level. She had to memorise several quotes for her exam, some of which remained in her head. One of these passages was:

"*Some are born great; some achieve greatness and some have greatness thrust upon 'em.*" (1)

Evanna certainly did not consider that she had been born

great; maybe that was reserved for the elite. Nor did she think greatness would ever be thrust upon her seemingly without knowing it! She wanted to achieve her greatness in whatever form that would come. She knew that she had the will and the drive to achieve this and to battle against the odds to succeed and be great, as she was a young and brave fighter as her name suggested — but in which particular arena she was unsure.

iii Petra

Petra was not bothered really about leaving school. She no longer viewed it as a safe haven, yet it was what she had "known" for her life thus far minus four years. It had been a constant round: the journey there and back (a quick five-minute drive or a 20-minute slow walk), the terrible uniform that students from the local schools laughed at and teased the Catholic School Girls on their walk home! The girls did not mind, they knew their red and white stripped blazers with matching ties resembled tubes of toothpaste and they knew most of their "taunters" as friends outside school. She loved the actual school building which was built in the shape of an old sea ship, as it had been built by an admiral for his beloved wife in the 18th century and as a consequence was a Grade 1 listed building. She loved the school's grounds with its orchard. She had grown up with the majority of her teachers, most of whom she liked. She would miss some of them, especially one female teacher on whom she had developed a crush, and how she would miss Alison Moore! She would miss the structure of the school day. But there would be other buildings, other structures, other crushes and other Alison Moores.

She knew it was nearly time to leave school — it was the outside world she feared more than the fruition of her school years. None of her friends spoke of similar concerns. They all seemed excited at the prospect of entering the big wide world. Most had decided on university, but Petra wanted something different for herself but remained unsure as to what that exactly entailed.

She did know that she wanted to help other people in some capacity. She craved to do so in a form she had yet to receive herself. She despised injustice and considered herself a good advocate and mentor. In her final year at school, she had been appointed House Captain and as a result was given the opportunity of advocating for and mentoring those in younger year groups. This was in spite of her own difficulties that she was experiencing at the same time. She proved an excellent counsellor, excelling at listening to others and providing superb advice and empathy. Petra, however, was unable to help herself. Indeed, when she tried to, she did not do so in the right way as had been proven.

Petra was also a very good and loyal friend and was often required to lend a supportive and listening ear to her friends who sought her counsel. They called her their "Rock".

All Petra really desired was simplicity: a peaceful and quiet personal life without any drama but recognised she would thrive in a working environment where she could deal with the drama that other people found themselves in. She knew she would be able to support such folk well. She wanted to get stuck into a role that showed off her skills but also promoted a sense of possibility and hope in others. She wanted to inspire other people and to be a role model perhaps.

As regards her own life, Petra realised that at some point she would need to tell someone that she was a lesbian, although she preferred to use the term "gay". She had finally realised what her feelings towards certain other females were and what that meant but she had not told a single soul. She was not about to do so just yet either. She was not ashamed, she simply felt uneasy as to the reaction of her friends who often make snide jokes about the "lesbian" PE teacher, who turned out not to be a lesbian at all! She knew that some of her friends would fear she was attracted to them and then would be disappointed when she told them, "no". Not that they, themselves, were gay but because they would not understand how Petra, a lesbian, could not be attracted to them — surely, she would be attracted to every female that she came across!

Primarily, she feared the reaction of her parents. Mostly that of her mother who was not quiet with her thoughts and opinions. She could be cruel. Petra knew she would be told: *"Don't be so stupid"*; the *"it's just a phase"* line and the *"how dirty and disgusting"* tack when her mother came to realise it may not be a phase. Petra would be surprised if her father had any reaction whatsoever. He never really said that much, never voicing his opinion. In fact, he hardly said anything of importance or thoughtful, hateful or kind at all.

iv **The Oak Tree**

So, our three had very important decisions to make about their future.

The fearful Bodhi faced so many challenges. The huge changes that he was being forced to make in his life, for his life, made him feel totally crippled. At times when things became too much for him, he would retreat into himself, closing his eyes in order to try to block everything out: the world around him, every person, every sight, every sound, everything. Whilst doing so he pictured his oak tree in his mind's eye. Sometimes it proved difficult to concentrate but he had established and practised a method of grounding himself by breathing in and out slowly and deeply counting every breath. Whilst doing so the tree would begin to appear, first, in a misty haze far in the distance but gradually there it would be standing tall and proud in all of its glory in front of him. He viewed himself as this tree's roots buried far beneath the earth feeling cool from the soil that lay on top. He was not scared about being buried as these roots were the tree's life source — feeding it and supplying it with water. As the roots fed the tree, they also fed themselves. It came to Bodhi that the roots were the first part of the tree to be given this life source; in doing so did they feed themselves the part with the best nutrients? If so, he was well placed to remain there — as a root being fed and watered, hidden from the world, until he felt strong enough to stop being the person he had been and to become the person he was meant to be.

The roots were the foundations of the tree and he hoped to feel that he would reach the foundation of his life. At this point he would climb higher up the tree. Deep down he wished he could be the highest bough surveying all that surrounds it for miles around. It had the best vantage point to survey its estate and was best placed to be warned of any foes or danger that may approach. Yet it was also best appointed to admire the view and to feel the elements, thus with that to feel life. Bodhi wanted to feel life — he just feared doing so.

Evanna was courageous but she had yet to appreciate this. She continued to view her oak tree from her bedroom window. She loved everything about this mighty tree. Evanna spent a great deal of her time in deep thought considering what part of the tree she would be at this particular juncture of her life. Evanna decided that she would be a leaf on one of the lower branches where there wasn't too far to fall. When it was time for that leaf to fly, the wind would take it. At times it would just fall to the ground and wait for the wind when it would swirl around on the windy currents without a clue where it was to land or what adventures it would have on its way. The leaf may look frail but as it tossed, turned and fought with the wind, falling, landing and later taking off again it would gather strength and see the world around it even if in mere glimpses. It may look weak and inconsequential on the outside but on the inside housed a stronger braver soul. Evanna wished she could be that leaf — perhaps she was, she thought!

Evanna wanted to truly be and feel alive before she died. Deep down she believed that she would live that life — that fulfilling adventurous life, seeing sights that not many see.

Petra felt tentative about the changes ahead. Now she was old enough she would take her dog out for a walk, on her own, in the common with one destination in mind — her Lollipop Tree, her oak tree. No matter the weather she and Rupert, her white West Highland terrier, would playfully walk and run to this tree. Rupert knew the way off by heart. When they reached it, Petra would feel totally at peace and free, happy and reassured that there it still stood after all these years. On the more clement days she would sit down in between the tree's thick roots, those that had unearthed themselves in part, and lean her back against the bottom part of the trunk. There she sat examining the moss-encrusted gnarled roots which Rupert skipped and ran around until he tired and lay beside her with his head in her lap.

She bravely decided that she would be the trunk holding up the rest of the tree, supporting its whole frame. How strong and powerful it was! Nutrients also flowed through it to every part of the tree, so it also gave life. With a few strikes of his axe a woodcutter could fell this tree in two leaving the wreckage on the ground. The woodcutter was the tree's main predator. Yes, Petra was strong and was able to support herself in every way, but she also knew that it would not take much for someone or something to tear her in two and there she would be lying next to the remnants of the oak on the ground. However, she wanted to live a little before she was taken and ripped apart (as she imagined would happen eventually). She wanted to help, support and be a rock to others as the trunk was to the tree.

Chapter 4
Planted Seeds

A Levels had finally been sat, which could only mean one thing — school days were finally reaching their fruition with mere weeks to go.

Bodhi, Evanna and Petra were all caught up with the general wave of furore that this elicited in their peers. Lessons had finished yet 100% attendance was still mandatory, which meant that the students had a great deal of free time to use, although it was expected that they mentor and aid the younger years with their studies. With this free time came long hot sunny days with which to soak up the summer sun, break school rules and play tricks on pupils and staff alike, all in good humour, of course. Alongside this lay universal, yet commonplace for students of that age, feelings of utter glee mixed with trepidation and concern.

Most had achieved some form of place at university or an alternative higher educative establishment.

However, Evanna and Petra had other well-laid plans afoot whilst Bodhi's future still hung in the balance.

i Evanna

After reading through the numerous careers brochures and leaflets that had been thrust upon her, Evanna grew steadily irritated with her lot — her lot as a female! Where were all the glossy brochures of exciting careers that suited a female of her personality and wanting? She was more than aware that the nuns only "advertised" the stereotypical jobs that they considered to be ladylike. Note the word "jobs" as opposed to "career". For these Dominican Sisters the role of a woman was to meet a man of good breeding who possessed religiosity and community zeal, who held down a safe yet prodigious career and one whom the girl's family would welcome into their fold as they knew their daughter would want for nothing and be well cared for materially if not emotionally. The couple would "court", become engaged, marry, move into their new home together, begin to procreate and have children (in that very order) whom the wife, now mother, would love, nurture and bring up (basically single-handedly) in the same vein as her husband when a child himself. The wife had vowed to remain obedient and faithful to her husband, thus she would be throughout, whereas if the man should stray or lift a hand to her, she should not make a fuss as divorce was not ever, not in any circumstance, an option. She would be expected to relinquish her "little" administrative or retail job as soon as she had wed in order to fulfil her duties as a wife, then as a mother. All this despite having obtained a good university degree which would now go to waste.

Some of Evanna's peers were happy with this path that had been paved for them. They viewed their three or four years away at university as their last "brouhaha" before they donned an apron or if they were "good" wives their recently gifted diamonds, but faux ones would be fine providing they received the real thing at Christmas. Others, who were not in the same financial league as the "gem getters", knew that they would never be on the receiving end of such opulence if their mothers were anything to go by, and simply accepted their lot. This necessarily entailed being a good wife and mother, attend church every Sunday, perform all wifely duties and if lucky one may be awarded a new floor mop as a surprise gift!

Suffice to say, Evanna was not and would never be content with either style of life. Frailty, she decided, was definitely never going to be the woman she would become. It was her belief that: *"frailty thy name is woman"* (1), as Hamlet denounced all womankind, to be was simply an aberration of thought in Hamlet's (or should it be Shakespeare's) world view and she was certainly never going to condescend to anyone who tells her: *"Get thee to a nunnery"* (2) because of the fickleness of all women in order to preserve her chastity and cause the least amount of damage or on the opposite scale to join a brothel through her being not chaste enough (whichever meaning Shakespeare had in mind). Evanna was no Ophelia!

So, as was her wont, Evanna went against the norm, such as that was from the Sisters' viewpoint. Her immediate consideration was to find herself not only an exciting, physical, demanding, fulfilling career but one where she felt that she was truly changing lives (including her own). This, she knew, involved supporting others whilst making a positive impact on her environs and which took her away from home (if not all that far).

Evanna was keen to become as successful as she could be in a male-dominated world of work — to prove a point (mainly to herself) that she could keep up with and even beat the "best" and the "strongest" colleague. Her reasoning for this was twofold. First up was that after her childhood, where she was repeatedly made weak and vulnerable, she made the very marked decision never ever to be *"that"* person again. Secondly, Evanna aspired to reach her nonpareil potential.

She deliberated over joining the military, primarily the Royal Navy, as that would certainly take her away from home. However, she reckoned that in spite of the Navy's supreme role of protecting Queen, Country and their Waters — keeping them free from invading armadas, aiding other countries in times of need and even perhaps going to war, the Navy was maybe not for her.

She was alive on April 2, 1982 when the British armed forces fought to defend the Falkland Islands against the Argentines. Evanna knew that, from the British perspective, this conflict was predominately a naval campaign comprising a large task force of vessels. Evanna was in full knowledge that she might die for said Queen and Country and indeed was willing to do so. During the Falklands War six Royal Naval ships were sunk and the brave lives of 88 Royal Naval seamen, eight members of the Royal Naval Auxiliary Fleet, 27 Royal Marines, eight Merchant Navy sailors and one RAF officer aboard these vessels were lost — killed.

She did aspire to be amongst and considered to be one of the courageous and was willing to make sacrifices, even of her life, whilst endeavouring to set this feat, but at the same time she wanted to connect with and have rapport with individuals and their daily lives. She had visions of making a difference to these people and to fight for and protect them. She wished to right wrongs and to fight for justice for those that needed it. Thus, the Navy, which protected and supported at a distance and as a whole was not the career for her. She realised that opposed to her want of making a tangible difference to tangible individuals she would be making an intangible difference to intangible strangers whom she would probably never meet, let alone know their names.

A spark suddenly brightly shone a radiant light in her mind. There the answer was! It lay right there in front of her! Evanna would, of course, join the police — the Metropolitan Police Force (as it was known in 1988 as opposed to Service) naturally!

ii <u>Petra</u>

Petra knew where her vocation lay. She just did not know in which particular sector. She had only ever wanted to help, support and empower others; to fight for other people's basic human rights, welfare and justice — to fight against any injustices done to them. She wanted to be an advocate, a supporter, an enabler, to help others become independent where they lacked independence, to help them in times of need and strife. She wished to provide for such people a service that was a) non-judgemental and b) person centred. Above all she wanted people to feel believed and listened to by her and not to ignore cries for help, no matter in what form those cries came.

Petra was aware that her strengths lay in helping children. She considered entering the social services. As she kept herself abreast of news, politics and general current (and not so current) affairs she had no little knowledge of the previous two decades comprising feminist campaigning which had managed to bring childhood physical and sexual abuse to the forefront in various professions, including the social services. However, as she was also aware that public support for any social work intervention was extremely low after the Cleveland scandal of 1987-1988 during which it was concluded that 94 out of 121 children had been removed from their families incorrectly, being finally returned but not without unnecessary trauma to both child and family, she began to have doubts. As the huge media coverage caused outrage and criticism from the general public towards the social services Petra concluded that she did not want to be part of a "body" that no one supported (at that time). It took her a while to reach this consensus as she also believed she could change public opinion because she was "Petra". She would not be there to blame but to find out the truth for such families and children but realised she could not change such opinion in isolation as the whole profession was viewed negatively. She did not much care for her own viewpoint as she knew that she was giving up before she had even begun — but so be it.

Petra was still in her teenage years, so reckoned that supporting those in their teens would not be something she would be able to do just at that moment but was willing to try if required. In order to gain experience, she felt there must be positions available, of a similar ilk, at the local community centre. When she investigated such roles, she discovered that a support worker, who would *"receive all the necessary training"* was required at different groups and clubs that the centre held. Groups for pregnant women, babies and toddlers, OAP lunches, coffee mornings for the local community, "soup kitchens" for the homeless and a youth club for the under 13s and another for the older teenagers. Basically, a group or club for every section of the community. Petra decided that this would provide her with a wealth of experience, a place where she could find her niche, home in on and improve upon her skills and talents. Therefore, a thoroughly good place to start.

It was a pity that this would not enable her to move out of home as the role was locally based. Nor would it provide the finances necessary. However, through having a monthly salary she would become increasingly financially independent and would also be able to save at the same time. So, she needed a bank account!

She would also become more personally independent — she was due to leave school imminently; she could drive plus had been given her mother's old beaten-up Fiat Panda! Not only this but she knew she would grow as a person — in her confidence and assertion. Moving out may take a while but not too long a while, she thought.

Now all she had to do was actually get the job!

iii Bodhi

Our poor Bodhi just had no ideas. No ideas about his immediate present, let alone his distant future. He could not even bear to consider the bits in between. Those interminable hours, days, weeks, months and those intangible years ahead. He would not allow himself to contemplate the next minute or even second.

He was practically strong-armed and frogmarched into school each day where he found himself phlegmatically sitting anaesthetised against the world around him as his noisy excitable peers planned their end of school parties, their future and, above all, the mayhem they would cause on their last ever day at school!

Bodhi could not even conjure up his tales of brave knights or his fantasies of stars and lakes. He felt nothing. It was as if he no longer cared about anything — not even his perfect death. He had no tears; he had no anger, and he felt no pain, physical or even mental. In short, Bodhi was barren.

Yes, people noticed but did they attempt to cajole him into their gay abandon or did the teachers try to instil in him a sense of confidence or even reality as regards his future — even for the next few weeks? No! To his credit, Bodhi did sit with his peers and laughed in all the right places despite not knowing why. He would also take himself off into the school library, primarily for solitude but where he also gazed at booklets that may somewhere hold the key to his tomorrows ahead — his working tomorrows that were. However, in reality, all that Bodhi was able to muster was to flick through these glossy pages — gleaning not an iota.

He was not interested in food, he was not interested in speaking or reading, imagining or dreaming. He was interested in nothing and disinterested in everything.

It is hard to pinpoint exactly what brought Bodhi to this — his years of abuse, his fear of change, his trepidation concerning his future, the loss of his friends when the majority went on their merry ways to university. Or was it a mixture of everything wrapped up in this package of emptiness and atrophy? Bodhi did not know nor did he much care.

He felt so tired — tired of everything. Exhausted of being forced to make choices, tired of the incessant excitable banter of his peers, tired of waking up each morning, tired of sleeping yet all he wished to do was sleep. Sleep and never wake up — that much Bodhi did know.

His mother was on her very last tether, it seemed, but not a word, not even an utterance or sign of upset, encouragement or understanding came from his father. Bodhi preferred his mother's angry shouting to that wall of silence.

So, was it to be that Bodhi was to leave school and go on to do nothing? That still lay heavily in the balance. It would take some miracle for the scales to measure a more positive upswing.

iv The Oak Tree

It seemed that Evanna had planted her seed — to join the police.

She had decided that as she would be moving away and would no longer be able to look out onto "her" oak tree from her bedroom window she would grow one of her very own, albeit imaginary. She would watch it grow as she grew with it. This seemed way better than looking out onto a tree that in reality did not belong to her and one that she was unable to touch.

Petra had also planted her seed and in her joy at reaching this decision after school, she walked out onto the common along with her four-legged faithful companion. As she reached the open space and approached "her" Lollipop Tree she smiled a soft, yet slightly sad smile, realising that she no longer needed it to grow sweets and lollipops but acorns, leaves and branches as it was now, they were sweet enough. She was growing up as her oak tree was forever growing in age. They had been "playmates" now for almost 18 years and as such had grown together and would continue to do so but no longer as playmates but as cherished compatriots.

Bodhi had yet to plant his seed but let us plant some for him — as one is bound to take root and grow. Let us not give up hope in him.

Although at present he was not able to reach "his" oak tree in his mind's eye he could see the dense foggy mist that enshrouded it. Bodhi knew that it was there, hiding somewhere as he was hiding. He had buried himself deep inside his entire form and mind but that dense foggy mist was bound to evaporate as Bodhi was bound to unearth himself eventually.

Chapter 5
Roots, Shoots and Broken Branches

Evanna and Petra were now in the process of planting their roots in the hope that shoots would form, and they would begin to grow in maturity, experience and in life. Each girl had a million dreams, it seemed, which they had promised themselves they would fulfil.

Evanna would become Police Commissioner because of her awesome ability to track down and apprehend the most wanted; her intricate and exhaustive investigative skills; her supreme bravery and, of course, her passion for protecting and serving the public, preventing crime, upholding the law, meeting justice and her well-accomplished adeptness of man management creating an equally passionate, driven, skilled, enthusiastic workforce whose morale could be no higher.

Her dreams also drifted to sporting prowess, her body would be a professional athlete's pipe dream, and she would flaunt her many gold medals that had been hung around her neck.

At present her dreams did not include serious relationships but her fantasies were somewhat on the erotic side!

Evanna dreamt of being the best of the best, fighting her way up the police ranks with a little fun on the side!

Petra's dreams were more "lowly". Her ambition was such that she felt she would be far more than content if she touched, changed and made a positive difference to one single person's life.

She dreamt of making a home for herself where she ruled

supreme but in a quiet, polite and easy manner. A place where those fortunate enough to be invited inside felt at home immediately. It would be her safe haven — her security blanket — the one she never had.

Petra also dreamt of having a family. A wife, possibly, although this was not legal, but a person whom she would consider to be her wife in her own right. One whom she loved beyond all measure. Children would also be part of that equation although she had no idea how that would happen — she did not fancy the "turkey baster"!

Simple dreams yet truly perfect dreams to Petra.

Did Bodhi have similar dreams? We already know that he is caught up in himself. Did he have roots to set in the earth? No, not quite. He had yet to plant a single seed.

However, Bodhi did have his "Perfect Death" and if picked apart we can see that his dreams lay in finding an awakening in himself. As he fantasised about lying in an open field or in clear waters drifting away from this finite world, whilst gazing at the infinite stars and skies above he felt at peace both with himself and whatever or whoever dwelt in the clouds and heavens above. It could be said then that actually Bodhi did dream. He dreamt of finding his peace, his tranquillity and his place on the earth and in the universe. He dreamt of finding beauty, paradise and of glimpsing a moment in time with the ancients who, he believed, held the keys to the multiple mysteries that would unlock all the doors to the questions he needed answered.

He wanted to behold all the ancient wonders and to touch history in its most classically ancient form. He wished to travel to all the far-flung hidden places that he hungered to visit. Bodhi's enlightenment would guide him through his life. Bodhi the neophyte to his docent.

Did our three achieve their dreams? If so, how did they arrive at them? If not — why? What happened along their paths?

Did Evanna reach the highest of heights professionally? Was Petra able to touch the life of at least one living soul and settle down with her love? If Bodhi was ever able to plant his seed, in what form would it grow?

Seeds sown, roots set, and shoots grown, dreams dreamt (or not), this is now for us to contemplate.

i Evanna

Having researched the facts, Evanna discovered that she was too young to join the police "proper", but she could apply to join the Metropolitan Police Cadet Corps. This enabled her to transfer directly up to the Police Training School providing she successfully completed this gruelling year!

The Metropolitan Police Cadet Corps consisted of a 46-week residential course starting with a four-week induction, followed by a set of modules consisting of such things as intense physical and adventure training, drill, academic studies to do with the criminal justice system, psychology and the police in general. Each academic module concluded with an adventure training week in Derbyshire or North Wales. A Cadet was supposed to be immaculately turned out so they would be expected to be expert ironers, shoe cleaners, bed makers, wardrobe organisers among such things! It was advertised as being character building.

Evanna had all the necessary academic qualifications, was the correct weight and height. Well, almost the right height. She grew an inch when she went to be weighed and measured at the designated police station. The policeman advised her to stand on her tiptoes whilst being measured and bingo! She was 5ft 5 inches tall! She realised she would have to train herself up to reach the required physical standard but felt sure she would be able to this with some hard work.

She attended the Cadet Corps open day in Hendon with her mother. Evanna noted the smart uniforms and the mirror-like shiny shoes. She gazed in awe at the parade square which was home to the Union Jack and the Metropolitan Police Cadet Corps flag, and at that moment, some new recruits being drilled during a drill lesson.

A very confident and smart female cadet showed them around. First stop was the gym which was decorated with ropes, wall bars, mats, benches — everything that a PT session required. She was able to watch part of a lesson during which the cadets were "beasted" by a fearsome PTI who shouted and hollered at "his" exhausted looking charges, but they still managed to stand to attention when shouted at to do so. Evanna noticed that even the laces of their plimsoles were gleaming white.

They were then taken to see the assault courses which appeared terrifying in Evanna's eyes. There were two of these — one apparently low and one extremely high. Each consisted of an assortment of obstacles: scramble nets, high and low ropes, walls, planks, monkey bars and such like with only a thin layer of sand to break a fall.

The dormitories, she considered, looked frightening in themselves as the cadets had to keep them orderly — without one thing out of place. Each bed, covered with sheets and itchy looking blankets, were made exactly the same way without a crease or lump or bump. The wardrobes were all ordered correctly; each part of the uniform (which were numerous) looked ironed to perfection. Shiny bulled shoes lined the wardrobe floor. Personal items were also expected to be ironed and ordered. These wardrobes, Evanna considered, were art forms in themselves!

Each cadet that she managed to speak to oozed confidence, enthusiasm, strength and maturity, but she was warned that this course was not for the faint of heart. It was, however, an opportunity simply not to be missed.

When home, Evanna immediately filled in and posted the very detailed application form and waited an anxious age for the reply. Finally, a letter arrived inviting her to attend a three-day selection comprising PT tests, written tests, medical tests, observations in leadership and problem-solving skills and finally a formal interview with the Corps' commandant. Included, in the envelope, was a detailed list of what kit she would need to take, highlighting that all candidates would report to the Duty Inspector on such and such a day and date at no later than 17:00hrs. Any late arrivals would be dismissed immediately unless a reasonable reason was given.

Her heart beat with nervous excitement. The day arrived. Evanna's stomach was alive with zillions of very fluttery butterflies. This was her dream which she could not banish — she could not fail.

On her arrival, after she reported in as advised and her documentation was examined, a cadet led her to a six-bedded dormitory in which she would sleep for the following three nights.

The selection process proved extremely tough. On meeting the PTI all her group, including the brawny supposed "tough guys", visibly quaked in their trainers! She knew that if she did not pass one single thing, she would fail everything and not get in; thus, the lights on her dream would be out.

She found the written tests quite easy but the art of problem solving proved problematic. She also questioned herself as to whether she had led well enough when it came to her leadership skills.

She enjoyed the formal interview with the commandant who was a very measured imposing and seasoned-looking senior police officer, dressed in his full regalia. However, he proved to be an amiable and encouraging man.

Evanna did not take to sharing a dormitory with five others too well, having never had to share a bedroom before. She also found the communal showers embarrassing. Her school did not possess any showers at all, so having to be naked in front of strangers was extremely difficult.

When the selection days had finished, she was advised by a member of staff that there were 100 excellent possible recruits who excelled themselves over the last three days. There were to be five other three-day selections each with 100 young people, from all over the country, which would be completed in five weeks' time. After that a decision would be made. She was also told that there had been 2,000 applicants in total, all fighting for 21 places. He said, "*We only consider the best of the best.*" That was it. The selection was over. Evanna knew she had done her level best and more.

Once at home the anxious wait ensued. During the middle of week eight a brown envelope was posted through the letterbox landing on the doormat. Evanna rushed to it. She nervously fingered the seal of the envelope: "*Should I open it now or later?*" she thought. She could not bear to do it. The envelope was thick: "*Is that a good sign?*" she questioned. Suddenly and with a flurry she tore it open. With trembling fingers, she opened the folded bundle. Her eyes immediately averted to the Metropolitan Police Cadet Corps crest centred at the top of page 1. She found it impossible to lower her gaze to the written words but finally she caught the wording: *"I am pleased to inform you that you have been successful in all aspects..."*

This was not merely good news — it was simply the greatest news ever!

She was to join Course 40 in four weeks' time.

A highly precise kit list was provided down to how many pairs of knickers she would need! The other pages detailed other information and a few more forms.

Evanna was leaving home, but more importantly, she decided, this was the beginning of the rest of her life — her dream was becoming a reality. Now all she had to do was go up the ladder each rung at a time until she had fulfilled it. She was aware, at the back of her mind, that as time progressed more dreams would appear, but she would tackle them as she would tackle this — one step at a time but above all she would never give up.

ii <u>Petra</u>

Petra proved to have a far easier application process than Evanna.

One windy afternoon she strolled down to the Community Centre where she spoke to the member of staff on duty. She immediately recognised him! PC Mike Hamilton happened to be the home beat officer for both the centre and Petra's school, so they were already acquainted. He was off duty that day and explained that he spent a great percentage of his off-duty hours volunteering at the centre. Mike extended his welcome to Petra, who then explained her interest in the advertised role. Mike immediately invited her to join him in the office where he produced an application form which he helped her complete on the spot! He informed her that she would, no doubt whatsoever, be called in for an interview very soon.

The interview was held the very next week. Petra ensured that she dressed appropriately, not too casual yet not over the top. This was her very first interview and regardless of all the advice given to her by her parents her stomach was churning at a rate of knots and she felt sick to her toes.

She left the house in plenty of time. As it was a still, bright sunny autumnal morning she decided to take a slow walk to the community centre whereas she had originally intended to drive to save her hair from the wind, should there be any. As Petra walked, she felt as if she was taking the final steps into a chamber for her execution. She was so riddled with anxiety. Her head was continuously answering millions of questions that she would "undoubtedly" be grilled with: *"What experience do you actually have?" "Why on earth would we want to employ you?" "What do you really have to offer anyone?"* The more questions that bombarded her mind the more she was certain she would vomit. To calm her nerves, she smoked a cigarette but then freaked out as her clothing and breath would now stink of stale smoke. She dug deep into her mother's handbag that she had reluctantly agreed to use as her mother almost forced it upon her saying: *"You must make the right impression, dear."* She found the packet of Wrigley's spearmint flavoured chewing gum that she remembered popping in there before she left. As she put it in her mouth, she noted to herself: *"Please, please, spit this out before entering the bloody building!"* Petra also found some of her mother's "Poison" perfume which she, with great disdain, sprayed all over herself with no little generosity. *"Fucking marvellous!"* she cussed. *"I may not smell like an ash tray now but I sure reek of a whore house!"*

When she arrived, she was greeted by the jovial, rather stout and rotund Mike who showed her round the centre before leading her to the office where the interview was to be. On entering the room, she was equally jovially greeted by a very smiley, statuesque woman sporting a Roman nose. She introduced herself as Coral. The three of them sat down. Little did the two ladies know that they were to share a great friendship with plenty of laughter and tears over the many years to come.

The interview proved to be the complete opposite to the interrogation that Petra had envisaged. It was a most friendly chat spattered with some pertinent yet simple questions. It lasted 20 minutes. Petra was invited to wait in the cafeteria where she could get herself a drink, *"Hot or cold."* Before she knew it the two interviewers were in her sights. Both were smiling. As Mike patted Petra on the back Coral asked her when she could start. Because of Petra's rather questioning face, Mike exclaimed: *"You've got the job! Actually,"* he chuckled, *"you got it before the interview, but we had to go through the motions."* The start day of the following Monday was agreed. Petra would receive a few days training and then *"be let loose"* assisting the different and varied groups for the local community and a youth club at the weekends. Obviously, hours of work were also squared.

After a mere 45 minutes, Petra left the building and had *"only bagged"* herself the job! She felt elated as if she were walking on air. *"So, this is the start of the rest of my life,"* she whispered to herself as she almost skipped down the street grinning widely from ear to ear. She lit herself a congratulatory Silk Cut wondering how she would celebrate that evening.

iii Bodhi

Bodhi lay numb in bed. At times he slept, otherwise he merely drifted in some kind of haze. He tried his level best to ignore his mother's admonishments and remonstrations. He did not receive the encouragement, warmth, help, support or love that he so badly needed and indeed cried out for internally.

He craved his Beautiful Release. To be at one in the arms of his angel — whoever or whatever that may be. He felt as if he was sinking deeper and deeper down into his mattress; into what or where, he was unsure. He believed in God and Satan and firmly believed that Satan believed in him. However, he also believed that wherever he may be going would be better than the cold world in which he currently found himself.

He lay praying to his secret God. He prayed for an answer, for a clue as to how he could "be like Houdini" (who, of course, died whilst attempting a Great Escape of his own). Whilst sleeping he dreamt of an island in the clouds, the inhabitants of which had reached a state of Nirvana. The state that Bodhi longed for — this was his Island of Ataraxia, Awakening and Enlightenment.

He was never hungry but ate only to appease the wrath of his mother. He did not wish to wash but did so for similar reasonings. The droplets of water that fell down from the showerhead felt like shards of ice on his head, shoulders and back. They seemed to pierce his very skin. Drip, drip, drip — pierce, pierce, piercing him. He felt weak in body, mind, spirit and soul.

He cried, he slept. He felt rotten to the very core as he stagnated in his pit. He wished for and waited for a quick release but no matter how long he wished and waited that release just did not come. He lacked the energy to perform this for himself, which only exacerbated his desire. Bodhi was desperate to be lifted from the place he was in. He wished to be pulled under the undertow. He wanted to simply let go — he prayed: "*Please, please, let me go.*"

It may be possible that this lack of strength combined with the fact that his prayers were not answered served a purpose. As he continued to lie for days so infernal and countless, he slowly began to consider his life, such as it was. *"Perhaps,"* he thought, *"I need to work for my Nirvana. For my Ataraxia, for my awakening. For my enlightenment. I have to seek it out. I need to serve out my time in a way no other has served. After all,"*, he mused, *"true awakenings and enlightenments are not merely granted. They are not easily gained. They are earned."* As he lay in deep thought he considered: *"I have to plough my way through this mire, step boldly along this endless darkness before I am considered ready to reach my beloved Island of light and hope — my Ataraxia."*

Bodhi had no thoughts as to how he would overcome the darkness and emptiness that had surrounded and consumed him for such a length of time he felt unable to comprehend.

That night he began to write a letter to an anonymous reader. He wrote about his plight, about his helplessness. He wrote with solemnity about his deepest darkest thoughts and feelings. He wrote furiously about his abject hatred and fear he had for his mother and his father whom he considered as amorphous. He wrote with some trepidation concerning his desire and wishes. He wrote pages and pages almost without thought. What he did not detail was the actual abuse he had borne. After having signed his name at the fruition, being sure to plead for the utmost confidentiality, he felt confused as to how to feel. Surprisingly, he did not find this cathartic. He did not feel relieved or indeed released. If anything, he became overwhelmed with anxiety but as to why he was unsure.

Conceivably, it was because he had overstepped a line somehow. In doing so he knew he had placed himself in a latitude from where he could not return. This filled him with fear — a fear that he had never experienced before.

Eventually, he realised who this letter was intended for. He inscribed, with no little hesitance, the name of his chosen audience — his chosen reader who was his old German tutor, now a family friend whom he considered to be a very special person — one who may be his angel, his saviour of sorts — but an earthly one. Ironic, as he hated German at school but actually enjoyed his private tuition that Marika gave. The letter began: *"Dear Marika..."* He then washed, dressed and summoned up the courage to leave the house for the first time in what seemed like forever and walked into the hot bright sunshine of summer. He walked, letter in hand, albeit slowly and tentatively. Upon finding his destination he pushed his letter through Marika's black letter box. He then breathed in deeply, turning a hoof before retracing his steps.

iv The Oak Tree

One could say that the oak trees "belonging" to all three of our adults in the making were beginning to firmly lay down their roots and if one spied closely, small shoots could be seen forming and shaping themselves on the body of their structure.

Evanna said a quiet farewell to "her" tree as she looked upon it fondly from her bedroom window. She knew that this wouldn't be a real goodbye, so long as her parents didn't move and as long as the tree remained upright, but she was also aware that the next time she saw it she would possess a different set of eyes — albeit still her own — as tomorrow she was to start her adventure — to start her new life.

The day prior to when Petra was to begin her new life she went to visit "her" oak tree. For the first time she did not see it adorned with lollipops and sweet tasty treasure but simply as it was — strong, sturdy, proud, faithful, nurturing, giving yet tinged with a slightly darker side which made Petra smile as it reminded her somewhat of herself! She saw this tree in its full glory — it was truly beautiful.

When Bodhi returned, after having posted his letter, he went straight to his bedroom and to his bed yet did not retreat to either. He lay on his now freshly made bed. Despite his obvious anxiety concerning his having to wait for whatever the consequences of his soon to be read letter would be, he experienced a feeling flowing through his body that he had never experienced before which he could not quite put a name to. But for you, dear reader, it was a complete restfulness that filled him with hope — positivity. He may indeed, finally, receive the help he needed. This would be from Marika, who he had entrusted his scribing to. Bodhi had placed his whole trust into that one woman, which may not seem fair, yet he knew that she was made of stern stuff! He appreciated that Marika would not be his rescuer but the conduit to his future here on earth which he was more than aware would not be an easy channel but one in which he was willing to try to navigate his way through.

Bodhi conjured "his" tree into his mind's eye. He saw its broken branches slowly begin to fix themselves and then he watched as new shoots formed upon its very boughs. He even felt the roots digging a firmer hold.

Chapter 6
Family, Friends and Foes

"Some people are worth melting for." (1)

Contrary to what you might have thought, dear reader, an oak tree can be said to possess family, friends and even foes.

Let us explore such phenomena more closely, although by no means too scientifically.

"Rejoice with your family in the beautiful land of life." (2)

The oak tree belongs to the Fagaceae family, which could be said to be akin to a surname — Fagaceae.

This family is made up of a salmagundi of flowering plants including the beech tree. Just as a human family consists of a mishmash of people related by blood, the family Fagaceae consists of a mishmash of species, some 927 to be exact which are related by some commonalities and are either deciduous or evergreen.

What binds the Fagaceaes together, despite their differences, are their alternate simple lobed leaves and their unisex flowers known as catkins, for example. Their fruit are in the shape of cup-like nuts lying in scaly spiny husks which are absent of endosperm. This is the nutritive tissue, or food store, which contains starch and protein along with other essential nutrients surrounding the embryo inside the seeds of the flowering plant.

This large family also contains five or six sub-families which are generally accepted to include eight to ten genera. A genus is placed below a family but above a species. These are groups of the same species sharing similar structures.

On siblings:

"Your only enemy you can't live without." (3)

Or:

"Sibling relationships are complicated. All family relationships are. Look at Hamlet." (4)

The Fagaceae family reside in many different parts of the world. They could all be said to be related to each other: some close relatives whilst others distant.

At the very foot of the Glastonbury Tor in Somerset, England, stand two of the most ancient oak trees. Twins, perhaps. These have reputedly reached over 2,000 years old. They are considered to be the very remnants of a beautiful avenue of their siblings which once led up to the Tor itself. This grand avenue was named The Oaks of Avalon. The two remaining giants bear the names Gog and Magog Fagaceae, of course. Sadly, in the year 2011 Gog, who had technically already passed away, was severely burned by fire. This fire was considered to have been started accidentally by a burning candle, but thankfully, it was extinguished by the Fire Service who did not allow it to spread to Magog.

Thus, this goes to show that siblings can indeed grow, even take root together, for the whole of their lives — until one dies. Then how the other must grieve.

On friendship:

"There is nothing I wouldn't do for those who are really my friends. I have no notion of loving people by halves, it is not my nature." (5)

And:

"A friend is one that knows you as you are, understands where you have been, accepts what you have become and still gently allows you to grow." (6)

Do oak trees have friendships? You bet they do! Maybe not in the conventional human sense but they display such nurturing, giving, unselfish, unconditional and loving friendships which should leave us humans in awe.

The oak tree has made friendships of insects, birds and mammals alike. Oak trees do not discriminate such as the likes of us.

Its winged friends, such as jays, have taken to the wild oaks in order to feed off their fruit, the acorn, as do squirrels, badgers and deer. Other of God's creatures partake in the rich nutrients of these generous branched structures. Caterpillars, of the Purple Hairstreak Butterfly (no less) feed from the oak's buds. The tree's soft leaves break down with great ease in the autumn. These then go to form a rich mould which descends and goes to rest beneath the oak thus enabling invertebrates, such as beetles, to feed from it.

The seemingly nurturing nature of the oak also allows its many and varied friends to dwell on or within it. Holes and crevices, in its very bark, provide the most perfect nesting spots for the Pied Flycatcher and the March Tit. Bats come home to the oak to roost in old woodpecker holes or under loose bark. They also feast on the rich supply of insects that have found homes in the tree's canopy.

"I'm as free a little bird as I can be
I'm as free a little bird as I can be
Gonna build my nest in a big oak tree
Where no one else can bother me." (7)
"Every little swallow, every chickadee
Every little bird in the tall oak tree
The wise old owl, the big black crow
Flappin' their wings." (8)

On enemies:

"If you don't have enemies, you don't have character." (9)

It cannot be denied that the ruling majesty of the woods, the oak tree, oozes such character. What, or who could possibly claim the title: Enemy of the Oak Tree? Alas, it does have them, yet it keeps on giving, to that very same foe, all the same. Possibly, they see each other as friends — but whilst making a friendship with the oak, it may be a cunning plan because it is also its enemy:

"Your worst enemy could be your best friend and your best friend your worst enemy." (10)

So, let us complete a quick examination of these "friends" also known as "Foes of The Oak".

Our first culprit: the Oak Processionary Moth, which begins its life as a caterpillar nesting in the oak tree. This is not indigenous to the United Kingdom but can be found to dwell in various parts of the "The Green and Pleasant Land". This pest damages the tree's foliage thus increasing the oak's susceptibility to disease. The caterpillar feeds, almost exclusively, on our beloved oak, as it makes its home on the tree's trunk and larger branches. In spring the caterpillars, which are covered in small hairs, being a health risk to human beings, hatch and descend lower down the tree as they grow and develop. Come summer they retreat into nests in preparation for pupation. Finally, with the arrival of late summer the adult Oak Processionary Moths emerge. Here, it could be said that the oak gives the moth its life but also the karma it deserves as once an adult these moths live for a mere four days with the sole purpose of mating. However, the cycle is only set to repeat itself when the female lays her fertilised eggs high up in the oak's canopy.

What about humans? Are they friend to the oak? Once again,

the oak's generous nature and unconditional love for all leads it to its own demise. Humans took the leaves, bark and fruit as they once believed, perchance some continue to believe, that they could heal various human medical ailments such as: diarrhoea, inflammation, even kidney stones. Acorns were also used to make flour for bread. Tannin, found in the bark, has been used to tan leather since prior to the Romans.

So, nothing too disastrous, right?

As the oak is so giving (apart from, it is agreed, the somewhat "criminal act" of stealing sunlight from others) one would not think it would mind giving more of itself for the purpose of others. Sadly, this all too often leads to its own destruction and death. Humans fell our oak tree: cut it in two, for their own use. Not for the ecosystem or the circle of life. The British Royal Navy was often described it as "the wooden walls of Old England" because of the habit of constructing naval ships out of oak.

Humans use the oak's wood for other construction forms and for fermenting, for fuel, for furniture ...

The oak can only hope that its murderer comes into close contact with the poisonous hairs of the caterpillar of the Oak Processionary Moth — now that *would* be karma!

The British species of human does, however, claim a deep affinity with the British oak tree by declaring it their Symbol of National Strength.

Thus, this from Aesop can also be said to be true:

"*We often give our enemies the means for our own destruction.*" (11)

Here, the oak tree gives its human foe its strength.

On humans:

"*Someone to tell it to is one of the fundamental needs of*

human beings." (12)

It will seem obvious to you, dear reader, that human beings have relationships involving those of family, friends and foes. Some find relationships easier than others. Human relationships are about communication and compromise which are vital for the overall wellbeing of an individual. Such interpersonal relationships often grow into strong, deep and close associations or acquaintanceships, between two or more people, that range in length: from brief to enduring. The context of such relationships varies from family, friendship, marriage, work, clubs, community, places of worship and so forth.

Human relationships are far more complicated than that of the oak tree. In short, the Human Relations Management Theory is a researched belief that people desire to be part of a supportive team that facilitates development and growth. As we are all too well aware relationships, of any kind, can be hard work. Often, we argue, often we hate. However, often we love and laugh, so it would be good to remember that:

"*No road is long with good company.*" (13)

On the human "family":

"*In time of test family is best.*" (14)

The common use of the word "human" most often refers to the only extant species of the genus Homo — anatomically and behaviourally modern Homo Sapiens. Extant human populations are historically divided into sub-species but since the early 1980s all such extant groups tend to have been subsumed into one single species thus avoiding such divisions. Homo Sapiens is Latin for "*wise man*" which sounds like a perfect surname for some humans but sadly not all. The extant species of the genus Homo date back from roughly 1.9 to 0.4 million years ago, including a number of other species (or sub-species). Thanks to evolution we are those "*wise men*" or "*anatomically modern humans*" of today.

Are we all related? Well, in form we are. Modern humans have a lighter build than our more robust archaic human ancestors. Contemporary humans exhibit many physiological traits. Their cranium is larger in order to house a bigger brain; they have a steeper and even vertical forehead which has a vital role in communication through eyebrow movements and the skin wrinkling of the forehead. We have smaller, different shaped teeth making the jaw line stand out producing a prominent chin. Modern humans have smaller lower faces. Contemporary humans have a less robust skeletal structure than that of the Neanderthals, for example. Neanderthals are an extant species, or sub-species, of archaic humans in the genus Homo from circa 400,000 until 40,000 years ago.

Obviously, there are many more differences even down to the evolution of behaviour.

In essence, yes, we are all related but not necessarily by blood of family. Modern human beings are divided still and are diverse, but they are united by family — all humans were born into a family.

Unlike the oak tree, being unisex, human beings have two basic genders, male and female with titles to suit, e.g. Mr, Miss, Mrs, mother, father, daughter, son, sister, brother, aunt, uncle, grandmother, grandfather with the "nonbinary" cousin making up the basic human nuclear and extended family. In our times the lines of gender and gender identity are becoming blurred. Some now identify as non-binary or transsexual, for example. However, as this is a very basic homily on familial relationships (more importantly the author is no expert) the author will not complete a detailed explanation concerning gender for fear of upsetting others.

The writer can safely say, though, that family relationships are diverse and are far from simplistic. Their make-up comes in multiple forms. Some families are large, others small. A basic family consists of the "Nuclear Family": mother, father and two children with an extended family of grandparents, aunts, uncles, cousins and so forth. Even this example is not necessarily the "norm". No family is perfect, but all are equal.

We do, however, tend to share some form of physical or behavioural "likeness" to one or some members of our own blood family:

"My father's in my fingers, but my mother's in my palms.

I lift them up and look at them with pleasure

I know my parents made me by my hands." (15)

Human siblings have multifarious relationships. It can be said that:

"Children of the same parents, each of which is perfectly normal until they get together." (16)

Or that:

"Siblings are the only people in the world who know what it's like to have been brought up the way you were." (17)

However, one can wholeheartedly state that the relationships humans have with their siblings are far more intense than those of the oak tree.

On human friendships:

"Love is blind, friendship closes its eyes." (18)

The oak tree appears to provide unconditional friendship, even to its enemies. However, humans tend to be more selective, but not all humans can be said to behave as if a "good" friend to others. Maybe this says more about the individual, but humans are more complicated than the oak tree.

Human beings are often heard to state, something along the

lines of, it's only in a crisis that you find out who your true friends are. Elizabeth Taylor adeptly summed this up when she declared:

"You find out who your real friends are when you're involved in a scandal." (19)

Likewise, true friendship can be described:

"Friendship is born at moments when one person says to another: 'What — you too? I thought I was the only one!'" (20)

Human friendships are more two-way, reciprocal, than those of the oak. What gains are there for the oak tree in any friendship as it gives, gives and gives whereas its friends take, take and take.

Some human friendships can last a lifetime whilst others a matter of days, but each "type" comes into one's life for some reason or purpose.

On human enemies:

"Always forgive your enemies, nothing annoys them so much." (21)

Human beings naturally adopt enemies; those whom they may cross at school, and in later years. The oak tree's enemies appear to injure and kill whereas human enemies are not necessarily quite so fearsome. However, human beings would not wish to make an enemy of those akin to the Kray Twins! But why turn someone into an enemy when one may not need to?

"Now, now my good man, this is no time to be making enemies." (22)

So, oak trees may have relationships akin to humans, yet they are not actually comparable. Human beings can lay claim to two-dimensional, deeper and interchangeable relationships.

For the time being, the pause button will be pressed on the lives of Evanna, Petra and Bodhi as their relationships of the familial, friendship and even foe type are examined, even if just for a little while thus far.

i Three in one

As is already known, the lives of these three had the capacity to be mirror images; thus, their families did also.

Evanna, Petra and Bodhi all had the stereotypical nuclear family: mother, father and one sibling, in each case an elder sibling of three years who also happened to be a sister!

None worried much about being the youngest, although Petra and Evanna were known to become just a little annoyed with their sister's hand-me-down clothes, especially the pink party dresses, black patent shoes and the like! Bodhi did not have to endure this, although he always had to deal with the phrase: *"my baby brother this…"* and *"my baby brother that…"* which irked him so!

As it happened, each was blamed for any wrongdoings, arguments, breakages or upsets at home. In truth, each would concur, they would often be the culprits but at the same time disliked the automatic impeachment that was laid upon them!

Their extended families were reasonably large. Their mothers had one sibling each who was married with two children. Their maternal grandparents, "Nanny" and "Grandad" were still alive when our children were very small, as was their maternal great-aunt who was their grandad's sister.

Their fathers each had four siblings who in turn had seven children in total. Their paternal grandparents, "Grandma" and "Grandpa" were of eastern European descent. They happened to be Jewish immigrants who escaped the Nazi pogroms. Neither Evanna, Petra nor Bodhi can recall ever having met them as they were babies when they passed. The obligatory paternal great-aunt was still alive but her "lights were not really on", if you understand what is meant by this (however not unkindly).

So, that is the general familial structure of each. Now, let us probe a little deeper into each as despite the framework and bare bones being similar the flesh and sinew are very different.

ii Evanna

Evanna was definitely her own child! For the more mature readers, she was Kato to her sister's Chief Inspector Clouseau; however, only in the manner in which she used to find superb hiding places just to pounce out and leap upon her poor unsuspecting sister, Gianna, when she least expected it. Gianna never saw the humorous side to these escapades which often got Evanna into immense trouble with their mother!

The sisters had a love/hate relationship. Evanna often wondered why it was that she loved Gianna so much but believed it evident that Gianna's feelings towards her were not reciprocal — indeed, she even felt hated by her sister! There was no real evidence for this, however. In truth they were just two very different souls. Evanna the "tomboy", the Action Man lover, who had aspirations of changing her sex when she grew up. Gianna, the Barbie and pink frilly dress lover. Evanna the mud and worm eater. Gianna, the pretend tea party hostess. Evanna the imaginer, Gianna the common sensical. Evanna the violated and abused to Gianna's pure and virginal.

The two siblings also had very different relationships with their parents. Evanna exhibited an often cheeky, rebellious nature when in their presence. She refused to show her more vulnerable side despite knowing she was the more so of the two sisters. Evanna loved the attention she received when she donned her "comical" hat at family gatherings. She enjoyed being in the limelight on these occasions despite feeling like a shrinking violet within. Gianna exhibited a more mature nature and an always sensible persona when with other family members. Evanna considered this fake. It was as if Gianna did not wish to identify with her younger sister and cousins. Gianna was never the wallflower. She always tried her best to join in with the more adult conversation but failed to excel as she never knew anything about the topic in question. However, she was happy in the knowledge that she wasn't scrabbling on the floor playing with the "kids".

If either was going to achieve in the academic field, it was to be Gianna. If either was to find success athletically, it would be Evanna. It seemed neither was pushed to absolutely excel and become dominant in their field, but it was academia that was considered the most vital. Sporting prowess was unimportant. It was not encouraged, either at school or at home, although a fine hobby to follow if one felt so inclined. Gianna was the scientist and mathematician. Evanna the athlete and sometime historian.

Evanna's parents worried about her future: what successful career could be mapped out with these subjects whereas Gianna had an endless list of opportunities. Evanna always felt second best to her sister because of this and when Gianna left their private convent school in the sixth form to attend a rather exclusive public school in order to study the three sciences, Evanna hoped that she would be afforded the same or similar opportunity when her turn came. She was not!

So, the siblings had a difficult dynamic. In short, Evanna wanted to be loved by her parents which, despite everything, she did not doubt she was. However, she lived in constant fear that she buried deep down which is possibly the reason behind "her" Kato and often the cause of her troublesome behaviour in comparison to the staider demeanour of her elder sister.

Evanna always felt a great affinity towards her Jewish

relatives. There did not seem to be a definitive reason, but she was always told that she resembled this side of the family. She could only agree; was it the nose, the darker thicker hair, the slightly darker hue of skin or the mono brow? Evanna also shared certain personality traits with this family set who were known to exhibit behaviour related to some form of mental illness, namely: hypochondria, depression and bipolar. She began to show signs of the latter condition in her teenage years which were only to increase as she grew into adulthood.

Evanna felt very close to her maternal grandparents: Nanny and Grandad. Sadly, both died when she was a young child. She wished that she could remember them in greater detail or in any detail at all rather than that gleaned from photographs or family tales. Nanny and Grandad both held a very deep place in her heart and soul which she carried with her forever. She still cried for them as an adult, yet she could not, with clarity, recall one single memory, not even of their deaths. To Evanna, they simply vanished. She knew that they were the most wonderfully kind people because when her heart pulsated, she sensed their kindred beats of purity and love.

She never met her paternal grandparents, which upset her as she never got to hear "their story" whilst in Poland with the rise of Hitler and their rush to emigrate to the safety of England. Family history fascinated Evanna, but she never knew too much. No one really spoke of it. She was aware, however, that one of her father's young cousins and his family decided to remain in Poland only being forced to wear the Yellow Star. One morning this 15-year-old male cousin merely went out to collect a pint of milk, which had been left by the milkman, on the front doorstep. He was never seen of or heard of again. It was assumed he had been rounded up by the Nazis but the story of his extermination, or otherwise, was never discovered.

Evanna was also aware of some Jewish relatives who were kilt makers in Edinburgh, Scotland, and the fact that her family came from a solid stock of Polish horse thieves. Her maternal ancestry also came from thievery as the infamous English highwayman Dick Turpin was amongst their number. This filled Evanna with glee as it gave her a certain twinkle in her eye, mirroring Dick's perchance! She was also proud to be related to a Vice Admiral John Warren, of the 17th century, who was buried in Westminster Abbey. She felt so excited, as a child, to know that she literally walked over his grave when she went there!

Evanna enjoyed her popularity. She was naturally funny, vivacious, vibrant, kind, well-meaning and supportive.

Her first "friend" was Joy, whom she really did not like that much, and the feeling was certainly a mutual one! Joy was the youngest of three daughters. Her mum, Jeanette, was her own mother's best friend. The two women met at ante-natal classes when Evanna's mother was pregnant with Gianna and Jeanette with her second daughter, Michaela. Their friendship blossomed, which inevitably led to the great friendship between those two girls. When the time came for Evanna, who was six months the elder, and Joy, the two were "thrust" together with little choice! They attended the same nursery school where each morning they would argue over the rocking horse! When Evanna had her feet in plaster casts she would kick everything in her sight including the poor unsuspecting Joy. The two families spent many days out and even holidays together. Until Evanna and her family moved to a new house they lived within very close proximity, about a two-minute walk. Even upon moving the journey time between the two houses, by car, was a mere five minutes. The two young girls did get along at times. They had sleepovers when they were little. Evanna enjoyed staying over at Joy's as she got to eat Angel Delight with tinned peaches for pudding. However, they often got into "fist" fights, fortunately without injury! Eventually, when school age was reached, they attended different places of education, which was of immense relief to Evanna and if truth be known, to Joy as well.

Sadly, Auntie Jeanette was diagnosed with breast cancer which later spread throughout her weakened body and into her bones. She did not make it past the Christmas of the following year leaving behind her three young daughters and their hopeless father but her kind husband. Evanna's mother lost her best friend and confidante when Jeanette died, but Evanna never once saw her shed one single tear although she undoubtedly did when alone. Evanna felt this loss hugely but being so young herself she did not process it. However, Jeanette's passing did remind her somewhat of that of her grandparents. Despite this "hatred" of Joy she felt such empathy for her from then on, although she always thought her a little odd!

Evanna's first school was a junior middle and infant school close to her new home. Much to her disappointment she only spent the first two years there as her parents decided to "upgrade" her schooling to a private one, where she remained until the fruition of her school career.

Evanna loved her first school. She made a wonderful friend in a blond-haired, blue-eyed Swedish boy, who often wore a Kermit green knitted jumper at weekends. His name was Lars. She shed many a tear when Lars and his family moved back home to Sweden at the end of the first year. She enjoyed the friendship of boys more so than girls which resulted in being pals with Dom and Jason but admittedly there was also Kaleigh and Elizabeth. She simply adored her teacher who was young and so very kind, fun and encouraging. Evanna was never able to pronounce her newly married name, so Mrs Dauphin became "Mrs Dolphin" which she never corrected; indeed, she laughed (in a kind way) about it.

Great hilarity was caused in the classroom of four-year-olds when Dom and Jason were caught measuring their "willies" with a ruler whilst changing for PE. Dom was the obvious winner and due to his rather callous gloating was made to stand, stark naked, on top of the table for all to see! Even at this age Dom was very proud of his lengthy shaft but the thought of this punishment being dealt in the world of today would be unthinkable! Still, these were different times in the 1970s and nothing much was thought about it.

Evanna was six when she moved schools. She detested this prim and proper girls' school with its scratchy brown pinafore dress, blue shirt with a tight collar around which she had to wear a red and white striped tie. In the winter there was a heavy camel coat, brown gloves and a ridiculous blue hat. The summer uniform wasn't much better with its stripy blazer, boater and white gloves which never stayed white for long! She still remembers the mantra of: "*indoor shoes inside, girls, and outside shoes outside*".

She found the transition from a relaxed mixed school to this strict all-girls' school tiresome and very difficult. Plus, the teachers at her new school were old and old fashioned in comparison. Some of these teachers, including the Headmistress, were nuns from the convent attached. For that first year, Evanna made various escape attempts when her mother dropped her off, so it was decided that instead of accompanying her into the playground each morning she would deposit her into the firm hands of the Headmistress who would then escort Evanna to her seat in the classroom and stay with her until the bell sounded for the start of the school day. Little did the young Evanna know but Sister Rose kept a kindly but distant vigil over her all day and indeed until she was of the age to go up to secondary school. Despite this transition proving highly difficult Evanna grew to accept her new surroundings, rules, teachers and classmates. After that first year she never looked back.

Her sporting prowess began to be noticed in Prep 1 (first year of juniors). She was nurtured by her wonderful PE teacher, Mrs Jenkins. Although the only sports they did were netball, rounders and tennis, Evanna was spotted as talented. The school also offered swimming lessons once a week. Already a competent swimmer, Evanna was quickly sent to the deep end with five other classmates during their first lesson. These excellent swimmers also happened to excel at netball, proving to be wonderful tennis players and First Place "sticker winners" on sports day. Because of this a little clique was formed which Evanna enjoyed but was also careful to socialise with her other classmates. Her popularity was born through her ability to get on with everyone and never to consider herself better than others.

Out of school Evanna had a very good friend in her next-door neighbour, Mark, who was two years her senior. They bonded over mud spending many happy hours in it whilst finding incredible joy in building roads using "Matchbox"-style steamrollers, trucks and diggers in the rockeries situated in each other's back gardens. Both mothers despaired over uprooted plants that the two children discarded as they got in the way of their intricate roadway systems. Each had a huge collection of cars and Action Men. Evanna owned a plethora of Action Man paraphernalia but was still slightly envious of Mark's helicopter. However, her favourite of all toys was her Scalextric set. Oh, the many, many, blissful hours she spent, some with Mark, designing different tracks, building the grandstand, adding new pieces of equipment and road-testing cutting-edge cars, which she received as presents, for many years, at Christmas and for her birthday. This was her pride and joy which she was only too glad to share with her neighbour who was delighted to discover that despite being a girl, Evanna did not "act" like one.

Evanna also appreciated her own company, playing solo football in the garden with an actual ball and solo rugby, in the living room, with a balloon for some reason.

When she attained her 11th year, Evanna left the prep school "graduating" to its senior school which was situated within the exact same grounds. She was actually sad to leave the smaller school but soon found her footing in the bigger. Once again, she became greatly admired because of her sporting capabilities, although the school was not best known for its sporting prowess — possibly the reverse! She immediately became firm friends with those on the various, actually four, sporting teams. These girls were known as the "cool crowd" but to Evanna they were just normal girls. Naturally, being Evanna, she mixed with everyone and proved popular and well-liked by all.

As she grew in age, as well as height, her social life also began to grow. Her friendship circle became more diverse, especially upon joining the local youth club where she befriended, in both the friendship sense and in the "boyfriendish" sense, a number of the opposite sex. Her first "love" was a lad of Italian descent, to whom she lost her virginity in the conventional sense; however, through "the man who visited her room" she had actually lost it years prior. But there was also the girl whose parents had emigrated from Australia to whom she lost her lesbian virginity! There were others, too, over the years!

During the long hot hazy days of the summer immediately after the completion of her O Level examinations, Evanna discovered a person who was to become one of the best friends she could ever hope to have. This friendship, despite its various ups and downs, lasted the test of time. Georgia, who had always shared a class with Evanna, was someone who Evanna had never spent any time with for reasons that the two never quite understood. At school they had different friendship circles, but both stood out, albeit for alternative reasons. Georgia was loud, gregarious, loving to be at the very epicentre of attention yet she was also marmite to others — either loved or hated. Evanna was ambivalent towards Georgia throughout their years at the same school. However, after their final exam of that summer, the two girls happened to find themselves walking home together. Despite living only four doors apart they had never socialised but soon wished that they had. On that walk home they laughed the whole way and from then on, a firm bond and friendship was born. They spent the entirety of that summer together, enjoying their freedom from school and studies whilst they basted themselves in olive oil and lemon juice before roasting in the sunshine. Evanna, inevitably burnt whilst Georgia turned a lovely shade of brown! When Georgia visited Evanna they would raid the drinks cabinet and Georgia would never hesitate in raiding the fridge as, apparently, Evanna's fridge was always stocked with far tastier and more plentiful food than her own, which wasn't exactly true. It is strange, though, how other folks' refrigerators appear more exciting than one's own! The evenings would mostly be spent at Georgia's playing Trivial Pursuit in the lounge or in her bedroom smoking and drinking sweet sherry. It was in this room that Evanna sampled her very first, and far from last, joint. Her friend had an en suite bathroom in which they would puff on a joint, blowing smoke out of the large open sash window whilst seated on the carpeted floor listening to Simon and Garfunkel. However, on one occasion they became a little careless and far too cocky as they smoked a thickly rolled joint in the bedroom, windows firmly shut. All of a sudden, Georgia's mother could be heard knocking on the bedroom door stating: "*I've got your washing dear!*" The two girls sat stone still, aghast as they watched the door open, as if in slow motion, and in entered Georgia's mum, Kate, with a pile of freshly laundered clothing. The girls watched her as she inhaled the marijuana fog that had enveloped the room. She said not a single word but merely left the room. As soon as they breathed out a sigh of huge relief, however, they heard Kate call Georgia down the stairs. Evanna could just about hear the heavy debate going on in the kitchen at which she swiftly and rather nimbly, although rather unfairly, took flight, making her escape via the front door and running home where she went straight to her bedroom, as she always did when high, so as to avoid her parents seeing her red heavy eyes. Evanna nervously sat on the edge of her bed with sweaty palms awaiting the dreaded knock on the door which would inevitably be Kate with Georgia in tow, sporting bowed head, to tell the sorry tale to Evanna's parents. There never was a knock on the door. Not that night or any night.

Kate proved to be as if a proper mum to Evanna. She gave her what she lacked at home. Kate realised, without ever being told, that life at home was not good for her daughter's best friend. She did not know why and nor did she ask, which Evanna was eternally grateful for.

When term started again, the two girls entered the sixth form. Evanna stayed in the same school but Georgia left for another. However, their friendship remained only to grow firmer and stronger as the two girls matured.

As for enemies — Evanna did not have any. Yes, at times she fell out with friends and indeed even "disliked" Georgia when they argued but only for a few days when one or the other relented. At such times, hugs were in abundance and tears would flow followed by the inevitable laughter and vows of being best friends forever and never to fall out again. Despite these times they loved each other unconditionally and knew that their bond would never die no matter what may happen and so indeed it continued and fermented with age.

iii <u>Bodhi</u>

Bodhi came from the stereotypical family of four, consisting of his mother, father and sister three years his elder. He had little to do with his sister. This was mainly because she never had time for him, which caused Bodhi no little upset. He seemed permanently scared of his domineering mother resulting in him doing his utmost to please her. He also tried to accommodate his quiet passive father.

Bodhi loved his maternal nanny and grandad who came to live with him when he was four years old. They lived relatively short lives, both dying in their early-to mid-seventies when Bodhi was still a young child. He was unable to recall a great deal about either grandparent but remembered them both with a heart full of warmth and love. He would always miss them feeling such envy when his friends, no matter how old he was, spoke of their still living grandparents.

He did remember his nanny possessing a multitude of hearts: kind, soft, warm, whole and heart felt. She was a short lady with dark curly short hair who always wore a sunny smile despite being a Type 1 diabetic, which resulted in her having one leg amputated above the knee after which the other was also taken off just below the knee because of gangrene caused by the numerous daily insulin injections she had to give herself over the years. He fondly remembered how she taught him how to inject an orange, as that was how she learned. Nanny appeared like a little old lady by appearances of today. His grandparents had their bed and bathroom on the ground floor of "his" three-storied house. Bodhi's father would carry Nanny up and down the stairs so that she could join the family in the kitchen and living room. Bodhi knew that his nanny died in hospital but cannot recall much more. In fact, she only lived with Bodhi and his family for six weeks before she died by choking on a chicken salad whilst in hospital. Through her diabetes she developed oral thrush, the consequence of which was that she was not supposed to consume any solid foods. Hence, she was on a strict liquid diet for that time. However, one supper time, a nurse mistakenly provided her with the aforementioned chicken salad. Nanny was old school. A lady who was brought up never to complain but simply to be thankful for what one was provided with. She had survived wartime with its bombings and rationing — one just did not complain but retained the British stiff upper lip. She was also too timid to mention to the nurses that she was not able to eat this. Hence, she choked to death. After the funeral, which Bodhi was considered too young to attend, his mother and uncle complained to the hospital authorities, but he never knew the outcome.

Subsequently Bodhi became too frightened to sleep at night for he feared that his nanny's ghost would appear to him in the corner of his bedroom dressed in a long light blue sheet, reminiscent of the Virgin Mary. Of why he harboured such a fear he had no clue as he loved and missed her so much. All he actually wished to do was have her wrap him up in her arms and look after him. Despite this, the fear lasted several years. That's where Bodhi's recollection ends of his maternal grandparents. Of his paternal he had nothing, merely a false memory of his grandpa visiting the house with his pet caged budgies whom he allowed to fly freely around the room downstairs. However, Grandpa had passed away before the family had moved to this house and he kept pigeons, as opposed to budgies, who never came to visit!

Including his childhood abuse, Bodhi could recollect two other scenarios that he firmly believed added to his depressive ways and his continual search for enlightenment and awakening although he was unsure how they fitted in with that.

The first occurred during one breakfast time before school when Bodhi had reached his thirteenth year. His sister, having finished her Ready Brek, had left the table leaving him disgusted, as was the case every morning, due to deliberately opening her full mouth containing the gloopy, grey looking porridge. This being the reason why Bodhi had never been able to eat the stuff! So, there he was on his own sitting at the kitchen table whilst enjoying his two soft boiled eggs and toasted soldiers. His mother had, mistakenly, left the television switched on, probably because morning television was a brand-new phenomenon which took some getting used to! Bodhi did not normally take any notice of the news, which was the bulletin on which the television had been left in between the Commonwealth Games from Brisbane, Australia. However, during this particular news broadcast he happened to look up having just sunk his teeth into his last soldier which was soaked in thick golden yellow yolk. At that particular moment what he saw and heard proved to lie etched into his brain forever. His eyes gazed, almost spellbound at the screen. He was simply unable to remove his stare which latched onto the black and white photograph of a young woman who appeared to be in her twenties, with dark wavy hair which she wore down to the nape of her neck around which she sported a pearl necklace. She donned a dark coloured cardigan with a lighter thinner jumper underneath. Her beautiful features and bright radiant smile shone out at Bodhi such that they spoke to him somehow. It was a simple headshot. It seemed to Bodhi that the picture had been taken by a professional photographer by the way she was seated at a sideways slant, yet her head faced forward looking directly into the camera. He did not have the time to truly appreciate this beautiful woman because as he sat mesmerised, he heard the newsreader say the words, which obviously went alongside the photograph: *"found... patch of long grass...raped...murdered"*. He did not hear any more of what the reporter had to say, just these words which were vivid enough. He needed to hear nothing more. He could not turn his head away or his ears off. He could not make his brain stop. He could not rid himself of the unwanted images of this poor, poor, woman whom he imagined laying naked, somehow neatly arranged, hidden in long wet grass. There she lay, her limp neck to one side as it had been broken through force of being strangled. It was a sheer horror to him. She died in abject terror.

That very photograph and those exact words continued to manifest inside his brain producing a vivid film at intervals throughout the rest of his life. He never would or could understand how one human being could do "THAT" to another human being and one who looked so innocent and happy. A young woman whose life had been stolen, dispatched in an instant after been subjected to such a traumatic, humiliating, degrading, painful, harrowing, terrifying (and so much, much more) event. Bodhi felt so deeply for that hapless woman who he almost fell in some form of love with as she remained with him forever. This was his first "experience" of such evil and horrific happenings in the world outside his own.

The second scenario was a series of brief events that he happened across. These left him terrified and scarred. It is fair to say, however, that they would have made an impression of some sort on most people.

Bodhi mostly lived a sheltered life. Sheltered, in respect of the television news and "unsuitable programmes", sheltered from the newspapers that were delivered each morning and such like. Apart from the aforementioned "mishap", which his parents never knew about, his mother and father did manage the content of his viewing and reading well. For example, Bodhi was unaware that he was born in the midst of the Cold War.

In 1980, when Bodhi was fast approaching his tenth birthday, the government of Prime Minister Margaret Thatcher produced a "programme" entitled: "*Protect and Survive*". This, owing to the said Cold War, was to advise the citizens of the United Kingdom of the safest way to protect themselves in the aftermath of a nuclear attack. It consisted of a mixture of pamphlets, radio broadcasts and public information televisual films which were authorised for free dissemination to all households if the risk of such a nuclear attack were to increase. The advice given was widespread and detailed. It was meant to be taken on board and acted upon by each and every British civilian immediately in order to improve their chances of survival.

The pamphlets prescribed how to build domestic nuclear shelters including technical guidance for the design and indeed construction of long-term and even permanent shelters.

The first page of the original pamphlet warned:

"Read this pamphlet with care... Your life and the lives of your family may depend on it."

"Protect and Survive" was also adapted for the television in a series of no fewer than twenty short public information films, similar in content to the pamphlets. They used voiceover narration, sound effects and a combination of simple stop motion and illustrated animation. These were only meant to be televised if the government determined a nuclear attack was likely to occur within seventy-two hours. The "programme" would also be disseminated by radio.

The Wartime Broadcasting Service had scripted a broadcast in event of an attack which was to be transmitted on the BBC radio waves. It warned:

"Remember there is nothing to be gained by trying to get away. By leaving your homes you could be exposing yourself to great danger."

And:

"If you leave you may find yourself without food, without water, without accommodation and without protection."

Also:

"Radioactive fallout, which follows a nuclear explosion, is many times more dangerous if you are directly exposed to it."

Including:

"Make your food stocks last... may have to last for 14 days or more."

"Radioactive fallout can kill you. You cannot see it or feel it, but it is there."

Combined with *"Protect and Survive"* was the *"Four Minute Warning"* which was a public alert system conceived by the British Government, during the Cold War between 1953 and 1992. The name was derived by the approximate length of time from which the Soviet Union launched a nuclear missile attack against the United Kingdom to the time it was confirmed that the missile had exploded on its target. The population was to be notified by air raid sirens, television and radio, urging it to seek immediate cover. In actuality, the warning would have been three minutes or less.

This proved how world tensions were rising at this point in history. In 1980 nuclear war seemed closer than at any time since the Cuban Missile Crisis of 1962. Despite only being intended for distribution if the government determined there was likely to be a nuclear attack within 72 hours, news of *"Protect and Survive"* was leaked to CND and other organisations including the BBC who subsequently broadcast it on *Panorama* on 10th March 1980 which was shortly after the Soviet invasion of Afghanistan.

Who do you think watched this whilst being baby sat? Bodhi, of course. Who do you think caught glimpses and snippets of newspaper reports, radio broadcasts detailing the information? Bodhi, of course. Who do you think had such fear put in him, whilst playing in the playground, by his school friends who had also been exposed to such material? Bodhi, of course. Who do you think was taught the meaning behind the early 1980s pop hit *Two Tribes* by the band Frankie Goes to Hollywood, with lyrics such as *"mine is the last voice you will ever hear"*? Bodhi, of course.

When he reached 14 years old, in 1984, who was allowed to stay up late and watch television only to view *Threads*? Bodhi, naturally. From this he gleaned, in the most graphic detail, the full horrors of a nuclear attack and its aftermath, including the cataclysmic impact it had on all human beings and their way of life. From having no electricity, running water, sanitation or supplies, to looters of shops and homes, to murder, to the reinstatement of capital punishment, to radiation sickness, to having no manpower or fuel to burn or bury the forever mounting dead thus amounting to a widespread epidemic of a highly contagious and deadly disease. To a nuclear winter to an uninhabitable Sheffield to ultraviolet radiation to a vast reduction in the population. Ten years after the attack the British population had dwindled to between 4 and 11 million. At this time those left alive worked the fields with primitive handheld farming tools, children spoke in broken English because of the lack of education and family life. Basically, humanity lay near barbaric squalor.

This film fascinated, numbed, and horrified almost every viewer but for Bodhi, combined with *"Protect and Survive"* and his vivid imagination, made him crumble internally. He so desperately longed to seal every window in his home with duct tape. He may have wanted to die — but not that way — never that way. Bodhi turned fatalistic but from his imaginings of the mushroom cloud and the bright, bright, nuclear light he came to envisage his own bright light of Enlightenment and Awakening. His quest, as odd as that may sound, to find the true meaning of life.

What has this got to do with Bodhi's family? Only that through this one learns part of the reason why and how he came to be as he was — and yes — his family were involved in his entirety, as has been discovered.

Bodhi always enjoyed quiet popularity at school. Despite being relatively shy he still had a boyish mischievous side to his nature which rarely got him into trouble as his teachers found him endearing. They considered his features angelic and his nature so kindly and warm. Throughout his school life he favoured the company of girls over boys for no particular reason. However, he did spend time with the boys who were less lively and popular.

His main recollection from primary school proved rather distressing, as only Bodhi's recollections could be! He recalls the sight of Russell Carter picking up the class pet gerbil, appearing to stroke it for a time, only to hurl it against the farthest wall breaking its fragile frame — dead. He remembers the screams and tears of his classmates. He sees this incident in his mind as if a dream. He had no idea what became of Russell Carter as he grew into adulthood and beyond although he was still allowed to attend the same school.

In secondary school, two bright girls "claimed" Bodhi as their third wheel, which he was thrilled about. This threesome developed a very close bond which lasted until the end of the sixth form when they went their separate ways. From the second year onwards, on the first Friday of each month, the three friends went out on a "*cinema and pizza evening*" in the local town. This friendship enabled Bodhi to feel part of something giving him the sense of belonging he never felt before. Attempts were made, by all, to keep in touch when they left school, but both Caroline and Fatima experienced their very own traumas. Sadly, they lost contact. Bodhi often thought about them, wishing he knew how to find them, but he had no idea how.

Bodhi was never interested in having either a girl or indeed a boyfriend. He felt nothing in that way. He presumed, as he grew older in the years to come, that he was asexual. This realisation did not bother him, but he wondered how he would create the family that he so desired. The one that he longed for. He knew he could happily settle down with a best friend, whoever that happened to be, but still where would the children appear from!

After he had left school, as we know, Bodhi became a recluse. However, one special person turned out to be his saviour who he remained in contact with from there on in. Laughter, wine and good food proved to be the medicine they eventually grew to share no matter the situation or crisis. Bodhi detested German at school. He hated, no feared, his teacher as he simply was not good at it! This teacher, who was German herself, could not tolerate this. However, for some reason, he seemed determined to take on this language as a subject for his O Levels which his teachers did their utmost to dissuade both him and his parents from as he would be "*bound to fail*". In the back of his mind, Bodhi knew that these teachers were more concerned about league tables and exam statistics than his personal failure. Because of this, Bodhi's mind was even more determined to study German and "*fuck them all*"! His parents sought out a German home tutor with which he was not best pleased. However, as soon as Marika entered his family home, sitting down with him at his desk, he knew that he would enjoy these weekly lessons and possibly learn something too! His mother baked a cake each "*Marika Day*" which both student and tutor enjoyed with a cup of tea whilst going through, for the hundredth time, the nominative, accusative, dative cases and so forth. He was introduced to Marika's husband, Edwin, a Scot, whom Bodhi liked equally as much. Marika came to have four children over the years whom Bodhi had the privilege of witnessing becoming wonderful adults — just like their parents whom Bodhi considered to be "*purely perfect parents*".

Bodhi confided in Marika about school and basic teenage angst but that was all, until "*The Letter*" (the result of which will be detailed in a following chapter). What will be said now is that Marika saved Bodhi. She saved him from himself, from ending everything. He proved eternally grateful to Marika, which he did express, at the time, but again in his adult years long after. Owing to the longevity of their friendship and close connection, Marika exudes an inner and outer beauty to be sung about out loud with a smile spread wide.

Partly because of Bodhi's quiet and passive demeanour and partly because of his ability to appear almost invisible, Bodhi never had any enemies or even near enemies at this time.

Despite sometimes appearing invisible, Bodhi had friendships. He had the capacity to make good friends which he treasured. He did not have a vast collection of these but those he did have made an effect so profound which remained true for the entirety of his life.

iv Petra

Petra enjoyed being the younger sibling to her elder sister of three years.

She had a great affinity with her mother's older brother, Derek, who was the total opposite of his sister. Larger than life in both build and personality, boasting locks of dark hair with one thick streak of brilliant white which, as he grew in age, invaded his whole scalp and what with his beard to match he really was the spit of Father Christmas! When Petra's maternal grandad died it was Uncle Derek who took over the role of Santa at Christmas. Petra enjoyed being with her accordion-playing uncle who was definitely a "glass half full" person despite his own financial struggles and strife. He was married to the very lovely Auntie May. Together they "gave" Petra two slightly younger cousins, Warren and Eliza. This family lived quite some distance away, but they all got together as often as they could.

Petra loved her maternal grandad. She had no recollection of her other grandparents. Grandad Ron lived with Petra and her nuclear family. He had a mass of bright ginger hair in his heyday, but by the time Petra came into the world his head of magnificent hair was very much balding, but she could still spy a sprinkling of fine ginger strands. However, he always kept hold of his huge "Toby Jug Handle"-like ears which were inherited, much to Petra's relief, by her sister. Grandad always smelt of the wonderful Old Spice aftershave, the smell of which was always like "home" to Petra. Grandad was wholesome, fun loving, albeit a teller of rather bad jokes, kind, a great hugger and so very loving. His soul was the epitome of everything beautiful.

He was not conscripted into the army during World War Two for which reason Petra never did know — too old perhaps? Instead, he was an air raid warden. Every night during the Blitz he would mount his old rickety bicycle to ride the streets of Tottenham, north-east London, in the pitch dark of the blackouts. The aim of his job was to protect the local residents from the danger of the nightly air raid bombs. One night, however, he needed protection from himself as it proved so dark, he failed to see the rather large tree in front of him which he proceeded to crash into, knocking himself out and breaking his nose. His family spent the whole night taking shelter from the Nazi bombs underneath their sturdy dining room table, as their Anderson Shelter took to flooding. However, they were not scared for themselves that night but were terrified that Grandad had been struck by one of the numerous bombs that had exploded during the night destroying copious homes and lives. Grandad managed to hobble home, sometime after daybreak, broken bicycle in tow with a bloody nose, black eyes, a large bump with added bruising to his forehead and various other cuts and grazes. He entered the house whistling a happy little ditty, as he was prone to do, seemingly oblivious to the anguished night spent by his beloved wife and children! That was Grandad. Uncle Derek took after him

— but cups were actually never half full as they overflowed with all the joy, wonders and beauty of life in spite of everything.

Grandad died when Petra had turned six, two years after Nanny. Petra remembered their last birthday present to her — the biggest most magnificent box of Lego ever!

The day prior to his death, it was a Wednesday, the family minus Petra's father, who was working, spent the most fabulous day out in London Zoo along with friends. This memory, although not a clear one, made Petra feel warm as at least she knew that her grandad's last day on this Earth was one spent with those he loved the most and was a day she knew he enjoyed immensely. Early on that next fateful morning, Petra's father took a cup of tea to Grandad's bedroom as he was due to accompany her father to work in the shop, which he liked to do. After knocking on the door several times and, unusually, not hearing Grandad's cheery "*good morning*" voice echoing through the door Petra's father anxiously opened it. There was Grandad Ron, who looked as if peacefully still sleeping but in fact was having the longest and most permanent sleep — he had died.

When Petra's mother woke her up, Petra recalls being told that "*something very sad has happened, darling*". Petra's immediate concern was that something awful had happened to the rabbits, but reality hit her when she was told the truth. Her grandad was the *real* victim of the Grim Reaper — of Death Himself. Death was a concept that Petra had yet to come to terms with but understood that Grandad would never wake up and he had gone away. The rest of that day was surreal. It was the height of summer. Petra and her sister were requested to play in the garden, which they duly did. They knew better than to battle this request. The curtains to Grandad's bedroom were closed, as they had been all morning, and the girls had been firmly ordered not to enter this room. Petra did not understand why but did as she was told. Part of her longed to go into this room as subconsciously she knew that Grandad was still in there in some form or other. "*What did death really mean?*" she thought, which was why she wanted to see for herself. Death doesn't mean much to most six-year-olds; Petra was no different. The doorbell rang several times and different people were invited in and shown into Grandad's bedroom. One such person was a policeman, which confused this six-year-old, but she asked no questions. After what appeared an age her parents joined the sisters in the garden. Their mother advised them that they were going to the local shops with their father to buy each of them a small present. Petra remembers choosing a blue plastic gun-like toy which fired red circular discs from its frame when the trigger was pressed. These discs were like frisbees sailing through the wind until they dropped to the ground. On their return from the shops the house was back to normality. The door to Grandad's bedroom, which Petra was now allowed to enter, was open, as were the curtains and windows. Grandad, however, was gone, but his scent lingered on. The bed had been made up with, judging from their fresh smell and starched appearance, newly laundered sheets. Lunch was ready and on the kitchen table: ham sandwiches alongside homemade leek and potato soup. No mention of Grandad, no tears, just chit chat about the girls' new purchases but the conversation had a sad sombre tone and Petra's mother looked drawn, exhausted and so very sad.

Petra was considered too young to attend the funeral. Grandad was cremated. Her mother and uncle planted a rose bush in the crematorium's beautiful gardens in memory of both Nanny and Grandad. And that was that. Petra was allowed to attend her great-auntie Gwen's funeral when she died seven years after her younger brother, who was Grandad. Gwen had been a picture of beauty in her youth. She was engaged once only to be jilted at the altar, from which she apparently never recovered, remaining a "spinster" for the rest of her days. Petra loved it when Auntie Gwen came to stay, but the rest of her family did not especially, as she could be a difficult woman. But Petra felt a certain closeness to her and as she became more aware of her own sexuality wondered if Auntie Gwen had really been that devastated when jilted as Petra suspected her a lesbian too, owing to her demeanour and language she used. Petra recognised parts of herself in Great-Auntie Gwen — the parts that she recognised as gay. Was it a family trait!

Gwen battled with stomach cancer which eventually beat her. A few days after the funeral Petra and her mother went to the warden-controlled flat in Acton, London, where her auntie had enjoyed living for several years, to sort and clear out her worldly goods which did not amount for much. This struck Petra as somehow so sad. Great-Auntie Gwen and Grandad were always with Petra — every single day of her life.

Petra was always flowered with friends. She had a good "following". There was Jemma Thompson, who shared her love of Smurfs and Snoopy; Ashleigh Brown with her huge Alsatian dog and Joanne Franklyn with her perfect singing voice to name but a bare minimum of friends. Of course, there was the gorgeous Alison Moore who Petra fell in love with!

Petra broke a few hearts herself. This was unintentional, but she just could not help but get herself embroiled in love triangles, of her own making, as she found ending anything so very hard but especially relationships no matter how trivial or even how bad. When young she dated boys but also girls, which she preferred but realised it would be the *"wrong thing"* to come out to anyone at this stage as it just would not be understood.

Her mother always mocked Petra calling her a *"collector of lame ducks"* because of her ability to attract anyone and everyone who had some problem or difficulty that they believed Petra could solve for them. Petra did not mind being a shoulder for others as it provided her with a sense of being needed and liked which she never felt at home. She was a confidante to all. A peacemaker when friends fought. A supporter when support was in order. An ear and a shoulder. Petra was forever there for others.

She was never confident about her own body. She was almost too aware of it in some sexual sense which felt uncomfortable and embarrassing to her. In her junior school play she was to act as a parrot in the school's production of *Alice in Wonderland*. Her three minutes of stardom entailed, along with four other "parrots", singing the *"AEIOU"* song whilst dancing and jigging about. Dressed in only a red leotard emblazoned with brightly coloured feathers, a pair of red tights and with a parrot mask complete with beak Petra had to stand at the very front of the stage with her hands on her hips whilst moving them from side to side in time with this song, which she considered so so awful and the height of humiliation. She had day and nightmares about it for weeks on end. The worst was the actual performances themselves when proud fathers were taking photos during the performance. Nothing sinister, let alone sexual, was meant by them. However, Petra felt, even at that young age of ten, that her "sex" was on display in full force for all to see. It was the hip wriggling that she felt most uncomfortable with. It disgusted her and proved to be a constant foul memory for the rest of her life as she remembered that discomfort and awkwardness as she performed what she saw as her *"sexual display"*.

Like her counterparts, Bodhi and Evanna, Petra sailed through her early years without making any enemies or any that she ever knew or heard about!

Friendship made her happy but being a rescuer made her happier still.

v The Oak Tree

We all have family and friends of some description which, in the most part, help us through our lives. It is said that:

"You can't choose your family, but you can choose your friends", which as a saying, rang true for all of our three. None ever felt comfortable or happy at home but found love, solace and whatever else they needed as individuals in their friendships.

They all went through the death of a loved one early on in their lives which certainly made a hole in the hearts of each of them although they were too young, at that time, to realise how deep those chasms actually were.

Thus, the similarities between the oak tree and our three "actors" may seem as if a strange analogy but if one looks deeply into it, the similarities are there, especially as each had their own beloved oak tree which figured so strongly throughout the whole of their lives.

In a sense each of their oaks represented a kind of family member that they desired or at least a very dear friend — with their constant strong sturdy dependable presence.

Book 2
Mighty Oakes Of Little Acorns Grow (1)

The Mast Years

As the human parent allows and encourages their maturing offspring to move away in order to live their lives and fulfil their dreams, out in the big wide world whilst standing on their own two feet, so too does the oak tree.

Young adults go out into the world to face what life has to offer and what chance deals. Some survive better than others. Some thrive whilst others do not.

In the months of September through to early November the parent oak tree bids a fond farewell to its mature acorns which fall from their progenitor's boughs so to disperse their single seed. Some do not make it as other residents of the forest dine on them whilst humans also collect them for their own purposes. But some are gathered by squirrels and jays who scatter — hoard such prizes in caches for future feasts. Unbeknownst to these creatures, by hoarding these acorns they are acting as botanists conserving this magnificent tree by planting the acorns in a variety of locations in which it becomes possible for them to germinate and thrive. Even though such jays and squirrels memorise mental maps of the locations of their stockpiles with the plan to return and consume them at some later date, the odd acorn may be lost, thus allowing a small number to germinate and survive, which in turn produces the next generation of oak trees.

So, there we have it. Humans let their children go in order to survive, grow and perchance aid in the production of the future generation. Some succeed with their own goals, some manage, some fail, some die prior to doing anything. Likewise, the oak does the same, the consequences of which are equal to their human counterparts.

Evanna and Petra's parents have enabled them to enter into the world whilst Bodhi's desperately want him to go.

So, let us now see within these following pages what befalls each. Do the fruits of the *"enclosed land"* (i.e. the acorn and in a sense our three individuals) survive, thrive or do we witness their demise?

Chapter 7
i Evanna The Akerne

The light blue "hair shirt" with a collar and three small white buttons that stretched from breast bone to collar bone itched at her skin made worse by the tight-fitting woollen, army style, navy blue jumper worn on top (without the navy blue and white striped material snake belt as that was issued, alongside the established cadet uniform upon the successful completion of the four-week Induction phase). Her legs were covered with three-quarter length, basic tactical navy trousers tapering off at the calf with a Velcro fastening. Her feet, dressed in thick woollen navy walking socks pulled up to the knee, were not yet accustomed to the new, stiff and yet to be broken into brown leather walking boots. It took a while to master the correct positioning of the beret, also navy, so that the silver Metropolitan Police Cadet Corps badge faced to the front. Any other positioning, even if a millimetre out, was not correct and meant punishment.

The jumper was only to be worn in unison with other course members; if one wore it all wore it, but if one did not all did not. The beret was to be worn at all times whilst outside but never inside unless ordered to do so. An army green cagoule complete with high neck and hood which, on appearance and texture, was made from the exact same material as the huge rucksack which was also issued alongside a black balaclava, one spare set of all clothing, apart from the boots where one pair was sufficient. All of this formed the Induction kit but was used during all Adventure Training exercises during the next 46 weeks.

Alongside this, a standard PT kit was issued: two white Air tex T-shirts, a navy-blue sports skirt underneath which was to be worn the huge navy PT "modesty" pant and bright white plimsoles.

New recruits were told to bring brown and black shoe polish plus white plimsole whitener with them. Brown for the boots, black for their eventual issue black shoes to be worn with the official cadet uniform issued after Induction and the whitener's use is obvious! An assortment of shoe brushes and cloths was a must.

Course 40 consisted of twenty-four young 18-year-olds fresh out of school. Seven young women and seventeen vernal men stood to attention in three ranks of eight in the pouring rain, dressed in their Induction issue plus jumpers being shouted at by Colour Police Sergeant Willard because they were twenty seconds late for their first drill lesson. Upon first sight it could not be recognised which cadet was female and which male as the uniform was the exact same. As punishment for their lateness twenty press ups, by each, were performed on the puddle-spattered parade square. This admonishment was a "let off" in actuality!

Castigations were dished out at regular intervals; for a single "tramline" on a trouser or shirt; smudges on boots or the eventual black shoes; slightly dirty white plimsole laces; tardiness... if one cadet should make even a small snafu of this ilk, the whole course tended to receive a "beasting" ranging from press ups to "show parades" to sunrise nine-mile runs or six-mile log runs which consisted of one heavy log being placed onto the shoulders of four cadets with which they were to run through the muddiest areas of parkland possible and wade across often rat-infested streams and rivers. Character building, they said! The individual guilty party was never blamed, well at least for the first time, as they were all in the same boat. Each single one of them ended up receiving a whole course punishment at some point!

Evanna shared her dormitory with the six other girls on her course. There was Vicky the bonny Yorkshire lass, Ellen the wonderfully funny yet profane Glaswegian, Elise the Stones and Roses fan from Hull, Tracey the athletic Mancunian blonde bombshell but a "space cadet" (in a good way), the highly organised, efficient and brilliant Eva from the Home Counties and Rosalind the lovely, quiet, old-fashioned, posh girl from Surrey. Then there was Evanna who had no clue where or how she would ever fit in with these girls who all appeared so much more capable than herself. These girls, who heralded from vastly different backgrounds with the most diverse personalities, not only had to get on with each other but also with their seventeen male counterparts coming from equally mismatched upbringings and boasted sundry dispositions. Somehow this was achieved. Somehow each individual cadet served his or her individual "purpose" within this cohort. As a result, the course as a whole shone thanks to its monumental ability to support its members as they embraced their individualities, differences and eccentricities. They supported each other throughout and each discovered that the strongest glue-like bond had been created which was never to break. Each had twenty-three new siblings, brothers and sisters, who knew one another better than anyone had or indeed would ever manage to do. This was owing to the often extreme, conditions in which they were put that tested each individual to the max. Each cadet became strangely familiar to each other's fears, strengths, weaknesses — to the whole personality as they each metaphorically "undressed" themselves in front of each other sometimes without even realising it. Even after thirty years those tight connections and bonds remained. True Cadets — *"one for all and all for one"*, forever there for each other, proud, strong, tenacious, supportive.

Each evening every cadet throughout the Corps was fully engaged intricately ironing and defluffing their uniform (including PT and AT kit), shining shoes until faces could be seen in them, polishing boots, whitening plimsoles including their laces in preparation for Parade the following morning and associated lessons throughout the day. Coupled with this hive of activity was the organising and tidying of dormitories including personal cupboards in case there was also a surprise dorm inspection.

Course 40 was in Rowan House and was privileged to have the best staff: Inspector or Ma'am Trooper, Sergeant Hilary and Staff Jefferson, a Police Constable who was the cheekiest, kind, funny, just a tad sarcastic, encouraging and such a respected man. He was one who gained that respect without instilling fear and dread but who garnered his authority in a quiet and unimpeachable manner. He also proved to be the most sought-after pin-up for most of the female cadets! These three amazing people were Course 40's core instructors. Bill Jefferson and Evanna would become the most wonderfully close friends in the years to come but for now he will strictly be referred to as Staff Jefferson as that bond came after the Cadets, and remains for future reporting.

Course 40's main Physical Training Instructor, or PTI, was the no-nonsense, punctilious, rigorous, uncompromising authoritarian Staff Daley who managed to propagate a great deal of angst and trepidation yet reverence and fealty in each cadet who came across him. In actuality, when not "performing" as an instructor he was a funny and caring individual. He became legendary in his own right. Evanna spent her time in the cadets, as did they all, trembling before each Physical or Adventure Training lesson, but Evanna especially dreaded the assault course. However, over the years to come, she became most grateful to this awesome man who gave her the sheer will to do things she otherwise would never have tried or achieved. She owed her future tenacity, mental strength, determination and courage to him. He certainly was character building and an individual she grew to truly admire.

It wasn't until Evanna experienced her first Adventure Training (AT) lesson on the assault course that she even realised that she was afraid of heights. Staff Daley ordered groups of six to climb The Tripod which was an extremely high scaffold structure. Her group was the first to climb. She began to do so confidently and without fear but once at the top, Staff Daley instructed them to release their hands from the scaffolding and to "*stand tall*". As they did so he proceeded to shake The Tripod so hard that Evanna thought she would fall all the way down onto the thin layer of sand which was supposed to break such disasters! She did not fall, but here lay the birth of her acrophobia which was really basophobia, FOF — fear of falling. If a cadet should fall, falter or fail at any given obstacle, they were to lie face down in the sand then roll like a log whilst their fellow cadets kicked sand all over them. That sand got everywhere, in every bodily crevice and orifice!

Evanna also discovered that she had never learned how to climb a rope. Not only was this a mandatory requirement which was often performed but cadets had to complete it in a set style and in three shifts. At first, Evanna could not even get onto the damn rope let alone climb the thing. The fear this produced in her at every PT lesson did not enable her to improve. Her sweaty palms and the derogatory shouts aimed at her by Staff Daley did nothing to aid her! The rope climb was a key component in each PT test at the end of each module's work. She was determined to master this, as it was the only constituent that prevented her from passing this test. So, for the remainder of the course, until the very last and most important PT test, Evanna was in the gym at 0600hrs seven days a week practising the rope climb and building up her upper body strength as Staff Daley did not hold back in ridiculing her. It did not take long until her nemesis cottoned onto the fact that she was no quitter but an ardent and impassioned striver to succeed. Over time, Staff Daley began to come out of his office and help her during which time a real mutual respect was formed.

Each morning began with Parade on the Parade Square during which uniforms were inspected by senior instructors and the flags were flown. If a uniform should be spotted with even the slightest crease or tramline, a fleck of fluff, a belt not centred correctly or there was a tiny scuff or blemish on a shoe, the guilty cadet was to attend Show Parade that evening when their uniform was to be perfect as expected at all times. There was also often a punishment dished out for the whole course. If it was raining, dormitories were inspected alongside individual cupboards and uniforms. If anything was considered out of place or imperfect, residents of the entire dorm were punished and a Show Parade for the individual.

Another dread that was realised in Evanna was that of "*Trogging*". This was a night-time exercise whereby one dormitory, housing another female course within the same block, would raid another dorm whilst they were sleeping. As they would rush in, each bed would be upended whilst the occupants slept causing their heads to bash onto the wall behind. It would also consist of water guns, flour and sometimes treacle. Trogging was performed in good humour but did take some getting used to until Evanna found herself as a "*Trogger*" during which she found she thoroughly enjoyed herself and realised that she would have to just deal with being at the receiving end.

Back to the Induction which proved to be four weeks of hell: marching, PT, AT, beastings, punishments, sunrise nine-mile runs and log runs, endless kit and dorm inspections and finally a week spent in the wilds of Derbyshire adventure training. This involved: rock climbing, abseiling, canoeing, walking for miles and miles wearing the heaviest rucksack imaginable. Staff would joke that all that they could see of Evanna were her little legs "protruding" from the pack on her back. On her first abseil, Staff Selwyn literally pushed her off the cliff as her legs were trembling as if jelly and all of her courage seemed to drain from her soul! It proved a hard week for all; there were blisters galore, sore aching backs and feet but also laughter and camaraderie as the course bonded and grew together. They began to love one another as brothers and sisters.

On their return, after a weekend of nursing their wounds it was time to begin their first proper module. All twenty-four had passed the Induction phase, none were back classed, and none invalided out or decided to leave.

First, and the most exciting thing of all, was the issuing of the proper Cadet Corps uniform now they were true cadets. This consisted of navy trousers, white shirt, the same navy jumpers worn on Induction, but they were now allowed to wear the navy and white snake belt. Blue epaulettes denoting the Cadet Corps were now worn on the shoulders of both jumper and shirt with a blue lanyard, denoting Rowan House. Female Cadets were to wear the WPC bowler style hats with a blue band and Cadet

Corps badge whilst the males wore a cap with the same appendages. Black shoes were also issued as well as Number Ones which consisted of a dark navy skirt for the girls (trousers for boys), and tunic with which the white shirt and hats were to be worn with white gloves for the hands. These uniforms were for special occasions only.

The next two months were, again, based at the Cadet Centre. They consisted of academic studies, namely, basic law and police procedure, multicultural studies, psychology and First Aid. At the end of the module's work projects were to be completed. Naturally, there was also PT and AT every day, swimming and drill twice a week, parade every day and many a "surprise" thrown in for good measure, such as early morning runs, log runs, dorm inspections, extra fitness lessons and so forth. PT, First Aid and swimming tests also awaited them at the end of the module. Their days were packed and exhausting with the obligatory clothes washing, ironing, shoe cleaning, dorm and cupboard tidying each evening.

The following module was their first opportunity to go off on their own and perform some service within the community. Each cadet was given their own environment in which they would be attached for the next few months. Evanna was sent to work at a school for special needs children in East London. She loved this and excelled at the work. Each Wednesday the cadets remained on site for PT and AT in the morning followed by a fun sporting afternoon in which the whole corps participated.

After this module came another academic one, similar to the first but harder and more involved with the usual exams and tests at the fruition. Next to come was further Community Service. The final module was an academic one at the end of which each cadet had to complete a presentation to do with the police service;

a project for each subject studied, the final PT and swimming tests plus other certificates.

In order to pass each academic module each cadet had to successfully complete Adventure Training weeks in Snowdonia, North Wales. The first was entitled Intermediate Wales (the Induction adventure training being called "Basic Camp") which was followed in the final module by Advanced Wales. As their names suggest each week grew progressively harder.

Their base was the Metropolitan Police "cottage" high up in the mountains where it always rained. This cottage was basically a shack in which the instructors got to sleep in proper beds, albeit bunks, whilst the cadets were relegated to tents. Washing and cooking facilities were minimal and basic!

Intermediate Wales proved tough going for all. Prior to leaving their base in order to go anywhere, all of their kit, including tents, had to be packed away and loaded into their rucksacks which were then hoisted onto their backs which by the end of the week were crippled by the weight. AT kit was worn and expected to be cleaned, somehow, each evening after their day's toil ready for use the following day. A stream which flowed along the bottom of the site was where this was completed but needless to say no kit ever appeared spick and span after the first day. Spares were also obviously carried and worn but nothing stayed clean for long in the wind, rain, mud and even snow! Evanna was introduced to Mount Snowdon during this Intermediate week. It was on a cold, foggy morning in February at 0600hrs when the bugle announced reveille. Having completed their ablutions, eaten their breakfast of porridge and packed up their belongings it was time to vacate their shelter of the week and head for Snowdon. Needless to say, the cadets were led up through the Grade 3 route, being the toughest and hardest going.

These routes are considered rock climbs as opposed to mere scrambles. This particular one tackled the notorious Crib Goch. The traverse required using both hands and feet leading up from the "Pyg track" which was followed by an ascent to the arête prior to tackling three rock-pinnacles to a grassy col and Bwlch Coch. The initial part of the ridge, of Crib Goch, is exposed with precipices below. Just before the cadets went across, Staff Jefferson gaily informed them of the number of fatalities that had occurred here of even the *"most experienced of mountaineers"*. Each cadet then took their turn to traverse the ridge. It was impossible to cross two abreast. Finally, it was Evanna's turn but when that time came, she froze to the spot. The fog had gone revealing bright sunshine, but it was cold and rather windy. It had not long since snowed leaving rocky, uneven ground underneath to freeze in part. Even before crossing she could already see the severe drop on either side. One false step or slip could bring about her falling to the earth way beneath and thus her inevitable death. Unable to walk across it through sheer fright she had no other choice but to crawl in which she duly, at a snail-like pace, succeeded. At either end cadets shouted words of encouragement whilst staff were taking the unavoidable yet, Evanna considered, unnecessary piss out of her! It seemed an age to reach the other side but when she finally did, she was helped to her feet by the very calm, trustworthy and loyal Cadet Simons.

Advanced Wales proved to be the most *"character building"* of the three Adventure Training weeks. Evanna recalled, in future times, what she appellated to be *"her most torturous three consecutive days ever"*!

These occurred in the middle of that week in December.
The First Day:
One lengthy and hilly route march with full kit plus rucksack

to the beach. Followed by sea canoeing navigating through rather rough and cold waters.

After this, the hopeful cadets stood in line waiting to be allowed into the bus nicknamed the "*Green Goddess*". However, staff duly laughed at them, instructed them back into rank and file before route marching them safely back to camp the way they had come. Exhausted, the cadets cleaned their uniform, polished their boots, then, after supper of some kind of stew, went directly to their tents, wrapped up warmly against the night's elements, and went to sleep. Camping in December is no laughing matter at the best of times but high up in the mountains of North Wales it proved rather nefarious as the ice cold attacked their very bones. It was roughly 2300hrs when the cadets retired. It was approximately 0130hrs when the bugle rudely awoke them, and staff could be heard yelling: "*up — get up, you, ugly lot. Everyone up and out. Get dressed and packed up. 5 minutes GO.*" In double quick time twenty-four bleary eyed, boreal, benumbed and bewildered cadets were stood in ranks. They were then ordered to reverse their balaclavas so that the gaps for their eyes were now at the back. All that could be seen was the black of the wool and they were thus blind. Then herded into the rear of a Land Rover they were instructed to empty their pockets of all money and were divided into groups of two. Each group was provided with a map and compass and were informed that, in these groups, they were to reach Britannia Bridge, Anglesey, some thirty miles away by 1000hrs the following morning. They were able to use any method they chose to arrive at the grid point.

Evanna was coupled with Cadet Simons. The duos were dropped off at their designated start points. Evanna and Cadet Simons were the third to alight and it was when their feet touched the stony ground that they could right their balaclavas. Still, they remained both literally and metaphorically in the dark. They found themselves on a small snowy track in the middle of nowhere. As they heard the Land Rover's engine and saw its rear lights disappear into the distance, they knew they were now on their own. They both stared into the pitch black of the night with only the night sky's decoration and their map and compass to guide them.

Being cadets, they had each placed their issue torches in easily accessible places which once switched on did not immediately illuminate them as to where they stood on the map! After much orientation of map and compass they managed to pinpoint an approximate place which they considered "*good enough*". On discussing their next move, they came up with a plan. They were to walk the next seven miles, give or take, to the nearest A road where they would hitchhike as far as a kindly driver would allow. They began to walk but the going proved tough. Legs were aching from not only the previous day's events but from the beginning of the camp, feet were blistered and heels cried out in pain, backs broke with the load they were carrying and hunger was on their minds despite being provided with rations. Finally, they reached their initial destination. Neither having hitchhiked before they huddled together, mainly for warmth, held a brief discussion concerning the most assured way of getting their desired lift. Their strategy was precise, well organised and coherent. It involved Cadet Simons hiding behind a bush leaving Evanna to stand by the roadside, seemingly alone, thumb up in the hitchhiker pose whilst looking forlorn. The theory behind this master plan was that a trucker would more likely stop for a lone female in distress — not that anyone would be able to tell that Evanna was in fact a female, with her balaclava, AT attire including heavy walking boots and rucksack, especially in the depths of the night. Despite this, their plan was not only successful but proved to exceed even their highest expectations as the very first lorry that came into view pulled over and very happily allowed both cadets inside. The trucker told them that he would be able to drop them off after 15 miles and then it would be a hike to

Llanfairpwllgwyngyllgogerychwyrndrobwllllantysiliogogo goch where they could catch the first morning train which would carry them to Britannia Bridge Station after which it was only a short 2.8-mile walk to their allotted grid reference. On inspecting their map, the terrain looked flat which pleased them. After the two weary cadets jumped into the kindly trucker's cab, he took pity on their bone-tired and beleaguered appearance. He suggested they get some warmth and possibly some "*shut eye*" in his makeshift bed behind his driver's seat. Whiskey, coffee, sandwiches and crisps were also on offer which both Cadet Simons, whose first name was Terry, and Evanna consumed with glee and no little cupidity! After a brief yet welcome doze the truck driver pulled his horn to announce their arrival at their drop-off point. They never did discover his real name as he merely went by the name "*Baloo*" — possibly because of his heavy-set tattooed structure which belied his gentle and kindly nature. The cadets thanked him profusely and off Baloo drove into the dark.

Terry and Evanna hoisted their rucksacks, which now felt as if they had been filled with bricks, and began their hike to the train station which boasted the longest name in the world. Once there they found a lonely looking guard, sporting heavy eyes, sitting on a chair with his feet up resting on a wooden desk whilst nursing a steaming cup of tea. On spotting the two, equally heavy-eyed, uniformed cadets he chuckled whilst saying:

"there's more like you up on the platform! We see you poor lot here every so often. Up you go — Platform 2. Travel's free for you." True enough, on Platform 2 were six other members of Course 40 lying there fast asleep using their bulky rucksacks as pillows. One had bagsied the bench whilst the rest were lain close together, to keep out the biting elements, on the platform's concrete floor.

On hearing Terry and Evanna's footsteps most woke enough to offer a grunt and there were pats on the ground, amidst the huddle of bodies, to say "come join us — keep warm" which neither hesitated to do. A broken, frozen sleep came. At dawn they were woken by the now wearier-eyed guard with offerings of his cache of hot chocolate and Bourbon biscuits. Once the obligatory photographs were taken of the group crouched beside the station's fifty-five-lettered nameplate their train eased towards them. The journey was not long, but it was welcome and just long enough to melt their frozen frames. The seats had padding. It was a relief not to be walking. After disembarking at Britannia Bridge Station, as directed by Baloo, they began the flat 2.8-mile walk to their end point which they arrived at with plenty of time to spare. Time enough for yet more group and individual snapshots whilst relating tales of their various night-time adventures and wait for the rest of their number to arrive as this group of eight were the first. The last had walked the whole distance as they did not know how else to get there. On hearing this the remainder laughed so much it hurt. Those two poor cadets, two males as it happens, were forever marked and were even more upset upon discovering that one duo somehow "bagged" a lift from their exact drop-off point all the way to the final grid reference — although it took a while for a trucker to stop for them.

Bang on 1000hrs the "Green Goddess" arrived with a cheery and annoyingly refreshed looking Staff Jefferson at the wheel. Each cadet dragged their chaffed, raw, tender feet and abscessed bodies into the vehicle. Glad to sit down. Relieved to think that they would soon be back at base where they would, no doubt, be debriefed and then allowed to rest at least for a while. However, consternation mounted when the vehicle turned towards the coastline instead of the mountains. Echoes of *"what the fuck — where are you taking us now, Staff!"* and *"You must be having a laugh!"* filled the Goddess's small and now rather smelly interior. *"Don't worry, 40. We're off for a jolly,"* announced Staff Jefferson. Course 40 did not quite believe this as Staff was known for his light-hearted manner but sometimes blind omissions of the truth! He was the one who would declare, whilst on a long run: *"nearly done — just around the corner"* but that corner was either many miles further in the making or round many different corners. However, he was a man who truly could make vodka out of raw potatoes. Knowing his sense of humour, which actually was appreciated by all cadets, they knew only too well that they were about to embark on no *"jolly"*. Indeed, it was not, especially for Evanna for the fear of heights that continued to betray her was about to do so once again. They disembarked at a large cliff overlooking the cold Irish Sea where other members of jocose staff awaited them.

Evanna was not able to spot the familiar climbing equipment or canoes or logs that usually accompanied the AT staff. Staff Green finally announced: *"Gals and guys, we're not climbing up this rock, but we are traversing around this rock — so get your pretty selves together."*

As it turned out sea traversing, as it was called, required no equipment. No rope, no helmet, no nothing despite the rather high and ragged rock face which dropped at such a height into the icy and not particularly calm sea underneath. Basically, the premise was if anyone should fall, no harm done, just a wet and sea-battered cadet.

Evanna gingerly began to take her turn, trying to find hand- and footholds. Trembling she began her junket. They were to traverse quite a distance. Evanna had no idea how her sore aching feet and freezing cold hands would manage to stick fast to any abutments. The mid-December Irish Sea did not look overwhelmingly inviting. Needless to say, it did not take too long until she felt herself suspended in mid-air yet hurtling, at a turtle's pace, closer and closer to that exact same mid-December Irish Sea. Suddenly the ice-cold waters engulfed her and shocked her into life. She found it too deep for her feet to touch the seabed, so upon realising she had no other option dragged her tired but also uniformed and booted body to the shore. Front crawl proved to be the best stroke for this endeavour. Despite being a very proficient swimmer, it was as if she was swimming the Atlantic Ocean, although in reality the shore was not far away. Both uniform and boots weighed her down — it proved a struggle. She eventually buoyed herself to stand up. As the waves broke about her feet she staggered onto the wet sand. Her uniform soaked and her boots filled to the brim with water, inside which upon emptying them her feet could be heard squelching. She then heard shouts of: "*Cadet Michaels,*" as was her surname, "*the cold and wet never hurt a fly. No pain no gain. Back to it.*" PT and AT staff only seemed able to use short sentences! Evanna prayed he was joking and that once she had climbed her way back above sea level, she would find dry clothing, a hot drink, maybe a bacon sandwich and even a hug awaiting her. That sadly remained a dream — even the hot drink. Every time she found herself fall back into that damn sea only to wend her way back up, six times in total — yes SIX times, she had to begin again. On her seventh attempt, somehow, she managed, the whole traverse but even then, her dream was not realised at the other end apart from hugs and cheers from her comrades. She was far from the only one to fall in but was the only one to fall in six times, bar one who did the dreaded deed once more than her! That was poor Cadet Barker, Rosalind, who looked even colder than the ice-cold Evanna.

Fortunately, this was the end of Evanna's self-entitled "*most torturous three consecutive days ever*". The last two days proved as if a holiday in comparison but in reality, they weren't much different from the initial two. Anyway, that was it — Advanced Wales, with all of its horrors, yet laughter and camaraderie had been passed and completed by all twenty-four cadets of Course 40.

Back at the Cadet School, Course 40 had a very busy few weeks writing their individual presentations; practising the drill routines for their Passing Out Parade and ensuring that they pass their final PT test, Community Sports Leaders Award; Gold Life Saving and other swimming certificates, their First Aid exam et al.

Evanna decided to complete her project and presentation on India 99, the Police Helicopter Division, which searched for criminals, missing people and such like from the skies using thermal imaging and infrared devices. This entailed having a visit to their headquarters as well as a "tour", an eight-hour shift, in the helicopter. She enjoyed this immensely and during her time on it her crew were directed to attend some exciting and ultimately successful jobs.

Every cadet dreaded each PT test but the final one was the

most nerve wracking of all.

Evanna felt confident that she would easily pass all elements well — bar one — the rope climb. She had given every ounce of effort to this over the course of the year. From being unable to even get her feet onto the rope she could now reach the top, using the prescribed form, in 3.5 shifts. However, 3.5 was not good enough to pass. A solid 3 was the only way she would pass. Her technique would then be judged out of 10. She had lifted so many heavy weights in her undertaking to develop her upper body strength which she had more than achieved.

Evanna stood poised in front of the rope, in the middle of a line of three. Each of those three cadets were standing at ease with eyes front anxiously awaiting the order to "*climb*". When it came, they immediately burst into action. She pulled her way expertly through the first shift, then the second. She went straight into the third knowing it was now, make or break. She heaved her way up leaving room enough only to touch the top leather strapping at the very top, as was the correct procedure, before she made her way back down in the uniform three shifts. Whilst she was performing this task, she could actually feel the tension of her fellow cadets who telepathically willed her to the top. Once there she was not able to scream aloud with euphoria, nor were the rest of her fellows but she could sense their joy and pride as if it was her own, and her own was in abundance. Her feet landed on the floor alongside the other two climbers whilst the rest of the course were lined up in three lines, one behind each rope awaiting their turn. Evanna stood at ease waiting for her fate, the marks out of ten. She wanted to punch the air with her fist and shout with glee as Staff Daley announced: "*Cadet Michaels — 9*" in his very formal and stern tone. All she was allowed to say was "*thank you, Staff*" in a neutral voice as if he had completed the climb in her stead. However, as she marched past him, to take her place on the floor, Staff Daley acknowledged her efforts with a deadpan face but with a big wink from his left eye. Evanna achieved top marks for all of the other exercises that made up the test — job done!

She passed every test, every exam, every project, every presentation with flying colours. All of the hard work was done. Now it was just relentless drill lessons to perfect their marching for the Passing Out Parade. However, there proved to be a spanner in the works in that the Police Training School "*proper*" did not have a course available for Course 40 until a few months ahead, meaning that they were to be "*held over*" at the Cadet School for that time. As, in effect, they had completed the course, they were allowed certain privileges but were still expected to attend morning Parade and behave as a "Cadet" should. They continued to be put through their paces in the realm of fitness, but this was done with more joviality and humour as it was Staff Jefferson who took charge. One day they were supposed to be attending a day clearing rubbish from a parkland, but Staff was informed en route by the local council they were due to help that this was now cancelled. Without asking his superiors for permission he immediately took a detour to Thorpe Park and what a fabulous day they had! Sworn to secrecy the cadets arrived back with huge grins plastered over their faces. It was questioned how a day's rubbish clearance could possibly make twenty-five people, including Staff Jefferson, so happy. Then there was the scabies outbreak. The culprit of which was none other than Course 40's Cadet Downing who had a penchant for female nurses, female paramedics, female anything! As a result, the whole of the Cadet School, including staff, had to "paint" their whole bodies with this rather revolting gloop resembling light blue emulsion paint. Cadets painted each other with literal paint brushes ensuring that every nook and cranny had been covered. The gloop then required time to "set" before it could be showered off. The purpose of which was to kill off any bugs. All uniforms, bedding, mattresses — everything had to be burned after which the cadets were sent home for a long weekend whilst new equipment was procured. Poor Cadet Downing just could not keep it in his pants but as a result he never did live this "*incident*" down!

Course 40 was also used to help out the police "proper" mainly for searches. This normally entailed the rather grisly task of searching for dead bodies, often weeks or months old, who had fallen victim of murder, had gone missing or had received some other fate. This also included searching for murder weapons, other evidence, articles of clothing or anything that could possibly be related to the job at hand. The cadets travelled all over the Metropolitan Police area in order to do this as they had been fully trained as part of the cadet course. The police, however, were not routinely search trained, resulting in the cadets being used for their expertise. Donned in their AT attire, carrying long wooden poles for searching through long grasses, marsh lands, rivers and ponds they would carry out their duty. They also completed intricate fingertip searches. Course 40 were often successful with their "finds" which could be gruesome sights. Their first search entailed searching for a 16-year-old boy called Darren Ball who had gone missing, presumed murdered by a gang. He had nothing to do with this gang but was merely protecting another young person whom the gang were threatening. No body was found but some clothing was. The cadets were shown a photograph of Darren and informed of the background to the case prior to the search. Evanna absorbed this until it was literally etched into her brain. This was an image and a story she could not and would not ever forget. Darren was never found. Nor was it ever discovered what truly befell him.

The course was also called upon to aid the emergency services when various different body parts needed to be found, collected and bagged after someone had thrown themselves in front of a train. They found body parts strewn for miles along the railway tracks. This was not a pleasant job. However, these young cadets performed everything professionally whilst quickly learning that a certain rather dark sense of humour was required if they were ever to survive as police officers.

Evanna, herself, was used as a decoy so that detectives from a station in the East End of London could detect and arrest a male who preyed on teenage schoolgirls by flashing his appendage at them and asking them to fondle it! As she looked so young Evanna was chosen to act as such a schoolgirl. She had been provided with a school uniform from the local school, short white socks 'n' all. As it was summer the detectives ensured that they kept her cool with phallic-type rocket ice lollies for her to lick, while she stood in the predator's "patch". She was there for days but made friends of sorts with the two officers in the case, who were always in her line of sight. Each day they treated her to lunch in one of the local Pie 'n' Mash shops where she was introduced to the traditional food of the East End — Pie, Mash and Liquor. The "sting" was a success. Evanna was even invited back to the CID office for a celebratory drink — namely whiskey.

So, the next two months of the Hold Over carried on in such a manner but let's go back and consider the "other" lives the cadets had throughout the course.

There was Additional PT after the "working day" for those who needed extra input. These were harsh sessions held three times a week in the gymnasium with Staff Daley at the helm. Because of struggling with the rope climb, Evanna found herself in this group for several modules.

However, down time was obviously required during which cadets headed for the "Blue Lamp Club" which was, basically, their onsite social room which housed a tuck shop, pool table, general seating area and the obligatory smoking area. The latter was mostly filled with male cadets — and Evanna! Cadets were allowed off campus during their free time — evenings and weekends. Their curfew from Sunday to Thursday was 2230hrs but this was extended on Friday and Saturday nights, by a whole half an hour, to 2300hrs. Lateness, even by one second would mean some form of punishment early the next morning, and usually with a hangover from hell!

The Cadet School had many official mottos, such as: "*Integrity, Compassion and Courage*", non-official ones, such as: "*no pain no gain*", "*no planning or preparation means piss poor performance*" (Staff Daley's delight), "*the wheel's come right off*" (a favourite of Staff Jefferson), and "*it's goodnight Vienna*" (again often to be heard by Staff Daley), but of course, Course 40 had one of their own which was their preferred "motto" of choice:

"*Don't despair,*
Have no care,
All will be fixed
In the White Bear."

The White Bear being the local public house where many a fun-filled, alcohol-fuelled evening was spent.

Cadets also took part in extracurricular sporting events. Evanna represented the Cadets in swimming, triathlon, long distance running and Olympic-style wrestling. Her preference was the triathlon in which she went on to successfully compete for the Metropolitan Police for the length of her service. Overall, she won many a gold medal and trophy often beating the armed services teams.

The Corps also hosted inter-class sporting tournaments and events in which all cadets were expected to partake. Some of these were fun whilst others were taken more seriously. Off curricular was the inevitable "inter course" which most cadets took time to enjoy but some were more successful than others in this event!

Course 40, as a whole, also represented the Cadet Corps in a range of events: the Chichester March, the Devizes to Westminster Canoe Race, Ten Tors, the Lord Mayor's Show and Remembrance Sunday.

There were also Dining Out Night, which was a formal dinner at the school where Cadets donned their No.1s, had "posh nosh" in Simpson Hall, followed by a disco in their civvies. Then there was the Corps Christmas Party where staff served the Cadets their dinner.

Whilst on their Hold Over, Staff Jefferson was able to get his hands upon twenty-five tickets which gained them entry to join the audience for various televised quiz shows including *Blankety Blank* with host Terry Wogan. These tickets included admittance to the television's studio bar where they got to meet the show's host. How he managed to obtain these tickets was a mystery!

As a result of these varied experiences both at work and at play, each course, but especially Course 40, developed tight knit and treasured relationships with each other which were to last a lifetime. As they said: *"No one knows you like another Cadet"* — as no one truly knew an individual — ever — like a fellow Cadet Course member regardless of the time that passed without seeing each other.

Evanna and some of her fellow cadets appeared in several national newspapers in an advertising campaign for the Cadet Corps. Accompanying the blurb, the headline of which read:

"It starts with an adventure and ends with an education."

Going on to say:

"The end product is a group of mature, well-balanced and physically fit individuals, ready to start training as police officers."

Accompanying this was a picture of Evanna being stretchered down part of the Snowdon mountainside. She was chosen for this role because she happened to be the lightest of the group!

The truth behind the written statement rang true but The Cadet Corps was far more and meant far more than those few words. It was character building for sure; it could be gruelling; scary at times; exhausting and exciting. It was learning about taking pride in oneself; about giving 100% of yourself in everything you did; it was learning the art of working as a team and also as an individual. It was about respect and trust for others and oneself. It was about friendship, camaraderie, supporting others and toughening up. It was about staying the course when all you wanted to do was give in and give up. It was about acceptance and confidence. It was gaining a family of 23 siblings who would be there for each other come what may and for the long haul. It set Evanna up for life, with its many twists and turns, and indeed was her proudest achievement.

The Passing Out Day arrived. The Day that Course 40 had been practising for so long. Smartly turned out in their No.1 uniforms they made their entrance onto the sunny parade square where family and friends awaited them to see the parade, and their review and inspection by the Metropolitan Police Cadet Corps Commandant. Course 40 chose their final march to be accompanied by the Simple Minds song *"Don't You Forget About Me"* which actually saw them through the course as a whole. The first two marches were alongside the Metropolitan Police Band which they were apparently privileged to have, another of Staff Jefferson's "requisitions"! The Parade went off without a hitch. It was then into Simpson Hall for the Awards Ceremony where Evanna was presented with the Endeavour Shield for her hard efforts whilst to her utmost joy Cadet Terry Simons won the Best Cadet Baton. Alongside this, all of their numerous certificates were awarded.

Evanna gained 98% in the First-Class Physical Training Tests and her final Cadet Profile for PT, written by Staff Daley read:

- *Confidence — Good*
- *Leadership -Good*
- *Compassion — Good*
- *Reliability — Strong*
- *Punctuality — Strong*
- *Courage — Strong*
- *Tenacity — Strong*
- *Fitness — Strong*

Alongside this he wrote:

"This young woman has given 100% to the gymnasium work. She has improved because of her efforts and is a credit to herself and the Cadet Corps."

This was the icing on the cake.

Afterwards, cadets were allowed to take their guests on a tour of the centre followed by a buffet lunch. Finally came the moving Sunset Ceremony, the final March Past and the tossing of hats to mark the end.

Evanna would be returning home — but just for one week after which she would be returning to the Peel Centre to attend the Metropolitan Police Training School for twenty weeks.

Once home she went straight up to her bedroom, which she had not seen for the entirely of her being a Cadet. She began to read the Passing Out Day Programme and came across the brief passage that Staff Jefferson wrote about each member of Course 40. Using his tongue and cheek tone he wrote:

"Evanna joined the school as an accomplished runner but had difficulty with strength exercises like canoeing and rope climbing. However, her true character showed through to overcome these problems. Her community service module saw her dealing with mentally and physically disabled young people and later in an old age people's home. Evanna has already experienced active policing when she assisted CID in South London to act as a decoy for a local flasher. She admits to being quite frightened but relieved when he finally took the bait — could it have been the white ankle socks!

She has represented the Corps in Olympic wrestling, running, triathlon and swimming.

Evanna looks forward to becoming a Woman Police Officer and one of the fittest no doubt."

Whilst she sat on her bed, Evanna took time to reflect upon her year as a Police Cadet or *"Gadget"*, as ex-cadets were called in the rank and file of policemen and women she was yet to discover! For the first time in her life, the Akerne believed that life truly did have possibilities, vast ones at that. When a child she felt so weak, powerless and vulnerable but now having found her courage she had become the Brave Fighter that she was conceived to become. For she had: beaten the rope climb;

conquered the abseil; out-flanked the sea traverse; bamboozled Crib Goch and conquered the Night Hike. All of this having been achieved whilst staring into the face of adversity. She had proven to herself, if no one else, her strength of courage and tenacity but deep down she knew that she had not only demonstrated these attributes to herself but to the whole course including the instructors, but most importantly Staff Jefferson and Staff Daley. Her wish of wanting to feel alive before she died was already partly satisfied, as she felt it whilst braving the icy cold Irish Sea; the fear she felt whilst mountaineering; the exhaustion she felt whilst running as a team with telegraph poles on their shoulders in a log run; the joy and pride she felt on completion of that final rope climb and at her passing out parade. She was now convinced that there was a myriad of other ways to feel truly alive. Now she had felt this she wished to turn such as thing into a consuetude but one that she felt in awe of each and every time. She did not want this feeling to become a mere habitude.

Evanna had also begun her athletic "career" within the Cadets coupled with being afforded the opportunity to try out new sports such as Olympic wrestling, canoeing and triathlon, all of which she discovered she had a certain knack for.

She had not yet achieved the true greatness that she had planned for herself but was "*well on the way*", she figured. She was yet to discover what form that greatness would take but was sure that she would achieve it somehow.

Out of all the new recruits at the Metropolitan Police Training School it was the ex-cadets who found things relatively easy going in comparison to the rigour they had recently endured. Evanna was no exception. Yes, there were still morning parades and inspections, but perfection did not appear to be required. Actually, it was, but not the Cadet Corps style of perfection.

There were no dorm inspections. Yes, they were put through their paces but not nearly as harshly during PT, plus the assault courses were not used.

Difficulty lay, however, in the constant and intricate learning of all aspects of criminal and traffic law. Progress Tests were held every other week and there lay the constant threat of being back classed if one were to fail, even by one mark. The pass mark was 95% and the tests were hard. There were no excuses for failure.

Recruits also took part in practical lessons which involved role play in every conceivable situation a police officer may find themselves (or so they were told — in practice these lessons were far from reality!). There were lessons in how to write evidence in the proper manner and how to fill out the never-ending forms and report books. They were taught how to give evidence in the mock court. There were Arrest and Restraint lessons, "Truncheon" lessons and even "Handcuff" lessons.

Recruits were housed in tower blocks which denoted the training site to passengers on the Northern Line as their train passed by. Evanna was glad to have the privacy of a single room, which all recruits had, but found herself missing the jocularity of the dorm.

Evenings were spent ironing uniform, cleaning shoes which did not take ex-cadets long and lots of studying. Then everyone headed over to the Recruits' Bar with its cheap prizes of alcoholic beverages. This also proved to be a vital part of their education as police officers — drinking! There was no curfew for recruits, so the familiar White Bear was still frequented as were clubs and other venues in London, especially Soho.

The courses were divided into ten classes of twenty recruits. Evanna was in F Class of Blue Intake 1989. She was fortunate enough to have four other members of her Cadet family in the same class. The others were nice enough, all older than the ex-cadets, but good bonds were born, although they proved nothing like those within the cadets. Although the support and camaraderie were still strong, and much fun was still had.

Evanna was content, confident and yearned for her first day out as a proper police officer patrolling the streets of London.

She worked hard but did come across some difficulties with certain aspects of her legal learning but once again her tenacious personality shone through.

She chose to be stationed in 7 Area which covered north and north-west London but did not get a choice of station in which she was to remain until the fruition of the two-year probationary period after which she could transfer if she so wished. Finally, the day arrived, towards the end of the twenty weeks, when stations were allocated to the individual recruits. Her first was to be West Hendon and her shoulder number was SV 205. On passing the final exam with flying colours she could safely "Pass Out". The actual parade was not nearly as much a spectacle as the Cadet Parade, but it was still a great day. No.1s were worn, loved ones attended, the Commissioner reviewed and inspected the recruits, which was followed by the March Past and the celebratory throwing of hats in the air. There was also a presentation ceremony at which all received their coveted warrant cards and signed the Official Secrets Act after which they had to stand, en masse, to recite the Declaration of Service:

"I... do solemnly and sincerely declare and affirm that I will well and truly serve our Sovereign Lady Queen in the office of Constable, without favour or affection, malice or ill will; and that I will, to the best of my power, cause the peace to be kept and preserved and prevent all offences against the persons and properties of the Majesty's subjects and that while I continue to

145

hold the said office I will, to the best of my skill and knowledge, discharge all the duties thereof faithfully and according to law."

This declaration reminded Evanna somewhat of the Brownie Guide Law:

"I promise that I will do my best and do the Duty of God, to help other people and to keep the Brownie Guide Law"

and investiture during which she was handed her badge and allocated to the Gnomes. *"Mind you,"* she chuckled, *"I only lasted two weeks before I was asked to leave!"*

Once again, she was awarded the Endeavour Shield, having been voted by other recruits and staff, which was another moment of pride.

So, Evanna's adventures at Peel Centre had ended. She would return in the following years for training courses to enhance her career, but for now, she was to leave and venture out into the big wide world as a Woman Police Officer.

But first, she had to move herself into the Section House!

Training School proved far tamer than the Cadet Corps, in the physical sense, yet far harder in the academic. Through this Evanna realised that courage did not necessarily have to be born out of *"jumping out of a plane"* when scared of heights but also through strength of mind and the determination to do one's level best even when unsure of one's mental capabilities. She had somehow passed all of her progress tests and her final exam, which was no mean feat as this had not been easy. She had also put herself to the test during the practical assessments which she disliked through fear of making a fool of herself in front of her class and instructors. More to the point, she realised that if she should make a mistake, she was not only able to laugh at herself but also to take the constructive criticism afforded her.

By the fruition of both the Cadets and Training School, our

Brave Fighter had grown. She had grown in stature as she was finally able to stand tall and proud but also in mind as she had learned many a thing, both positive and some not so, about herself, not least that she carried a wealth of courage and tenacity inside herself.

ii **Bodhi The Acharn**

Little did Bodhi know at the moment of putting pen to paper that his letter to Marika would, in time, serve as the catalyst for his eventual rousing.

Initially he did not actually even consider appointing an addressee, preferring to keep it open. This decision was trifold in the making.

Firstly, he was unsure as to his exact intent for the letter. He may keep it hidden safely in a locked box, he may decide to rip it into tiny pieces or even burn it as if it never existed. He considered that it may be a letter one wrote but should never send or give to a soul.

Secondly, an open letter meant that he could write freely without need of revision, redaction or compromise. There would be no familiar face at the receiving end; no other's feelings to consider; no other's personality to envisage or keep in mind. No one else to scrutinise his every word or question his thoughts and feelings. No one to confront him, empathise with him or even possibly help him. He was not sure he was ready for any of that.

Thirdly, was his deep concern regarding the principle of Trust as in: who to trust; why he should trust someone, indeed even himself. He examined the advantages and disadvantages of trusting God alone as opposed to others. At first his many varied beliefs surrounding this matter, of Trust, caused him huge conflict. This was mainly because of his wide-ranging readings from religious texts. As he attended a Catholic school, he was familiar with the Bible; being "half" Jewish he had a good knowledge of such scriptures and because of his research of Buddhism and his constant search for Enlightenment and Awakening he was familiar with the religion's tenets and precepts.

He realised upon contemplation that, in effect, all three religious beliefs concerning Trust highlighted the same or similar basic characteristics.

Bodhi scoured his mind and Biblical texts for The Book's teachings on "Trust". He listed different passages that he considered pertinent.

On trusting God:

Psalm 20:7

"some trust in chariots and some in horses, but we trust in the name of the Lord our God."

He interpreted this as: seeing isn't believing when it comes to the Lord. It may appear to be easier to put one's trust in tangible things that surround you but God's love, which is intangible, is the only love that can be counted upon.

Psalm 56:3

"when I am afraid, I put my trust in you."

This, he believed, meant that fear is a normal part of life; but with God on our side we can turn to Him in our darkest moments and know that He is there for us always. However, he also considered that such trust could, possibly, be put in a trustworthy human in such dark hours despite humans being tangible which was in conflict with the first passage.

Then he read:

Psalm 60:11

"oh, please help us against our enemies for all human help

is useless."

Despite having no tangible enemies Bodhi acknowledged that his intangible fear felt so raw and real that it was actually tangible; thus, it was indeed his foe. Here he posed this question to himself: *"is all human aid actually useless — if so, what is the point of humanity?"*

He continued his search:

Jeremiah 17:5–6

Agreed with the principle that one should not trust mere human beings as:

"this was what the Lord says: 'cursed are those who put their trust in mere humans, who rely on human strength and turn their heads away from the Lord. They are like stunted shrubs in the desert with no hope for the future. They will live in the barren wilderness; in a salty land.'"

"What is wrong with the strength of human beings?" Bodhi wondered. Surely, if God created us, in His image, He would have recognised the human potential for helping other humans. Surely, He would have given us this purpose, and if He did, one would not be turning away from Him but turning towards Him as we embrace His creation and all of the attributes He gave it. We would be His channel.

Bodhi then turned the wafer-thin pages to Micah:

Micah 7:5–6

"trust not in a friend, put your confidence not in a guide."

What is the point of friendship if not to love and trust? What is the point of a relationship if one cannot allow oneself to be guided and indeed guide? Why did God create us if we are such amoebas? If He did create us, in His image, surely that must mean He gave us the power to trust and guide through Him.

On trusting others versus God.

Bodhi read in **Proverbs 11:13**

"a gossip betrays a confidence, but a trustworthy person keeps a secret."

"So, one can trust humans after all!" he delighted. Sure, Bodhi knew "The Gossip" — he also knew "The Trustworthy" but was unaware how to differentiate between the two.

On to **Romans 8:28**

"and we know that for those who love God that all things work together for good."

It is fair to say that Bodhi did not necessarily believe in the one Christian God per se. However, he did believe in some kind of ethereal entity which he thought to be one and the same for all religions. He felt some kind of attachment, some kindred, if you like, towards this entity, but was it love? Were his feelings towards this enough for the forces of nature to combine and for the cogs of the universe to work in harmony for the good and for the greater good?

Or does the passage mean that if one loves God, He will ensure that goodness comes? Bodhi was unsure as to whether this was true as he knew those who loved God but had yet to receive much good. However, maybe they eventually would when they entered the Kingdom of Heaven.

Bodhi then switched his attention and deep thought to Buddhism.

As he turned the pages of the *"Buddhaniti Sangaho, A collection of Buddhist Wisdom Verses",* he happened upon the chapter entitled *"Trust"*. He read through the verses finding three, initially, that found resonance within him.

220

"do not trust the untrustworthy
be wary even of the trustworthy

there is danger following trust
like the lion and the hunted deer."
This reminded him of **Micah 7:5–6**
Then he digested **221**
"*do not trust one who is wicked*
do not trust one who speaks falsely
do not trust one who is selfish
or he who makes a show of peace"
which made him mindful of **Isaiah 2:22**

"*don't put your trust in mere humans. They are as frail as breath. What good are they?*"

Finally, he came to **Buddhist Wisdom Verse**
"*do not place your trust in such as*
only appear to be your friends
having smooth words and various means
they have no intention to act."

"*This could be akin to* **Numbers 23:19,**" he thought,

"*so, God is not human, that He should lie, not a human being that He should change his mind. Does He speak and then not act? Does He promise and not fulfil?*"

All of this left the exhausted Bodhi reeling. He found it near impossible to trust himself, let alone anyone else, and these passages only seemed to confirm to him that mere mortals should never place their trust in another mortal as that trust would go unwarranted, and would be unconfidential, misunderstood or suffer some other appalling betrayal, as humans are so weak. Therefore, it is best to place such entrustment with God or other omnipotent, more sentient being.

With that in mind, Bodhi concluded that his letter should be open as he found himself unable to place his trust in another living mortal soul. In part this originated from his history, his life experience thus far, and in part merely from being Bodhi. Whilst contemplating this issue of Trust he became totally disillusioned, as he had hoped that his studies would shed some more positive light on himself and his fellow human beings as opposed to the negativity that he felt he received.

So, he had been correct all along. Trust No Man! Trust belongs only to and in The Divine. But when would that Divine Power, whatever and whoever that may be, answer him? When would it hear him? How long would it take him, Bodhi, to attain Enlightenment and receive his most longed for Awakening? His patience was waning. The path ahead could be long, treacherous even. He may become lost along the way or take the wrong fork. He might never succeed.

Despite this, he collected a pen, some fresh white writing paper and began to write.

It took some time to detail everything he chose to write about in his letter. He wanted it to be "just right". The best representation of his thoughts and feelings that he could muster, which took no little courage. All this despite the possibility of it going to the flame. Upon reading the finished article out loud to himself he found himself wishing that he were able to hold the absolute assurance in someone's trust and be courageous enough to allow his vulnerabilities to be seen by that individual as he realised, he needed help. He sat on the edge of his bed contemplating. He searched his mind for some other temporal or empyreal teachings that might just lend him the bravura to actually address his letter to such a trusted individual.

As he sat and pondered two words seemed to pour into his mind, *Bitachon* and *Emunah*, which he recalled were principles, if you like, concerning Trust and Knowledge of sorts. A Knowledge based on the state of understanding within Judaism.

He reached as far back into his brain as possible until he realised his goal — that of remembering the varied Jewish festivals and celebrations at which and over the years his paternal relatives would school him in teachings concerning their faith. They never pushed these upon him. On the contrary, he always considered himself "mostly" Jewish and as a result relished these times. He craved to learn what Judaism with its many laws, wisdoms and traditions, was all about. Thus, he was now able to recall the basic precepts of *Bitachon and Emunah.*

Bodhi envisaged himself sitting in his uncle's kitchen lapping up the "teachings" of his great-aunt, aunt and uncle one Sabbath.

Bitachon, meaning Trust, has two forms. The first being a reliance on G-d, spelt in this form as a sign of respect and reverence, such that He will assist us in our efforts to help ourselves.

The second is the more simplistic Trust that G-d will perform a miracle when appropriate. Based on *Emunah,* which Bodhi had yet to unlock the memory of just yet, G-d is good, thus is the only one in charge. Therefore, there is no need to have any fears or frets. For the mega rational person holding such a belief, the positive side of life will forever remain in the forefront.

However, his or her *Bitachon* is not actually based upon this as it is not a belief based on experience but one that creates experience. *"Things will be good because you believe they are good,"* his great-aunt had told him.

It is not a strategy to manipulate the universe with. One's belief does not create good as the good in which one is so confident is already the underlying reality. One's belief only provides the means by which the reality can surface.

There are various degrees of *Bitachon* according to an

individual's degree of *Emunah* (knowledge). One person may have such *Emunah* that although things in the immediate present are not good, they are all for the good eventually. However, a more enlightened *Emunah* considers that everything right now is good despite it appearing terrible.

Unlike *Emunah, Bitachon* does not reside within a person in a uniform-like state. For the majority of the time, it remains in the background whilst one has utter faith that G-d will bless you whatever you do, so therefore it will not be your own smarts or handiwork that will provide success but G-d's blessings. Then situations begin to arise, from time to time, which seem impossible to resolve by any natural means; this is when *Bitachon* needs to wake up and step up. Rather than cries of: "*woe is me!*" or "*why me!*" or even "*who can help me!*" you must say, "*my help comes from G-d who made heaven and earth, so He can do whatever He wants with them.*"

Even a more simplistic Jew believes that G-d provides our needs against all the odds. You are healed by a good doctor who is a mere channel for the real healing by G-d.

So, we find in *Bitachon* a G-d beyond nature yet within nature. *Bitachon* is a source of tranquillity and happiness, thus meaning *Trust*. It relies on G-d. Trusting Him entirely with a sense of depending on Him to watch over and protect you. He created you in order to give His love, kindness and mercy. Whilst you are still responsible to be proactive you are NOT in charge of the outcome. Nor are you the determinant of the results.

Thus, while you do your part, you rely on G-d to care for you. "*So, take your heavy burden, Bodhi,*" advised his uncle as he pointed to the Heavens above, "*and place it in G-d.*"

Emunah is the Knowledge that G-d created and with which He continues to run all creation. Nothing can exist and no activity can occur without G-d. There is no such thing as happenstance. There are no coincidences or random occurrences. G-d is intricately involved in the running of the world and His creation. *Emunah* is that Knowledge that G-d is involved in the minutiae of daily life, 24/7 365 days a year. No human mortal or other power can change anyone's destiny apart from G-d who decrees the fate of man and is there, on the scene to carry out that decree.

There is a clear understanding that G-d runs the world. From big, to little. From global to local. Across all platforms and stations. He is there controlling every outcome.

Thus, *Bitachon* is a state of Trust that comes from recognising that the Creator is good, kindly, wise and cares deeply for His creations. Whilst *Emunah* is a state of understanding that comes from studying this world and seeing that there is a Creator. A person, however, can know that G-d runs the world but does not trust him. This person has *Emunah* but not *Bitachon*.

As Bodhi reminisced and recollected these "principles" that had been taught to him when a child, he realised that based on his very simplistic understanding both *Bitachon* and *Emunah* struck a highly personal chord. His own Ethereal Entity, his "God", did create the world. Maybe not as described in Biblical terms but more as Darwin prescribed. However, it is possible that his Entity directed the Big Bang — thus creating the world. This "God" then continued to run His invention, as it was of paramount importance to Him. Bodhi appreciated the viewpoint that *Bitachon* is a source of Trust and his Ataraxia and beatitude. His belief that his Ethereal Entity created the world in some manner and, therefore, controls everything within it, awakened his mind in such a way that he realised he had been "made" to write his letter. Now a decision was being made "*for*" him, but not against his wishes, to actually address it to someone whom he could entrust to deliver some kind of help.

This may not be the exact premise of either *Bitachon* or *Emunah*, but it "suited" Bodhi, as this was what he was able to glean from it at the present moment. After all, he could not be wrong if God did actually control everything. Plus, he had been proactive, as required by *Bitachon*, by setting pen to paper. Now God would provide the means for a miracle of a sort. The chosen addressee would be His channel just like the doctor.

Bodhi then delved even further into the recesses of his mind searching for other pieces of wisdom that may hasten him to find that trusted soul. He found three further verses, two Biblical and one from the Buddhist Verses of Wisdom which aided him to affirm his thoughts.

James 4:14

"you do not know what tomorrow will bring. What is your life? You are a mist that appears for a little while, then vanishes."

Although Bodhi knew this only too well and it was a prospect that usually caused him angst, now he viewed this passage with more courage. He supposed: *"I do not want to merely vanish without achieving one solitary thing. Tomorrow may be my new beginning. I may not disappear for some time yet so I may as well become 'mistier' not 'foggier', so I am not so easy to blow away."*

Proverbs 28:26

"those who trust in themselves are fools but those who walk in wisdom are kept safe."

Well, he did not trust in himself, so he was certainly no fool! Nor was he about to trust some unwise individual. The one he had in mind oozed wisdom so safe he would be kept.

Faith: Wisdom Verses 219

"in that one in whom he has trust
in whom his heart has devotion
although he is unknown before
he should willingly place his trust."

Despite having known this person for a few years, as opposed to being a stranger to him, once upon a time they were indeed strangers. He certainly trusted and loved her with all his heart — so in this person he would surely place his Trust.

Bodhi's letter read thus:

Dear Marika,

To be honest, I originally wrote this letter in two minds as to what to do with it once completed. Did I rip it up into tiny pieces, burn it or simply lock it away in a box hidden from prying eyes? Otherwise, did I muster the courage and post it to someone I totally trusted? However, if I were to do the latter what was read could never be "unread", which filled me with terror. A fear I thought I would not be able to conquer. However, after much searching of the soul I came to the conclusion that you were my person — My Trusted Person.

So, please allow me to state how much I trust you and how much faith I have in you. You have already, subconsciously, instilled in me such a sense of warmth, fun, trust, friendship and love that I hope I will always have the privilege, joy and pleasure of knowing you for as long as is permitted.

I apologise if what you are about to read causes you upset, anger or confusion as to what to do. I do not require you to do anything, if you should find yourself in a dilemma, but merely to read what I have written. We never even need to speak of it again if you so wish.

At present, well, for the majority of my so-called life thus far, I have felt such isolation from my family, my friends — the world.

To state that I feel lonely does not do any justice to the word.

I feel deeply depressed. I think I was born so! I may make a joke out of it, but my suicidal ideations are severe. I want to die. It is all I want to do. I have no other ambition. No other dream. No other hope.

I have given up on my relentless search for some kind of Spiritual Awakening. Enlightenment eludes me. Neither are forthcoming.

I live in constant fear and dread. They fill me up. They appear to have a predilection for my soul.

I fear everything but mostly my mother. I understand your hesitancy in believing this. How could I possibly be scared of this lovely woman who bakes cakes, makes cups of tea and laughs? She appears so warm, friendly, caring, empathetic and loving. I, however, do not experience her this way. I find her injurious, neglectful, merciless and hateful. I am unable to explain exactly why, but it is simply just the case. These words may seem harsh and mean when it seems that I want for nothing upon appearance. However, I feel I lack love — the love of a true mother.

As for Dad — he scares me too but in a contrasting way. I fear his quietness, his silence, his seeming lack of joy or even personality. I do not feel his love either, due to his oft ambivalence towards me or his then "over the top" affections which are at a huge variance to his timidity.

I fear for my future as I know I am doomed to fail. Doomed in life if I continue on in this manner.

I live in a void. I am a void. Empty.

I have friends but do I TRUST — really trust them? No! Until I wrote the first draft of this letter, which was going to be an open one, I thought that I had no one person in my life in whom I really trusted. But then I went on a journey in my mind, searching my *soul for the Truth in this and for the reasons against my addressing this letter to someone.*

I already knew who the addressee would be — you naturally. But I had to be certain. This is my 2nd draft. Similar to the original but with you, as the reader, in the forefront of my mind. I realised that I do indeed trust you, Marika. I trust your judgement, your senses — I just trust you. In saying that I am taking a leap of faith as despite not boring you with all of the gory (!) details, which I consider unnecessary to impart, I am placing all of my trust in you as I believe I am able to do.

I realise I need help, which is the reason for this letter. It is not meant for you to feel sorry for me. I guess I am asking you, though, for some practical help as you feel fit to provide.

I am requesting your total and utter confidence, especially when it comes to my parents, but I am aware that this may put you in a very difficult situation, for which I apologise. Of course, you can share it with them if you feel you need to. This will not affect our friendship as I will understand. I would not be angry with you but above all my faith in you will not have been lost as I trust your judgement entirely. Obviously, you can share it with Edwin if you feel it would help you.

If you feel unable to help, that will not make me feel or think any the less for you either. I hope you know that. I am not asking for you to send a lifeboat — I do not want rescuing of that sort. I am requesting some help with a plan of action; I suppose as I am unable to do such a thing for myself. I do not appear able to get out of bed, wash myself, look after myself or think clearly. My head is full of noise yet full of nothing.

Thank you for being you and for reading this letter to the end.

Bodhi

Bodhi didn't hear from Marika immediately. This wasn't too surprising, being back in the day with no mobile phones or computers, but this did not prevent him from being no little anxious. Four days after he had posted the letter through Marika's letter box the family landline rang. Bodhi's household had two such phones, one being in the living room whilst the other was out of bounds in his parents' bedroom. He was forever unable to have a private conversation on the phone as he was never allowed to use the one in his parents' room as they disliked him talking in "secret". After answering the call with the usual: "*hello*" to his pleasant surprise he heard Marika's comforting sincere voice at the other end of the line.

"*I'm glad it was you who answered!*" She spoke kindly. "*Thank you for the letter. I'm so sorry I didn't get back to you sooner, but I really wanted to digest what you had written. I'm flattered that it was me who you chose to write to. Please, come over tonight. I'm sending Eddie out with the kids and I've cooked the two of us dinner.*" Bodhi, relieved, nervously agreed. "Nervously" purely because he had never divulged his feelings to anyone before and had never felt so small and vulnerable.

When Bodhi arrived, he was greeted with the obligatory Marika-style hug, always one in which he felt safe, warm and loved, all of which were infused with joy and laughter. Also obligatory upon greeting was the finest glass of French red wine. She had prepared a luscious supper consisting of a rack of lamb with roasted vegetables; Marika really was a wonderful cook. Over their feast they entered into a deep yet relatively easy conversation. Easy because Bodhi suddenly felt free to talk and air his soul. Marika listened attentively but more than that she actually heard what he had to say. This made him feel justified. Finally, he was being taken seriously. At last, someone did not dismiss his introspections as banal. They spoke till long after midnight, Edwin had since put the children to bed and sensitively did so with himself after having arrived home from the cinema and a meal at Pizza Hut. Despite Bodhi's protestations, Marika managed to persuade him to book an appointment with the GP. She would go with him if he so wished. At first, he built up barriers making numerous excuses as to why seeing the GP was the "*worst idea*" although deep down he was only too aware that this was the "*right idea*". Eventually he consented, feeling secretly relieved that a plan had been arrived at and that Marika had promised not to speak to his parents unless she became even more concerned but would tell him first. Bodhi was to book an appointment with the GP in the morning. An appointment that Marika would gladly accompany him to.

Despite the heaviness of the conversation just had, on his short walk home, Bodhi felt lighter than he had done in an extremely long time — years maybe — possibly ever. This may have been the wine, but he did not think so.

The following morning, he did as promised, and dialled the number for the doctors' surgery. His heart missed a few beats as he turned the dial. He was also aware of a large lump appearing inside his vocal cords and he wondered if he would be able to speak. He was privately hoping that he would not be able to get an appointment for weeks but to his bewilderment he got one for that very morning. Part of him felt relieved but the most part of him was currently overwrought with nerves. Every part of his body felt tremulous. "*What if I'm carted off in a straitjacket to the local loony bin?*" he cried internally.

True to her word, Marika drove Bodhi to the surgery and joined him in the consultation room for moral support. She was also there to ensure he was able to say what he needed to say. So, with his consent, she would act as his prompter. Notwithstanding her other role as a shoulder, Marika would make provision for their shared sense of humour, especially of that in dire times!

The GP listened. She appeared a compassionate, helpful middle-aged lady with a slightly cross-eyed left eye which left Bodhi wondering where best to look. But he felt able to talk with her, albeit with a little help from Marika. Overall, however, he managed to stumble out how he felt and what he thought with no little discomfort but as he could feel Marika's presence by his side, he felt unusually strong and brave.

The doctor prescribed him antidepressants. Initially he would start on a small dose after which she would slowly bring the dosage up. They should take approximately two weeks to begin their "*magic*", but they would not be able to do the work alone. She then proceeded to tell Bodhi about the benefits of attending the Day Hospital situated in the psychiatric wing of the local general hospital. Bodhi had already declined the offer of more intensive inpatient treatment, for he was not feeling that brave or indeed mad!

Henceforth, it was agreed that the GP would refer Bodhi to the Day Hospital where he would receive excellent treatment five days a week, initially, for as long as it was felt required. He would not have to wait long as within the referral she would highlight the urgency. In the meantime, he would take the antidepressants as prescribed; get at least thirty minutes exercise, each and every day in the fresh air; eat properly; shower daily and try to make contact with some friends.

Upon leaving the surgery, Marika wrapped her arms around him crying: "*I'm so proud of you, my boy!*" That was the time when Marika saved his life and for which he was forever thankful.

Bodhi was a patient at the Day Hospital, as it was known by professionals or the *"bin for the part-time loonies"* to its "inmates".

His junket to recovery wasn't easy, and there were times he resented having to attend the various groups he was allotted to. In theory his attendance was not mandatory but in practice, it was almost like school, in that participation was noted and lack thereof could result in being politely asked to leave *"as there were others on the waiting list who would better take advantage of the treatment on offer. Those who wanted to help themselves and recover."* However, on the whole he did not mind going. Indeed, he actually enjoyed it at times, although would only reluctantly voice this out loud.

It was not particularly the mixture of groups he attended such as: drama (which he thought ridiculous but could be a laugh); the talking therapy group, where everyone sat in a circle in which one was supposed to bare their innermost thoughts, feeling and problems. Bodhi would make himself appear as small as possible in his chair, squirming when the therapist invited him to speak. He could just about bear the outpourings of emotions, the tears, the shouts, even the hostility between patients that was often tackled as apparently, they mirrored certain causes of rancour on the "outside". He soon recognised those who revelled in the attention they received by these outbursts of emotion as they demanded pity compared to those who attempted to offer their opinion and to those, such as himself, who spent the hour and a half in silence wishing themselves invisible. He partly enjoyed the creative writing group until the part where each were expected to share their manuscripts which he would often decline to do. He also enjoyed the Games Group on Wednesday afternoons, especially on the more clement days when rounders or hockey would be played in the garden. This was more of a fun session with some actual smiles and laughter! He attended art therapy and jewellery making once. The reasoning behind him being entered into either group betrayed him. Alongside these groups were weekly individual sessions with his key worker, Hazel, and another with a psychologist, Beth.

Despite all of this, so-called, therapy, Bodhi found that what helped him most of all was having a routine and making friendships. Routine he discovered was very important to him and his recovery. He did not understand this whilst at school but now he was older recognised the importance of getting up at a set time each morning, going out for a brisk walk, going to the hospital. He was also eating regularly and going to bed at roughly the same time each night — apparently, he was practising "*great sleep hygiene*" in his bedtime habits!

During his first week whilst outside playing hockey he caught his very first glimpse of who he could only describe as a beautiful heavenly being who he later learned was named Laine. The sun hovered over her head, as if a halo, whilst she dribbled the plastic ball with her plastic hockey stick towards the makeshift goal. He considered her to be Perfection Personified. It was not necessarily sexual attraction, but it was a somewhat physical attraction, nonetheless. After the tightly contested game and several plastic cups of orange cordial, Bodhi summoned the courage to strike up a conversation with this beautifully formed, almost feline woman with long brown hair who was simply clad in blue denim jeans, a loose red Nike T-shirt and flip flops, it being the beginning of summer. He thought, because of her appearance of "normality" that she was a therapist or a nurse whom he had yet to meet. However, as it transpired, she was "one *of them*". Not that the patients were abnormal in any way at all but there was something they all seemed to share. It was hard to discern what this "something" was but it may be an aura that denoted sadness, madness or something of that ilk which the staff or most of those "on the outside" lacked — maybe they merely hid it well or were not ready to put it on show. As he tentatively approached Laine, she was advancing towards him. "*Are you staff?*" she questioned *him!* She proffered her genuine surprise when he told her the contrary declaring: "*Gosh! You're one of us — no fucking way!*" He was surprisingly grateful that he did not resemble the mad lunatic that he considered himself whilst Laine mirrored these exact same thoughts about herself. Thus, they embarked on a friendship which was to last many years until Laine decided to change her name after graduating from Fashion School and somehow, they lost contact. However, Bodhi was not too upset as he realised that some people enter our lives for a reason and then make an exit for a reason too. He was content in the fact that she was then happily married to her long-term boyfriend and had begun a career that she was to excel in. The reason they entered each other's lives, at that exact time, was to support each other through those tough times; to learn more about friendship; to have fun; to socialise with one another and to discuss their shared favourite topics of history, religion and politics.

Initially, he attended the Day Hospital for five full days a week with weekends off. He found these weekends hard to cope with, at first, owing to the lack of routine and being almost tied to the house with his parents around him. He would confine himself to his bedroom sleeping on his bed. However, slowly but surely, he began to venture out with Laine whose boyfriend often accompanied them, which Bodhi also enjoyed.

The days at the hospital mostly consisted of lounging around with little to do but Bodhi did strike up some conversations with other patients who also then became friends. These lazier times were interspersed with the odd group, individual sessions and lunch which was provided. However, after a while Bodhi decided he wanted, indeed needed, something more. So, in consultation with Hazel his days were decreased to four and slowly they continued to be reduced until the day he "*graduated*".

He liked Hazel, who took no bullshit but at the same time listened whilst appearing to understand. Her mission was to enable Bodhi to become more independent and not so reliant upon others. Despite fearing and disliking his mother, Bodhi was reliant on her for doing all of his washing, ironing, cooking — everything. She, it was considered, made him feel almost totally dependent upon her even down to needing her approval concerning everything he did or wanted to do. When she did not give it, which was more than often, he simply either stopped doing whatever he was doing or did not pursue what he had planned. Hazel was keen for him to move out of home but despite all that he had endured and continued to endure he put obstacles in the way as he feared leaving home so much but could not explain his reasonings. More than that, though, he was terrified at the thought of telling his mother.

As for Beth, he grew dependent on her too. In hindsight this, so-called, therapeutic relationship proved antipodal of such. He spent at least three years having weekly therapy with Beth but if one had to be missed, he felt bereft. They did form a bond but an undefinable one. It was not strictly a therapist/client one; nor mother/son; nor sister/brother. Nor could it be described as a friendship, although that was what Bodhi longed for. Strangely, it could be described as dominatrix with submissive lover of sorts but not a lover. She was not strict with him — in fact, her way with Bodhi was diametrically opposed to this. However, it was as if she metaphorically cradled him in her arms. She called him "*little one*"; she cried when he cried or indeed even if he did not. She was not a mother to him but did treat him as if a child. He had his very first sexual fantasy, obviously about her, which shocked him as he did not think he was capable of such things. Although he was not actually sexually attracted to Beth, Bodhi found himself in love with her. His emotions became very confused, especially when she hugged him and kissed his cheek, never his lips. She told him that she loved him, which gave him no small measure of hope that their "relationship" would somehow blossom past his days of therapy. He considered her to be "The One". Deep down he realised this was never to be, which was the reason behind his constant pain, the constant ache he felt in his heart and stomach for the entire length of time he was her patient. Indeed, he was only a mere patient, although possibly a favourite one.

Never to contradict, challenge or oppose these feelings which Bodhi often gushed out to her or wrote about in lengthy, rather graphic letters for which she would thank him stating that she would "*cherish*". His confusion and pain were, therefore, understandable. He was able, however, to tell her about his execrable erstwhile past in some great detail. She appeared to almost "delight" in his abhorrent memories which he mostly gave in written form, finding this medium easier than the tongue. In a way dismaying, he felt as if she were encouraging him to colourfully describe the horrific acts done to him. Neither found this sexually arousing or erotic but he did sense an arousing of some sort for both parties that he was never able to explain or expressly nail down what it was or even why. It certainly never expelled his memories, his painful flashbacks or his hatred of his parents yet he so wanted to please Beth that it did provide him with a certain need to tell her more. It appeared to Bodhi that she seemed to end every session on a cliff hanger. They laughed and cried together, they held hands, they kissed cheeks. She also expressed some of her own thoughts, feelings, wishes, desires and difficulties in life to him, which gave him more "hope". Despite loving Beth, and despite it feeling as if an eternity between each weekly appointment which he clung onto, Bodhi discerned that her style of therapy was not good for him, but he needed it like a drug. His psychiatrist gave permission to extend the number of sessions not once but three times, as Beth requested, because of his "*progress*" and "*commitment to therapy*". Yet these extensions were unhelpful to Bodhi as he became more and more reliant on his therapist, but no one noticed.

However, Beth, together with Hazel did perform one good therapeutic aspect for Bodhi. They both convinced him that it was time to move out of home. This took some time, partly because of his reluctant dependence on his mother but also because of his terror of telling her.

A local hostel, or halfway house, had an available bed which Bodhi agreed to view with Hazel. Immediately he set one toe inside the threshold he knew that this was not the place for him. He was only too aware that this would be the end of him. Owing only to his sense of politeness did he allow himself to be shown around by the manager but the more he was shown the more he wanted to run and hide. The institutional décor, the staid communal areas, the institutionalised residents, the bromidic bedroom and the stereotypical hospital-like supposed nourishing offerings made Bodhi want to scream. He declined the offer with the utmost pleasantry but with astonishing assertion.

Beth and Hazel then returned to their task of finding him somewhere to live with the now definite exception of any form of such communal living. After a brief while their task proved lucrative. They approached Bodhi with looks of cautious glee handing him a brochure which he began to flick through lacking much lustre at first. However, he soon sat down as he realised that he may actually have landed on his feet. A small estate, consisting of houses and flats in equal measure, had just been built. Some of these would be privately owned yet some had been set aside for a housing association. The more he read and the more he gazed at the glossy photographs the more his heart did joyous leaps. On visiting what was his flat to be, he did not need to stay long to jump at this opportunity that was being handed to him on a plate. The flat was of a good size; one double bedroom with fitted wardrobes; a large kitchen with white goods, oven and hob already installed; a lovely sized living room complete with a brand-new settee and a good-sized television stand. The bathroom was all kitted out with white toilet, sink, bath, overhead shower and chrome towel rail. The flat had its own front door which opened out onto a front garden and parking area. Just inside the door a flight of stairs led up to the flat itself. It was totally brand new, still smelling of freshly coated magnolia paint and carpeted throughout. Along with the flat came a support worker whose role it would be to help Bodhi become more independent. He met Stephanie that day and they hit it off straight away. Before he had time to even ponder on how he would summon the courage to tell his mother, he leapt at the chance to move into his first home of his own.

To his pleasant surprise his mother took the news extraordinarily well and both parents along with a close friend helped Bodhi move in. It was akin to a military operation, run by his mother, but by the end of that busy day pictures had been hung; a desk had been erected in a suitable area of the living room; the television had been installed and tuned in, all boxes were unpacked and disposed of; food and other essentials had been put in their place; plants bought and watered. Even a grey coloured beautiful kitten, which Bodhi named Demi, had been welcomed into what was now her new home too. It had been a good day!

Bodhi actually hated his mother more than he did his father owing to the fact that she declined him any help when he was most in need. In fact, she ignored all of the signs which were so visible. She retreated into a state of self-imposed ignorance choosing to simply take no notice of what must have been staring her in the face. He feared her for her dictatorial-like nature and her ability to make him feel stupid, silly and ridiculous, which were words she would audibly and frequently call him. He resented the way she was able to strip him of any ounce of independence he might have had making him feel utterly emasculated. Thus, he was unable to voice his wishes, his opinion — anything. But the day he moved there was no fear, no animosity, no hatred — there was just action, all hands to the deck. A union of sorts between parents and child, now adult.

His mother disliked the fact that he attended the Day Hospital and had a therapist. Possibly it was because it was what they represented to her — The Truth. The Truth coming out and being exposed leaving her reputation and that of her husband in tatters. But more so her own. Nor could she cope with Bodhi's diagnoses of anxiety, depression and schizoid personality disorder (distinct from schizophrenia). She believed mental illness to be an excuse for lethargy — nay laziness and what she referred to as "*self-indulgent claptrap*". She did not believe in illness per se, let alone mental ones. She would rather sarcastically and nastily call those suffering from mental illness as "*neurotic*". In short, she had no time for it despite her own husband displaying obvious and deep signs of depression. Many of her in-laws also had some form of mental health difficulties. Despite liking these relatives, she considered them "*ridiculous*", having no time for their ills.

Having moved in Bodhi decided he wanted to study. He enrolled in a BA(Hons) degree in the Humanities with The Open University. He was not yet ready to attend actual university and as he learned better studying on his own; reading rather than being lectured and taking notes which were never legible, his chosen style of further education suited him best all round. He decided to do this on a part-time basis, meaning it would take six years to complete instead of three, but this did not matter to Bodhi as his study was due to be a hobby, yet one he intended to work hard at, devote time to and excel at. Which he did on all counts.

He continued to attend the Day Hospital but was now down to two days per week. He also purchased his very first computer which were slowly becoming commonplace in everyday households.

He began inviting friends over for coffee and eventually dinner. His first guests, for an afternoon "tea", were Beth and Hazel. He felt so proud to be able to invite them into his home which was immaculate and remained that way. His support worker, Stephanie, visited twice a week. She took him shopping, which terrified him owing to the immense and confusing interior of supermarkets; the fellow shoppers; the sheer amount of choice available on the shelves, but most of all he feared the placing of his soon to be purchases on the conveyor belt ensuring to pack everything into the plastic shopping bags which always failed to open, whilst sorting out the money to pay the cashier often leading to loose change spilling all over the supermarket flooring all whilst ensuring that the queue of faces behind him did not register their displeasure at his slow and clumsy ways. Over time he learned that not only would the floor not create a sink hole down which he would fall if things went wrong but that he was more than capable of multitasking. Stephanie had advised him to make *"chit chat"* with the cashier as that would distract them a little, hence slowing them down whilst in turn this would put himself more at ease. By doing so he grew to discover that the task was becoming increasingly more manageable, although he had yet to go shopping on his own which he would eventually do, taking baby steps and with Stephanie on standby.

His mother proved unhelpful in his fight for independence. She insisted that each Thursday would be *"housework and shopping day"* whereby she would take over, dragging Bodhi along with her. The arguments they had were ferocious. Bodhi dreaded these days with such passion, but he felt he had no choice. At this point she continued to hinder his personal growth. She would even take away and do his washing which he was more than able to do himself. He struggled with this, deeply resenting his mother for continuing to cause his emasculation. This did cease but it took time with Bodhi fighting against his mother, insisting he was very able and capable. At times she refused to leave his flat when he asked her to. She would scream in his face telling him how *"selfish"* he was. Over a lengthy period of time, he grew to find his voice in front of her so that she was not all triumphant in their numerous battles. She was known to retreat on occasion but never — ever to proffer any attempt of or form of apology!

He was soon to leave the Day Hospital after he and all

professionals involved in his care agreed. He felt highly nervous and unsure how he would cope on his own without the now familiar faces and place he regularly saw. However, in truth he would not be alone as he had Stephanie for support and his friends. Plus, he still had Beth. He was also known to attend the odd meal at the family home where he dined with his parents and at times his sister. In short, Bodhi was coping. Depression would never be far behind but here he was in his own home; fending for himself (well almost) and dealing with life for the first time which, for now, was good enough.

Towards the end of his time at the Day Hospital whilst in group therapy he happened to voice that he wanted to begin working in schools but lacked the confidence to even apply. This is where fate came into being. Another patient announced that her sister was a primary school teacher in the reception class of a local school and was looking for someone to support one of her young pupils who had a very rare life-limiting genetic illness giving her physical disabilities. As a result, she required support in and around the classroom and playground.

It was arranged for Bodhi to visit the school, meet the teacher, the little girl, who was beautiful, and the rest of the class with whom support would also be required of the successful candidate. Initially the role would be part time, an hour prior to lunch, during the hour and a half lunchtime period and then half an hour afterwards. As Bodhi was leaving the school, which was small yet very welcoming and charming, the Headmistress, Mrs Morass cheerfully approached him. *"What do you think?"* she enquired of him. A perplexed Bodhi did not quite know what to say. Although he wanted the job, he knew he still had to apply, which frightened him as he did not feel *"good enough"*.

"It's a lovely class with many different personalities, isn't

it?" she continued, "*and Magdala is a super yet rather headstrong little girl, and of course, Theresa is a great teacher who everybody loves. Plus, this school is absolutely wonderful. It sounds trite, I know, but we are a family and a close-knit one at that. You can start on Monday if you like or another day that suits you better. Magdala's funding is due to be increased very soon so the post will go up to a full-time one. It's yours if you want it.*"

Bodhi, now even more perplexed hesitantly replied: "*I would love the job but surely I need to be interviewed at least.*"

Mrs Morass replied: "*I watched you with Magdala, and with the class. It was obvious that you hit it off with all of them. As for Magdala, she listened to you immediately, which is a rarity! You were brilliant. Just what this school needs. I don't need to interview you — I've seen you in action. We can do the CRB forms on Monday. Whilst we wait for them to come back, which will take no time at all, we'll just have to ensure there's another adult within eyeshot of you.*"

Bodhi then reluctantly said: "*But don't you need my CV or even be told about my experience and things?*"

She knowingly patted him on the shoulder replying: "*I have been told what I need to be told and it's all good.*"

With that — Bodhi had landed himself a job!

So, now it can be seen why Bodhi's letter, addressed to Marika, was "the catalyst for his eventual rousing". He received the support he needed for his emotional health; he formed friendships; he learned how to deal with his mother on more equal terms; he gained independence; he gained confidence, a home of his own, a job and began to use his "little grey cells" by studying. He found a form of contentment.

Bodhi was far from his Ataraxia, but he was edging forever

closer. He had yet to answer even one of life's ultimate questions. The secret behind the meaning of life and existence in general continued to evade him. Yet ultimately, he had survived the overwhelming prospect of leaving school, albeit a bumpy path. He had realised that nothing bad would happen should he make a mistake when in a group of people. As a child he detested afterschool clubs for fear of making himself look the fool but the drama and games groups, at the Day Hospital, necessitated a certain amount of risk taking where mistakes were often made, which Bodhi coped with well and found that he could laugh at himself.

Although he was far from forgiving his parents, the buried roots of his oak tree were slowly unearthing themselves, as he no longer wanted to hide away quite so urgently as before. Part of this was due to the new friendships he had formed, his first job which he was due to start and the fact that he had a new-found freedom with living on his own.

His junket this far can be compared to Evanna's in that they each went on an adventure of sorts that built up their characters and one which taught them how to fight for themselves; how to endure and how to achieve despite all the odds that appeared to bar their way. Evanna's was more physically arduous whilst Bodhi's can be said to be as equally arduous but in the mental and emotional sense. More to the point they both progressed in and with their lives to a point where success and happiness seemed plausible.

Bodhi began working at the Stuart Meade Primary School on the Monday. That is where his life really began.

iii Petra -The Akran

At this point in their lives, Petra was definitely having an easier time than either Evanna or Bodhi. There being no physical or emotional beastings. Although it is fair to say that times would eventually become harder — but that was a way off yet.

Despite receiving next to nothing in her monthly pay packet, Petra was loving her work at the Community Centre. She opted to support mainly the elderly at the various groups, lunches and tea dances that ran throughout the day. She also had a support worker role at the two youth clubs. One, for the 11 to 14-year-olds which was held each Friday evening and the other held on Saturday evenings for 14 to 16-year-olds.

She enjoyed helping to make and serve lunch at the Old Age Pensioners Lunch Club every Wednesday. After serving she would settle down at a different table each week and chat to these wonderful gentlemen and women whose lives she loved to hear about. They had their friendship bases and as a result their own seats and tables each week. They chose to sit at the exact same table and in the exact same place every week, so woe betide a newcomer who dared to occupy one of those seats! Most of these elderly folks had lived in the area for all of their lives thus far, so therefore, had built up their friends and even enemies over those long, sometimes, hard years. Their bonds were tight as they would often have known each other since childhood. They had their cliques, their best friends and their rivals. They gossiped, they discussed, they debated, they enjoyed telling stories long forgotten or often retold stories not so long forgotten! They reminisced, they cried over their dearly departed, they picked clean the bones of the latest funeral they attended, how they found the vicar, the service, the flowers, the coffin, the hymns, the prayers, the food and beverages served at the wake compared to the funeral they attended the week prior. They laughed, they joked, they complained, and they ate.

After lunch had been eaten and the tables were free from their remnants, Petra would start drawing the Bingo balls. This game was always hotly contested and thoroughly enjoyed by all.

Petra was liked, even "loved", by staff and clients alike. They embraced how she was always willing to listen; to hold a hand; to pat an arm. They loved how she showed such great interest in their histories, their lives, their families and how they lived their present in comparison to their past — "*oh my, how things have changed, and not for the better,*" they would protest.

The other OAP groups of yoga, singing, film and games carried on in a similar vein to that of the Lunch Club but without the lunch. The theme of the group carried on albeit secondary to everything else. The topics of conversation and seating plan remained the same. The real reason for attending any of these groups was for the friendship and chatter.

It was at the youth clubs that Petra met Coral, once again, who was the life and soul of everything.

Coral was twenty — one year Petra's senior. She had a slim athletic frame, tall in stature with a mass of black hair, slightly Afro in appearance with its various curls, coils, kinks and frizz which almost shimmied down to the nape of her neck. Her hair and very large Roman/Jewish nose were her trademarks, yet she was neither of colour, Roman nor Jewish! Alongside this was her sense of dress. Always attired in loose-fitting, brightly coloured, cotton summer dresses with brown sandals in the spring and summer with a bright jumper and brown or black boots in the autumn and winter. Her entire wardrobe was acquired from various charity shops, although she had the money to buy from more expensive shops, which she was never shy about declaring. Why should she be? Coral boasted a slightly dishevelled and mismatched appearance, but no one noticed as it suited her well and that was Coral. She would not have looked half as wonderful in anything else.

Her personality was radiant, effervescent, effulgent, incandescent and sanguine which filled the corners of each room. Her deep, almost manly, voice boomed, beamed and reverberated through each room and echoed through each wall sending vibrations all around the community centre. As for her laugh and her sneeze — they were just something to behold!

Coral loved children and young people. Her aim in life was to make a difference in their lives. To nurture, to enthuse, to inspire, to teach, to mentor, to advise, to counsel and rescue many a time. She gave up each weekend to run these youth clubs on a totally voluntary basis. She organised events and nights: film nights, discos, games, party nights; each different night always ended with the obligatory music and dancing. She organised the tuck shop buying all of the snacks, sweets and pop. She was the chairperson, the treasurer, the manager, the secretary, the arbiter and the sometimes chastiser. Coral was the most loved woman. She was loved by all of the staff, the other wonderful volunteers, the children and young people alike. She did not shy away from her responsibilities or from voicing her opinion. She was certainly no pushover! Thus, she was treated with some trepidation by certain committee members but always with love and respect. Coral returned that love and respect to all she enveloped into her life, which was pretty much everyone she came across, no matter the capacity.

Coral, who had suffered over the years with relationships, was a single mum to her daughter Emma. Coral worked full time in a primary school, taught swimming three evenings a week and organised the youth clubs at weekends. Emma was Coral's younger self. Eventually, she fell in love with Paul who was a quiet, retiring but wonderful man. One who also gave up his time to volunteer at the youth club. His role was to deal with any fisticuffs should they arise which they sometimes did over a girl! It was the best day when Paul and Coral married.

Coral's other loves were her five dogs. Over the years this number dwindled and rose but on average she maintained a steady five. She would inevitably rescue these loveable rogues from the local animal sanctuary and were normally ones that no one else wanted, those that people merely walked past without giving them a second glance. She rescued the three legged, the blind, the deaf, the moth eaten and those with "issues".

She never sat still, unless she was reading or listening to *The Archers* on Radio 4 which was a guilty pleasure.

Petra warmed to Coral in an instant as Coral did to Petra. They became real buddies, partners in crime. When they were both around people would sing: *"there may be trouble ahead..."* Neither were the greatest of planners yet everything they arranged turned out to be successful even the week-long barge holiday for the Saturday youth club which did become ever so slightly hairy at times, but no damage or injury occurred, apart from some stomach muscles due to excessive laughter. Paul also went on this holiday which was when the spark was lit between the two.

Petra and Coral's friendship remained strong for just over twenty years until Coral died extremely suddenly and totally unexpectedly. One minute she was cleaning the bathroom and the next minute she lay dead upon its tiled floor. But Petra never would forget her smile and laughter. She would always remember her beautiful friend.

Financially, working at the Community Centre was not proving exactly fruitful. Petra had her responsibilities and had been promoted. She had gleaned much knowledge and a great deal of experience from working with and supporting the elderly and children who required very different approaches with the very wide canyon between their generations. Her niche, she discovered, lay with the younger epoch.

Despite her lack of remuneration, she enjoyed her varying roles. However, she was quick to realise that her hopes of moving into a home she could call her own would not be realised for a long while yet. But she was not only doing exceptionally well as her probationary and annual reviews attested to; she was making friendships with the other workers and superb team of volunteers without which the Community Centre would not have been able to flourish, indeed exist at all. Not only that; she was able to walk to work, thus saving money she would otherwise be spending on petrol or bus fares.

For obvious reasons Petra preferred to be out of her "parental home", as she referred to it as often as possible. She joined the local gym where she met a whole different set of friends, plus with her long distance running, socialising and work she was able to limit the time she spent within her parental home to the bare minimum. This infuriated her mother beyond belief whose shrieks of *"you're treating this house like a hotel"* Petra believed could be heard streets away.

Her sister had managed to escape the clutches of her parents, so she was left on her own. Having said that, her sibling was not in the greatest of hurries to flee the nest, but the opportunity to purchase a house with two of her friends just seemed too good a one to miss. As the two sisters had quite a fractious relationship, Petra chose not to visit her too often; likewise, her sister chose not to invite her over too often either!

There was one good point about still remaining in her

parental home, however. Her mother suggested, much to Petra's great surprise, that the room downstairs become her bedroom. This room and the whole of the downstairs floor, being part of a three-storied town house, had served many functions over the years. Starting out as a bedroom-cum-living room for Petra's grandparents it evolved into a playroom-cum-homework room complete with desks for the sisters with the kitchen being converted into a utility room for mother. For a brief while the room then transformed into an office and storage room for Petra's mother so she could work from home on occasion. Then it metamorphosised into a bedroom for Petra, so a sofa bed was purchased along with a television and stand. Petra decorated this room as she wished; it was her den. Her bedroom also became her social expanse, enabling her to entertain visitors. She, though, soon came to realise, much to her chagrin, that her mother hated her spending time alone in her heavenly private space. It seemed she was expected to join her parents, who were unable to comprehend the concept of privacy and personal space, at all times when she was by herself. As she dined with them in the evenings, which Petra admitted she did not mind as her mother did produce the most amazing meals, she considered this would satisfy her parents, but they had different processes of thought.

Despite her father keeping himself at a distance for the majority of the time he did, upon occasion, continue to pay her the odd "visit" at night when her mother was out. Petra hated herself more than ever as although being a fully-fledged woman, an adult, who was mentally and physically reasonably strong, she found herself unable to fend him off. At such times she did not fight. She flew within herself — she flew into her mind whilst her body froze. She thought it must have felt like shagging a corpse to her father, but she did not speculate him to be a necrophiliac, although under the current climate nothing would surprise her. She blocked it out. It just was not happening. She retreated into a different world, a safe world that she had created for herself. She despised herself for this. She felt unable to voice what was happening to a soul. She was so deeply, deeply, ashamed believing that if she should confide in even her closest ally, she would be judged a harlot, a cocotte, a tart, a whore. It was herself that was undoubtedly to blame. As for *him,* he would merely be considered a chancer, opportunistic, possibly unscrupulous but not necessarily at fault. This was her true belief. Had she viewed this at a deeper level, Petra would have realised that this was simply not the case. If she had the wherewithal to put herself in the shoes of another, she would have realised that her perception was entirely erroneous. However, most victims of sexual abuse and assault are unable to rid themselves of these thoughts and the guilt. Somehow, they are just not able to process their beliefs and thoughts correctly.

In order to keep herself out of the house, especially on the nights she knew her mother would not be in, Petra became immersed in her social life. She was in a social whirl! Economically permitting she went out a great deal, to restaurants, the cinema, pubs and bars. Most of all, she enjoyed frequenting the local gay-friendly public house which she had been introduced to by her male gay friend, Angus, whom she had met at the gym. During one training session whilst they sat side by side going forward and backward on rowing machines, Petra managed to pluck up some courage and asked: "*Angus, will you take me out?*" to which he replied: "*I'm very flattered, but you do know I'm a homosexual, right?*" He said this with a very strong emphasis on the word "*homosexual*"! A red-faced Petra acknowledged this fact and advised him not to worry; she was not hitting on him! She then retorted that she was actually trying to ask him if he would introduce her to some of his gay haunts. Thus, they began to go to The Ship and Anchor on a regular basis. Every night was party night at The Ship and Anchor with lock-ins galore for their trusted regulars of which Angus and Petra were two. The pub hosted the most eclectic mix of people including "hetros" as the "homos" called them and vice versa. Everyone was welcomed. It was an establishment way before its time. Although upon appearance it was not decked out with rainbow flags or other such paraphernalia. The only "reminder" that it was a gay pub was the stacks of *The Pink Paper* and *The Gay Times* piled high on a table in an alcove next to the much-loved juke box. Scattered along the bar were leaflets regarding safe sex and information about HIV and AIDS since this was so deadly and prevalent during this time.

The Ship and Anchor was situated in close proximity to the nearest town. It was easy to get to on foot, by vehicle and public transport. It made such an excellent reputation for itself that people travelled to it from miles and miles away. At that time, it was the only such venue or meeting place in the county or even those located near to it. The only other place to go was London. As it was a "normal"-looking pub for all intents and purposes it did not receive much negative attention from homophobes. Petra and her fellow punters viewed this not as good luck or chance but knew that if they kept themselves to themselves, hidden away in the safe confines of the pub and its surrounds without advertising their sexual identity or presence, they would receive no discrimination. The pub and indeed its environs were considered "safe zones" by all who drank and partied there. Their heterosexual neighbours became friends. It was a safe haven where the sounds of the 1980s and 90s could be heard blasting out of the juke box and sound system 24/7, it seemed!

Petra had always worn her hair short, apart from a brief interlude when she was aged about seven. One day she went into London with some old friends from school when she saw the most attractive-looking female sporting a completely shaven head. This was also the age of Sinead O'Connor, who Petra had a crush on, with a sheared coiffure of her own. She happened to say to her friends something along the lines of how she would like to do that to her hair but did not have the nerve! They laughed together, and that was that. However, on returning back to one of their flats, where they were all to stay over that night, they decided to smoke a few joints and drink some chilled white wine. It was during this that they decided to shave Petra's hair completely off. Petra sat, quite willingly, upon a wooden dining room chair whilst her friend began to shave her dark brown locks which she could see as they fell onto the light beige carpet. Behind her was a mirror in which she could just about see her friend poised over her scalp with electronic razor in hand. The cackles of laughter, bordering on the hysterical, filled the room. Marijuana and alcohol do not necessarily go together especially during an "operation" such as this!

That night Petra went to sleep. She snuggled into her sleeping bag on the living room floor which was littered with her hair as she was herself. The hoovering, they decided, would wait until morning. When she woke up at 0800hrs she automatically went to brush her fingers through her hair only to find she had none. What she found instead was a bristly bald scalp. Her first consideration was: "*How the fuck do I tell my mum?*" As it was, her mother did not say too much. She didn't need to as her face said it all! Her father just laughed.

As it happened, Petra's new appearance went down rather

well with everyone else. Fortunately, her head was such that her new hairstyle suited her face and that her scalp was well rounded with no lumps or bumps. It also "bagged" her many new admirers, especially certain females in The Ship and Anchor. However, there was only one woman who Petra had eyes for, but she did not appear to evoke the same eyes for Petra.

The Ship and Anchor was packed to the rafters one Saturday night. There she spotted the woman she had eyes for. She was "butchish" with a head of naturally grey hair which looked as if it had been highlighted with silver streaks, which it had not. She was dressed in dark blue denim jeans, a white well-ironed shirt, a dark blue waistcoat and black DM boots. She wore glasses and a prognathism which strangely complemented her face. She was of medium build and just a little taller than Petra who proved to lack the courage to approach her! Angus spent a good part of the evening trying to persuade her to go and speak to her, but she lacked all nerve. Out of sheer exasperation he ripped a corner off *The Gay Times* that he had been glancing at and after promptly writing Petra's phone number down on it he rose from the table, made a bee line for Sarah, as was her name, pressing the number into her hand. It didn't take long for Sarah to approach Petra offering her and Angus a drink and she invited them to join her group of friends, which they duly did. Petra had a wonderful evening. Sarah exchanged her phone number with her which she nervously phoned the following day. Thus, a relationship was born which was to last twelve years.

Sarah owned a ground floor flat. Not much time had passed when Petra spent most of her free time there. She stayed over regularly, which meant she needed her car for work.

Sarah was a construction engineer working for the country's top engineering company based in London. She was dedicated to her career working very long hours. She had the capacity to be fierce and formidable at times but soft and gentle at others. She was "going places" in her profession. She enjoyed flashing her cash but somehow, she managed to do this in an unbrazen manner as she never tastelessly boasted about her wealth.

After quite a short while Sarah suggested to Petra that she move in: "*You practically live here anyway!*" she reasoned when, for some reason even Petra did not understand, her invitation was greeted with hesitancy. Finally, Petra agreed with pleasure and indeed some excitement, moving in the following weekend. She didn't have much in the way of furniture and only a few bits of kitchen equipment and some other small personal effects, so it was mainly clothing that required packing.

Petra's mother was none too pleased when her daughter began to socialise with lesbians, so her daughter decided to keep her socialising at The Ship and Anchor quiet from her family.

Although she had known herself to be gay, as she chose to describe herself, for many a year, she decided to keep this to herself. Never in a million dreams did she think she would actually be able to live that life. She presumed it would have to remain forever repressed, but she would refuse to be with or marry a man merely to keep others happy and for societal norms. So, when she began to go to that very special drinking establishment her feelings began to be realised and her eyes were opened as until then all her friends were strictly heterosexual. She did, however, tell her mother and sister which pub she went to, although they were blind to the nature of its clientele. One day her sister, having recently discovered the above, quizzed her about why she chose to go to "*that particular place*". In response Petra blurted out the truth but asked for her sister's discretion which, as it turned out, she did not get. It was only the following day that her mother asked, *"Why do you go to that awful pub? Are you one of those lesbians?"* Realising that she was not best pleased by the mere thought of this Petra bit her lip but then found herself exclaiming, *"Yes I am! And,"* she continued, *"I have a girlfriend!"* Her mother did not say too much in that moment as the tears prevented her from talking. But Petra was not free from her wrath for long. Her mother was sure that Petra would live an *"isolated, lonely, childless life";* she would lead *"an awful existence on her own"* and would be known as *"weird by everyone"*. She would also *"look like a lesbian"*; be *"unemployable and..."*

As soon as she moved in with Sarah the 3am telephone calls commenced during which Petra learned from the caller, her mother, that she was, *"dirty, disgusting"* and *"immoral"*. These calls continued every night for months on end but eventually they decided to keep the phone off the hook until her mother had calmed somewhat, which she did.

Petra realised that her mother was "old school" and that it was she who feared what her own friends and neighbours would think and say. As for Petra's supposedly childless life, that was said more because her mother wanted grandchildren in her life. The fact that she was suddenly dirty, disgusting and immoral were words she never expected her mother to aim her way and with such venom. At first it deeply upset Petra but with Sarah's support she was able to put those feelings to rest. As for the surmise that she would lead a lonely life, Petra considered that anyone could do so. Maybe that last quip meant that her mother actually did care about her. She wanted her to settle down in a conventional relationship and be happy as that was how life was led.

As the relationship between Petra and Sarah began to mature

and flourish Petra's mother conceded defeat, a miracle in itself, but remained stoic in her hypothesis that her daughter was merely "*going through a phase*".

Sarah could see that Petra enjoyed her job but was becoming increasingly frustrated at her lack of monetary reward. This did not cause Sarah any vexation apart from the fact that Petra saw it as an irritation. However, more importantly, she knew that Petra was becoming increasingly frustrated at the lack of fulfilment in this role as there was no career path for her there as the two managers were unlikely to move elsewhere any time soon and Petra had already been promoted to deputy manager. Her bosses were both lovely but rooted to their posts and set in their ways. Petra's various new ideas were all greeted with enthusiasm but ultimately nothing was done to put them into being. They feared change, as did Petra in fact, but she could see the merit of such in this case.

She was still young, full of enthusiasm and ambition. She wanted to alter lives, to support others and to be that fighter for justice by being the voice of the underdog. She was beginning to feel that her job at the Community Centre was becoming stale despite having now been there for several years; had made some good friends; good relationships with the clients; had managed to achieve some change and high praise. Through this Sarah encouraged her to begin job hunting for a more demanding role with a defined career structure.

Behind the scenes, Sarah had put her flat on the market whilst they both began to search for a house together. The plan was that Sarah would buy, therefore, own their new home, but Petra would make other financial contributions. Petra realised that she would basically become a "housewife" although one with another job outside the home as Sarah found any domestic chore highly disagreeable!

The sale, house hunt and purchase went smoothly, which must have been a first for such a market, despite actually having to move on what proved to be the wettest day that month. Their new home was a terraced Victorian cottage. All of its features were original. The living room was front facing with a beautiful large bay window and open fire. Being a large room, the kitchen became a kitchen/diner, each area taking up equal halves with plenty of room. The patio doors led out from the dining area into a good-sized garden with flowerbeds and leylandii which Petra was none too keen on, but Sarah loved. Upstairs were two sizeable double bedrooms and a small single room. They took the front bedroom, leaving the other as a guest room and the single room as a gym for Petra and gaming room for Sarah. It was placed in a quiet road not far from Petra's "parental home". This was not planned. However, it was also within walking distance of The Ship and Anchor, which was kind of planned! Petra decided that should her mother ask she was never going to have a front door key if her life depended upon it! Sarah proved handy with a drill, paint, sander and lawnmower, which made up for any lack of skill at housework and cooking. Sadly, she was not so handy with superglue, having stuck her fingers together multiple times. It did not take long for the house to be torn apart and resurrected, refurbished, renovated, revamped and even extended. All of the carpets were taken up being replaced with floorboards, new doors were hung on every frame, the kitchen overhauled and the whole of that room's floor was tiled by Sarah who also overhauled the garden although the leylandii remained firmly rooted. Petra could not regard them as a replacement for her oak tree. The new addition was the huge conservatory leading off from the dining area. It was to become Petra's reading room, sometime joint wildlife watching room and general wonderful place to sit especially in the evenings with a bottle of red wine whilst they chatted about their day and life. The couple were content in their new home and in their togetherness.

Obviously, The Ship and Anchor remained a focal point of their life. To their delight a new all-women's "disco" was now held on the last Saturday of every month in the town centre. It was named "Girls On Top", but the regulars referred to it as "*The Dyke's Disco*"! So much fun and laughter, was had there. It wasn't as corny as the name conjures up in one's mind. It was actually the first of its kind for miles around. The attendees, who were mainly lesbians, were tolerated by the local community as long as they were discreet. Some years later it moved to a different town where sadly they were not tolerated quite so much and closed when too many revellers were attacked, even hospitalised on occasion. It was sad to see this event reach its end. It welcomed all from the ages of 18-100 all of whom mingled together. It witnessed many occasions from make-ups to break-ups but never any violent incident inside its walls. The toilet cubicles did sometimes harbour the noises of sexual activity to which those queuing to use the toilets applauded and cheered upon the exit of the red-faced couple. Most of all, however, "Girls On Top" offered a sanctuary for lesbians.

Sarah treated Petra to many delights: expensive restaurants, exercise equipment and gadgets which she loved. They went on numerous city-breaks both in the United Kingdom and Europe where they always stayed in top hotels. Sarah did not believe in doing things by halves.

Their first proper holiday was a three-week road trip through Florida, USA. Beginning in Sawgrass, in St Johns County, then on to Orlando and Disney World and ending up in Key West where they swam with dolphins. Whilst they were staying in Orlando, they met an English lesbian couple heralding from Blackpool, Lancashire in the North-west. They became firm friends, so much so that they visited each other often, went on weekend breaks and holidays together. Alice and Shannon were the only two guests invited to Petra and Sarah's wedding. At this time in Great British history, gay marriage was still illegal, but the loving couple wished to make that commitment to each other regardless. Upon some investigation, Sarah discovered a few places in the world where such marriages had been legalised. As chance would have it, Hawaii was one of these places! Although they considered a more public pledge to each other, what they yearned for more was a quiet ceremony. Neither of their parents wanted to go, so they came to the conclusion that they would ask Alice and Shannon to act as their witnesses and that would be that. Of course, a huge celebratory hen party was held where all of their friends ate, drank and danced until the very early hours of the morning. Fortunately, the restaurant staff were only too happy to oblige them in this.

Petra and Sarah headed to Maui, Hawaii, a few days prior to their two friends. Their hotel room was magnificent, as was its private beach that it looked out onto and was a mere five steps away from them. The first thing they did was to kick off their shoes and run down the hot sandy beach to paddle in the clear warm waters of the Pacific Ocean. The next thing they did was to run back the way they had come, don their swimming attire, grab their snorkels and run back over the sand until they reached the water which they skipped into until it was deep enough to swim. Petra was awestruck. She just could not believe the sight before her eyes. It was as if she was swimming in a tropical fish aquarium. All these wondrous, shapes, colours and patterns swimming beneath her made her hold her breath in total rapture. She literally cried with the sheer wonder and delight of what she beheld. Petra became addicted to her daily snorkel. On her second trip she met a turtle who befriended her. Each day Terrance The Turtle waited for her and then led her on a magical mystery tour of his reef.

Maui is the second largest Hawaiian Island inhabiting a diverse landscape which is the result of a unique combination of geology, topography and climate. It is characterised by only two seasons each year. Half of the island is situated within five miles of its coastline which, alongside the extreme insularity of the islands as a whole, accounts for the strong marine influence on Maui's climate.

Whilst there the four friends also attempted windsurfing and actual surfing. They attended a Luau, went humpback whale watching, sunbathed on beaches which could only be described as heaven on earth. They ate in magnificent restaurants dining on the most exquisite seafood, drank copious amounts of fabulous cocktails and attended a wedding — Petra and Sarah's.

They arrived at the isolated beach in style. A limousine drove them along the coastline whilst they sipped champagne. They were dressed relatively casually but nonetheless smartly. Petra wore a simple turquoise sequined knee-length dress, with thin shoulder straps. She had on a pink mother of pearl necklace around her neck and went without shoes. Who needs shoes on a beach! Sarah donned a flowing pale green silk trouser suit with a cream silk shirt underneath. The officiant met the wedding party of four on the deserted beach. They married as the sun was setting on the horizon with the sea's horses gently breaking over their feet. The officiant led them through the ceremony as they held hands whilst taking in the glory of it all. Champagne was corked and poured into four crystal glasses. A toast was made whilst they drank their drinks and they gazed seawards, listening to Dido and Joan Armatrading which was playing on a CD player. Other than that, and the sound of the ocean, all was silent. Any added noise, even a whisper, would have been sacrilege. It was a wrench to leave this perfection, but they had to depart as a chef was awaiting their arrival at a different, indeed even more perfect location. As the limousine approached their next beach, Petra cried tears of absolute delectation as she saw fire torches planted in the sand surrounding a beautifully laid table with a chef illuminated by the fire of the torches and his hot plate which was heated by its own flame. This dreamlike scene welcomed them as they approached the chef who immediately handed them yet more champagne. The evening was so perfect — so perfect it was almost tangible. They dined on scallops, lobster, crab, fish cakes, mahi mahi, ahi, hapu upu u, all of the seafood family. The finest fillet steak with salad was also cooked by the chef, on his fire-heated grate, in front of their very eyes. The most glorious desserts were gobbled down as was the most beautiful red and white wine. It was a day taken from a fairy tale.

Alice and Sharon remained with the newlyweds for two more days celebrating the union in further style after which they returned home leaving the happy couple to embark on their honeymoon. They hopped onto another island, Kauai, which geologically is the oldest of the main Hawaiian Islands. It boasts a tropical climate, mongoose and more glorious beaches. It is known as the Garden Island owing to being draped in emerald valleys, sharp mountain spires and jagged cliffs. It houses tropical rainforests and their amazing inhabitants, forking rivers and beautifully cascading waterfalls. Some parts are only accessible by sea or air which the wedded pair took advantage of, by kayak, only to have revealed before them views beyond their wildest imaginations.

Their third holiday of a lifetime was a six-week tour of New Zealand where they decided they could easily emigrate.

Petra was fulfilling her wish of being able to help others through her work at the Community Centre. She certainly made the O.A.P.s' day when she was on shift for their various groups through her happy demeanour and her art of listening attentively to their many tales of the past, groans about the present and sometimes fears about the future. At both youth clubs she was a very good role model for the youngsters to follow. She was also able to take those who needed to be taken under her wing to mentor, empower and also advocate for when required. She was definitely true to the meaning of her name — The Rock. Despite this, life outside work had not been an easy path because of her mother's abhorrence of her discovering her sexuality but Sarah had eased the way forward for her.

So, Petra was safely settled in her life. In theory she had no need to work. She could have been a lady of leisure as Sarah earned enough money for at least four people, but she chose to work in order to fulfil her dreams in that area of her life.

However, over the horizon life-changing decisions, changes and strife lay in wait for Petra. Why do things simply never run smoothly?!

iv The Oak Tree

Evanna, Bodhi and Petra continued to resemble, even represent in part, their individual oak trees.

When Evanna, The Akerne, visited home she continued to look out onto her welcoming Oak Tree. In times of hardship, whilst climbing up and traversing down mountains or ropes she envisaged her tree, sharing its courage and strength. She had still to recognise or even appreciate her own.

Her year as a cadet, then whilst in Training School, brought with them many changes and challenges, both mental and physical. Just as an oak tree faces changes and challenges during each season throughout the year.

It is true to say that Evanna was proud of her achievements, especially those as a cadet. Both introspectively and corporeally she felt stronger. On one particular occasion, as she contemplated her tree, she internally noted that she was beginning to resemble its trunk. Not in its form or structure but owing to its strength in the physical sense. She also acquiesced that her mental strength may possibly be growing stronger too. In a way she also felt "taller", although she did not quite tower over others stealing their life force or their view as the oak bestrode other trees, appropriating their sunlight.

There was once a time when she reckoned herself a leaf attached to her tree which fell to the ground waiting for the wind to sweep it skywards, swirl and toss it around on its currents. This leaf, *"or me,"* she thought to herself, *"had absolutely no idea where or when it would eventually land or what adventures lay in store."* In actuality, Evanna was not this leaf or any leaf for that matter as she was not so fragile, yet she was ignorant as to where she would finally end up or as to what exploits she had yet to experience. Her future was truly unknown, even her next minute or second. This small frail leaf appeared so weak upon first sight but was, in fact, the antithesis of such an adjective. It was a durable member of foliage as Evanna was no flimsy flower. However, she did not consider herself brave like the leaf which seemed content to be tossed and turned in the breeze, small or mighty, only to drop out of the sky in a place unknown where it would possibly cease to be. Evanna was not quite so intrepid but now she was less afraid. If she continued to consider herself that leaf, then possibly she too would be that brave soul. She still depicted her leaf to fall from a lower bough as its plummet to the ground would not be great. *"All those years ago, when I thought myself a leaf — did I know then that I was afraid of heights!"* She sniggled.

Sexually, Evanna had three "boyfriends" as a cadet and a few of the female variety. Some were cadets, others not. She still viewed herself to have two genders within her soul just as the oak tree did. She never thought herself bisexual, however. Nowadays she would be labelled *"pan sexual"* which can be described as being sexually attracted to a person, an individual, of any sex or gender. Just as the oak tree has its two genders.

When the oak's seeds had landed and planted themselves deep within the soil so had Evanna now planted herself within the Metropolitan Police. Now she had to grow in that position and within her life as a whole. She began to reminisce about when she said goodbye to her oak tree just as she was leaving for the Cadet Corps. She remembered it, as never meaning or feeling as an actual *"goodbye"* as she would surely see it again, both in reality and in her mind's eye.

But now she thought: *"I am becoming my Oak Tree."*

Bodhi, The Acharn, carried his Oak Tree which continued to withhold its pain as Bodhi did, with him at all times in the rooms of his elan — vital. He tried to put his best foot forward in times of pain so that no one saw his torment but gradually his mask was to fall as the tree creates a stiff upper lip when its leaves are ripped from its mainframe, or its bark is shredded and etched with the etchings of bladed articles.

The Oak protects, shelters and provides for others. Bodhi

needed protection, sheltering and love which he found in Marika who protected him from himself. She provided him with warmth and love and in her Bodhi found a safe shelter.

He recalled that there was a time he wished he acted as a root for his oak tree, buried deep down underneath the earth's damp soil which was his protection and temperature gauge. There he would be fed and watered as all flows through the roots. He would be hidden from view yet kept alive so when he felt ready, he could begin his ascent, as the nutrients ascend the tree to its highest heights. When Bodhi reached the tip of the tree, he would have found his Enlightenment and Awakening. He could finally "feel" life in all of its glory.

As he sat on his bed, having posted his letter through Marika's letterbox, he began to breathe deeply and slowly counted each breath. He was attempting to ground himself. To root his feet firmly on the ground in order to feel safe, stable, unshakeable, steady and strong. The roots, his feet, were beginning to unearth as his life was slowly starting to disentomb — to resurrect.

Bodhi considered himself asexual as opposed to the sexuality of the oak tree, despite his feelings for Beth which he did not quite understand.

He had the "Trust" (Bitachon) and the "Knowledge" (Emunah) that G-d had created all creation. Thus G-d had not only created himself (Bodhi) but his Oak Tree. So, such as that was G-d would continue to make plans for His Creations — all Creation. He may even perform a miracle or two in the process.

Bodhi thought: "*I am becoming my Oak Tree.*"

As for Petra, The Akran, she remembered her Oak Tree, once Lollipop Tree. How patient it was to wait for her for all those years. Waiting for her to come and say "*hello*", to sit resting her back upon its trunk amidst the roots. To tell it her sorrows, her achievements, her joys and her dilemmas. It offered her shelter on many an occasion, from the elements, from others and from herself. It always stood there waiting, continuing to offer her its goodness and protection. Oh, how dependable it was and how it continued to be so.

This tree, so strong and durable. It fought the climate's extremes with such bravery and dignity. How it remained standing tall and proud. Over the years Petra had gained her strength from this tree for when she was unable to touch it; like Bodhi she *"saw"* it in times of need.

This tree used every tool it possessed, all of its parts to reach its best potential and to help others. It served to protect animals, birds and plants alike. Likewise, Petra was now beginning to use all of her tools to reach her best potential. The oak tree fought even for its own survival, albeit selfishly, in order to stay alive by reaching heights higher than all the other trees and plants in order to access the better part of the sunlight. So, Petra was also fighting to beat the horrors of her childhood. However, she was not mercenary in so doing. She merely needed to remember to keep using these tools — these attributes that lay with her soul which were sometimes awake, but sometimes they lay dormant.

She recollected thinking herself as the trunk of her Oak Tree which held up the rest of its sturdy self. It took nutrients up from the roots, then up again into itself until they reached its highest height. Thus, it looked after and protected itself as much as it possibly could. Petra was not yet able to care for herself as well as her Oak Tree but was beginning to. In looking after others, the oak was strong, sturdy, faithful, nurturing and so giving. Just as Petra was. She supported and served others such as the elderly and the youngsters who attended the youth club. She wished to continue doing this for as long as she was possibly able.

Sadly, the Oak had its enemies, as we know it does. Such as the woodcutter who could strike it down and chop it into pieces at any given moment. Petra knew it would not take much to tear her down and cleave her into two parts. This may be metaphorical, yet her feelings and emotions were more than capable of doing this to herself, as were her parents, but her mother to a greater degree.

She differed from the Oak Tree in that she had only the one sexuality, that of a lesbian and a Gold Star one at that!

Despite this, Petra thought: "*I am becoming my Oak Tree.*"

The bark of the oak tree, indeed any tree, serves as a protective layer as the skin is to a human being. Evanna, Bodhi and Petra needed that skin to be as thick as possible, even in the allegorical sense, as children. They would continue to use it as they grew both in age and in mind, even in wisdom.

The bark bleeds sap as the skin bleeds blood and as the eyes bleed salty tears. It can be assured that the oak tree has experienced this "blood loss" as have our three "Acorns" who have bled from their oculi.

These "Acorns" of ours all want justice in some form. To fight for it, to earn it and to help others battle to receive it for themselves. They want to help and support these others. They have each embarked upon this or are about to imminently. Evanna the policewoman. Bodhi the special needs teaching assistant to be. Petra the community support worker. They each support and care for others in some capacity. These roles will flourish and change as time goes by, but the theme always remains the same. Likewise, the oak tree represents such humanity.

Since their births the oak tree has assumed the role of an

anchor, a foundation and a rock to the "Acorns" and its circle of life has been a mirror, of sorts, to each of their lives thus far. Yet they all have so much more in store.

Evanna, Bodhi and Petra are merging with their own tree.

So, now onwards to see what is in store for the "Acorns".

v Evanna

WPC 205sv stood on parade in the Street Duties portacabin on her very first day on division having been transferred from Training School. PC Gavin Harrogate was doing the inspection of uniform and "*appointments*", although not nearly to the standard of Training School, so way below that of the Cadet Corps. Nevertheless, The Akerne was nervous. She feared being not up to standard, and being picked up on any single thing.

The day prior she had taken some of her spare uniform and her "*appointments*" to her new police station in order to put them in her locker.

The uniform consisted of:

2 x tunics — dark blue with 4x silver metal buttons embossed with Metropolitan Police crest

2 x winter skirts — dark blue

2 x lightweight skirts — dark blue

2 x cravats — (clip on) dark blue and white checks

4 x shirts — white

2 x short-sleeved shirts — white

1 x police hat — bowler style, with hard top and chin straps, dark blue, dark blue and white chequered band round rim with Metropolitan Police badge pinned to centre — silver metal

6 x pairs spare tights — black

1 x gel tex jacket — luminous yellow with "POLICE"

written in, blue block capitals on rear

4 x pairs epaulettes — dark blue with 205sv pinned to them — silver metal

1 x lightweight long coat — dark blue with 6 x silver metal buttons embossed with the Metropolitan Police crest

1 x heavy weight coat — dark blue with 6 x silver metal buttons embossed with the Metropolitan Police crest

1 x pair gloves — leather — black

1 x pair gloves — cotton — white (for ceremonial duties)

And her "*appointments*" were thus:

1 x shoulder/handbag — dark blue

1 x truncheon — wooden — dark brown

1 x pair handcuffs — silver metal

1 x handcuff pouch — leather — dark brown

1 x whistle — silver metal

1 x whistle chain — silver metal links

The tunic, or jacket, was fitted, so it was not entirely practical when it came to wrestling with someone on the ground as there was little give. The skirts were of the not so trendy A line variety and again not entirely fit for purpose whilst climbing fences as the male officers behind could see right up it. Could this have been the C20 version of up skirting! It did, however, have a concealed truncheon pocket in which the ridiculous piece of wood could be hidden away and pulled out at all but a moment's notice, provided one's tunic did not impede it.

The shirts, well, they were just shirts but had tight collars apart from the summer ones which had an open neck. The summer shirt was worn without the cravat unless worn with the tunic.

Evanna was not alone in detesting the two coats. Also, highly impractical. They both reached down to the bottom of Evanna's calves. The heavyweight coat was big and cumbersome whilst the lightweight one was slightly less awful! Each had small side pockets which, again, were not fit for purpose. The luminous yellow gel tex jacket was only to be worn during road traffic accidents, public order events and otherwise at any scene or situation where it was desired to stand out and be highly visible. The hat had a hard top similar to that of a riding hat to protect the head should it be hit with a hard weapon. The chin straps were worn in times of a public order situation in which the hat was likely to fall off or be taken off by someone other than the officer wearing it. The cravat was clipped onto the neck of a shirt via a plastic device to prevent strangulation by another. The dark blue epaulettes which had Evanna's shoulder number pinned onto them were to be worn on the shoulders of all outer garments in order to denote the officer's identity to members of the public should they wish to complain or perhaps commend the officer to their superiors.

Also, to be worn by WPCs were black tights or stockings, most opting for the tights. These were also impractical as they were easily laddered. Black police shoes were also a must.

As for the "*appointments*", the ridiculous dark blue handbag with shoulder strap was detested by all female officers as it not only got in the way — it also looked bloody idiotic! The PCs had big pockets in their trousers which housed the necessary report books and other such necessities whereas the WPC's uniform lacked these. Inside the handbag, and the PC's pockets, should be kept:

Warrant Card

Accident Report Books (ARBs)

Incident Report Books (IRBs)

Process Report Books (which did not have an acronym)
Fixed Penalty Notices (FPNs)
Penalty Charge Notices (PCNs)
The all-important notebook in a black plastic wallet.

The WPC had the option to keep her truncheon inside it too. This wooden truncheon was smaller than that of the PCs and really wasn't worth the tree that was cut down to make it! It wasn't great protection — it was of little or no protection when it came to having to defend oneself against a marauding crowd but super for smashing windows!

The metal handcuffs were kept in a brown leather pouch worn around the belt at the waist. These were the old-style cuffs with a linked chain connecting each cuff thus joining them together.

The whistle was placed onto the whistle chain which was attached to the top button of the tunic. It was really worn for tradition and ceremony so in those modern times was just a decoration and a reminder of "*the olden (possibly golden) days of policing*".

Also worn around the waist belt was the extremely inefficient, bordering on the useless, Storno Police Radio. This was always destined not to work. Batteries went flat sometimes after a few hours' usage, they cut out, and refused to work in the multitude of black spots. They also failed to work anywhere underground and in lifts. They did not have an emergency button as they do now and had only two frequencies. They weighed a tonne. The battery dangled down from the belt clip to which it was attached. A thick black rubber tube ran from this battery to the radio itself which was attached to the shoulder epaulette via a clip. Needless to say, it always fell off this fixing when most needed.

Evanna's uniform was always too big for her as the police store lacked any of her size — in fact, they always did, so she continued to look like a sack of potatoes for most of her career unless wearing plain clothes.

Over the years, as a policewoman, Evanna saw some positive changes to the uniform, especially to that of the WPC. The coats were replaced with a more "fashionable" and practical rainproof jacket. The tunic was changed to a jumper but continued to be worn for ceremonial duties in which No.1 uniforms were obligatory. Damn that lost white glove! The truncheon was to become a rubber baton, which did not fit inside either the skirt truncheon pocket or the handbag. So, all officers wore it around the waist via a loop ring which was attached to the belt. The handcuffs also changed in style. The chain, now null and void, was replaced with a thick, solid static bar which proved better for securing and controlling prisoners. The skirt underwent various different prototypes: first the culotte and finally the trouser, both heavy and lightweight. The day these were issued was akin to a day of victory for all female police officers! The waistline was now being weighed down by the sheer amount of equipment the belt had round it. Utility belts were a thing of the future!

As soon as Evanna was able to drive a police car she ditched the handbag in favour of a clipboard which felt so much better for she was not a "handbag type of person"! The area car, being the only vehicle, which was double manned, was eventually kitted out with one stab-proof jacket and one bulletproof jacket. This was the only vehicle that was double manned, which proved highly interesting when it was known that a perpetrator and/or assailant was armed but it was unknown which type of weapon they had. To solve this problem one officer wore the stab-proof jacket whilst the other donned the bulletproof and then "danced around" around each other until it was ascertained exactly what weapon the suspect was "tooled up" with. It saw many a great dance routine and indeed much hilarity, even in some rather dangerous moments!

Nowadays, police "people" appear to be so much better equipped with more practical clothing which seems fit for purpose.

That proved to be the first and last "proper" inspection of Evanna's police career although one never got away with a shoddy turnout.

Evanna had now embarked on her eight-week Street Duties course alongside six other "probbies" otherwise known as probationers. This course was run by two PCs (Police Constables) who were under the direct command of PS Edmunds (Police Sergeant). She immediately warmed to Sergeant Edmunds, who was nearing the end of his 30-year career. Like most sergeants, he answered to the name of "Sarge", "Skipper", or plain "Skip". However, she found both PC Harraday and PC Mark Thomas rather arrogant individuals. "*A little too much up their own arses!*" she considered.

This course was designed to acclimatise all new probationers to their ground and "*how the job was really done*". They were told to "*forget most of what you learned in Training School because this is how it's really done. This is the real world. You're not in Toy Town now,*" Mark revealed.

Each was handed a small yellow booklet entitled "*Probationer's Record of Work Book*" in which for the next two years they were to record literally everything they did, from vehicle checks on the PNC (Police National Computer) to arrests. This book would be regularly scrutinised by their sergeants and inspectors (otherwise answering to: Guv, Guvnor or Boss). On the wall of the Street Duties Cabin was a wallchart upon which each of the new probbies' name was written. Alongside this there was to be a detailed tally chart of everything they had done from week to week, much like the small yellow book. At the end of each week, the one with the most tallies was awarded a beverage at the pub.

Street Duties, or Puppy Walking as it was otherwise known, was also to enable the new probationers to familiarise themselves with their soon to be colleagues on relief (or team) as they were of a different breed to civilians.

Evanna's first arrest was a murderer, who had murdered his girlfriend by strangulation in a fit of rage, which put her high on the scoreboard for that initial week for "best body" (body, being slang for the arrested person). Although she was pleased to get her first arrest under her belt, she was a little deflated because it wasn't as if she chased this guy down herself. On the contrary, he was handed to her on a plate. There was a warrant out for his arrest and CID (Criminal Investigation Department) wondered if one of the new probbies would care to execute it. Despite that she was still nervous as she had never cautioned or handcuffed anyone, let alone arrested someone in the "real world" and she wondered if she would do it correctly. She even wondered how she would feel about depriving someone, no matter what they had done, of their liberty. On arrival at this murderer's hideout a CID officer rammed the front door open and in they bundled, and it was a bundle! She was accompanied by four CID officers. She began to feel almost sick with nerves with her mouth becoming rather dry. However, to her amazement she was able to explain, to the alleged murderer, why he was being arrested and administer the caution without stumbling over one single word or momentarily forget them. Word perfect, professionally and with no little authority she stated:

"You do not have to say anything unless you wish to do so, but what do you say may be given in evidence."

She also remembered to note down the time she gave this caution and his reply which was: *"fuck off!"*

After that first arrest, none were quite of that calibre whilst on Street Duties. The course were "given" the dregs that those on relief didn't really want to be "tied up with" (i.e. too busy for anything else for at least the next eight hours!). As the station was situated close to a busy shopping centre, they were often called upon to deal with shoplifters, which once arrested and after searching them, interviewing them, doing all of the appropriate checks on the PNC may result in their being arrested for additional offences. During those eight weeks, all off the back of one shoplifter, she had to further arrest many for a multitude of offences including: possession and/or supply of a controlled substance (drugs), handling stolen goods, fraud — the list went on. Outside shoplifters she arrested others for the above offences but also for a wide range of others including robbery, TDA (taking and driving away), theft, burglary, criminal damage and various public order offences. One such arrest whereby she had to "nick" (arrest) a young woman for "Theft Employee" (she stole money from her employer) greatly upset her as this girl had no previous convictions, was polite, well-mannered and completely devastated at her behaviour. She admitted what she had done, which made Evanna think she had simply made an error of judgement, albeit a large one. During her interview it transpired that she stolen the money in order to help out her mother who had recently been made redundant and was struggling at home with three other young children. This account was verified. Evanna felt deeply sorry for this girl as she wiped away her tears, which were far from crocodile, on being charged. Evanna knew that with this on her record the girl may well now be unemployable. The effect this had on Evanna surprised her greatly.

Other jobs she was required to do consisted of stopping vehicles the drivers of which had committed some misdemeanour but once stopped she had to check the vehicle for any defects ensuring that no other offence had been committed. She reported RTAs (Road Traffic Accidents), an assortment of crime, neighbour and domestic disputes to list some of a very long list. She had cause to stop and search a fair few people, mainly males, for going equipped to commit a burglary, carrying an offensive weapon or bladed article, drugs and so forth. She also had to report sudden deaths which came across her police radio as a "locked (or collapse) behind locked doors" which was basically code for *"there's a suspected dead body in this house; go and deal with it!"*

One day, whilst still on Street Duties they were driven to the local hospital where they watched a real life post-mortem. The probbies were in the "theatre" whilst this grizzly task was executed. Two of her colleagues, both male, fainted and two walked out leaving her and one other to finish viewing this slightly gory yet highly interesting procedure. She disliked the sound of the rib cage being cracked open but the sight and sound of the skull being scalped and then sawn open after which the face (well, facial skin) was pulled completely down towards the neck was a sight truly to behold but a rather unpleasant one. Each internal organ was taken out, examined and weighed. However, it was the sight of the brain lying in the hands of the coroner as he walked to the weighing scales that Evanna found most profound and beautiful. Its form appeared perfect to the eye and the mere thought of how it performed in life was simply amazing. This post-mortem was where she was taught the sometime necessity of smearing Vicks underneath the nose to "drown" out some of these repulsive malodours.

For each and every "job" came the mountain of paperwork. There were no computers for the police back then, so everything had to be written by hand, which was slow and laborious work. Then they had to be typed out on an old-fashioned, often part-broken typewriter and placed in a bundle for court. When interviewing suspects everything that was said had to be detailed on the form verbatim. A simple arrest could mean eight hours of paperwork, often meaning overtime which Evanna could do without, especially if it meant having to forego a training session at the gym.

The probbies also had various attachments, including to the CID, traffic divisions (or Black Rats as they were known by others as they were hated) and mounted branch.

Having completed Street Duties, she was put on Relief (team). Her relief was C relief, which was supposed to be the best, but according to those on A, B and D theirs were also the best! The probationary period was two years in total. Evanna had twenty-two months left to complete now that she had reached the fruition of Street Duties.

Becoming familiar with the "Canteen Culture" of the Police, Evanna was finding some of this difficult to imagine she would ever be party to. Canteen Culture entailed a set of conservative and possibly discriminatory attitudes which appeared to exist within the Police Force (as it was known at that time as opposed to Service). This, she discovered, included, but was not limited to, male chauvinism and sometimes racism. The "banter" often proved rather dry, cynical and dark; Evanna was to realise that in order to be an effective police officer one required a certain propensity for a rather twisted and macabre wit, which she found shocking, disrespectful and insensitive at first. However, in time she found her sense of humour changing to this manner, out of necessity to cope with some of the terrible situations she dealt with and the sights she was subjected to.

As for misogyny, Evanna soon found herself answering to "*Doris*" which was the blanket term male officers used to "name" each and all of their female counterparts until, at least, they had proved themselves to be "*up to the job*". This was also true of the term "*plonk*". No WPCs rid themselves entirely of these epithets, no matter what they did as a group of more than two of them were known as "*Doris*'" or "*plonks*". As Evanna was one of only ten WPCs at her first station and one of only two on her relief it was difficult, as a probationer particularly, to admonish her male colleagues, especially the "*old sweats*" who were male officers who had been in the job for many a year and were very set in their ways. When women were first able to join the police, they were only seen fit to deal with children, old people and to make the tea.

Despite these obstacles, Evanna managed to prove herself reasonably quickly and in style! First, there were the Poll Tax Riots in which she proved that she was more than able to hold her own and then whilst out on foot patrol she was first on scene to an officer who had called for "*urgent assistance*" over his radio. She found this PC wrestling with a male brandishing a bladed weapon. She did not consider her own safety when she managed to disarm, secure, handcuff and arrest this male. By doing so she possibly saved PC 457's life. For this she not only earned herself the loyalty, trust and respect of all, she was also awarded the nickname "Zolbic". This was an amalgamation of two "names". "Zol" was after Zola Budd because of her speed of foot in arriving at the scene so quickly and "bic" was after the Bionic Woman because of her strength physically and her courage. Nicknames were commonplace but one had to prove oneself in order to gain one. They tended to stay with an officer for their entire career no matter how many times they transferred to different areas! A WPC was also categorised into the pigeonholes of *"bike"* or *"dike"* unless she happened to be in a steady relationship with a male. As for racist and cynical discussions, yes, they occurred but never out of the mouth of Evanna. She never witnessed any racist behaviour when "out and about" by any officer.

As for the conversations at mealtimes or in the pub which verged on the downright gruesome but always with a sick sense of joviality over a fatal RTA or something of that ilk, Evanna doubted she would ever join in with but she soon caught herself joining in with them as a way of release and the only way to survive. As there was no form of counselling this was their version of it. No one ever admitted to feeling upset or scared — that just was not done.

Evanna likened this canteen style culture to walking a tightrope. If she failed to participate, she would be vilified, but if she joined in too much, her opinion of her whole self would diminish to zero. There was a very fine line to tread.

However, slowly but surely, she found her place and she was accepted as "herself". She was fully accepted into the fold without having to compromise. As a result, her "family" grew as she obtained a whole host of brothers and sisters. There proved to be nothing akin to the camaraderie of these "siblings" who relied on each other to save their lives if needed. In short, they "had each other's backs at all times".

At first, Evanna found the four-week shift pattern of Early Turn (6am – 2pm), Late Turn (2pm – 10pm) and Night Duty (10pm – 6am) tough going, especially the weeks with quick changeovers mixed in for good measure. These meant that if she finished work at 6am, on the last night duty out of seven, she had to be back on shift at 2pm that day. The other meant finishing at 10pm and back at 6am. This was even harder when she incurred overtime. During the winter months she hardly saw daylight during the week of nights. She detested early turn but loved night duty. This was partly because there were no senior officers above her Inspector around, meaning when quiet the pack of cards and a bottle of whiskey were enjoyed. Somehow the dark was more exhilarating than daylight. The quality of "calls" seemed better leading to more high-speed vehicle chases, owing to the empty roads. It was the time for "suspects on premises", pub fights and public disorder in general, which Evanna quite enjoyed. The adrenaline flowed more during night duty somehow. This shift pattern changed a few years after Evanna had passed her probation. This was owing to the advent of Sector Policing whereby each team (as reliefs were now to be called) had their own beat to patrol during certain given shifts but not the core ones. The only time they were ever out in pairs was in the area car and in the van.

Overtime was much sought after and easily achieved. There was no limit to it. In reality, one never finished their "tour" exactly on time.

There was a huge array of personalities, each a treasure in their own right. Most shifts ended with a visit to the station's "local" which had regular lock ins for their "resident coppers" and in turn the pub landlord knew they would be well looked after. The pub, alcoholism, extramarital affairs, sleeping around, incestuous behaviour with colleagues and chain smoking were the policeman's lot — their way of letting off steam. Evanna did go to the pub regularly but not after every single shift as she preferred to let go of her steam at the gym. After a night shift some, including Evanna from time to time, would head for Spittlefields Meat Market, as there, cheap beer could be purchased at 6am.

After passing her probation with flying colours, Evanna was able to become a Basic Driver, meaning she could drive a panda car, a Mini Metro, but was not allowed to use the "blues and twos" or break any road traffic law. This regulation was often discarded, which was all well and good unless one was involved in a Polac (an accident when driving a police car) whereby The Black Rats (the reviled Traffic Division) had to report the accident and duly suspend the driver while he or she was investigated.

Over the course of Evanna's police career she completed a multitude of courses enabling her to become qualified and partake in different areas of policing. She had no desire to join the CID. Her first course was to take the IRV (Instant Response Vehicle) Course which upon passing allowed her to upgrade the police vehicle she drove to an Astra. She was now able to use the "blues and twos", to respond to all emergency calls, using the appropriate policing driving techniques she had been taught, and to break driving laws using extreme caution and only when necessary. She was also able to drive the van which she enjoyed doing. Next, she passed the Advanced Driving Course whereby she drove the Rover using advanced techniques. The Rover was the Area Car, the fastest car on division and the only one that was double manned or "two up". The area car drivers, who were few in number, held such respect of all of those who did not hold this status.

Evanna also became a SOIT (Sexual Offences Investigation Trained) officer, which made her responsible for acting as a first responder to allegations of a sexual offence. Her role was to gather evidence and information from the victim in a manner that contributed to the overall investigation, preserving integrity and securing the victim's confidence and trust. This also required her to offer support and information, in a sensitive and compassionate manner to victims whilst ensuring they were given timely advice about other police departments and support agencies.

Alongside another WPC she was given the task of forming and setting up the first DVU (Domestic Violence Unit) in the country. This role enabled her to use much of the SOIT training as she supported victims of domestic violence, arresting the offender and bringing them to justice, if the victim wished this to happen, but they often retracted their statements, which Evanna found frustrating, as she had no doubt she would be meeting these people, time and time again.

After a few years, Evanna decided to transfer to the CPT (Child Protection Team) where she was able, once again, to use her SOIT and DVU knowledge and experience. It proved tough going, often heart-wrenching and gut-twisting work. However, this was the reason she joined the police, to win justice for others — those that had been through what she had been through, but she did not receive the justice she deserved. She felt proud to be able to provide this and she gave it in abundance, winning commendations for her tenacity and excellent results. Whilst in the CPT, where she was to be for five gruelling yet satisfying years, she completed her sergeant's examination after which she was required to go back onto division where she was to be in charge of a team. She was attached to two different stations whilst a PS, being Brixton and Kilburn. She was well liked and well known for her firm yet fair, friendly, approachable and amiable leadership.

She also became POLSA trained which meant she was a Police Search Advisor. She went down hundreds of drains searching the sewers and numerous other odd, sometimes disgusting places, for bombs (namely of the IRA type) and such like. This normally took place prior to a big public or ceremonial event.

She attended an assortment of other courses but the one she treasured most, just edging the Advanced Driving Course from the top spot, was the SOIT course as it enabled her to support victims of such crimes and to help bring the offender to justice which was what she was almost reared to do.

From the very beginnings of her career, Evanna began to note down each of her arrests but when it numbered way into the hundreds, which was quite early on, she stopped doing so as she came to the realisation that this number would keep on rising, the thought of which depressed her as she never thought there would be so many "bad" people out there. It did, however, give her a sense of satisfaction that justice was being served and she was known for being a great "thief taker".

She policed many a football match, rock concerts, marches, protests, ceremonial events, Notting Hill Carnival — you name it, she policed it. The IRA were prevalent at this time, so she was also sent on searches for bombs and whilst at Kilburn and Cricklewood arrested and came across a fair few, IRA members, or those affiliated to it.

She worked the mundane to the absolutely ridiculous and

when a sergeant did the same but had the added pressure of managing her team whilst ensuring their safety.

Leave and Rest Days could be cancelled at a moment's notice, which could be infuriating, especially when she needed a break.

Evanna saw some horrific sights, dealt with some horrific people but also had some wonderful and jocular times. Here is just a mere snapshot of some of those occasions which always stood out in Evanna's mind.

The Akerne was not long out of Training School when she was seconded to attend Central London on 31st March 1990 in order to police a march against the Poll Tax.

The advent of the Poll Tax was due to an effort to change the way the system of taxation was used to fund local government in the United Kingdom. The system that was in place until that time was called "rates" and had been in place in some form since the early seventeenth century. This system was described as a levy on property, which in more modern times meant each taxpayer paying a rate based on the estimated rental value of their home. In 1989 the then Prime Minister, Margaret Thatcher, and her government had promised to replace such domestic rates, which were unpopular as they were viewed as an unfair way of raising revenue for local councils by levying on people rather than property. Thatcher promised that in their place would be a flat-rate per capita community charge a head. A tax that saw every adult pay a fixed rate amount set by their local authority. This was widely called the Poll Tax. This charge proved highly unpopular; while students and the registered unemployed had to pay 20%, some large families occupying small houses saw their charges go up considerably; and the tax was thus accused of saving the rich money whilst moving the expenses onto the poor.

The march that Evanna was to police was arranged by The All-Britain Anti Poll Tax Federation. The senior police officers anticipated the march to be peaceful despite, only three days prior, organisers informed them that it would be larger than 60,000 people. Owing to this, and unbeknownst to the regular officers actually policing it, the Federation's request to divert the march due to the volume of people had been denied by the police as the policing had been arranged for Trafalgar Square and there was no time to alter this. A building site, on the square, with easy access to supplies of bricks and scaffolding had been left largely unsecured while the police set up their centre of operations on the opposite side of the square. Thus, it was destined for disaster even before it had begun but no one bothered to let this information filter down to the rank and file.

Here is Evanna's report of that day:

"Incident: Poll Tax Demonstration
Day: Saturday 31st March 1990
Time: 1530 hrs
At: Whitehall SW1 Junction with Trafalgar Square
Notes not made at the scene due to personal safety.
On Saturday 31st March 1990 at 1530hrs I was on duty in full uniform as a member of Serial 469 in Whitehall at the junction with Trafalgar Square SW1.

I was at the Poll Tax demonstration in Central London. At about 1530hrs I was formed as part of a single lined cordon across the top of Whitehall at the junction with Trafalgar Square SW1. My job, along with that of my serial, was to prevent people from going down Whitehall due to a disturbance at the further end of Whitehall. A large crowd began to form in front of me and I heard them chant and felt them push against me as they surged towards us. There were 10 of us in the serial. We were holding tightly onto each other's belts to prevent us from being pulled into the crowd of what looked like 1,000 people. A few people said to me that they wanted to get through the cordon, but I was told I could not let them through. I saw and felt the crowd push against us and saw some raise their clenched fists. They were shouting words such as: 'Maggie's boot boys' at us and were trying to break down our cordon. Missiles were then thrown at us. These included: bottles, bricks, scaffolding poles, pieces of wood, stones, plastic traffic cones and drinking glasses. People were spitting at us. At this point I became aware of another large crowd of people approaching us from the rear. When the crowd in front saw this their chanting became even louder, and they became more violent and told us to turn around so that we could see the large crowd running towards us in a menacing manner. I heard them shout: 'You'll be the filling to the sandwich.' At this point PS 8sv Brown, who was the sergeant in charge of my serial, ordered us to take out our truncheons. We did so. Missiles were being thrown at us from all directions and angles. We were then ordered to retreat. The sergeant told us to 'run, run as fast as you can and jump in the river if you have to' as we were so vastly outnumbered which we had been since the moment we arrived. We managed to run in a direction where there was a clearing.

I saw policemen and women being hit with the missiles being thrown by the crowd. I was hit by many of these, but I am unable to state exactly what hit me. I saw a mounted branch officer being pulled from her horse and set upon by 6 people, but she was rescued by colleagues. I saw many officers being helped out of the crowd with varying injuries. Each time a police officer was carried out, the crowd cheered and jeered. We were then told to push the crowd toward the Embankment now that some

218

reinforcements had arrived. I do not know at what time we reached the Embankment, but we were still outnumbered. However, I do know that it was a very frightening situation to be in.

I felt disgusted at the way some members of the British Public acted towards the police, who were there to protect and serve. They were certainly not there to be beaten in such a savage and violent manner.

When I arrived home and began to undress, I noticed that I was bruised on my right hand and on my left side. My legs were also covered in cuts and bruises. I noticed a large lump and bruising to the right side of my forehead which was very sore. These injuries must have occurred during the melee in Whitehall Junction with Trafalgar Square SW1.

The crowd surrounding me were scruffy white youths. I do not know at what exact time these injures were incurred but they must have been induced between 1530 and 1800 hrs. Nor do I know who actually gave me these injuries."

What Evanna did not include in her report was the fact that when staff inside the Whitehall Theatre saw her serial run in retreat, they opened their locked doors to enable the serial to find some safety from inside. She was able to use their telephone to inform her sister that she would not be able to join her, that evening, for her birthday celebrations. Gianna was rather cross, so Evanna advised her to turn on the television and watch the news! Nor did she include that one rioter had thought to bring his white pet mouse to the protest which he carried in the palm of his hand. He was imploring Evanna to rescue the mouse from the very missiles he was throwing at her!

Evanna worked an 18-hour tour of duty that day. When she

returned to the section house she soaked in a steaming hot bath. The events of the day did not really hit her until she caught a glimpse of herself, truncheon in hand, on the BBC News. Her mother, who was visiting friends in the USA, called her as she was so concerned having seen televised reports she had watched. It was then that she reflected upon what she had been through. She decided, somewhat surprisingly, that this was the single most invigorating and exciting albeit frightening experience she had ever had. This was despite having lost a shoe in the riot and having her tunic torn and buttons ripped off as the crowd attempted to pull her into it. She was rescued by Big Trace, a member of the TSG (Territorial Support Group) who were not brought in until the very last minute with their riot gear and shields. Big Trace was an amazon with long flowing curly ginger locks. She was not someone to be reckoned with! This amazon simply lifted Evanna up by the scruff of her neck and plonked her back down onto the pavement with minimal if no effort. She then waved at Evanna before she turned her back and returned into the fray, as did Evanna.

Over the years she saw hundreds of bodies in all states of disrepair. Some recently deceased, others who had been left for months were consequently maggot ridden, some had black tongues. However, it wasn't this or even the swarm of bluebottles that flew around her head that got to her, it was the stench, especially from those that had been left there for a long time. It proved near impossible to rid oneself of that "death smell". It clung to the uniform literally soaking through it and into the very pores of the skin. Evanna could cope with the bluebottles, the maggots and the odd black tongue that protruded from its owner's mouth but that stench...

In the years to follow she dealt with a few cot deaths which were so, so sad, made even worse by having to question the parents, despite doing so as sensitively as she could, to check that no major crime, or any crime for that matter, had contributed to the death. Alongside that the delivery of death messages was hard, especially to anxiously awaiting parents. Evanna was to see many a dead body outside the home. The worst types were those found washed up along river or lakesides. They were bloated, decaying, ridden with water life and putrid. She became used to the sight of dead bodies. The tell-tale signs of the "collapse behind locked doors", which in reality meant there was a dead body on the other side, were the stereotypical milk bottles building up on the front doorstep and old newspapers and post sticking out of the letterbox and piled high on the indoor welcome mat. But the dead giveaway was the smell. When the nose edged through that letterbox. The smell of death. There is no smell quite like it. The longer the corpse had lain there the stronger and fouler this stench was.

She grew to accept that death was an inevitable part of life, but it was never pleasant dealing with sudden deaths. With the deceased and often their relatives. However, it was when these dead people had been left alone sometimes for weeks, even months, on end without one single person noticing that really floored The Akerne. It wasn't the state of their rotten, maggot-infested flesh or even the mephitis. It was the mere fact of the matter that not a soul had noticed. Not a soul had bothered. Was it really the case that not one solitary soul cared about this life — this life now gone? This light that had burnt out — no one cared about? This haunted her from there on in, about herself. She feared this would happen to her. She would probably be childless, her parents (such as they were would probably be dead), her sister didn't give a toss and her friends would be the same age as her.

So, who would notice? Who would care? Who would bother? Would it matter because she wouldn't know anything about it as she would have ceased to exist, but one never knew the truth about that — maybe in death they would. Most of all she didn't want to rot and smell like that and be left there with "*no bugger giving a toss*". Oh, the indignity. In later years, she spoke about this fear to two of her closest friends both of whom assured her that even if they lived to be one hundred years old, they would check on her every day so as to avoid this from happening. Naturally this was said in some jest and irony but Evanna knew that if they could, they would. This, though, did make her think about her own mortality in some depth.

So, on the whole Evanna could cope with dead bodies, especially those of the elderly in that she was able to get on with the job at hand without dwelling too much on it. It was dealing with deceased babies and children, taken way before their time, way too soon, that really knocked her sideways. It wasn't just seeing their tiny, fragile, innocent bodies which often appeared merely asleep. It was also dealing with the understandably distraught and angry parents. Having to go through the formalities and then to ask them awkward questions, for evidential purposes, which she was all too aware sounded callous, uncaring and accusatory.

Nor did she much care for attending suicides: drug overdoses often with vomit and spittle everywhere, hangings, wrist slittings and so forth. However, the sight of two types of suicide left her with this awful taste in her mouth and cringe deep inside.

The first of these was a one-off experience for her. After "breaking into" a house, having answered a call to a "collapse behind locked doors" she was greeted, to her profound distaste, with a white male who had committed hari-kari. This is the form of Japanese ritual suicide by disembowelment This young man was not remotely Japanese, however. He was definitely of English descent, not that it mattered. There was blood and guts everywhere. The deceased had plunged a short-bladed kitchen knife into his belly, then drew this blade from left to right; hence slicing his belly wide open. Everywhere she looked there was blood. The room was washed in the stuff. Everywhere she placed her feet she stood in it. The most ridiculous thing of all was that she had to call and then wait for the FME (Forensic Medical Examiner) to attend in order to pronounce life extinct. The post-mortem revealed that he had managed to perform this cut so deeply that he had severed the descending aorta causing a rapid death of blood loss as was his intent judging by the suicide note he had scribbled.

The latter form of suicide which she found loathsome were the "jumpers". Those poor souls who felt the need to end their lives by jumping in front of a high-speed train. However, she never knew who she felt most sorry for: the actual jumper, the ill-fated train driver or the unfortunate people who had been going about their everyday mundane business who had then been forced to witness this or the emergency services including herself and her colleagues who had to clear up the mess. This meant crawling underneath the train and walking along the tracks locating, retrieving and bagging up bits and pieces of body which could be strewn a mile or so down those tracks. The one who found and reclaimed the head had to get the beers in later. It was a most truly gruesome task. Evanna came to the conclusion that she felt pity for everyone involved. She also considered "the jumper" to be truly selfish owing to the fact that they had involved so many people in their own demise. If she were ever to commit suicide, she would never involve anyone else, she determined.

On 11th April 1992 at 1309 hrs, Evanna was standing on the front outside steps of the police station with some colleagues. They were to be off duty at 1400 hrs and were busy discussing who would get the all-important first round in. At 1310 hrs they were lying in a crumpled heap at the bottom of the steps deafened by the almightiest blast which no one mistook for anything other than a bomb. Which it indeed was. The bomb had been placed in a white Bedford van near the Staples Corner Junction in north London. The attack happened only a few hours after the major bombing of the Baltic Exchange seven miles away which had killed three people. Both bombs were homemade. The IRA, who had claimed responsibility for these bombs, had given telephone warnings 50 minutes prior to the attack.

Although, miraculously, there were no fatalities or injuries caused at Staples Corner, the blast was extremely powerful causing significant damage to roads leaving a crater in the North Circular flyover. People felt the blast from several miles away. The bomb damaged a three-storey DIY superstore so badly it had to be demolished. It was later estimated that the explosive force was around 100kg.

Despite having been literally just blown off their feet Evanna and her colleagues were told by the duty inspector to dust themselves down and *"get on directing traffic"*, which they duly did for the next eight hours. However, joy and normality were restored when they finally made it to the pub for its official last orders but what was to be a lock in for them! Neither Evanna nor those who had been with her on the steps had to buy one single beer that night!

Obviously, Evanna saw the mundane, often dull and routine side of policing: the reporting of crime; the mountains of paperwork; the minor road traffic accidents; drink driving offences; other minor offences; neighbour disputes — indeed this list could continue ad infinitum.

Friday and Saturday nights were "Pub Fight Nights" and drunken street brawls often resulting in arrests for assault or public order offences. Evanna actually found herself enjoying these as they got the heart rate pulsing and the adrenaline pumping. However, fights between a group of women proved savage as nails and clumps of lacquered hair could be sent flying into the air.

She was always well respected amongst her fellow officers both as a PC and a PS. This was owing to her bravery, her willingness to get "stuck in", her work ethic and indeed her overall personality. As a sergeant she never allowed anyone to do something that she would not do herself. She led by example and for that she was given high praise. In short, she excelled at her job. Her courage and strength of character shone through many a time, such as when she disarmed perpetrators brandishing knives and even guns. On occasion she was known to verbally persuade the assailant to give up his weapon voluntarily without the need of force, which was always safer and, therefore, preferable.

She loved driving the area car. "Following" vehicles at high speed was her forte. Everyone clambered to be her crew member. The passenger's, otherwise known as the Operator's, role was to operate the MP Radio System (the radio for the entire Metropolitan Police area, not merely that of the division). They accepted calls as directed by the driver, operated the "blues and twos" as directed by the driver and in the absence of today's satellite navigational systems read the map if called upon to do so by the driver. In other words, the area car driver was The Boss! The thrills Evanna experienced when she drove this car, chasing those vehicles who failed to stop, breaking all speeds in order to attend an emergency call and being overall top dog. All clamoured to be her operator as they knew they would be in for an exciting, fruitful, fun and great tour.

She was part of numerous public order events which went "pear shaped", including the Notting Hill Carnival. She never shied away from any trouble or danger. On the contrary, she would be the first to run towards it — to run into it. None of "her" officers were going to get hurt or at worst killed on her watch. Much of the time, when wearing the police uniform, she felt invincible — she could do anything and could not be harmed. She was "The Protector" of all things civilian and all things police.

She organised various operations and raids which, mostly, produced good and fruitful results.

Her greatest satisfaction arose when she arrested someone for sexual assault or when she was involved in such cases. One of the best feelings was when a suspect was charged and proceeded to be found guilty at court. Her years on the Child Protection Team were tough going as they brought with them such horrific personal memories but the sense of euphoria she received when justice was duly served vanquished those memories, even if only for a brief while.

As a police officer whilst on duty Evanna found she lived in the moment. When dealing with a situation, no matter the type, all attention and focus had to be diverted towards that. She lived the trauma, smelt the smells, saw everything at that moment. She would feel the pump of her heart and the flow of her adrenaline. As a result, she experienced, lived even, everything that she came up against to her very core. In stereo Dolby sound and with the clarity of 20/20 vision. Thus, she found it near impossible to switch off. She lived the atrocities she saw, the traumatic events, the anger, the sadness and grief — all of the emotions belonging to the people she came up against or supported — she lived and breathed. She was not the person to put her feelings and emotions to one side as most of her colleagues were able to do, but she did bottle all of them up, which did not bode well for Evanna. No one discussed or even acknowledged their true feelings after a traumatic, portentous, fearful, atrocious or menacing incident. It was simply: carry on regardless and down to the pub later to dilute and wash away all feeling.

Evanna disliked attending road traffic accidents. She found them tedious. Especially when they were mere prangs with the drivers disputing who was at fault. She dealt with so many that they merged into one. However, this one left such a vast imprint in her mind. This one left her reeling. This one left her guilt ridden. This one she would forever be able to remember with acute recall. But had it not been for this one she may have never saved the lives of two young children.

It was 0530 hrs. Night duty was just about to finish with 30 minutes left on the clock. Evanna was sitting on the parade room table alongside her relief and some eager members of the early turn crew. In about an hour she would be in bed. A call then went over their radios. A call that would lead to the worst of her nightmares. A call that she would continue to relive for the rest of her life. It was described simply as an RTA (Road Traffic Accident). That night Evanna had been driving the IRV and had yet to hand over the vehicle, so the keys were still in her hands. She jumped straight up, telling the lads to stay behind as she would deal. So, off she sped on the short journey to the dual carriageway where the accident had happened. On her approach all her eyes could see was a wall of flame. A wall of fire. On exiting the IRV, which she had pulled to a halt at a safe distance away, she was able to feel the immense heat from the fire that had engulfed a vehicle. A top of the range Porsche, yellow in colour, which she discovered later as at that time she was unable to make it out because of the blaze that had claimed it. Once again, living in the moment, presence of mind and quick reactions sprang into action. She did not stand, stare and despair. She did the only thing she could. She called for the fire brigade, an ambulance and for urgent assistance from those back at The Nick (police station).

She was as close as she could get to the inferno because of the heat. It was a heat like she had never felt. As the sun woke from its slumber the flames met with it. She thought she could hear screams coming from inside the vehicle that had been swallowed by phlogiston. She listened intently. The conflagration itself didn't appear to make a sound. Instead, it was as if it were a blockade of energy. The noise was silent. To her terror she made out two voices, one high and one deep. Initially, she was certain that she could save those inside but upon approaching the vehicle the scorching, searing heat knocked her back. It was a force she was not prepared for. Twice more she attempted with her right upper limb outstretched so that the appendage on the end, for neither her arm nor hand felt as if it belonged to her, could somehow withstand the heat, happen upon and pull the driver's door handle open so that the occupants could be saved. This proved all but a fruitless effort. It would have taken a superhero to achieve this. Thus, all she could indeed do was stand, stare and despair. She was in a trance-like state. She was not really aware of her colleagues who had now arrived or the few witnesses, all of whom could only stand, stare and despair.

As her eyes searched inside the blaze, they grew to acclimatise to the flames enabling her to see into and through it. She saw the vehicle and into it through the driver's door window. There she made out what looked to be a female. She was screaming. Screaming in sheer agony as the flames lapped at her body. She shrieked "*HELP, HELP, HELP US.*" Evanna watched as the female's body slumped over the steering wheel. Her screaming and screeching ceased. The guilt she felt when she realised, she was thankful for this cessation which was the point at which this poor woman had probably died. Thankful because she was no longer subjected to it. Guilt that she felt relieved that this woman was now free from that suffering, which meant this woman would feel joy no more.

Evanna could still hear the deeper screams but not as loud now. She could not see the passenger but judging from the screams' depth of tone they belonged to a male.

It felt like decades before the fire crew arrived but in reality, it was only minutes. She could not understand how the vehicle had not already combusted. The firemen extinguished the flames leaving a scorched wreck of a Porsche. The woman was indeed slumped over the steering wheel; that had not been a figment of Evanna's imagination. Her once long blonde hair that was now blackened and seared covered her face which Evanna was grateful for. She also felt guilt as she could not bear to see the face of the woman she had failed so badly. Failed to save. Failed to even help. She imagined this woman would look at her with an accusatory stare. It was a sight she would see for evermore.

The male was by some miracle still alive but barely. He was silent but was just about conscious and breathing although each and every breath was laboured. Evanna saw the ambulance crew gently evacuate him from the vehicle and lay him on a stretcher.

She chose to stay some distance away but could still see that his clothing had been burned off in part with the rest having melted into his skin. His body was of different hues of red, black and a creamy pus. He looked blistered from head to foot. His head was left with clumps of singed hair. It was a sight she would see for evermore.

As he was being rushed into the awaiting ambulance, Evanna heard one PC mutter: "*He smells like roast lamb.*" Indeed, he did smell; she could smell him even at the distance that separated them but not ever of roast lamb. He smelt rancid. Smelt of burning and burnt human flesh. She could not describe that smell, but it was not even remotely akin to roast lamb but maybe of some kind of rotted meat. It was a smell she was to get hints of for evermore.

The wreckage of the vehicle before her had been stripped of all of its former glory. It was nothing but steel rods forming some kind of shape — car-like, perhaps. It was black. Each window had blown leaving shards of glass everywhere. The area was saturated with water and foam.

Evanna was in shock as she stared at this scene which almost seemed peaceful now apart from the slow drip drip drip from the water freeing itself from the wreck. All around her was in slow motion. Movements and noise all slow. She knew she had to "*come back*". There were witnesses to deal with, reports to write, traffic police to liaise with and fellow officers to assist. Slowly but unwillingly, she noticed her view return to normal and with that her duties.

Stuart died a few hours later.

Upon her return home six hours later, after witness statements had been taken, accident report books written, the wreckage being taken away and such, she lay down on her bed.

All she could do was cry. All she could do was cry. Cry. How useless was that! Back at work that night it was business as usual. None spoke of it. Being a main carriageway, Evanna was forced to drive along it several times that night. She froze inside each time she did so as she imagined the atrocities of the scene that had occurred before her very eyes.

Later she was to learn that the driver of the Porsche was named Annabelle Stevens. She owned an exclusive nightclub in the centre of London. Annabelle had been 52 years old. Her passenger, one Stuart Wright had been celebrating his 21st birthday at the club. It remained unclear as to why he happened to be a passenger in the vehicle as they were not related and did not appear to have been acquainted prior to that night. As they were driving back from the club they hastened upon another supercar, as witnesses evidenced and traffic police confirmed, which for some godforsaken reason ended up in a race down the dual carriageway which was deserted of traffic at that time of the morning. Annabelle lost control, hitting the roadside barrier. Her Porsche flipped in the air several times before it landed right side up and ablaze. The other vehicle made off.

The guilt that shrouded Evanna for the rest of her life never diminished. The guilt of not being able to save the lives of those people. Those people who died such horrific deaths. The guilt that all she could do was to merely stand, stare and despair. The guilt of truly believing she should have done more. The guilt of relief she felt when the screaming ceased. The guilt of disgust she felt when she saw Stuart's repulsive looking body. The guilt of joining in with the sick, vile jokes back at the station. The guilt of that disrespect. But what else could they do? She lived with that guilt and the night terrors for evermore, but those terrors were not just at night. They were to haunt her at unexpected times and events when least expected with such depths of clarity that never seemed to fade. The images before her eyes were slowed-down videos of this incident but with such clarity that targeted all of her senses. From there on in she developed a fear of fire, even that of the flickering from a candle for she had seen, all too up close, the dire consequences of fire. *"I will never die that way,"* she promised to herself. The worst way to die she was now certain. Although, ironically, she continued to want to be cremated in death.

It was a mere few weeks later when Evanna was on a Late Turn driving the area car. A call came up as a *"house fire. Fire Brigade have been called."* She was literally 30 seconds away and on arrival first on scene. She could see and smell smoke coming out from a terraced house. There was a gaggle of onlookers. She heard the anguished cries of a man and a woman who were the parents of a toddler and a five-year-old who were still inside the house upstairs sleeping. They had fled the house leaving their children in bed! Evanna managed to control her anger instead directing her operator as to what to do, then ran towards the smoke, towards the house without a thought except: *"No one is going to burn to death ever again on my watch!"* She knew she would not, nay could not, allow these children to die the same torturous death as that of Annabelle and Stuart. As she ran towards the house, the smoke became denser both in vision and stench, but she did not really notice this as she was fixated on one thing and one thing only — the lives of these children. In truth she was never able to recall much about what happened next. She knew the smoke filled her lungs which caused them a burning sensation and she was struggling to breathe. She felt heat. She felt her heartbeat. She kept low to the floor. She knows that somehow; she climbed the stairs. She knows that halfway up she could make out, through the smoke, two tiny figures standing on the upstairs landing holding hands. She is aware that she scooped these two figures up, one under each arm. She knows she returned down the stairs. She does remember hitting the fresher air outside but has been told that she did not stop walking with these two children until she was physically stopped by her Guvnor. She remembers a feeling of relief flood into her that she had rescued this brother and sister from the black, dense smoke and fire that had started in the kitchen. She got reprimanded by that same Guvnor as she was being attended to by the ambulance crew, but he did save her from the tirade of anger from the fire chief as to how she should have waited! She had no option but to allow the ambulance to take her hospital for smoke inhalation.

Later, as her Guvnor drove her back to the police station, he apologised for shouting at her. As he explained that he could not allow any member of those under his command to *"die on his watch"* she knew exactly how he had felt. This big, burly man was in tears as he spoke. He later was able to speak more calmly, repeatedly stating how brave and selfless she had been — is. What a credit she is to The Job. Although this was meant wholeheartedly, Evanna did not pay any heed nor did she to the reprimands at the time. She simply did what she had to do. Anyone would have done the same. So, when she was awarded commendations for bravery she felt like a fraud. It was her job. It was her duty. Had it not been for that fatal car fire — would she have rushed into that smoke-filled burning house so quickly or would she, in reality, have hesitated which may have caused two more deaths? She could not possibly know.

Naturally, Evanna's years in the police did not pass her by without some hilarity. Actually, there was much of it even at times when really one should not be caught laughing. At times she likened experiences to The Keystone Cops! She cared to highlight in her brain a few of these times but there were just too many of them that she could consider her "favourite" moments. Although she would often find herself giggling at the same ones there was no particular rhyme nor reason as to why these came to mind. Perhaps they were just snapshots of the bigger picture that she chose to see first.

Despite not being rib-ticklingly hilarious she used to chuckle, to herself, owing to the fact that her big burly male counterparts always sent her in first to a "*suspects on premises*" or a bar brawl. The theory behind being that no self-respecting male, no matter how drunk, would hit a female let alone one with such a "Lilliputian" frame such as herself! This theory proved highly mistaken on many an occasion, especially the time, she recalled, when she was sent through a regular-sized cat flap for a "*suspects on premises*" shout. The fitting through this flap of her shoulders and hips proved an experience in itself notwithstanding the way she was greeted once inside the property — by a young male swirling a baseball bat in the air, then a blow to her head! It wasn't a major bow as she managed to grab hold of said bat, pull the burglar's legs from underfoot, restrain and handcuff him before she led him out by using the front door which could have been opened from the outside as it transpired much to the shock of the policemen waiting for her to let them inside and then search the house. You see, Keystone bloody cops!

Then there were the ridiculous calls, such as some so-called "*domestic incidents*" on Christmas Day. This one stood out. The couple in question had opted to call 999 which Evanna received whilst driving the area car. Risking life and limb to the scene thinking that a major assault was occurring because of the crying and screaming the operator had heard coming from the other side of the phone, Evanna arrived at the house where there had been no assault of any kind. The husband and wife, aged about 50, advised her that they had been quarrelling as one wanted to watch BBC1 and the other ITV. That was it! After giving "words of advice" she promptly switched off the television set via the mains, confiscated the remote control and suggested they stick to playing charades! It was all she could do but not to smash the TV with her baton (truncheons now being obsolete but one was not supposed to smash glass with a baton as sharp pieces of it would embed themselves in the rubber — so what was the point of them in the first place!).

That same year she was on duty in Trafalgar Square at New Year's Eve. This was the place to be on this night of the year at that time in "history" despite there being no fireworks or music, just a crowd of drunken folk who stood in the bitter cold, cheered and kissed total strangers at the stroke of midnight, then dispersed and went home. On this particular New Year's Eve Evanna was stationed on one of the, now drained for the occasion, fountains. In order to reach this fountain, they had to climb over a police barrier, then onto the brick wall which run its circumference. It was a bitterly cold night. Freezing in fact. She was one of three officers policing that particular location. At 2215 hrs they were able to go off for a quick tea break until 2230 hrs. Now, this is important to keep in mind, that this preceded the advent of trousers for WPCs, so although Evanna's legs were covered in thick black tights they still felt ice cold. After battling her way through the alcohol-fuelled throng of rather raucous, yet merrily happy crowd, she nimbly clambered over the barrier, then mounted the brick surround. Much to her horror, as soon as her feet stood on the fountain's ice ridden and slippery surface, she fell straight over landing on her backside with her legs akimbo.

2355 hrs had just ticked by on the clock, five minutes before midnight. Trafalgar Square was awash with drunken revellers who, she could've sworn, were all facing her direction at this precise moment. They all issued one enormous cheer which was just for her. A rather red-faced Evanna, who was now so hot she was sweating with embarrassment, stood up and did the only thing she could so. She gave a very regal curtsey after which she promptly but very gingerly, lest she was to fall again, walked to the other side of the fountain where PC Leon Hargreaves ripped the piss out of her! The following morning, she admitted to feeling rather relieved not to have found any photographs of the incident in the tabloids.

Evanna swore that icy conditions had something against her, as there was the time she happened to be double "manned" with PC Daniel Harper, nicknamed Zebedee, from the children's TV programme *The Magic Roundabout*, due to his incessant bounciness. It was another cold winter's Night Duty. They were off to report a simple theft of vehicle, the car of which belonged to a rather well-off gentleman who lived in a mansion situated in a highly exclusive road. After telling Zebedee to stay warm in the car she got out and approached the house which boasted a pure, large, marble doorstep which happened to be a thick sheet of ice. Without anticipating this, obviously, Evanna rang the doorbell at the exact same time she set foot on this *"godforsaken doorstep!"* and with that promptly fell over. In an effort to heave herself up she clung onto the nearest drainpipe just prior to the "victim" of the crime she had come to report opening the front door. He found her lying there crying with laughter as was Zebedee who could be heard from the kerbside. She had not managed to stand up when the front door opened. In fact, she was gripping the drainpipe for all of her life whilst lying on the floor guffawing.

All she heard herself say to the well-dressed gentleman, amidst this carnage was: *"you called the police!"* through her tears of laughter. The man did not laugh, he did not smirk, he did not smile, and to top it off he did not help Evanna to her feet, which after several disastrous attempts she managed to do.

It was summertime now, and a different year. Evanna and her colleagues had been sent to the American Ambassador's residence in London to await the arrival of the then American President Clinton. Her role was to "protect" him — not personally but to ensure that no member of the public broke through the cordon and entered the grounds. They were situated on the front lawn located in Regent's Park. They were there at the most beautiful time of the day in Evanna's book — sunrise. The scene seemed perfect, so picturesque as Marine One, the Sea King, helicopter transporting the President and his entourage flew into view as it came into land. One of the mounted branch's horses took fright at the sound of the whirring blades, but his mount soon got him back under control. It was not long before Evanna saw some trenchcoated males exit the residence and walk down the front steps each making a beeline for individual PCs. Evanna was joined by one such male who was very tall and athletic in appearance. He wore an earpiece and had pinned to his lapel a badge displaying the Stars and Stripes of the Star-spangled Banner. He introduced himself as Special Agent Anderson explaining that he formed part of his President's security detail. He would be partnered up with Evanna for the rest of the tour. Special Agent Anderson took his role extremely seriously. He only spoke to ask Evanna a set of questions. The first being: *"So, what gun do you carry?"* Desperate to not disappoint, she tried to wrack her brains as to what gun she may be secretly hiding about her person but decided that the truth would out, so she replied: "*I'm not carrying a gun. The British police don't routinely carry them.*" Special Agent Anderson was not suitably impressed. Then he continued: "*So what weapons do you carry?*" Evanna then delved into the truncheon pocket of her trousers producing the said police's weapon of choice. Special Agent Anderson looked aghast as he surveyed this short piece of wood. Refusing to give up he asked: "*What type of bulletproof vest do you wear?*" Once again, the look of pure astonishment invaded his face when she answered: "*The British police don't wear them.*" Then just so he could not fail to understand she retorted: "*We don't carry guns and we don't have stab-proof vests, let alone bulletproof ones!*" Special Agent Anderson resumed his nondescript facial pattern as a car horn could be heard coming from the road. Upon looking up at the car, a silver Ford Cortina, driven by a female in her sixties Special Agent Anderson saw the driver wave. He then noticed Evanna wave back. He asked her: "*Who's that?*" By this time Evanna who had noticed the irony of the whole conversation thus far, merely stated: "*Oh, that's my mum,*" and just for good measure: "*She's on her way to work.*" Special Agent Anderson did not utter one more single word to her for the rest of the, what now proved to be, long and dull day. Evanna considered that he could not have imagined a worse scenario. His President being "protected" by a group of unarmed "*fools*".

On the ground of one of her stations to which The Akerne was attached was an animal testing laboratory which, because of receiving a variety of small letter bombs and several bomb threats, rightly called the police every time they received a package through the post which they considered suspicious. Now, as it took an age for the bomb squad to arrive and as it was a right pain to set up cordons directing traffic both vehicular and pedestrian away from the area the bobbies routinely decided to bypass all of that palaver. Instead, the majority of the shift would attend. On seeing the package, they would draw matches, the copper with the shortest one got to open the parcel, package or envelope whilst the rest offered words of rude encouragement from the relative "*unsafety*" underneath tables. They did wear their helmets or caps, though, for extra "*protection*" and as they said as a mark of respect for the parcel opener should the "*wheels come off*"! This was always done with great hilarity. It was not as though they failed to recognise the potential danger, even stupidity of their actions, and consequences if a bomb should explode, but they continued in this manner for many a year until the site was forced to close. This course of action was passed down to the newcomers, so until it closed bouts of mirth and nervous laughter could be heard coming from the postal room as the poor PC or WPC gingerly, often with sweaty hands and forehead, opened the package and declared it safe, at which there was a roar of applause! Thankfully, a bomb never did explode at such times.

These examples are just mere fragments of the funny and fun times that Evanna had during her time in the police. Times when more decorum perhaps should have been displayed but such is the sense of humour of a copper!

Despite disliking labels and not being aware of that of pan sexual, Evanna realised that she was not exactly heterosexual. She was attracted to the person — to *all* genders. She described herself as being gender blind. She did not consider this the same as bisexuality, not that she cared what she was labelled as but the topic was of interest to her, because as far she understood bisexuals were attracted to multiple genders rather that ALL. So, pansexuals may find themselves attracted to *all* possible gender definitions whereas a bisexual would not. *"It's a complicated matter,"* she thought, *"and what does it matter anyway? You are who you are!"*

Although she had her fair few encounters and dalliances there had been no one special or serious in her life. She had no one special or serious until she joined Training School and even then, she did not anticipate or even mean for that relationship to go the way it did. As it did not do for a police officer, male or female, to be anything but heterosexual at that time, Evanna chose to keep her sexuality to herself. In any case being a WPC, she also had to contend with the adage of either being a "bike" or a "dike". Evanna wanted to be known as neither.

Whilst at Training School she had been dating a recruit, Jack, who had been also been a cadet on the course below her. Because she thought it pertinent to be in a steady relationship with a male, precluding her from becoming known as a "dike" or a "bike", she decided to continue with this relationship when she went on division. It wasn't merely a relationship of convenience as she loved Jack. He was a 6ft 4½ tall and 6ft 4½ wide rugby player. They loved each other, so when he asked her to marry him at her Passing Out Parade from Training School she said *"yes"*. She did have some reservations as our Evanna did like to play the field, but she thought it was about time she settled down. She considered herself fortunate not to have contracted an STI. At first, whilst dating Jack she had not been "entirely" faithful and did not always practise safe sex, but she came to the conclusion that she should see if monogamy suited her, which it seemed to! They bought a house together and a dog, a Jack Russell, called Rosie.

Despite agreeing to marry him for all of the right reasons and in good faith she proved to be most uninterested in any form of wedding planning. She did not care what kind of flowers or bouquet she should have; she wasn't really bothered about where the venue for the wedding would be or what food they would eat or what wine they should drink. She did not care for the invitations, the church, the bridesmaids or even her dress! She wanted it to somehow organically and magically come into being on its own. Her mother chose her wedding dress without Evanna even being present. She had to concede that this dress was rather lovely and without a single fitting was a perfect size. Although she was not strictly a wearer of dresses she had agreed to a full on formal white wedding. In a sense the wedding did happen organically and magically around her as her mother and mother - in-law-to-be organised the best part of it. She, on the other hand, only devoted an extremely limited time to it and even that was half hearted.

Two weeks prior to the "Big Day" she began to have cold feet. *"What the fuck am I doing?"* She panicked. She questioned herself so many, many times. Eventually, with one week to go, she summoned up the courage to tell her wedding-crazed mother that she could not possibly go through with it but proved unable to say exactly why apart from that she just did not want to get married… ever! She hoped that this news would be received well and that she would be heard, but she should have known better. Apparently, there was to be no going back as everything had *"been arranged, and what would people say!"* For a brief moment she even considered standing him up at the altar, but she quickly dismissed this idea as she was not that cruel. She would just have to deal with it and make the marriage work. She decided that she would have a "proper go" at married life. Once the day, which she dreaded, was over, normality would be restored, and life would carry on at its normal pace — normality would be restored.

The day came. Evanna looked beautiful, everyone said so, but don't they just to the bride at weddings! The church, the ceremony, the reception in a lavish hotel, the string quartet, the wedding breakfast, the champagne, the wine, the speeches, the photographs, the weather were all perfection. They chose not to have a disco in the evening so left the hotel and went straight to the airport for their long weekend of a honeymoon in Florence which was also perfect. Evanna never could recall much about that day apart from what she was told, which was mainly: "*It was perfect, darling*", and from the photographs.

It was not too long after they returned home from their honeymoon that Jack announced that he had been told either to resign or be sacked from the police. When Evanna asked him as to what grounds he did not proffer any real reply. He claimed that he did not know. In hindsight Evanna realised that she should have pressed him on the issue. But hindsight is truly a marvellous regret. As it happened, Jack never had the chance to resign as the very next day he was given the sack. She took this news as well as she could despite not being given a reasonable explanation as to why. She was worried about the mortgage and all of the bills now having to come out of one wage — her wage. She could tell his upset, so she kept her fears close to her chest. Shortly afterwards, Evanna was rushed into hospital with acute appendicitis. On her return home, the house looked as if it were a squat. Empty cans of lager took up each and every inch of space alongside overflowing ashtrays. The stench of stale tobacco hit her as soon as she entered the house. She had only been in hospital for five days! Jack did not pick her up from the hospital, her mother did. Jack was drunk on the day she came home. Jack continued in this same vein. He did not attempt to look for a job.

His days were spent drinking and smoking whilst Evanna worked and did everything that needed to be done within the home. But she could never get rid of that smell. Housework proved a fruitless task.

Then the beatings began. Well, they began the day after she arrived home. She had asked Jack to carry the hoover up the stairs for her. The surgeon had told her not to do anything at all energetic, no lifting and to rest for at least two weeks, but she didn't plan adhering to all of that! Jack was a big man. No matter how hard she may attempt to defend herself she had no hope against the hulk who was often a drunken one. Jack did not want to carry the hoover upstairs, so he advised her of this by punching her in the stomach bursting her stitches. She had to lie to her mother and then to the doctor as to why they had burst. She apparently had defied every piece of advice the surgeon had given her and had been weight training. The beatings persisted. He was careful not to mark her face — only her stomach, back and thighs oftentimes leaving bruising but always so very sore. He was jealous of Evanna because she was still in the police. Not only that; he could tell that she was a high achiever. He never doubted that she loved him, and he professed to love her, but how could he? The beatings and the bruising, even the odd broken rib and one broken cheekbone which was *"accidental"*. Yes, it was because he broke his own rule and smashed her face with his fist in a drunken rage. After five long and terrifying months she left him. It was News Year's Day. It was a rushed decision. He raped her on occasion which she found hard to define as rape, seeing as they were married but she did not consent. On the contrary, she pleaded with him to stop. It was always after a beating. She was in the right job to explain away any bruising. The difficulty would come if one of her police friends on her shift questioned her. They would've known about any assault on police. However, he normally kept his fists away from her face. This time, he went one step too far when he entered a place that was always out of bounds to him and he knew it. She had no option but to move back in with her parents. She did not want to bother her friends but once again hindsight is a marvellous regret.

She did learn, though, that Jack had been sacked for beating up a prisoner for which he had been arrested. How she didn't get to hear of this on the rumour mill she had no idea. Perhaps she did. Perhaps she chose to close her ears and mind. She chose not to press charges against Jack. She was too embarrassed and humiliated. She told not one single soul what had happened even after she had left. She knew her police buddies would seek revenge on her behalf and that revenge would not have been a sweet one as these friends would, quite possibly, have gotten themselves arrested.

The Akerne moved out of the frying pan back into the fire. She moved into the room downstairs. She had further affairs of differing measure with people who happened to be both male and female. Then to her surprise PC Daniel Harper, Zebedee, asked her out. Now, she was attracted to Zeb in all the right ways, so the two set out on what proved to be a very loving relationship. He was the complete opposite to her ex-husband in the waiting.

Her father took to "visiting" her on occasion when her mother was out. The same old pattern but not quite as often. Despite being a policewoman, her entire body froze blanking out completely as her father thrust inside her.

She was obviously sleeping with Zeb. They had a very healthy and happy relationship. They enjoyed safe sex most of the time.

To her horror, Evanna discovered that she was pregnant.

Well, it was horror at first which then turned to joy, for all but a brief while until it returned to horror upon the realisation that the foetus inside her could very well be her father's.

Zeb was beyond elated about the prospect of becoming a father. She did not tell him about her own feelings. She did not tell a *soul* about these. So, it appeared that they were keeping the baby. Zeb had not asked her if that was what she wanted. It was simply assumed that she felt the same way. Which she did in a sense and was able to feel some joy.

To think that there was actually a human life forming inside her own body was miraculous. She had never been or felt even remotely maternal until now. However, she was also confused. She put her father away in a box for the moment as she could not cope with what he had done to her. She had never really considered a baby especially not one so early on in her career. Was it her father's, or was it Zeb's? She would rather kill herself than it be her father's. Zeb insisted that they tell Evanna's parents together and immediately. Her father, unsurprisingly, said not one single word. For a mother-to-be to tell her own mother that she was about to become a grandma would, for most, be the best news on the planet. A moment to be cherished but not for this mother. All she could say was: "*You need an abortion.*" She was never one to mince her words.

It was not strictly these words, these commands, that led Evanna to have an abortion. Her reasonings were obvious and in a sense justified. But now that the news of the pregnancy had fully immersed itself in her brain through the most obnoxious morning sickness which actually proved to be "all day sickness" she was actually coming around to the idea of becoming a mum regardless of how the baby came to be inside her tummy. She had already decided that she would bring her child up in a diametrically opposed way to the way her parents had brought her up. She was suddenly and uncharacteristically becoming maternal. But then it hit her like a rock. The thought that the baby inside her could be her father's, was a thought too abominable to even consider for a second, yet she did.

Zeb was excitement personified. As far as he was concerned, he was a dad already. He was beside himself with the magnificent prospect of becoming a parent and having a family. Although he had been adopted to two loving people, he had always determined that he would have a family of his own and here was his opportunity. However, Evanna conformed to her mother's wishes. They were not entirely Evanna's wishes, but she did not feel able to bring a child into the world which could share the same father as herself. It blew her mind to even consider this a possibility. She told Zeb of her decision but not the real reason as to why. She did not consult him — she told him what was going to happen. He could not speak to her. He could not set his eyes upon her.

The day arrived. Her mother accompanied her to the hospital where the procedure was to be performed. She never did say why she wanted the abortion. She told no one. Nor was she asked.

Evanna knew that the only way she was going to get through this was by blanking it out, which she had a great deal of practice doing as her history attested to. As a result, her mother called her *"hard"* and *"cruel"*. Zeb arrived at her bedside pleading with her not to go through with it. He sobbed and sobbed. His tears uncontrollable. It was time. It was done. When she came out Zeb had gone. He ended the relationship soon after. That night, Evanna's parents ordered a Chinese takeaway for the three of them. As if she felt like eating. She was expected to sit at the dining room table with them, which she duly did but could not eat a single morsel.

The guilt then flooded through Evanna. This guilt did not subside. It swelled and at times it became very rough. The guilt of murdering her child and the guilt of going against Zeb's wishes and devastating him. Why hadn't she just told him the truth? Why didn't she tell him the truth now? She could not. She just could not.

Evanna grew to bitterly regret the abortion, especially as when she became older, she became truly maternal but there was no viable prospect of becoming pregnant. Thus, she would remain childless forever. This thought became hard to bear when she reached her 40s and worse still when the menopause hit.

After Zeb, she had a few "relationships" if you'd could call them that. She moved out of her parents', into a lovely brand new, two-bedroomed ground floor flat with wide patio doors opening up onto the garden which was ideal for her two cats. She was content. At least for a while.

Staff Jefferson who she was finally able to call Bill had contacted her. A lifelong beautiful friendship was formed. She referred to him as her Big Brother and had so much platonic love for him and him for her.

Life in The Police was just that, life — a way of life. Life was lived and breathed The Police. Your colleagues became your family. The trust that was embedded in each other was insurmountable. One's very life could depend on them. There was nothing like the camaraderie — nothing.

Being in The Police was a lifestyle. It could be incestuous. The number of affairs and "carryings on" were rife. The partners of a copper especially to someone outside The Job did not and could not understand The Policeman's Lot.

Because of the lack of counselling heavy drinking and

alcoholism as well as chain smoking were commonplace. Evanna did drink. At times she could be described as a binge drinker but far from an alcoholic. But she did smoke. No one took drugs or illegal substances of any description.

PTSD was unheard of at this time but Evanna and most of Evanna's "family" would have been diagnosed with it.

Evanna loved her life in the police. She loved everything about it. Her entire social life revolved around it and her "siblings", as was the norm. They were in each other's pockets — that was the life of a police officer. You see, they shared each other's days off; they shared each other's philosophies; they dealt with things that only their colleagues would ever see and would quietly understand the feelings attached without ever having to explain or voice a thing.

She was proud of her achievements. She believed that thus far she had bought justice to those who needed to be brought to justice and in turn she had achieved justice for those victims of crime, especially of crimes she had been subjected to herself but had received no kind of justice.

She was climbing the ladder whilst enjoying each and every minute of it. She had passed the initial parts of the inspector's exam and was awaiting the third and final part.

Then quite suddenly things began to unravel.

The end of a Late Turn was drawing in when there was a request, over the police radio, for someone to deal with and check upon an abandoned vehicle in an underground car park that a member of the public had reported. Evanna took this call as she was in the area and would "*tuck her up*" quite nicely for the last few minutes of the shift. On arrival she parked the car and proceeded to get out. She began to walk up the aisle of parked vehicles trying to find the one in question. She never did find it.

She never found it because it was never there. It did not exist. Instead, she was surrounded by five adult masked males brandishing metal bars and wooden clubs who set about her. Being underground her Storno police radio failed to work thus being unable to call for Urgent Assistance. She drew her baton in a hopeless attempt to defend herself. She managed to wave it around a bit connecting with at least one of her assailants before she stumbled and sank to the floor where they proceeded to kick her with their heavily booted feet. The cowards then ran off leaving her for dead. She was barely conscious.

Her team, back at the Nick, were waiting for Sarge to return as their shift had now ended and they were headed for the pub. They called her radio several times, but she did not reply. All they could hear was the crackle of white noise. They checked the location of her last call: *"What could possibly go wrong with an abandoned vehicle shout?"* one wondered out loud. They decided to go to the location to see if she was still there.

In truth they were not expecting to find her there. They secretly hoped she would be at the bakery buying doughnuts for them all as she often did but normally as an Early Turn treat. She was a fabulous sergeant. They were not prepared to see what they saw when they arrived at the carpark. A bloodied, broken Skipper lying on the cold, concrete flooring in a crumpled heap. Some knelt by her side whispering words of encouragement such as: *"You daft Doris — trust you. But keep with me. Keep with us."* Fully fledged male officers were forced to either hold their breath or bite their lip to prevent themselves from crying. But these tricks did not work as they unselfconsciously and automatically wiped away their tears. Tears of fear, tears of anger, tears of frustration and bewilderment. But also tears of love for their beloved Skipper. Some desperately searched the area for evidence but to no avail. The CCTV would produce some, if it was working! Finally, the ambulance arrived. It took no longer than a few minutes but for those policemen it was a lifetime.

Evanna was in a coma for two weeks. She had suffered from a major head trauma, multiple broken bones, her body was one big bruise internally as well as externally. Her face was pulverised. When she awoke, she could barely speak as each sound she uttered and each breath she took were of pure and utter agony. But she was lucky! Truly lucky!

Her recovery was slow but steady with great strides forward, then great strides backward. Her stay in hospital was lengthy after which she went to the police convalescent home in Sussex where she continued to recover.

Finally, she felt fit enough to return to work but against her wishes she was to have a phased return and was to be on "light duties", so was based in the Crime Desk. She continued to have physiotherapy which was going from strength to strength. Her aim was to return to the same physical prowess that she enjoyed prior to the attack. After all, she enjoyed thrashing the PCs at chin ups and press ups!

Eventually she was granted her freedom! She went back to work with her old team whom she had seen often during that year and a bit but on her first day back she was given a hero's welcome. She wasn't in the least bit scared to be back "out". She didn't have flashbacks because she had pushed the attack so far back in her mind, she was unable to access it. That fateful call had been a hoax merely to lure some unsuspecting copper into the lion's den. The assailants were never caught as their identities were never discovered.

Evanna appeared as if back to her old self but secretly she was struggling. All of a sudden everything began to implode.

Everything she had been through as a child; the domestic violence, traumatic and horrific scenes and "jobs" in the police, the abortion and the attack that rendered her useless for a while. She began to act strangely. She reverted back to her childhood habit of self-harm but now she cut herself with anything sharp and burned her flesh with cigarettes. Her relief and superiors grew concerned for her welfare and checked her into a private psychiatric hospital. They took her there under false pretences as they knew she would not agree to go by herself. Once there she agreed to stay for one week, which she did, but on the seventh day she promptly discharged herself.

For two years she suffered mostly managing to keep things under wraps, but she also often had to go sick. It took two years for the Chief Medical Officer to finally end her career in the police. She had been diagnosed with bipolar and was thus unfit to serve. She was "cast" as it was called. *"Thrown out and discarded"* in Evanna speak. She considered it to be as if she had been thrown away. She was medically retired, so at least she could claim her police pension immediately, one day prior to the final part of her Inspector's exam which had been postponed several times and she was not likely to pass.

Evanna was desolate. Her life — literally her whole life had been obliterated. She was now "nothing". It was as if her whole identity had been stolen. Now she was simply no one. Stripped of this she no longer knew who she was. After twelve years of service, she was out, and she had nothing and was nothing.

So, Evanna was now lost. Her very life, for the past decade plus two years, had been robbed from her. She was now spiralling into a hole, so deep and so dark. How could she ever scrape her way back up?

vi **Bodhi — The Acharn**

It took a while for the Acharn to lose the feeling of security and the need of the Day Hospital where he felt cosseted and safe. He felt it scary doing so without having it to hand, especially when he was feeling frightened, depressed and lonely. Despite not believing it would help him he had learned various techniques to cope with some of the hard times. Routine was paramount as was sleep hygiene. He discovered that exercise helped immensely, so he took up swimming and running to enable his endorphins to work their magic. He missed seeing some of the friends he had made there, but he continued to be in regular contact with Laine who he spent a great deal of time with.

He anxiously wondered how he would cope in the "*Real World*". He was able to recognise that the Day Hospital was nothing like the "*Real World*" in which people did not notice or particularly care if you were having a bad day, which suited him. In a sense it felt, to Bodhi, as if his security blanket had wrapped itself around him, then had been unceremoniously ripped from his person leaving him alone in this "*Real World*" stark naked.

However, he now had an actual job to concentrate on, even if in part, which would enable him to form some kind of routine. He began running or swimming prior to work after which he would study for roughly three hours. It was an insular life but one that suited him and one he slowly began to enjoy. He was soon able to push the customary groups and security of the Day Hospital behind him as work took over.

He continued to have his sessions with Beth although he was aware that she would not be able to ask for yet another extension. Because of this and that the fact that his "session allowance" was to end he felt himself withdraw from her and keep things that he would normally have discussed with her bottled close to his chest lest he should open a can of worms. Eventually, the sessions did end. A day which Bodhi had dreaded for some time. He felt so distraught during the build up all the way through to that final hour. *"How on earth can I cope with not seeing her — I love her,"* he simpered. He knew that he had become far too dependent on Beth although she had appeared to invite this. He had seen her approximately once a week for the last three years and now he was alone in this *"Real World"*. He was all too aware that his "love" for Beth went unrequited, which greatly saddened him. As a result of this ending, Bodhi realised that endings of any form were his "kryptonite". But truth be known, he felt a form of relief and release when these sessions finally culminated.

Lastly, Bodhi discovered that the techniques he had been taught at the Day Hospital were all very well and good but when it came to the heartbreak of a much loved-one's death, they were totally inutile.

Still very happy in his new flat, even occasionally asking people over, Bodhi on the whole was content in his own company. He continued to enjoy studying immensely finding that both that and exercise were his forms of relaxation. These were times when he could turn off the demons that still haunted him.

At the end of the first year of his BA (hons) he was to attend a summer school in Bath which he had been dreading for months. *"I won't cope with having to socialise," "I won't deal with all of the strangers," "Everyone will think I'm a complete idiot and stupid"* were his daily mantras in the build-up to the sojourn. He prayed it would be cancelled, he decided not to go but he did go, and he had THE BEST time! On recollection he thought that everyone, including the tutors, spent the week in an alcohol-fuelled haze having imbibed rather too much at the student union bar, which boasted student union prices, every night! He discovered that he coped extremely well with the socialising, indeed making some very good friends out of the strangers he feared. None thought him stupid or an idiot. He coped so well he surprised himself.

Thursdays continued to be *"Housework and Shopping Day"* with his mother which he dreaded as they always developed into the most awful arguments with her shouting at him with her face so close to his that he could smell her breath and feel her spittle fly at him. On many an occasion Bodhi tried to put an end to "Thursdays", but she would not listen. She even took to taking his washing despite his protestations which she definitely heard as her reply would be: *"yes, darling"* and carry on regardless. In truth she was happy to keep Bodhi's independence from him as it gave her control over him and enabled her to state: *"after all I do for you..."* when they fought. She hated those who were trying to help him become dependent upon himself as they would eventually steal this away from her.

Stephanie was still acclimatising Bodhi to supermarkets and shopping alone. The day had come for him to do this by himself with her waiting for him by the outer set of doors. His task was to walk around the whole supermarket, buy any eight items which he was then to pay for. He felt very nervous yet determined as he pushed his trolley up each aisle. When he finally reached the tills, out of seemingly nowhere, he felt a tap on the back of his shoulder whilst he was waiting in line. It was his mother, who instead of congratulating him, said in a very loud voice for all to hear: *"Where's the food? You've only got cleaning equipment in the trolley. What are you? Stupid!"* Upon trying to explain his task to her he realised that his words were falling upon deaf ears, so he simply left the shop leaving his trolley in situ. On seeing Stephanie outside all he was able to do was stand feeling forlorn with tears pricking and stinging his eyes with anger, humiliation and even fear. Fear of his mother. He had returned to his childhood, but had he really ever left it in that respect? On the way home, Stephanie tried to undo the damage his mother had just caused but today her words were not heard. Tomorrow or the next day they might be.

Bodhi's father was noticeably forgetting simple words and acting out of character. Finally, he agreed to go to the doctors who, after several tests and appointments with a neurologist diagnosed him with Alzheimer's. Once the diagnosis had been given the decline was steady. Finally, he lost his speech and the power of communication altogether. He left taps running complete with plugs in the sink; he pressed the "on" button for the waste disposal unit whilst someone's hand may be down it and he went walkabout. Bodhi agreed to "father sit" two evenings a week enabling his mother to have a break and go out. *"It wasn't so long ago,"* Bodhi mused, *"that **he** would be visiting me when mum went out."*

Over the course of time, whilst seeing his father deteriorate and become quite childlike Bodhi began to forgive him. It was not a conscious thing, but it was because of his father's newfound state, call it karma or whatever you may wish. It was the first time Bodhi had ever seen his father smile. He was not stressed in his decline — so, was it karma? Forgiveness came organically and it proved a release although he could not find it in himself to offer his mother any form of forgiveness, nor did he ever.

His father died in hospital two years after his diagnosis. Bodhi did not join his mother at the hospital to utter his final goodbyes. Over time, the old man had lost the ability to swallow but he died of pneumonia. Despite forgiving him Bodhi was not sad, nor did he shed one single tear. However, he did feel a certain pang in his heart which he was unable to quantify but which was perhaps regret. Regret, because he missed having a father he considered he deserved. He may have forgiven the man, but he continued to hate him for what he did — forgiveness can only go so far.

Bodhi's mother had been an excellent wife. She had managed to hide everything under the carpet. She excelled in the appearance of perfection. She was definitely the matriarch to her husband's non-patriarchal status. She nursed him at home. She was present at his passing. She was a brilliant wife, a brilliantly strong person; everyone said so.

During the last few weeks of her husband's life, she began to be a "companion" in an ex-boyfriend of hers some 45 years ago who had tracked her down using the services of a private detective who worked for a national tabloid newspaper. Bodhi thought this man, Malcom (no.1), to be the love of his mother's life and the two men formed a close bond, which somehow aided a certain thawing in Bodhi's relationship with his mother.

They got married, Malcolm (no.1) and Bodhi's mother, a few months after his father died much to his sister's abhorrence who considered it too soon as she was yet to recover from his passing. Eighteen months later Malcolm (no.1) was dead. He died from a brain tumour. Once again, Bodhi's mother acted as nurse. Bodhi was present at Malcolm (no.1's) death. He sat alongside his mother and even his sister. Malcom's own daughters did not feel able to watch their father die. It took all day for him to go. Bodhi considered it a strangely beautiful "thing" as suddenly Malcolm removed the oxygen mask from his face that had been helping him breathe, lift his head and look at each of the three at his bedside in turn and smile. He then laid his head back down on the pillow and breathed his final breath closing his eyes allowing his soul to go. Husband and wife had rekindled their love after forty-five years and now that flame had been snuffed out. Bodhi could not but help to feel sorry for his mother. He considered this to be the most profound and even lovely death as Malcolm, in that final moment, knew that he was surrounded with and by love and in turn reciprocated that love with that smile. He was to picture that scene forever. However, Bodhi was bitterly sad. That night Bodhi and his mother sat up crying together holding hands. This was not to be a new beginning for them but a truce for that particular moment of mutual pain.

Monday had arrived!

Bodhi felt nervous but all at the same time excited and positive about his new job. He only hoped that he would fit in well with the staff and that the children warmed to him, especially his primary charge, Magdala who he discovered preferred to be called Dala. He was greeted in the reception area by Mrs Bridget Morass. She was a good headteacher who was supportive of all her staff and popular with her pupils. She had been Head at the school for ten years. Bridget was an old-fashioned looking woman and on the larger side which was of no matter. Her penchant was for music, of the classical genre, evidenced throughout the school with many extracurricular musical activities and classes. Bridget, herself, was a cellist often playing for the children during school assemblies. Above all, however, Bridget took pride in her school with its magnificent wall displays which were completed by each class boasting their wonderful achievements. Bridget retired a year after Bodhi had himself left. She welcomed Bodhi with a warm handshake, then walked him through the bright colourful corridor to the reception class where Dala was just about to begin a lesson on the carpet where she and the whole class were seated quietly anticipating the story they were about to hear.

Theresa was seated at the front of the carpet on a small infant-style chair with the Big Book opened at the front page whilst waiting for the last of the class to stop moving. She had been the teacher of Reception at the school for five years after finishing her degree. She was reasonably strict but always fair. Theresa was wiry in frame with a mass of frizzy dark brown hair. She always looked quite sad but in actuality she was not as suddenly her smile would brighten her face. However, she did not cope too well in social settings, consequently finding the hubbub in the staff room difficult to contend with, so she tended to give it a miss. Bodhi hit it off with her immediately, which was partly owing to his similar insular traits. When Theresa's mother sadly passed away it destroyed her for some time but all of the staff, including Bodhi, helped her through this as the school was indeed a Family.

Dala was a very beautiful child with stereotypical Arian features: long blonde hair, big blue eyes and fair skin. These looks could destroy a cross person in a second by their pleading innocence when she was found doing something wrong, which was a frequent affair! She looked akin to a cherub with her often puffed out cheeks which signalled her defiance. She suffered from a very rare genetic condition which caused her brain to malfunction in certain areas: balance, eyesight, hearing and so forth. Her bones were weak and fractured easily, and she was prone to epileptic seizures. This cruel disease was degenerative and life limiting. This seemed so unfair. But Dala didn't seem to care. She was happiness personified! She understood her condition as far as a five-year-old could and as a result did play on it when she wanted to keep in the warm at playtime or hoped it would get her out of doing a piece of work! Dala oozed charm. She was a popular little thing with her classmates. She was spoilt by anyone who came across her. Those big blue eyes and angelic face spoke a million words and had the capacity to melt even the most frozen of people.

She remained at Stuart Meade until her parents moved out of the area, which was a sad day for all. Bodhi calculated that everyone from staff to pupils cried the day she walked out of the school gates for the last time. He worked well with Dala. He grew accustomed to her many "excuses" but more importantly to her difficulties and the triggers that appeared to worsen her condition. Together they made a formidable team.

In time, Bodhi was offered more hours and then a permanent full-time post which he could not quite believe but Bridget pressed the point that he more than deserved it.

He continued to work with Dala but was given a few other charges all of whom had special needs. Bodhi had no idea, until then, that mainstream schools housed so many children with special needs. Three of his students over the years and the most memorable for him included Michael, Curtis and Jake.

Bodhi worked with Michael for three years, from Year 3 to the end of year 6 when Michael went to senior school. Michael was a bespectacled boy who enjoyed picking his nose and either eating the bright green bogies or flicking them at poor unfortunate souls. He had Asperger's which prevented him from seeing, hearing and feeling the world as other people do. He was of average intelligence but was rather a lazy so and so, thus never reaching his full potential no matter how hard Bodhi and other staff members tried. Michael found understanding and relating to others, taking part in everyday group activities and social life very hard. He did not know how to communicate or interact with other people appropriately. Nor was he able to interpret verbal and nonverbal language and cues. He was highly literal when it came to understanding language automatically presuming that people always meant what they said such as: "*It's raining cats and dogs.*" He also found it difficult to use or comprehend facial expressions, tone of voice, jokes, sarcasm, vagueness and abstract concepts. He did have a good use of language but still found it hard to get to grips with the expectations of others within a conversation as he tended to take over. He did not recognise other people's feelings or intentions. Nor could he express much emotion. Despite all of these struggles Michael was popular with his classmates, but the girls liked to "mother him" and some of the boys enjoyed getting him to do things that would be bound to get him into trouble. Bodhi developed an extremely wonderful rapport with Michael who was so very, very, funny. He had a sense of humour like no other! He was the class clown but that tended to backfire. After Michael had moved onto secondary school and then "graduated" from there he obtained a voluntary job as a "DJ" within the local hospital radio. He was unable to hold down any paid employment, but he was doing well in other areas becoming more independent. He also coped very well when his mother had a stroke. Bodhi knew all of this because he had become a friend of the family.

Curtis and Jake were both autistic which has many traits similar to those of Asperger's. Those with autism see, hear and feel the world differently to others. It is a spectrum condition whereby all autistic people share certain difficulties but being autistic will affect them differently.

Bodhi supported Curtis for seven years. They developed a bond that shone. Curtis was not intelligent but what he lacked in acumen he more than made up for in his capacity to warm souls.

Curtis was a loveable rogue, but he often got himself into trouble through his behaviour. Bodhi felt that some of the teachers, through no fault of their own, did not properly understand his difficulties giving him no allowances. However, The Acharn managed to cope with Curtis' wellbeing by taking him out of the often busy and noisy classroom on "errands" around the school which this pulchritudinous boy loved to do as he liked being helpful. He also loved a hug. Sadly, he often arrived at school late looking unkempt and obviously hungry. This was not because that his mum did not care but she struggled hugely. Bodhi ensured that he always had a breakfast inside him as soon as Curtis arrived in the classroom. He used to take some in especially for him.

Then there was Jake who started at Stuart Meade in Year 4. Bodhi worked alongside him until Jake left at the end of Year 6. Jake was a rotund boy who did not recognise his own strength nor how to manage his anger. This meant that he had the capacity to hurt both his peers and staff, oftentimes not meaning to but occasionally he wanted to, when he went into a fit of rage, the triggers of which were hard to pinpoint. However, after the fact he was always so remorseful. Jake knew everything there was to know about James Bond, especially each and every car that the super spy drove. He was an expert on the subject which was his go-to topic if anxious. Bodhi and Jake also developed a good relationship. Bodhi managed Jake's outbursts very well, which enabled Jake to learn about trust and respect. It also allowed him to remain within a classroom setting rather than having to work outside the classroom.

Bodhi made great friendships with most of the staff, especially with those who were the oil and the glue of the school.

Susan was a wonderfully warm and bubbly Scots woman

who was edging towards retirement. She had worked as a teaching assistant within the school from "year dot!" She was highly respected and loved by all within the school's safe walls and those who knew her without. She was The Fixer at school — if something was broken, Susan would fix it; if you needed help with something, Susan would help. For anything — you simply went to Susan. She retired just prior to Bodhi leaving.

Then there was the effervescent Jackie, the school secretary whose often dry and sarcastic sense of humour was much loved. She had a heart of gold underneath that tough exterior and was often found to be crying at overhearing a child being told off. She had also worked at the school since the dawn of time. She was a very tall, slim, elegant lady who always enjoyed a natter and a joke. Jackie took early retirement and moved to Spain just after Bodhi left.

Anne was the Year 6 teacher who Bodhi worked with much of the time. She carried a "school mar'm" kind of persona. She was always so immaculately turned out. Anne was an excellent teacher but a very strict one. However, she never failed to get the best results. Anne was traditional, conservative, disliking any form of change, especially when it revolved around her class. Each year Anne and her husband, Bob, took the Year 6 class to North Wales for a week. Every year the timetable was exactly the same! Bodhi went on this excursion for six years out of the eight he was there. He enjoyed going. He loved North Wales and he enjoyed the company of Anne and Bob. He also enjoyed spending time with his allotted group of children. Like Bridget, Anne was a musician. She played the clarinet in several orchestras. Anne never did have any children of her own. Bodhi always wondered why but realised this was not a question he should ever ask as Anne was a very private, prim and proper person. She was a middle-aged lady but she never did declare her real age until she turned 70 when she told Bodhi. Both had left the school by this time but remained close friends. Sadly, Bob had passed away from cancer leaving Anne bereft for a while, but eventually she picked up the pieces and resumed her active lifestyle. She took to confiding in Bodhi, which left him feeling honoured and privileged as Anne was not a natural confider. Anne left the school one year prior to Bodhi. She took early retirement.

Dee was a very tall, big-boned woman with another heart of gold. She was also a teaching assistant with whom Bodhi worked alongside. She had worked at the school for ten years. Dee remained at the school for several years after Bodhi had left, as her son was a pupil there.

As the school was growing in number the reception class became two, each with twenty-five children. As a result, the wonderful Samantha, or Mantha, was employed to work as the teacher in the new class.

She was brilliant at her job. Every teaching assistant loved working in her class as she made everything so interesting and fun for both children and staff alike. Bodhi developed a crush on Mantha which, once again, confused him. First Beth, now this glorious blonde haired, slim, attractive new teacher. He felt that maybe he was attracted to women but was not interested in having any form of intimacy, i.e. sexual contact, with them as he found the thought of it rather petrifying and disgusting.

These five people were the stalwarts of the school. The matriarchs if you like. However, there was another who held even them together. She was the energy. She was the epoxy. She was the very foundations of the school.

Her name was Amelia. Amelia Black.

Amelia was the main teaching assistant in the reception class and had been for sixteen years. There was nothing Amelia did not know about her job or the children. She was Bodhi's mentor when he first arrived at Stuart Meade. Amelia was a beauteous soul. Indeed, Bodhi and Amelia became best friends in a short space of time. He admired her calm and peaceful nature. She was loyal, kind, helpful and such a joy to be around. She was all of life's wonderful things. Amelia saw the good in everyone and everything. Not once did Bodhi ever hear her utter one single bad word about anyone. Even when her husband left her for a younger model, she kept all dignity.

Everybody loved Amelia — that just could not be helped. She was one of life's magnets. She was the go-to person if one had a problem. For eight years she was Bodhi's "Person" and he hers. She coaxed him through several bouts of depression, and he coaxed her whenever she should come across one of life's stumbling blocks and falter. Each morning they shared a chat and a coffee in the classroom before the start of school and at the end of the day they did the same. They laughed, they cried. They set the world to rights every day. They always "hugged it out"!

It was early one Wednesday morning when Bodhi got the call. His 0645 alarm had rung, and he was just about to get up. Before he lifted his head from the pillow the telephone next to him rang. It was Susan. This was the worst phone call that Bodhi was ever to receive. The phone call that destroyed him for a long, long time. The phone call that he would never forget. The phone call that others received. The phone call that rocked Stuart Meade Primary School to its very heart.

Susan began talking, after ensuring that Bodhi was seated, almost immediately. He detected a rasp and quiver in her voice that was not usually there. Her words were brief and to the point:

"*Amelia's dead.*" The words almost bursting out of her mouth amidst her tears for she had been close friends with Amelia for over twenty years. Much to his shock and disgust, Bodhi's immediate reaction was to stifle a laugh. His first thought was that for some inexplicable reason, Susan was joking with him. But why on earth would she choose to do that! A shocked Bodhi, now slowly coming to his senses, could not reconcile this news because he had waved her goodbye only yesterday afternoon at the school gates as usual. She was fine. It transpired that Amelia had collapsed and died on her five-minute walk home from school from an aneurysm on the brain. One minute you're fine — the next — BANG you're dead — there it was. "*Seize the bloody day,*" Bodhi thought. He was in shock, complete and utter disbelief as everyone was. Then he was unable to stem the incessant flow of tears. The school was closed for the rest of the week and for the day of the funeral which passed Bodhi by as if in a trance.

The school was never the same after Amelia died. It had been rocked to its very foundations as indeed Amelia *was* the foundations. They began to creak and seemed as if they would crack and topple over at any given moment. This was felt by children and staff alike despite the staff's best attempts at behaving as normal. Children are intuitive. Plus, they had lost their own much-loved go-to person. Amelia could be felt in every corner of every room and in every flowerbed and every blade of grass on the playground.

Slowly but surely, staff began to leave. The close family unit had been ripped asunder and for some reason it could not be reclaimed. The memories were just too painful. Amelia had touched so many lives for the greater good but at that moment all people could feel was pain.

Bodhi struggled on for a year or so but in the end, he could bear it no more. He realised he was trying to remain as close to his friend as possible but as a result he was only hurting himself. He missed her so. For "Amelia's sake" he endeavoured not to crash. But he could not stay at the school.

He missed his friend. He missed her smile. He missed her laughter. He missed her very essence. He missed her very being. His heart ached.

He managed to get a job as a learning mentor in a secondary school for boys with emotional and behavioural difficulties. To say he hated working there is an understatement as he realised that it was the staff that should also be put under the banner of having emotional and behavioural difficulties. He found the staff intolerable, especially some of the male ones as they considered themselves incredibly macho. In Bodhi's humble opinion they were nothing but bullies to other staff members but worse to the boys themselves. The headmaster being the worst. After whistle blowing, Bodhi left the school under medical grounds — being depression and stress. As a result, Bodhi's mental health spiralled downwards.

To say that Bodhi did not process Amelia's death does not sum it up. To him it never happened although he knew she was not there. His depression returned in full force.

He wanted to be in the grips of Death's dark destiny. Death's sweet destiny. He felt he could almost hear Death's pure melodies which would finally reach his ears totally in the dark solace of Death itself. He pictured Death's honeyed embrace that would blanket him in its shroud. As he stood outside, not feeling the bitter cold, and looked up at the clear night sky he saw in it the starry moonlit beauty that only Death was able to conjure. The invisible veil which would be absorbed into his very soul.

He began to consider the Earth's nihility, its unimportance and nothingness in comparison to the magnitude of the heavens above with their dark silhouettes, their eternal passages — the passages of Death that one must pass through to achieve glorification. In Death's dark vibrant void is where he longed to be. His breathing settled, becoming steadier, calmer, from being rapid and shallow, as he pictured Death's long pale fingers reach out to his — becoming Death himself, going into the intangibility of Death itself.

Suddenly he thought of Hamlet and remembered him crying:

"To die, to sleep, to sleep perchance to dream — ah, there's the rub, for in this sleep of death what dreams come through."

(Shakespeare -Hamlet)

This was said by Hamlet to himself when he thinks he is alone. He is asking himself if it is better to give up and die rather than facing his troubles, but he is frightened that he will dream when he is dead and never get any peace from his earthly troubles. The speech starts with the even more famous: *"to be or not to be..."* which is the *"should I be dead part"*.

"To die, to grow, to grow perhaps to flourish — yes in this growth in death how one flourishes."

(Bodhi)

This was uttered by Bodhi as he questioned whether, in death, he would receive his "Awakening", his "Enlightenment", and if so, will he thus grow and flourish? If he dies, will he grow, will he flourish as he has not done whilst alive? Perhaps it is better to die. He returned inside not knowing what to do. Questioning himself all the while. He was so scared of doing anything by himself he believed himself useless as he was so often called by his mother.

His boxes of medication seemed to appear from nowhere.

His calmness as he began to take them like smarties — One. By. One.

Bodhi had experienced things similar to Evanna in their exposure to the *"Real World"* and the *"not so real one"*. The latter, in Evanna's case, being Training School and then the former with its harsh realities faced as a police officer. For Bodhi, the Real World was exposed to him when he left the confines of the Day Hospital. At first, he coped so well but then he faltered with the death of his dear dear friend. The friend whose one photograph he had of her stayed with him wherever he went. The friend who he would cry over so often and forever.

They had also both been medically discharged from their jobs thus seemingly spat out into this harsh world that suddenly felt so unfamiliar to them both. Unfamiliar and frightening.

In their work they both became part of a Family. The Family that both craved. Now that was gone. For Bodhi that Family was never to be restored with the departure of his most Magnificent Friend. His Amelia.

vii **Petra The Akran**

Despite being poorly paid, Petra had resolved to remain working at the Community Centre but would leave if a better job should arise, but she was in no hurry. Money was not her primary motive, however, as it was just not a motivating factor in her life. She came to the realisation that she wanted to somehow "give" more. Yes, she was giving something to these elderly folk and young people, but she wanted to bestow more of herself and in so doing accrue not financial gain but job satisfaction as reward.

What really motivated her was the prospect of supporting young people experiencing *real* difficulties. Those who were in desperate need of some form of help, guidance and support. The

Akran believed that she would succeed at this because of her own history. She also wished for a role where justice, in some description, could be served even if that justice meant that just one child was saved from their dark cruel world.

Her relationship with Sarah was still going strong. They were a very happy and loving couple although Sarah worked a great deal thus did not lift one solitary finger to help Petra in any domestic chore. She did not even put her washing in the laundry basket but simply left it on the floor for Petra to pick up and deal with. This was beginning to grate on The Akran.

In the next few years, Petra was to face some difficult choices leading to no little upset and confusion.

Petra and Sarah's life was a happy one. They complemented each other in the roles that they had carved out for themselves organically. Sarah, the highflying workaholic breadwinner to Petra the work lover yet more domestic goddess! Their wardrobes appeared to denote these "provinces" too. Sarah with her very masculine styled suits, starched shirts and waistcoats. Petra with her undoubtedly boyish yet more feminine attire. Even their behaviour within the bedroom depicted certain of these characteristics with Sarah being the more dominant of the two. Obviously, lesbian relationships come in all shapes and sizes. Some have such "roles" whilst others do not. It just so happens that this particular relationship did.

Some of Petra's friends, particularly her straight male ones, found Sarah quite imposing, even sometimes possessing when it came to Petra. They would often remark on her sense of dress, especially the waistcoats which proved to be a popular conversation point between these friends as they found it hard to understand why a female, harbouring no gender issues, should choose to wear one. The conclusion being that she was trying to promulgate a certain sense of authority which they considered to be over Petra who admittedly felt this could possibly be an accurate assumption. However, it was not just about the waistcoats because on their first encounter she wore one and Petra was still attracted to her. Sarah was naturally an authoritarian, at times more so than others. She thrived upon being in charge and being a leader. But she did not necessarily lead by example. She did not feel inclined to do anything that was remotely feminine. For example, she did not ever iron her own work shirts which had to be starched and have one single lined crease going straight down the centre of each arm. Her expectation was that Petra should do this. She refused to allow Petra to drive her new sports car in spite of her being more than capable. She did not much care for Petra's occasional nights out with friends, yet she went out with hers. Even if she worked very late, she expected her supper to be cooked and waiting for her when she finally arrived home. Petra should wait and eat with her no matter the time regardless of the fact that Petra had work the next day.

These were not rules that were ever specifically laid out. There was no written or unwritten "constitution" or "commandment". From the very beginning of their relationship Petra fell into some kind of trap setting certain precedents which now appeared to be set in stone. At first, Petra was happy to oblige but over the years she became tired of being the charlady, chief cook, bottle washer and scrubber. She wanted more equality in their relationship but felt guilty thinking such a thing as Sarah worked so hard for them both and she was generous with her money.

Petra did attempt, several times, to express her disgruntlement to Sarah in the hope of some kind of change but her wife was set in her ways and there was an air of: "*I haven't changed, you fell in love with this person so don't try to change me now*" going on. The kind of attitude which Petra did appreciate because she certainly did fall in love with this same person, so, therefore, it would not be fair to try to change her.

It was herself, The Akran, that had changed and her self-esteem "*transubstantiated*" with it.

Petra was not looking for anyone else. Nor did it even enter her mind for, in spite of there being obvious pitfalls in the marriage, she was definitely not cheerless. Put upon maybe, but she did not feel miserable. If anything, she blamed herself for the flaws. She loved Sarah and all in all she was not unhappily married. However, she found the use of the term "happily married" to be one she found difficult to state apart from to kid herself. Petra was one to keep her vows, especially that of fidelity. She was, however, becoming frustrated in her "given" role. All she wanted was some help now and again. However, she appreciated how hard Sarah worked but she did not work much over the weekends when the bulk of the chores were done. So, whilst Petra was busy doing everything, after a hard week at work and more to come that weekend, Sarah would be busy playing on the Play Station or Xbox.

It came as a complete surprise, a huge shock, to The Akran when her head was turned by another. It truly was the very last thing she expected. One minute to be in a stable monogamous marriage and literally the next to be thinking about someone else.

One of her managers, from the Community Centre, had since gone off long-term sick, so an interim had been employed. Her name was Cathryn. Cathryn was not dynamic. She was not at all butch. She was reasonably feminine, even wearing a spattering of makeup. She was not a power dresser. She definitely was not imposing. To be honest she was not a very good leader. She was Sarah's complete antithesis. She wore loose-fitting feminine trousers, blouses and shoes with a slight heel. She had shoulder-length, wavy, strawberry blonde hair which set off her pale green eyes and porcelain skin. She donned a pair of star-shaped studs in her ears, a small cross around her long neck and a dainty gold bracelet on her right wrist. Cathryn was softly spoken and did not swear. She was of a similar age to Petra, of medium height and with a pear-shaped figure. She was marvellous with the elderly, coped well with the younger youth club but found the teenage one, with its hormonal members, challenging. She shied away from confrontations between this motley bunch. Cathryn avoided any form of controversial decision making but she was kind, good natured, hardworking and obviously wanted the very best for the centre, the clients and the staff, both paid and unpaid.

Petra was aware that she lived on a canal boat with her boyfriend, Rob. She also knew that her new boss attended a Church of England High Church. She warmed to Cathryn — there was nothing to dislike.

The shock came when during a particularly busy teenage youth club night a lad deposited a small folded up piece of white paper in Petra's hand which, he stated, was a message for her sent by Cathryn. Before reading the note, Petra looked up to see its author merely a few feet away staring in her direction. Petra thought it strange that Cathryn had not walked the few feet and delivered the message in person. However, upon opening and reading the message she understood why.

The hand it was scribed in was neat and small much like Cathryn herself. The words, which were to be a bane of Petra's life for the foreseeable future, were direct and to the point: "*I am gay too.*"

Petra's first consideration was that Cathryn, being a member of a churchgoing family, needed some advice or help in how to deal with her sexuality which was currently closeted. Perhaps she was struggling with how to tell her parents or with how to come to terms with it herself. Petra being Petra resolved to approach her after the club had ended and offer her guidance and support if needed. She simply acknowledged the note by tipping Cathryn the nod before tearing it up and throwing it in the bin lest some prying young eye should read it. As she had resolved to do, Petra did approach Cathryn after the last of the club goers had left, the "clearing up party" had finished and the two of them were alone. She was unsure as to how to initiate the conversation. The note may have been merely to make her aware that she was not the only "gay in the building"! Petra began by thanking Cathryn for the message before her mouth dried up as she was then struggling for words. Fortunately, Cathryn intervened between Petra and the potentially awkward silence. Cathryn explained quite starkly that she was in a heterosexual relationship and had been for seven years but was not happy in it. She continued by explaining how she had been in a brief lesbian relationship prior to meeting Rob and felt that was actually where her sexuality still lay. She categorically insisted that she was not bisexual. Petra, still a little lost for words, managed to offer any guidance or words of wisdom should Cathryn need it. However, much to Petra's surprise Cathryn dismissed any offer of support; instead, she invited Petra to a canal boat festival that weekend. She touched Petra's hand, which gave Petra a slight tingling sensation down her spine, seemingly to entreat The Akran to say "yes". Without hesitation Petra said exactly that but made sure to make implicit that Sarah would be going too. Naturally, Cathryn appeared pleased with this confirmation.

Saturday morning and the day of the canal boat festival had arrived. It was a mild March day. Petra was filled with what can only be described as nervous excitement which she could not adequately explain. All she knew was that she could forego the festival itself, but she was extremely keen to be seeing Cathryn.

Sarah, who was always running late to Petra's punctuality, was characteristically taking her time, which proved to cause Petra no little infuriation and irritation. She was concerned that Cathryn would think that they were not going to go. At long last Sarah appeared dressed and ready to go.

When they met Cathryn, just the one hour late, she was duly introduced to Sarah who extended her hand in the expectation that Cathryn would shake it. She did not. After overcoming that slight awkwardness Petra suggested they all walk along the towpath to see the assortment of canal boats, barges and stalls. She could not but help to notice the absence of Rob but decided not to question her new friend about this. The afternoon proved enjoyable, the sun came out, flavoured gins and vodkas were tasted and bought. Lunch of wood-fired pizzas was eaten. It culminated with a tour around Cathryn's boat, *Lyrica*, which was bedecked with banners and ribbons. As Petra and Sarah had a house viewing in an hour's time, they thanked Cathryn for her hospitality, said their farewells and left.

As Sarah had received a promotion and with it a substantial pay rise, she decided that she wanted to move to a more befitting property.

They had already managed to sell their lovely cottage at a very good price, so they were now able to jump a rung or two. That afternoon they were due to view a new build in a village further out from where they were currently living. The show home was to die for, but it was really too modern for Petra and lacked the character of an older house. Theirs would be plot 12 out of 16. The building work had been finished but lacked some of the interior décor. It was built on three floors. The ground floor, Petra's favourite because of the kitchen, had a box room, perhaps a suitable bedroom for a child, but Sarah thought it would be the perfect study and gaming room for herself. Opposite was a small bathroom. At the end of a long hallway was a magnificent looking kitchen-cum-dining room complete with breakfast bar. The kitchen was not yet complete, but Petra stood in awe of what she saw before her eyes! That room, on its own, sold the house to her. Up the first flight of stairs was a huge L-shaped living room, another bedroom, which Petra made the bold suggestion of turning into her gym, a family bathroom, and a large double bedroom with an en-suite shower room. Up a further flight of stairs was an even larger bedroom with fitted wardrobes and an en-suite bath and shower room. The garden was small, which suited both of them as neither were gardening enthusiasts or green fingered in the slightest. What the house lacked in history and charm it gained in the space it offered; the fact that no work would be required upon moving in and the social standing that Sarah imagined she may gain. Petra liked the house well enough, especially the kitchen/diner coupled with the fact she would have a gym. She did not much like the modernity of the house. The house was situated in a quaint village; after checking out both it and the locality the decision was made to put in an offer which was accepted. Sarah would be the sole owner, as in the cottage, which Petra was fine with. She was happy because Sarah was happy. She would not be able to rave about the property but knew that once they had put their stamp on it the house would look more like their home which would be warm and welcoming rather than being cold and sterile. It would be a few months until the house was completely finished, so they had plenty of time to pack and get themselves ready.

That Sunday, Petra and Cathryn spent the majority of the day texting each other back and forth. Petra felt quite tired as she had not had a good night's sleep. This, however, was not through any excitement or otherwise because of the new house or even upset at leaving the old. She considered neither house as she lay in bed wide awake contemplating. Her thoughts only contained those concerning Cathryn. She felt guilty having any thoughts about her let alone the rather sexual ones she was experiencing. The texts began in an innocent enough fashion. Petra thanked Cathryn for having invited them to the canal boat festival; Cathryn responding by a *"you're welcome"* text. But throughout the course of the day these texts became slightly less innocent. They were not overtly sexualised, nor did they elicit any immediate hints of being attracted to each other. Yet the hidden agendas and meanings of both involved were certainly present. As the day progressed and the agendas and meaning became less hidden, Petra began to feel guilty once more. Guilt that she was somehow betraying Sarah, not only because she was having lustful thoughts about someone else but also because she was telling that other person. In truth, however, it wasn't just guilt she was feeling for she was also feeling rather exhilarated, nervous, happy, aroused and so keen to see Cathryn the following day at work.

Later that evening, after the texting had concluded, Petra reconsidered her actions of that day. She was enjoying a roast lamb dinner, which she had cooked, with her wife. Why and how could she possibly even think about someone else let alone consider the possibility of embarking upon an affair (which she was)? The Akran snapped to her senses allowing the pain of guilt to invade her body because that was what she deserved. Even the thought of betraying Sarah was in itself unthinkable; thus, she deserved that torturous feeling of guilt. She did not know how she would face Cathryn the next day.

Petra got up early the next morning. Despite her thoughts and feelings of guilt from the previous night she had a very spritely spring in her step and butterflies in her stomach but chose to ignore the reasons behind such things. She was also rather too excited about the prospect of going to work on a Monday morning!

When she arrived, Cathryn was already seated at her desk drinking her morning cup of tea for she detested coffee. Upon seeing her Petra realised, with some horror, that given the chance she would have an affair with this woman. She would even take her over the desk right now! However, despite the text messages of the day before, she didn't actually believe such a thing would become reality. She certainly wouldn't assume to make the first move and the quiet, seemingly reserved Cathryn definitely would not. Text messages were one thing. They can be deleted, as if they had never existed. A kiss was more tangible, and one cannot be "unkissed" — that cannot be deleted and forgotten.

How very wrong Petra was! Cathryn called her into her office, shut the door, walked the few steps towards Petra, embraced her and proceeded to kiss her on the lips. Petra did not push her away in shock or revulsion. No. She kissed her back. Willingly, very willingly. Almost too willingly. Thus, an affair was born. An affair that was to last just over one year. It was the best and at the same time the worst year of The Akran's life.

Over the course of that year Petra would berate herself. Her sense of self-loathing was acute, as was her sense of guilt. She detested herself for what she was doing to the oblivious Sarah.

This did not prevent her from continuing the affair. The sex was awesome for a start. In hindsight that was Petra's main motive — the great sex. But the sex was only so great because of the clandestine, illicit way it was perpetrated. They had sex wherever and whenever they could even in Petra and Sarah's home: against the fridge, on their settee in the living room...

Petra felt such guilt. Raw guilt all of the time yet this did not stop her either.

It wasn't long until Cathryn informed Petra that she had split up from Rob and that he had moved out of the canal boat. Petra was not pleased at all, as Cathryn told her that the reason she had ended the relationship was because she had fallen in love with her and wanted to be with her. There had been no discussion about this previously. Immediately, Petra began to feel the fear rise up inside her. It was not the word "love" or even the fact that Cathryn had suddenly split up from Rob, it was more the possible expectations that Cathryn may have of Petra who was definitely not ready to end her marriage. Although she cared for Cathryn a great deal, *"was it love?"* she tentatively questioned herself. *"Possibly,"* came the answer.

The affair carried on. When they were at work, the flirting and innuendo were both horrendous and gradually their co-workers began to realise what was going on. They all professed their pleasure apart from Coral, who was upset because Petra had kept her in the dark. Nor was she enamoured with the infidelity part because having met Sarah a few times she had warmed to her. She was not backward in coming forward with her disquiet which Petra understood, even appreciating her honesty although she felt upset that she had disappointed her friend.

The day came for Petra and Sarah to move into their fabulous new house — and fabulous it was. They moved in on Petra's 31st birthday. The move went smoothly, no rain this time, just glorious sunshine. It took a while for them to get everything straight but when they did the house lost its sterility and became a home. A welcoming one at that.

This move did not bring about an end to the affair. If anything, it became more intense as Cathryn was vying for Petra to end her relationship with Sarah. Speaking about Sarah, when she went away for a week for the purposes of work Cathryn moved in. They neither made love in nor slept in the marital bed but did in the one occupying the spare room. Although Petra enjoyed the week it was marred by feelings of fear and guilt which took their toll. *"What if Sarah came home unannounced and found them in bed?"* *"What if she suspected that another female was in the house when she phoned?"* *"What if one of the neighbours innocently mentioned Petra's female house guest?"* *"What if Sarah found a stray strawberry blonde hair in a place that was hard to explain?"* This fear and guilt came from the place where she knew what she was doing was wrong. It was completely against her moral code — up until now.

Petra knew that Sarah would be devastated should she discover this sordid affair. She was all too aware that she was betraying her wife by cheating on her. She knew it was now made worse by having it in "plain sight", that is within the marital home. Petra was only too aware that Sarah's wrath would be awesome should she discover it. This still did not prevent The Akran from choosing not to put an end to it once and for all. She considered it but felt that she could not live without Cathryn but could or would she ever leave Sarah? In essence Petra was having her cake and eating it. Also, in complete and utter honesty, could she really leave this wonderful house with its fabulous kitchen? Could she forego the marvellous holidays? Could she relinquish this privileged lifestyle to which she had become accustomed? These questions shocked The Akran as she had never before considered herself materialistic. Discovering that indeed she was made her detest herself all the more.

However, the more she thought about Sarah the more she was beginning to believe that Sarah was not being a "good" wife, herself, with her complete unwillingness to contribute to any chore or even get a cleaner, especially as they now lived in such a large house and Petra was struggling with its upkeep. One day, just prior to Christmas, Petra knew that she would be late home from work and that Sarah would be working from home. She asked her wife if she could take over her evening "jobs" of making a packed lunch for them for the following day and cook supper, the ingredients and instructions for which Petra had prepared. When a tired Petra arrived home late that evening, all Sarah had to say was: "*I've made the fucking lunch but I'm not doing supper!*" Petra felt as if she could cry but instead muttered an uncharacteristic "*fuck off*" as she headed for the garden to smoke a cigarette. As she took her first inhalation, she heard the patio door being locked from the inside. There she was, locked out of the house on a snowy December evening. It took one hour before Sarah deigned to let her back inside. Neither ate supper that night.

A while later, Petra decided to have an early night, but she made the mistake of leaving her mobile phone on to charge in the bedroom. At 10 o'clock an extremely angry and upset Sarah shook her awake with no little force thrusting the phone in Petra's face as she did so, whilst reciting some of the text messages she had read from Cathryn to Petra. These mostly consisted of declarations of undying love. Sarah confiscated the phone intent on ringing Petra's lover. In that moment she would not heed any of Petra's protestations of innocence. Sarah did not call Cathryn. The following morning, she was calmer and allowed Petra to be heard who stated, without a qualm it seemed, that yes, Cathryn was attracted to her, but she was a bit deranged. Of course, nothing had happened between them although Cathryn wishes it would and had begun to hound her. Sarah was taken in by this, which only added to Petra's guilt and self-loathing.

Then the time came for Cathryn to beseech Petra to leave Sarah. It grew into a full-on campaign. Petra proved too weak willed to say anything to the contrary but time and time again she would tell Cathryn that she was working on it. Cathryn then began to provide Petra with ultimatums which included attending couples counselling with her and to have left Sarah by the time the sessions had reached their end. Petra went along with the counselling but purely for purposes of appeasement. Each time she went she felt as if she had had a head on collision with an artic lorry. The deadline passed, as did several more.

The deceit, the guilt, the confusion, the self-loathing, the constant deadlines, ultimatums, the double life and sheer turmoil that all of this elicited inside her all contributed to Petra's demise. She was not able or perhaps willing to make any form of decision. She often wished that she had never met her "mistress" and berated herself for getting involved with her, yet she could not end the affair. Her anxiety began to hit the proverbial roof. She felt the guilt and self-hatred overwhelm her. She felt her mood plummet to an extent that she was unable to rouse herself; then she soared with euphoria all of a sudden. At these times she was *"as high as a kite"* running on pure adrenaline and ecstasy, but not XTC. She spent money like water at an alarming rate. She lost a great deal of money this way, like when she booked a trip to Las Vegas for ten people which was to depart the following day! This was booked without appearing to recognise what she was doing. There were other such purchases, too many to outline. Things went from worse to even worse within the home and Cathryn was still hounding her to leave. Petra found herself wishing that Cathryn would reach the realisation that she was on a losing wicket and finish the affair herself. She did not do this. Petra felt under so much pressure as if her head was going to explode at any moment. The depression, the mania — the overdose.

She loved Cathryn and she loved Sarah. Each for different reasons. She never knew, until now, that it was even possible to love two people at the same time. She wished it was not. She wished she had never set eyes upon let alone met Cathryn who continued to set deadlines and pose ultimatums. With one set gone unheeded another would be set again and again and yet again.

Years later, upon much reflection, Petra realised that she was actually in love with neither. She did love Sarah because of her steadiness. She knew exactly where she stood with her as she did not play games. Sarah and her steadiness, her certainty, her pedantic ways, her immutability, her resoluteness, her consistency, and her honest, simple love. Did she love Sarah or was it more comfortable, safe, secure? She was not in love with her.

With Cathryn everything was more complex. Why did she love Cathryn? Because she was everything that Sarah was not. They were polar opposites. Cathryn was hesitant, imprecise, cowardly and erratic. Her love for Petra was suffocating, demanding, even threatening but it was also intoxicating and addictive. It may be a wonder why Petra did not end this affair as it caused her nothing but guilt, anxiety and self-loathing but she found she was unable to do so. She could not find the words but there was a possibility that she did not do this because when she was in Cathryn's presence, she felt happy. She, Petra, was The Boss. She was the one who was in control including in the bedroom. But did she love Cathryn, or was it mere lust?

All of the guilt, all of the lust, all of the deceit, all of the pressure and self-hatred. All of the confusion and stress became too much for The Akran. She was being made to choose by Cathryn, but she could not choose. Petra knew she was being unfair. At home she began to argue with Sarah as her irritability grew. Her mood began to swing wildly as if on a pair of erratic scales. These moods ranged from being suicidally depressed to being manic, spending money like a fiend and craving excitement and danger. She "stole" Sarah's sports car one night and went on a joy ride thrashing it down the motorway. Fortunately, there were no speed cameras back then or very few. She swung between these two poles quickly. No one knew where they stood whilst Petra became even more desperate. So desperate, she slit her wrists and took as many paracetamol as she could possibly find in the house, washing them down with vodka. This was a serious attempt to end her own life.

She woke up in a hospital bed with her mother and Sarah seated either side of her wanting answers. There she was with her wrists bandaged up and a drip attached to her right forearm. She felt sick — probably from the vodka. She was visited by someone from the mental health team who proceeded to talk to her about her suicide attempt. Petra thought it unfair to be asked the hundred and one questions that she was asked when she felt so utterly awful. She was unaware of how best to answer this ridiculous bombardment of questions without incriminating herself. The list of questions was endless. Petra spoke the truth.

Yes, she did intend to kill herself. Yes, she has got more plans to do so. Yes, she did regret waking up. Yes, she did wish it had worked. No, she did not think herself fortunate that it hadn't worked. In truth she was gutted and so angry with herself that she was still alive. She wanted to die and that was the absolute truth of the matter. The next thing she knew, as she fell back to sleep, was the fact that she had been sectioned under Section 2 of the Mental Health Act meaning that she would be forced to go into a psychiatric hospital for twenty-eight days, for further assessment, as she was a risk to herself. No one heard her protestations. It seemed that in twenty-four hours' time she was to be conveyed via hospital transport to St David's, which was one of the local psychiatric hospitals. When she had been declared medically fit the following day, Petra was spirited away from the general hospital to St David's. Never having stepped foot inside a psychiatric hospital, she was scared stiff. After all who hasn't seen *One Flew Over the Cuckoo's Nest*!

She had with her the bare essentials including the information about her sectioning and the mental health act which she clutched tightly in her left hand. On her arrival her escort helped her out of the ambulance lest she ran away but on the pretext of her not banging her head.

St David's was a psychiatric hospital in the grounds of a general hospital, some distance away from the one she had just been discharged from. The building stood by itself far away from any of the other hospital buildings. "*So far,*" Petra thought, "*it looks kind of okay,*" as she saw no crazed lunatics in the surrounding grounds being chased by orderlies wearing white overalls. As she entered, she noticed how uncannily quiet the ward was. It was mid-morning. The only noise came from the abandoned television set in the corner of the communal living room where she had been directed to wait with her escort.

Upon glancing to her right, she saw a darkened room, which had been partitioned off from the one in which she currently stood, by glass panels (reinforced glass, naturally). It was not because of the lack of light but because of the very dense smog enveloping the room that hindered her from seeing what was inside. As one person opened the door to exit, the stench of cigarettes and tobacco bowled her over. "*So, at least I can smoke in this godforsaken place,*" she thanked someone inwardly. The smoking room, as that's what this was, apparently was the "*Place To Be*" as most smoking rooms and areas are. As she was gasping for a cigarette, notwithstanding she was still as scared as hell, she motioned to her escort that she was going inside. There was no escape route from inside, so she was allowed to go in. Not even halfway through the door she regretted this decision as her fear took hold, "*I'm going into this room with a bunch of loonies!*" She thought it would seem impolite if she should turn around; at any rate she was gasping for a smoke and as she was not exactly in the position to judge, seeing as she held a "certificate" of sorts in her hand she entered whilst attempting to admonish her fears.

It took some time for her eyes to adjust and inure themselves to the thick dense smoke in an already dark room. The same could be said about her lungs which rapidly filled with the smog that polluted this room. She noticed that her shoes literally stuck to the black flooring. The furniture, if you could call it that, consisted of one settee, two beanbags, two armchairs, some wooden dining chairs, and two tables, was old, ripped, uncomfortable, also dark in colour. People were sitting on the floor as the "comfy" seats had all been taken. The room was lit by one strip light; the bulb had gone in the second. Petra chose to stand as she did not wish to sit on the sticky, grubby flooring which was littered with chocolate wrappers, coke cans and fag butts. No one really spoke, but the radio was playing quietly. Yet the room did not seem quiet. It seemed extremely loud as she could somehow "hear" the thoughts of its inhabitants and the repetitive inhaling and exhaling as cigarettes were constantly being smoked, sometimes chain smoked by certain individuals. No one looked up. No one welcomed her. But it did not occur to her that they were being rude. Eventually a Pan-like character piped up. He introduced himself as David and then proceeded to introduce her to the other "*inmates*" as he referred to himself and his fellow patients. No one appeared as scary as she had imagined. Here were "normal" people who had suffered hardship and who were unwell.

The more she became acquainted with David the more Pan-like he became. Pan being of Ancient Greek mythology. He is the God of the wild, shepherds and flocks. Of nature, of mountain wilds, rustic music, impromptus and companion of the nymphs. He has the hindquarters, legs and horns of a goat, in the same way as a fawn or satyr. With his homeland in the outlands of Arcadia, he is also recognised as the God of fields, groves, wooded glens and is often affiliated with sex; because of this Pan is connected to fertility and the season of spring. The word "panic" ultimately derives from the God's name. The ancient Greeks also considered Pan to be the God of theatrical criticism.

Petra could not quite put her finger on why she quietly nicknamed David, "Pan". It may have been because of the various artistic representations of him that she had seen. David, obviously, didn't have horns. Nor did his lower half resemble that of a goat. It may have been his very upright way of sitting on his haunches, or the fact he played the tin whistle, or even his constant allusions to sex. He was a schizophrenic who, as it transpired, held some form of sexual inclination towards and passion for lesbians! In spite of that he reminded Petra of a lost soul. Indeed, the majority of patients at St David's were lost souls of sorts including Petra herself.

At long last a nurse and nursing assistant collected Petra. They chaperoned Petra to her "bed space" which was actually a room. They then searched through and itemised all of her belongings searching for anything with which she could possibly harm herself such as tablets, razors and other sharp objects or those which could be made to do so. Anything remotely of that sort was confiscated. Also taken were her shoelaces, earphones, phone charger, belt. These she could understand but: *"Why confiscate my shampoo, conditioner and shower gel?"* She was informed that some patients ingest these in order to harm themselves. All such items would be kept in a locker in the nursing office. She could have access to them but only under supervision. The Akran was most upset about her phone charger, earphones and lighter.

The nursing assistant then advised her of the never-ending rules and regulations she was now under including those of the section she had to adhere to. She wasn't really listening enough to take any of this in as she was still reeling from having her belongings confiscated but signed the appropriate form regardless. Finally, they left the bedroom. Petra refused to call it a bed space as that was so impersonal. She wondered when she would see a psychiatrist as she was not told that. Nor was she told who this person would be.

Nothing much happened inside St David's. Petra assumed that she would be undergoing some form of therapy at least once a day. There was no therapy at all. She was put on a long list of medication for something called bipolar for which she was merely given a leaflet to read. The drugs made her feel drugged and tired. Apart from sleeping and eating she smoked. She quickly became familiar with a handful of patients. Those like herself who spent practically every waking moment in the smoking room. She actually developed a good rapport with them, especially David and a man she secretly named Catweazle but was actually called John. John was an old-fashioned "tramp" as opposed to the time-travelling character of Catweazle. She was not allowed out of the unit. Nursing assistants made sure of that. Every half hour they wandered round ticking names off a list to ensure each patient was still there. Most of the patients, including Petra, were on a cocktail of medications that reduced them into zombie-like states. The theory behind this, they believed, was to keep the inmates quiet and docile so that staff had an easy shift.

She did not see a psychiatrist until the end of her first week. Both Catweazle and David had warned her about a particular shrink who, sadly for Petra, turned out to be the one who she would be under. It transpired that patients saw their shrink once a week at "Ward Round" which was an imposing experience as it basically entailed being ushered into a room in which were a host of strangers, who patients were not introduced to, seated formally around a long table where the patient was also required to sit. Then this group of professionals discussed the patient, with them present, decisions were then made, and conclusions were drawn without the patient necessarily opening their mouth. Even if they did, they were not really "heard" or taken seriously.

Petra's shrink was Dr Ephraim. A Palestinian woman who reminded her of Toad from "*Wind in the Willows*" and "*Toad of Toad Hall*". She disliked her on sight as she showed no mercy when it came to the feelings of her patients. She could be downright nasty and demanded that everyone agree with her, including those sat around that table. She often reduced her patients to tears or hyped them up into such a state that they had to be subdued with an injection of medication.

Dr Ephraim seemed to be sizing the nervous and bewildered Petra up at her first ward round. Petra was seated at one end of the boardroom-style table, as she had been directed to do. Sitting at the sides were complete strangers who she was not introduced to. Directly opposite sat, who she discovered to be, Dr Ephraim who began to shout at her almost immediately. Petra, who thought it best to remain quiet otherwise her anger may get the better of her, could not believe she was being treated in such a manner. However, the end result was that she had indeed been diagnosed with rapid cycling bipolar and was then ordered to choose between her "*two female lovers*"!

In brief, bipolar is a mental health condition that affects moods which can swing from one extreme to another. Those with it have episodes of depression, feeling very low and lethargic whilst the other pole makes them feel very high and overactive. Symptoms of depression can include an overwhelming feeling of worthlessness, hopelessness and can lead to suicidal ideation and suicide. Other symptoms of depression may include difficulty sleeping, irritability, lack of energy, difficulty concentrating and remembering things, lack of interest in everyday activities, feelings of emptiness, guilt, despair and pessimism. One can doubt oneself and become delusional, have hallucinations and disturbed illogical thinking. Mania can include feelings of euphoria. It can make one feel very energetic with ambitious plans and ideas. It may lead to spending large amounts of money on things one cannot afford and would not normally want, as Petra did. It is also common not to feel like eating or sleeping. Mania can induce rapid speech and becoming annoyed. It can lead to psychosis. Other symptoms of mania include feeling elated or overjoyed. Having boundless energy, feeling self-important and full of great ideas and important plans. One can become easily distracted, irritated or agitated and have delusional, disturbed or illogical thoughts. Hallucinations are symptoms as well. Someone with bipolar mania can do things that often have disastrous consequences or say things that are out of character and that others see as being risky or harmful.

Petra had been diagnosed with rapid cycling bipolar meaning she repeatedly swung from a high to a low phase without having a "normal" period in between.

Inside St David's patients were left to their own devices, which usually meant being cosseted in one of two places — in bed or in the smoking room. The communal living room with the television was rarely used. Meals, which were served promptly at 0730 hrs, 1230hrs and 1700hrs were taken in the dining room. Medication was dished out straight after this with an extra lot at 2200hrs. Patients had to form an orderly queue at meds time and wait their turn which could be a long wait depending on which nurse was doing the dispensing. Poor behaviour was not tolerated! Most patients, including Petra, were overmedicated to the extent that they were unable to really exhibit any behaviour at all let alone of the "poor" variety.

The days were long and monotonous. Petra managed to coordinate the visiting times of her two "lovers" so that they neither clashed nor could they possibly bump into each other. Although she looked forward to both visits, she also began to wish that neither of them visited at all so that she could have some proper thinking space. Seeing them just appeared to "blur her vision", confusing her all the more. Petra did not know how she was expected to think straight with all of the medication she had to take. She was constantly woozy, and her brain was fog like. She had also been advised, by a mental health care professional somewhere down the line that she should refrain from making any life-changing decisions whilst her bipolar was bad as her judgement was impaired. However, one morning she woke up and had a "eureka" moment! Cathryn was the victor. So, now all she had to do was tell Sarah. She would always be unclear as to what led her to that choice, but it felt right at the time.

It was a Sunday. Being a weekend, visiting times were from 1000hrs to 2030hrs. Cathryn was to visit first, with Sarah later in the afternoon. Before Cathryn had arrived, Petra could hardly contain her excitement for she was going to tell her that she had "won", although not in those terms. Naturally, Cathryn was overcome with joy, albeit not quite believing her ears as to why and how Petra had come to this decision. She also wondered if Petra would actually go through with telling Sarah, although she had promised to.

Petra kept her promise. Sarah visited later as planned. She was met by a serious and actually mournful looking Petra. Mournful because it was deeply upsetting, and she hated endings. She hated the finality of them. The feeling of loss despite no one having died. She also hated being the messenger. In that moment, though, she was certain that she had come to the right decision. It was the end of an epoch for another to begin with someone else which excited her. There is no ending without a new beginning. They could be no backing down. Not now. She knew she could not fail in this "duty", for if she did, she would surely lose Cathryn. This was the reason she told her lover that she would be ending her marriage, prior to speaking to Sarah. The theory being she would not be able to back down if she became too scared.

Petra had been practising her speech in order that she would not falter or leave anything out. She wanted to appear kind in this far from kind situation. Her first mistake was to use the sobriquet, "*Pootle*", that she reserved for Sarah. This was not in her speech. It just slipped out mechanically: "*Hi Pootle.*" At this point Petra jumped at the chance of Sarah offering to make them a cup of coffee as here was an opportunity to "man up" and do this without anymore "fuck ups".

By the time the cups of watery, putrid looking cups of NHS coffee arrived, Petra had managed to recover herself. So, she began her speech which went something like this:

"*I have given this so much thought. You are not to blame yourself as you've done nothing wrong. You are a wonderful person with so much to offer someone, but that person can no longer be me. I'm so sorry but I need to end this relationship. I have been very happy but now I'm just not and I know I can't be with you in this relationship anymore. I'm truly sorry.*"

She was too cowardly to mention Cathryn or the affair.

There she paused waiting for an explosion but what she received was far worse. Tears. Many droplets of them. Petra knew she had to get up and leave before she reneged upon her decision, so she very simply, but not the least cruelly, left the table they were seated at and went to her bedroom which was out of bounds to visitors. Adrenaline was pumping through her. With shaking hands, she called Cathryn to tell her about this momentous moment. It was exactly that — momentous — but she had thought she'd be more elated and that she'd perhaps feel relieved but all she felt was deflation and sadness mixed with uncertainty, but it was rather too late for that. Needless to say, there were no commiserations from Cathryn, no "*that must have been so difficult for you. Are you okay?*" Petra would have appreciated that, in this moment. What she did receive, though, was a long list of things they now had to do and plan for such as to find a place to live and rather insensitively that Petra had to retrieve her belongings from Sarah's as quickly as possible. She was also informed that she must speak to her mother so that she could stay in the parental home until they found somewhere together. Petra received not a hint of an indication that Cathryn had any realisation of how hard this had been or of how she felt. A relationship spanning over one decade, twelve years and six months to be precise, was a very hard thing to lose no matter the reason. Petra was very upset as she knew that Sarah would not want to be "friends", but she also knew that she did not deserve that, nor did she deserve any pity. She felt like a complete failure; she had failed Sarah; she had failed herself and she had failed to fight to fix their relationship. Did she regret her choice? Alas, she wasn't entirely sure but whatever, she now had to *"get on with it"* and focus on the immediate present. Only that did not look too rosy as her heart was heavy and all she wanted to do was have some PRN (as required) medication and sleep. However, she had done as she was required. *"But don't I always,"* she sighed, *"in the long run anyway?"* The immediate present felt so scary, the immediate future looked even scarier right now and the past looked terrifying. So, where was she to align herself? Petra had indeed done as she was required, for she had finally split up from Sarah as required by Cathryn and had made her choice as required by Dr Ephraim. She was supposed to feel better, right, not worse!

Later, that evening, Petra was taking a nap after supper when a nurse came into her bedroom carrying an A4-sized white envelope which simply had her name written on it. Upon immediately recognising the handwriting to be that of Sarah she felt a lump in her throat but with fingers trembling she gradually opened it. Inside, much to her surprise, were collage upon collage of photographs of them both over the years, their wonderful holidays, their wedding, more of happier times. Accompanying these was a brief note begging Petra not to end this relationship. Sarah was willing to compromise, was willing to do anything to get her *"beloved, her perfect Petra back"*. She would understand anything. Whatever — it could be fixed. Petra's eyes immediately became not pools but rivers as they overflowed. The guilt she felt. How could she have done this to Sarah? Had she made the right choice? Petra never answered these questions; instead, she took Cathryn's advice to live in the present. The photos were now in the past as were her thoughts and questions surrounding them. Now, to phone her mother to discuss the much-detested move back into the parental home, albeit on a temporary basis.

Petra's twenty-eight days of incarceration were finally over. She left St David's with her belongings and a bag full of medication. She did not much care for moving back into the parental home, voicing this to Cathryn who was driving her there having collected her from the unit. Keener than ever before to look to the future, Petra began talking about just that. Their future together which took her from the minefield that she'd left behind but would probably walk back into at some point but in a different pasture.

She was to sleep in what was her grandparents' quarters as before and was pleased not to have to return to the bedroom of her childhood. Her mother was happy that she was out of hospital, but things had changed as regards Petra's father. This change proved fortuitous to Petra although not so for him. He had developed Alzheimer's meaning that he probably would not "visit" her as before. He'd more than likely forgotten all about it!

More or less immediately, Petra decided to enlist her mother in helping her pack and move her belongings out of Sarah's house, which used to be her home. She was dreading this as she anticipated the pangs of regret that would undoubtedly besiege her. She was simply going to take her clothing, exercise equipment, books and other knick-knacks that belonged solely to her. Everything else she would leave and would not contest. As it had been arranged for Sarah to be out of the house whilst this chore was being carried out, Petra left her a note highlighting her regret at distressing her and her gratitude for the happy years they shared. She also detailed how she was now with Cathryn, missing out the fact that she had lied to Sarah for a long time, as she made out they had just got together. A cowardly act. Judging from the rather offensive and abrupt, but justified, text she later received from Sarah this was not believed. After over twelve years they would never be friends.

Fortunately, in retrospect there were to be no arduous filings for divorce as although Petra and Sarah had married in Maui this marriage was not legal in the United Kingdom. She was advised, by a family friend, that she may well be entitled to something as regards the house as she had done all of its upkeep. However, Petra was not interested in this as she did not want Sarah to undergo any more upset; nor did she, Petra, deserve a penny.

Petra returned to work almost immediately. She was glad of the distraction. Cathryn had since found employment elsewhere as her interim contract had come to an end.

As it transpired, Petra did not have to remain in the parental home for too long as both she and Cathryn had found a cottage to rent in a lovely, quiet, leafy village. After they had passed all of the appropriate checks, they moved in. They were without much furniture, but their new home came partly furnished with all of the necessary kitchen equipment. Cathryn had a dining table with chairs, they had bought a television and a blow-up settee between them. So, they were set. They were excited at the prospect of both living and beginning their lives together. Petra was now sure she had chosen correctly. All previous doubts had disappeared. Furthermore, she was not one to harbour regret as decisions were made for a reason and that should be that. However, she still could not think of Sarah without terrible guilt but not with regret.

Shortly after the move, Petra's father died. She ensured that she supported her mother and sister but she neither wanted nor received any support from them. The lack of that was noted but was not harboured with any upset as Petra was indifferent to her father's passing.

They remained in the rented house for one year. It was the most fabulous year. The two love birds were both caught up in their love for each other and their fledgling relationship. It all appeared perfect. Because of this happiness it was decided that they should begin to search for a house to buy together. Petra was pleased with this equality. As their budget was a tight one, they viewed many houses that were too small and "awful" in every respect but as luck would have it there was a Victorian cottage for sale at the other end of the road in which they were currently renting. Upon viewing it they both fell in love with what they saw and to their delight their offer was accepted. A few months later they had moved in but this time with everything they needed.

The cottage was perfect. An end of terrace which was built in 1890 to house the milkmen of the day. Back then the house would have been a "two up two down" but now it had been extended to include a bathroom and kitchen. The kitchen at the rear of the house was a galley style off which was the downstairs bathroom. The front door opened straight into the living room, complete with wood-burning stove, which led into the dining room with the original fireplace. From the dining room was a step into the kitchen which led out onto a petite but lovely courtyard garden which was paved in part although there was a small patch of grass. Also, in the dining room was a steep flight of stairs at the top of which was a tiny landing leading to two rooms: the master bedroom with fitted wardrobes and a single bedroom. The loft had been boarded, which was ideal for a study and Petra's gym. It was far from a big house, but it had everything they required, plus Petra loved the fact that it was old, had history and character. The floors were lain with some rather old beige carpet under which were the original floorboards. The kitchen floor, which Petra loved, was tiled with black slate. The kitchen, itself, was blue in colour and in desperate need of a revamp, as was the pink bathroom. The whole house needed a redecoration, the carpet needed taking up and replacing with new floorboards, as the old were just too old. A new kitchen and bathroom were also on the horizon. The garden needed a spruce up and some tender loving care. However, everything was in working order, even the old boiler. Thus, there was no immediacy for anything, which was good as money needed to be saved. It was agreed that the first big job would be the kitchen. In the meantime, they would decorate the living and dining rooms.

In the midst of the house move, there was a logical and mutual decision to get married. They had bought a house; now their home together; had a joint bank account and aspired to become parents. The romance came in how "The Proposal" came about. They each took their turn to get down on one knee to pop the other the question and to present a ring. The date of this romantic evening had been planned alongside a romantic meal for two in their favourite restaurant. Wedding preparations thus began. Truth is, although they called it a wedding, much like Petra's previous one to Sarah, it was in fact a commitment ceremony as gay marriage was still illegal in the United Kingdom. However, they treated it as one. They wanted the formality of a matrimony after which they would be "*betrothed*" to one another in indubitable "*wedded*" bliss. As a church service was out of the question, they opted to have the ceremony in the hotel in which they were to have their reception. Several food tasting sessions later they happened upon the perfect hotel for the occasion which best suited their budget, which was reasonable as both sets of parents contributed towards it. This came as a complete surprise to both of them. To Petra, because her mother had, originally, been so scathing of her sexuality, still continuing to believe it was just a phase but also because her mother was her mother! Cathryn was taken aback somewhat because her parents were reasonably religious. They were even members of their church choir.

For the big day, Cathryn wore a traditional white wedding dress but forewent the veil, whereas Petra opted for a silk ivory-coloured long Chinese-style jacket with pale green silk trousers and cream shoes with a slight heel. Both held posies of purple and white flowers. They chose against bridesmaids, but both of their sisters played important roles as did their closest friends. Petra's "big brother" was given the job as best man and chauffeur. He did a sterling job with his typically funny speech. They kept everything as traditional as possible with Cathryn spending the night prior at her parents' house whilst Petra spent it with her best man and a close friend.

It was a perfect July day. Nervously, Petra got herself

dressed. She had no doubts whatsoever. She was excited and nervous but most of all she could not wait to walk down the aisle with her bride-to-be. It was not only a prefect day in July; it also proved to be a perfect "wedding". Everything went off without a hitch. The ceremony was lovely; the wedding breakfast delicious; the speeches had the tradition, formality and hilarity in equal measure and were paced to perfection. Petra's speech was highly approved of. In the evening came bacon sandwiches and bowls of penny sweets. As Petra did not believe in having whom she referred to as "*second class friends — you were either friends or not!*" there were no newcomers to the evening reception. Everyone tripped the light fantastic well into the evening before the newly wedded found their way to the bridal suite which had been suitably bedecked with confetti, balloons and yes, condoms! The newlyweds were shattered that night but after retreating to their room they found it within themselves to share a jacuzzi bath to talk about their special day. Each oozed excitement and utter joy for not only had the day outshone their very highest expectations they were now "married" to each other. The honeymoon was spent in the Lake District for a week. They were lucky as the sun shone down on them throughout. Both were utterly certain that the metaphorical sun would continue to shine for them forever.

Petra actually revelled in the simplicity of the lifestyle she had forged with Cathryn in comparison to that with Sarah. They were living within comparatively meagre means, enjoyed doing simple things such as going out for walks in the woods. They only dined out on very special occasions. Petra's new life was contrapositive to the one she had shared with Sarah. She was fully content.

To make their lives complete they decided to get a rescue

dog. This was when the most beautiful wise soul entered into Petra's life. A collie cross, aged about two called Bacardi, as named by the rescue centre, whom Petra and Cathryn tended to shorten to Cardi. Nothing much was known about her, but she was brought to an English rescue centre from Wales having been found on the roadside with a litter of several deceased puppies, presumably hers. Cardi was to become Petra's saviour in so many ways. The love and bond that they shared was unconditional and pure. Cardi, with her beseeching eyes that could see into one's soul and knew everything and were so full of love and wisdom. Cardi saved Petra's life for sure.

A few years had passed. Now they were both ready to try for a baby. Somehow, they managed to save a substantial sum of money; thus, now was the time to begin a family. Obviously, this was a not a simple procedure for a lesbian couple but as fortune would have it a friend of a friend of Cathryn who was a gay male wanted to father a child. Details were duly swapped. When they were feeling a bit courageous, they called Martin in order to arrange a meeting with him. Two weeks later they were sitting in his elaborate but comfortable living room in St John's Wood, London. This was a man who was not short of money but was short of a child which he longed for.

It transpired that Martin was single, aged 50 and had a successful career as a psychologist. He wanted to be a father figure. Although he wanted to be in the child's life, he did not want to be there 100% of the time. This suited our lesbian couple. He was willing to help the child financially, which both Petra and Cathryn would rather he did not. The girls' stipulation was STI, HIV and fertility tests for both Martin and Cathryn as she would be the birth mother. No decisions were made straight away as each party needed to go away and consider the proposal. As it happened, they were all thrilled with the other. And so, it began. First the tests which came back negative and high fertility counts on both scores.

There were numerous ways in which to carry out the actual "messy" part, but they decided on the easiest for the first few rounds. Ovulation and pregnancy tests, folic acid, disposable syringes, urine test pots and a stash of gay magazines were purchased. Each month, Cathryn would test when she was ovulating. When she was, Petra would phone Martin who would make the journey to the girls' house every evening until ovulation had stopped. Martin would let himself in the house, grab a urine pot and a magazine then go into the bathroom where he would masturbate and somehow ejaculate into the pot. He would then leave shouting "bye" as he went. Petra and Cathryn had been upstairs being amorous until this point. Petra would go downstairs, collect the pot, take its precious liquid upstairs where the two would patiently wait for it to reach the right temperature. Petra would suck the sperm up into a disposable syringe before squirting it inside Cathryn who would then lie with her legs in the air for twenty whole minutes. Despite attempts to make this a romantic procedure it was anything but. It was all very mechanical. Both girls were finding the process hard with each month that went by with no positive result.

With some of the money they had saved it was time to buy a new kitchen. The guy next door, Nile, had kindly donated the services of himself and his brother, Jason, to fit it as they were handy with such things. As this was being arranged the baby-making process continued. It proved easier to move into Petra's parental home, whilst the kitchen was being done, her mother being away on holiday. Cathryn elected to help the lads in the evenings as she enjoyed DIY whereas Petra would have been more of a hindrance than a help. It took two weeks to complete the kitchen as it was only done in the evenings owing to everyone having "proper" daytime jobs. On completion it looked fabulous.

On moving back to the cottage, Petra noticed a significant shift in Cathryn. Something had changed but The Akran was unable to place her finger on what it was. Initially, she concluded it was due to the stress and indignity of baby-making. One evening, after such a deed being done, much to Petra's bewilderment and surprise, Cathryn asked Petra if they could stop the whole thing. Feeling very sad and shocked, Petra could only say, "*No, I want to carry on.*" At that moment she was so afraid that she was losing Cathryn so hoped that by saying "*no*" Cathryn would stay; otherwise, she would leave. In hindsight this made no sense. It was that fear alongside the desire to have a child that prompted Petra to say what she did and act as she was acting. It was Cathryn's body but surely, she, Petra, had a stake in the proceedings. It was evident that Cathryn had no intention of discussing the matter further. Baby-making continued but the already tense atmosphere became frosty.

Petra was becoming paranoid and confused. She guessed that her wife was gearing up to leave but did not know why for she had begun to change prior to the baby-making but Petra refused to acknowledge this at the time. Cathryn denied that she was ever going to leave. Furthermore, she had "*no intention*" of doing so. Despite this Petra's constant anguish did not diminish, which added to difficulties with the bipolar.

It was the night prior to the morning after. Cathryn and Petra were both reading in bed. Well, Cathryn was whilst Petra was staring at the words with her head in turmoil. She didn't know what made her say it, but she said it regardless:

"*Darling,*" she said endearingly, "*are you going to leave me?"*

"*Leave you?*" came the perceived terse reply, "*No, but can we talk about your worries tomorrow?*"

Petra should have been content with this reply, but she had a niggle — that itched and needed scratching. However, she realised she had to be content with her answer. And so, to sleep. Or try to.

As it happened, Petra had the day off work the following day but was awake when Cathryn left and said: "*Goodbye, have a good day. I love you*" in Cathryn's normal fashion. Petra's fears had faded. Fears are always worse at night. After dozing off again, Petra got up and headed downstairs. On the dining room table was an envelope addressed to Petra written in Cathryn's hand. Her immediate, indeed her only thought at that precise moment was, "How lovely, she has written me a love letter." She sat down with a cup of coffee and opened the envelope. She began to read. The first five words: "*I love you very much*" echoed her presumption of this being a letter of love. It wasn't until the sixth word, that being "*but*" that her beliefs began to change. When she read the whole sentence again: "*I love you very much but despite that I'm leaving*" her fears from the previous night were confirmed. That one short sentence not only brought Petra's world crashing down; it was also to be etched into her mind for evermore. In short, the letter was five pages long blaming Petra for the breakdown of their marriage highlighting that Petra had pushed Cathryn into carrying on with trying for a baby. It was her, Cathryn's, body, so she should be able to control what happens to it. Petra was confused. She never forced the syringe into her and was quite happy to have a proper conversation about it. Her initial impulse, at that time, was to say no, she wanted to carry on, but there the discussion ended and was not mentioned again. Petra only took that first line in. She screwed up the entire letter into a very tight ball and threw it away — there, it never existed — yet it did. The telephone then rang. Petra wrongly assumed it would be Cathryn at some attempt of an apology but instead it was her psychologist who had just received a voicemail from Cathryn advising her of what she had done. Elise was kind enough to go to see Petra at home straight after the phone call as she was concerned about her. What she found was a deranged-looking and acting Petra who had tried contacting Cathryn using all forms of media: calling her phone, texting her but Cathryn appeared to have blocked her. She had emailed her, but the email bounced straight back. She had tried to message her on Facebook but again she was blocked. Upstairs, Cathryn's wardrobe and chest of drawers were completely empty. There was no way she had moved everything out that morning so it must have been achieved over a few weeks in dribs and drabs without Petra noticing. She felt so stupid. Elise was highly perturbed about her client whose mania was coming to the fore. She deemed her a risk to herself so called for an assessment team. By this time, Petra was too far gone to appreciate what was happening as she thought she was the reincarnated Virgin Mary who was sent back to down to earth to heal the world of all its ills but by doing so had to kill herself. Petra was still ranting and raving when the team arrived. They sectioned her under Section 3 of the Mental Health Act as they agreed with Elise that she was a risk to herself. As she had previously been sectioned under section 2 it was considered pertinent to use the section 3 which meant a six-month detention.

Petra was transported back to St David's but in truth she was so far away with the fairies she had no idea what was happening, where she was going or why.

viii The Oak Tree

The word "*mast*" in relation to The Oak Tree is that used to describe the fruit of forest trees that produce fruits. A *mast year* is when these fruits have bumper crops and produce more than they normally would. Trees such as The Oak fluctuate massively from year to year in the amount of fruit that they produce. In some years they produce no fruit at all but in others they produce exceptional crops — the latter are *mast years*.

The word "*acorn*" is related to the gothic name *Akran* (Petra) which had the sense of "*fruit of the enclosed land*". Earlier versions of the lexeme "*acorn*" are *Akerne* (Evanna) and *Acharn* (Bodhi). The word is applied to the most important forest fruit which is that of the Oak Tree. As Chaucer wrote in C14:

"*achornes of oaks*" (1)

which is related to the proverb

"*mighty oaks with acorns grow.*" (2)

This puts forward the idea that great enterprises may have modest beginnings. It is intended to be an encouragement to persist with small efforts so that they may build to grander ones in time. It is similar to the more modern phrase:

"*a journey of one thousand miles*
begins with a single step." (3)

So far, Evanna The Akerne, Bodhi The Acharn and Petra The Akran have had such bumper crops in what they have achieved in their lives, especially when it comes to their careers and personal lives to some extent.

However, like when the oak does not produce many acorns, if any, meaning there is a famine for all the creatures who dine off them, there were long periods of time for The Akerne, The Acharn and The Akran when there was a famine, or a drought of

305

better times. They all suffered.

Like the nature of The Oak Tree human beings have mast years during which time their achievements, their happiness — their everything is in abundance. At these times smiles are bountiful and are produced in ampleness but there are others when all goes wrong and it feels like a famine or a drought of all good things. During such times all that is grown and produced is stress, unhappiness and problem after difficulty. Not even a smile can be produced.

ix <u>Evanna — The Akerne</u>

Evanna was not coping well. Not only did she feel naked without her warrant card; she felt as if she were a non-person somehow. Her life was *The Police* — now her life was empty. It was nothing. It was useless. She was empty, devoid. She was useless. She was devoid of identity and pride. She was barren of any purpose of being, she was barren of lifeblood. She was absent of quintessence — she was without substance.

The Akerne had been stripped of her uniform which was her armour, which in turn was her essence. In stripping her of that, they had also stripped her of her very skin. The skin being the human body's largest organ. The Akerne had lost her barrier of protection between the outside of her body and the inside. She now had no way to sense pain, touch, pressure or itchiness as her skin was no more. Nor did she have a way of sensing temperature as the dermis, which is the middle layer of skin housing nerves, blood vessels and sweat glands, had gone. The hypodermis, the very deepest layer of skin which is mostly made up of fatty tissue that helps to insulate the body from heat or cold, had been stripped. Therefore, she could regulate nothing. Through this "stripping" of skin Evanna felt depleted of all energy as the storage area for fat, the hypodermis, had been stripped away. The hypodermis also provides padding to cushion internal organs combined with protecting the muscles and bones from injury. In short — Evanna was vulnerable. She disliked being vulnerable.

The Akerne had been stripped to the core. She may as well be dead now for she had no identity.

That year was *not* a mast year for The Akerne.

Evanna had been experiencing the worst possible feelings. She believed that she was slowly going mad. Her head was so full it literally felt as if it would explode. Her ears felt as if a hot iron poker had been pushed inside one ear, then through the brain only to come out the other ear, then being pulled and pushed back and forth. This was causing squeaky rasping sounds. Then there were the faint voices. She could not quite hear what they were saying but they were communicating with her just the same. Her head and ears were so loud they hurt, so in a vain attempt to quieten their clamour she put her hands over her ears. She was also hallucinating. She could make out four distinct shapes that at this time were shrouded in a mist so that she was unable to depict their true nature. However, she was somehow able to appoint each voice an image. Her body shook with huge rushes of adrenaline that whooshed and cursed through it right to the ends of her fingertips and toes. Exercise did not diminish this adrenaline. It only made matters worse as more was produced but none dissipated. Instead, it was only added to. She could not sleep as that was a waste of time.

She began to hit her head with her fists yet cradle it in her hands whilst rocking to and fro. She began to burn herself with cigarettes and cut herself with anything sharp. This was not due to self-loathing but in the hope of expelling some of this adrenaline and noise from her body. But this was only successful for brief periods of time.

She felt energised and manic yet so very depressed all at the same time. She was so depressed she wished to die.

When Evanna went to see the GP, she found it almost impossible to explain what was happening to her. He recommended that she see a psychiatrist whom he knew.

As the Akerne had private medical insurance from her police days she decided to see this psychiatrist, Dr Michael Green. He was apparently a man who would give her the correct diagnoses and medication. She was not keen on seeing any shrink, but she was so scared she didn't feel she had much of an option. She felt distinctly nervous when she went to see Dr Michael Green but went regardless as she needed to be reassured that she was not losing her marbles or indeed already had!

He seemed all right enough. A ginger-haired man with a ginger slug for a moustache. Evanna had a hatred for such moustaches! Dr Green posed her a series of questions which she duly answered as honestly as possible. She neither mentioned the abuse, her hallucinations nor voices because that would have been a step too far for her. Anyway, this was only her first visit and, consequently, the first time she had met Dr Green, so she was not about to divulge such personal information. Near to the end of the consultation he suggested that she may benefit from a stay in his clinic. Evanna was taken aback. No way would she be going into any "nut house" even if it was a private one. Upon saying this, but in politer terms, Dr Green suggested she meet with an ex-police officer who had benefitted from an inpatient stay there. He was a persuasive man, so Evanna found herself consenting to this and agreeing to her phone number being passed onto this Paul person.

Paul was cogent too in his "selling" of the Larkin Clinic. So much so that Evanna considered he had shares in the place! Despite that, she decided to "commit" herself as she did not know what else to do. In truth she felt a bit bulldozed into going in by both Dr Green and Paul but if it helped, then what did it matter? This was possibly a grave mistake, as for the next ten years The Akerne found herself yo-yoing between such institutions, which did not help her at all. Becoming institutionalised was the only outcome.

Needless to say, Evanna's mother was not best pleased about her daughter's decision to go into The Larkin Clinic. Maybe it was through fear of the abuse coming out, for she did not hesitate in vocalising her displeasure, anger and utter disapproval. To Evanna's mother there was no such thing as mental illness, or of any illness for that matter, despite her late husband being a depressive along with other members of his family exhibiting some form of mental health issue.

The day came for Evanna to go in. There was only a short waiting list, so she was "invited" very quickly, too quickly for her liking, as it did not give her the chance to reconsider.

The Larkin Clinic was like a hotel. Evanna spent the first few days completing a recce of the joint. It had large comfortable bedrooms; the beds complete with duvets. Each bedroom had a sizeable en-suite bathroom. The dining room boasted an a la carte menu and waitress service. The kitchen had an actual chef. The only accompaniment missing was a wine list! It had two floors with twenty-five bedrooms in total. There were three therapy rooms each with large windows. By the reception area was a large sweeping staircase leading to Dr Gloria Davison's office-cum-therapy room-cum-healing room. So called as it was aligned and adorned with seemingly every curative crystal and salutary stone conceivable.

The patients were a mixed bag but in the main middle-aged women who treated the clinic as if a sanatorium as opposed to the psychiatric hospital it was. Although Evanna preferred the term "loony bin".

However, during her various inpatient stays at The Larkin Clinic Evanna befriended a handful of people, especially those who were in and out as she herself was. There were the very frail and very young anorexic girls, Zoe and Tamara. They were both nineteen years old who fought off their demons via the control of food and occasional self-harm. Then there were the alcoholics, especially Vicky who became a friend of many years until Vicky, a head injury nurse, sunk her head inside the bottle for good.

Together with Vicky there was Abigail with her mass of long black frizzy hair a la Amy Winehouse. Abigail, who was in her late twenties, was a severe anorexic. Together, the trio were firm friends until Abigail broke it when she died. The months leading up to her death were horrific. She had been discharged from the clinic as her funding had run out. Professionals attempted to section her but for some reason they weren't able to do so but Abigail did know the "right" things to say in order to keep herself out of hospital, but it was all lies. She was fiercely intelligent. The last time Evanna saw her she was so very, very, thin, emaciated. Her whole body including her face was skeletal apart from the sides of her neck that literally looked as if you could pick her up from the large handle-like shapes which had formed there because of to the swelling of her lymph nodes. Abigail looked grotesque with her pallid skin and her piercing green eyes that were now popping out of their sockets. She talked of suicide relentlessly having failed several times previously. The next time she tried, only a few days later, she succeeded. She was found in her car, a yellow Suzuki jeep, her corpse bathed in vomit and spittle.

There was Belinda, also an alcoholic, who had been procured by a paedophile ring as a child. She was on the London news after an air ambulance had picked up her broken yet still breathing body from a motorway having jumped from an overhead bridge. How she survived that "fall" was a miracle in itself.

Miles was a middle-aged man with chronic depression. He had been on antidepressants for such a long time that his kidneys were near to failure, so he had to come off them. He fared "better" than Belinda as his "fall" was fatal. He jumped from an overhead bridge under which was a railway line. He jumped in the path of an oncoming train which tore his body apart.

Tamara was a highly bred woman in her early thirties, but she completely rebelled against this breeding. A drug addict and alcoholic as well as being ever so slightly scary with her oft violent foul-mouthed tirades. However, Evanna warmed to her; consequently, the two formed a bond. Tamara overdosed on a concoction of drugs but mainly heroin. No one knew whether her death was accidental or otherwise, but her previous attempts were numerous in number.

Evanna's main friendships were that of Janice, Tom and Susan who she remained friends with for a long time.

Janice was addicted to exercise and suffered from bulimia. She was married to Richard, Rich, and had three young children. Tom Summers owned his own construction company and had ideations of shooting his religious parents with a game gun, a specialised rifle. The four of them, including Rich and Evanna, spent a great deal of time together between admissions. Susan, or Lady Perch as was her official title, was very depressed but such a lovely, funny lady. She lived in a large country estate in East

Sussex with her husband, Lord Perch, and their daughter. Evanna used to visit from time to time until Susan died of complications after an operation.

Finally, there was Sariah, a very quiet Muslim girl of twenty-one. Evanna was not particularly a friend of hers but there was something very endearing about her which made Evanna want to give her a very large hug, but she was never given the chance. Sariah apparently went absent without leave from the clinic, but it took several hours for this to be noticed by staff as she was always so quiet. In reality she had hanged herself in the wardrobe of her bedroom which was on the second floor. No one bothered to look for her there until when, forty-eight hours later, it was decided that the room should be packed of all her belongings so as to make her bed available for another unfortunate soul. There she was found in hanging in the wardrobe with a noose around her neck.

There were a handful of celebrities, some minor, others high profile from lords and ladies to television personalities to pop idols. The only person who treated these people differently was Dr Davison, Gloria, in her obvious favouritism of them.

Gloria was a large buxom woman whose presence was felt from miles away. She liked to think that she floated along her *"corridors of power"* and into rooms with her long flowing dresses and caftans. Gloria had an uncanny knack of making her patients reliant upon her, as if they could not do anything without consulting her first. She also had the "gift" of saying some excessively nasty things to patients, even telling one to *"fuck off"* in the middle of a therapy group but forgiveness was swift as she backed it up by saying: *"That is said with love."* Evanna knew that it was not said with any love. In her opinion, Gloria was simply a bitch who lorded it over her patients, who made her rich,

312

making them feel small and insignificant in comparison to her. Gloria favoured the celebrity, high profile patients whose money would never run out. They became her favourite pets whereas the rest were mere strays. Dr Davison considered herself a spiritual healer of some sort. The practical Evanna did not believe in such humbug but did not judge those who did. She did, however, judge Gloria who proclaimed to be healing her clients who were roped in hook, line and sinker. She also practised crystal healing. "Donning" her police hat, Evanna thought that Gloria was guilty of Obtaining a Pecuniary Advantage by Deception. Gloria disliked Evanna, but this feeling was mutual, probably owing to the fact that she realised that Evanna was not taken in by her fraudulent actions. No one ever dared disagree with Gloria, not even Dr Green her business partner, but Evanna would.

The nurses were okay but Evanna's favourite, indeed everyone's favourite, was Mary, an Irish nurse who took the time to talk and to listen to patients. The problem was that Evanna became too dependent upon her. They were of similar age and may well have been friends under differing circumstances.

Timothy was her psychologist. He was a very quietly spoken, rotund Irish man. He was supposed to be a senior therapist but Evanna found him ineffectual.

Evanna self-harmed quite badly. Her arms were laden with cuts and cigarette burns. Because of this she had a 1:1 whereby a nurse was with her 24/7 who stuck to her like glue — she was followed everywhere she went — literally everywhere. However, when this proved not to work, she was moved into the constant observation room. There were three such rooms in a row, by the nurses' station, which were glass fronted without curtain or blinds. Everyone could see in. When she needed to use the toilet, she had to be accompanied by a staff member. Humiliation personified. Dr Green also threatened to send her to a locked ward several miles away but thankfully that never transpired.

Evanna considered Dr Michael Green a money-grabbing charlatan; plus, he was "*slimy*". He was more about keeping the middle-aged housewives happy so that they would book in for the next school holiday.

He diagnosed Evanna with bipolar with mixed episodes for which he prescribed the appropriate medication which left Evanna feeling like a zombie. Bipolar with mixed episodes summed Evanna up. She reluctantly agreed with this diagnosis. These mixed episodes, or mixed states, are when symptoms of depression and mania or hypermania are experienced at the same time or quickly one after the other. Evanna suffered with them occurring at the same time. It can be particularly difficult to cope with and it can be very hard to work out what you are feeling. It can, therefore, be harder to identify what help you need. It might feel even more challenging and exhausting to manage emotions as it is more likely for suicidal thoughts and feelings to be acted on. Psychotic symptoms can also be present: delusions, paranoia and hallucinations, both auditory and visual. Evanna's mixed episodes definitely fitted this description. She was dangerous to herself in regard to her self-harm and could be said to be unpredictable and impulsive. She found these episodes so desperately hard to explain.

With her mania came the paranoia and the shadows, the voices and visual ghost-like figures who she believed followed her everywhere. There was no escape. Her fears amplified when in large groups as she believed that everyone was against her. These people were drawn into her web of paranoia and delusion. With the mania came paranoia, The Shadows, the thought of being stalked. Evanna's actions and thoughts were interfered with by "the others" — the Four Horsemen of the Apocalypse and Beelzebub or Satan.

The Four Horsemen of the Apocalypse come from the Book of *Revelation* in the New Testament (1). This is a story regarding a book or a scroll in God's right hand that is sealed with seven seals. The Lamb of God opens the first four of the seven seals which summons four beings that ride on white, red, black and pale horses. The four riders symbolise: conquest or pestilence, war, famine and death. The Christian apocalyptic vision is that these four horsemen are set to bestow a divine apocalypse upon the world as harbingers of the Last Judgement. The Four are important as they are associated with creation on the earth in the Book of Revelation.

The White Horse is for conquest or pestilence. The rider carries a bow and wears a victor's crown. Some believe it is Christ himself or even the Holy Spirit. Others are of the opinion that the rider is the antichrist. This horse and his rider symbolise war but of the "just" variety yet still a devastating one all the same. They can also symbolise pestilence, infectious diseases, plague and famine.

The Red Horse symbolises war and mass slaughter. The rider is in possession of a great sword which suggests that blood is to be spilled. His sword is held upwards in a declaration of war as they enter into battle, perhaps.

The Black Horse and its rider denote famine. The rider carries a set of weighing scales symbolising the bread that is weighed out, but now there is a famine. Or the scales could symbolise justice, which would suit Evanna, meaning the rider is a lord and a law maker. This rider is the only one that is accompanied by a vocal pronunciation. John, the author, hears a voice that speaks of the prices of wheat and barley, so his famine is to drive up the price of grain but leave oil and wine unaffected, meaning abundance for the wealthy whereas the staples for the poor run scarce.

The Pale Horse and rider represent death. The personification of Death. They are followed by Hades, the resting place of the dead. The pale colour represents the sticky pallor of the corpse perhaps.

This ties in with Evanna's other delusional thought. That of "*quintessence*".

The fifth and highest element in ancient and medieval philosophy that permeates all nature is also the substance composing celestial bodies. It is the *essence* of "something" in its purest and most concentrated form. Long ago people believed that the earth was made up of four elements: earth, air, fire and water. They thought the stars and planets were made up of yet another element. In the Middle Ages, people called this element by its Medieval Latin name "*quinta essentia*" which literally means "*fifth essence*". Our forebears believed the "*quinta essentia*" was essential to all kinds of matter and if they could somehow isolate this, it would cure all disease. We have since given up on that idea, but we kept "*quintessence*" which is the offspring of "*quinta essentia*" as a word for the purest essence of a thing. Some modern physicists have given a new twist as they use it for a form of so-called "*dark energy*" which is believed to make up 70% of the universe.

Thus, the Horsemen, particularly the White Horse of pestilence and the Pale of Death had some significance to Evanna, together with "*quinta essentia*" or "*quintessence*" as she was the one to cure all disease, infectious or otherwise, but would have to die in order to make it so. Evanna was the "*purest*" form who could cure all disease as Christ was the Pure One who forgave our trespasses in death. Attending a Catholic school did not help with such delusions.

Evanna had several long stays at The Larkin Clinic. None of which helped and much to her horror she found that she became dependent on the place.

Finally, her private medical insurance ran out in the middle of a lengthy stay. She was informed of this fact by Dr Green, and that she would be transported, as if cattle, to an NHS psychiatric hospital. His tone was very matter of fact and uncaring. But she was of no use to him now that her money had run out. The Akerne did not want to go into an NHS hospital. This was not out of snobbery; it was out of fear. She had no choice in the matter, though, as she was quickly put under Section Three of the Mental Health Act because of being a risk to herself, which was in regard to her severe self-harm and suicidal ideation.

On the way to Beech Ward, via hospital transport, The Akerne was feeling extremely apprehensive as she had no idea what to expect.

As she was being shown to her bed space, and it was a space as her bed was in a bay of four others, she could only but notice how dark the ward was. This was due to the darkish green walls, a dark threadbare carpet and very poor strip lighting. There were no windows in this "communal" area. What reminded Evanna of a 400m athletic running track circled this part hugging the walls. At the very centre, the field sport area if you like, was a large glass-panelled room, again dark, which was the smoking room. Wards consisting of four bedded bays and the odd office led off from the track. There were windows, two large ones in each bay, but they all had a dark film on their outside to keep out prying eyes. These windows only opened a crack, to keep the "*lunatics*" in but also meant that natural light and fresh air were kept out.

After having her prohibited belongings confiscated, lest she harm herself, and those she was allowed to keep catalogued, Evanna headed for the smoking room which was one hazy mass of cigarette-polluted air. The room was full of silent patients yet the "*noise*" from within was deafening.

As this was Olympic year, she hoped that she would be able to watch this on the television to pass away the time.

The only group on offer was the weekly psychology group which Evanna attended in order to relieve her boredom. During one such group, which Dr Ruth Shearer presided over, Evanna disclosed that she had been sexually abused as a child. It was relevant to the conversation and that was all she said. Afterwards, Dr Shearer kept Evanna behind who then imparted more of her history as an abused child and indeed as an adult. She felt relieved that finally she had told of this horrific tale to someone who believed her. A few days later during her mother's daily visit, which Evanna dreaded as despite her mother wrapping an arm around her daughter's shoulder in a seemingly caring fashion she was also whispering abhorrent things in Evanna's ear about how she should pull herself together, about how she was letting everyone down, about how stupid she was... Dr Shearer then approached them on the bench they were seated on in the garden, it being a hot sunny day. However, what Evanna really wanted to do was to watch the 400m race on the television. Dr Shearer proceeded to talk about Evanna's abuse which Evanna had thought confidential. She went into no detail but there was enough said. The doctor then suggested to her mother that she come in for a family meeting, which she readily agreed to do. Evanna was not asked or consulted about this whatsoever. Dr Shearer then strode off leaving Evanna in the clutches of her mother which was not a pleasant place to be in as an onslaught of wrath was directed towards her regarding how "*abhorrent*", "*repulsive*", "*shameful*" and revolting she was for talking about this.

The day of the family meeting came around quickly. Too quickly as far as Evanna was concerned. She was of the view that it would just be herself, her mother and Dr Shearer. How wrong she was as when she entered the room there stood, as there were only three seats in the small room, her trusty social worker, several nurses and Dr Carthagaser. Her mother and Dr Shearer were seated. The vacant seat was reserved for her, it seemed. The look of vengeance upon her mother's face struck Evanna in the heart.

The conversation, with Dr Shearer as chairperson, concentrated on her happier times as a child initially but if she said "*on that day I wore a red sweater*", her mother would contradict her and say it was blue. Thus, the conversation went. The inevitable subject of the abuse reared its ugly head. Her mother said of her daughter that she was deluded, cruel and a liar. No one listened to what Evanna had to say. At the fruition of the hour-long debacle, Evanna left the room presuming her mother would follow; instead, she remained seated. Evanna never did know what else was discussed but her social worker suddenly passed her on to someone else and no one ever mentioned the abuse she had suffered and endured to her again. Her mother was even more deranged in her behaviour towards Evanna during every visit from then on. So much so that she was asked to leave the ward, on several occasions, by nursing staff as she was causing upset to both Evanna and the other patients.

For several weeks after that meeting, Evanna's mixed episodes grew intolerable. One day she requested some PRN medication (taken when needed) but when she was merely given a child's picture, taken from a colouring book, of Cinderella to colour in instead the nurse could not understand Evanna's extreme disquiet. Not only did she detest art, which nursing staff knew, she found it demeaning to be given such a thing to colour in.

Evanna was also prescribed ECT. Electroconvulsive therapy is a procedure, done under general anaesthesia, in which small electric currents are passed through the brain, intentionally triggering a brief seizure. It is supposed to cause changes in brain chemistry that can reverse symptoms of certain mental health conditions. Being on a Section 3, Evanna had no choice but to go through the 24 sessions of this, which she found traumatic. They only induced bad headaches and short term memory loss – no sign of any improvement in her mental health. In short, she found it barbaric. However, several years later she was to undergo this treatment once more under similar circumstances – again, proving no positive result.

Some good things did come out of this stay. She met two great friends, Cilla who also had bipolar and Belinda who was physically disabled as well as having a personality disorder. These wonderful people continued to be friends of Evanna for the years to come.

When she was not in hospital during those years, Evanna was sometimes referred to the mental health crisis team as she had become unwell but not considered ill enough to be in hospital. She detested these people as they all spoke down to her and sometimes, they simply missed appointments without so much as an apology. She was, however, relieved not to be in hospital. She also went on holiday to Spain. Janice had mentioned that Dr Gloria Davison was holding a week-long spiritual healing week in that country. This was not strictly

Evanna's cup of tea, but it was in Spain, by the sea, and the place had a swimming pool. So, she decided to go although in place of Janice, would be her husband Rich. Janice, however, joined Evanna and a mutual friend, Ollie, in Spain the week prior for a holiday. It was not a good week for Evanna as she realised, she had little in common with either friend.

Evanna had known Rich for a few years but during the spiritual healing week they became inseparable. So much so that they were accused of having an affair which they were not. That came about later when they got home! During that week Evanna only had eyes for one person and one person only, Roisin, a famous pop star. But that was not why Evanna had eyes for her as she found Roisin a beautiful soul inside and out. As it happened Roisin also had eyes for Evanna. They consummated their "liking" for each other which continued for a year, but on a "friends with benefits" premise. They did not part in any way incriminatory — the "affair" had merely run its course.

Evanna had quite an appetite for sex but she fell in love too easily, which was her downfall. She had many "friends" with said "benefits" who certainly pleasured her but knowing that they did not want a full-on relationship only caused her heartbreak. Apart from Rich, who she did not want a proper relationship with, her lovers were all women.

However, there were two who did want a relationship, more's the pity! One was a fiery Italian who moved in on their first date and another who turned out to be a dominatrix of sorts, which Evanna was not averse to. Indeed, she quite enjoyed being the submissive for a change and actually found the cat o' nine tails, the rulers, paddles, clit and nipple clamps highly arousing. In the end, though, she had enough and both relationships ran their course and came to an end, which was Evanna's choice.

Evanna continued to struggle with her bipolar but she did manage to stay out of hospital for a few years after 2012. She was unable to work because of the copious amount of medication she was still taking, despite it being cut down somewhat.

x **Bodhi — The Acharn**

"To die to grow, to grow perhaps to flourish — yes in this growth in death how one flourishes."
(Bodhi)

One by one they slid down the back of his throat as if a sweet. But then, suddenly, he stopped as images of death and dying shadowed his mind. Would he really flourish in death? Would he actually grow in his passing into the afterlife? Was now his time to put this to the test? Of the latter he was uncertain, to the former two he was certain that the answer was to the affirmative. But they had to be so for all three of these questions. Thus, Bodhi relinquished his tools of medication and vodka, hiding them away for when the answer to the last question posed fell in line with the first two.

Lying on his bed, the Acharn shut his eyes and saw his oak tree still standing tall and proud. Today, it was sheltering some poor souls who had run afoul of King Henry VIII. There they were huddled in its lofty branches silently praying. Praying they would not be found as otherwise it would mean a certain hanging or beheading. Praying that their beloved families were safely en route to their safe houses where they would eventually be reunited. Bodhi pondered over the plight of these brave "outlaws" whose only crime was to speak against the king. They thought of their families first by arranging safe places for them to dwell prior to preparing their own flight from Henry and his soldiers.

Bodhi then thought of Amelia, his dear friend, and her zest and vitality for life despite her struggles and sorrows.

Now was not the time to allow "*the King*" to find him and commit him to a painful end. Now was not the time to flee. But now was the time to remain and try.

On some days the Acharn could not get out of bed. On others he struggled to. Physically he felt weakened. Mentally he felt destroyed.

He slowly began to set daily goals for himself with the unfailing help of the ever-patient Stephanie. In the short term, his goals were literally to get out of bed, attend to his personal hygiene, get dressed, ensure he ate healthy food little but often and drink plenty of water. His long-term goal was to return to work but at that moment he was unable to think of that. First things first, step by step he began to put one foot forward with the other close behind. On some days he was only able to take one step backwards, on others he sidestepped but slowly and surely, he began to breathe more freely.

Amelia was never far from his mind. He was unable to accept the fact that she was dead. However, in death she would undoubtedly flourish and grow. One day he would see her again.

Soon he would be ready to look for work after almost one year of languishing. But he was not just dolorous. Bodhi took up his studies once more, which he had neglected, but as he was so far ahead there was little cause to worry. He had finished his BA (Hons) in the humanities, achieving a 2:1, and had embarked on a master's degree in classical studies which he completed and passed three years later.

He also began to run again, which enabled his body to feel strong and his mind to feel restored. Running made him feel truly free and alive. He preferred to run across the fields and along the canal towpath, close to nature, just as the sun was rising in his part of the world in which the wildlife was just beginning to stir and preparing to welcome in the day. He embraced the elements: the mud, the frost, the puddles, the wind, the rain and sun — sometimes even the moon. This was freedom. He alone was in charge of which direction he would take, how long he would run for, where he sprinted, where he would stop and watch the rising ball of fire in the sky.

Bodhi began to believe that he was on the right path both physically and spiritually. He also believed, that no matter how hard his downtimes were, they were a necessary part of his journey to his ultimate goal of enlightenment and awakening. He was only too aware that this would not just come to him as he needed to work both for it and at it. He was ignorant as to what form this would come in or indeed when, but he had to believe that it would come eventually.

Having researched Buddhist beliefs, the Acharn had a small piece of knowledge about how his form of "Nirvana" — his Ataraxia — may be reached. He understood, though, that the different "sects" of the religion had varying paths that one ought to follow. He would be the first to admit, however, that his knowledge was indeed limited, maybe even misunderstood.

Bodhi's "ambition" lay in his own version of his enlightenment and his awakening which he believed was to be achieved by using certain precepts from Buddhism combined with elements from other traditions. This was not to decry the Buddhist religion. He knew there was a meaning to his life for everything that had and would happen, the good and the bad, so he searched for it in everything he did. Bodhi chose to reassert his knowledge of certain Buddhist principles that he had previously read. It must be added that although it may seem as if he was picking and choosing his way through these, it simply was not the case. This was a hard journey for him, and he was aware he may never attain his goal. Bodhi had a deep interest in religion as a whole, because of his upbringing. He took aspects from various ones which he believed applied to him as he felt that amidst this minefield called "Religion" there must be parts, in each individual one, that applied to him and others not so much. It was not merely the easy parts that he kept for himself.

First, Bodhi needed to reacquaint himself with the Four Stages of Enlightenment which are the progressive stages that culminate in full enlightenment as an Arahant. These are held in Theravada and early Buddhist beliefs. An Arahant is one who has gained insight into the true nature of existence and through that has achieved Nirvana.

He recalled that these four stages are called *Sotapanna, Sakagami, Anagami* and *Arahant,* but as he was unable to remember them in detail, he took each one in turn. *Sotapanna* otherwise means "stream enterer". To attain this phase one has to be free from the belief that there is an unchanging self or soul. *Sakadagamin* means "once returner" which entails the abating of one's sensual desire and ill will. *Anagami*, or "non-returner", means that one's sensual desire and ill will must be completely abated. One must be totally free of both. Within these stages one also has to learn to be free from an attachment to rites, rituals and any doubt about the teachings. Finally, the fourth stage is, when ones becomes an *Arahant* who is free from the aforementioned but also from conceit, restlessness and ignorance and upon death will never be reborn in any plane or world, having wholly escaped *Samsara*, the cycle or repeated birth known as "The Wheel of Suffering". An Arahant has attained awakening by following the path given by the Buddha. In Theravada Buddhism the term Buddha is reserved for ones who "self-enlighten" such as Siddhartha who discovered the path by himself. This was key for Bodhi.

The Theravada tradition teaches that progress in understanding comes all at once and that "insight" does not come gradually. Each of the four paths is attained suddenly, followed by the realisation of the fruit of the path. The Sutras, however, view this differently as the paths have a gradual development. An ordinary entity has never experienced the ultimate truth of *Dharma,* cosmic law and order, so therefore has no way of finding an end to his predicament of being trapped in the endless cycle of Samsara whereby the endless rebirths can be of any form: human, animal, male, female, neuter, ghost or even a being from hell.

The Acharn then chose to refresh his memory regarding the Noble Eightfold Path to liberation which takes the form of Nirvana. Bodhi remembered most of its concepts but still continued to read and digest them lest he misunderstood.

The first path is known as *"Right View"* which concerns our actions because they have consequences. This includes karma and rebirth and the importance of the Four Noble Truths when "insight" becomes central to the Buddhist. Karma means that every action has consequences, karmic results, influencing the future rebirths and the realms a being enters.

The second path, *"Right Resolve/Intention"* intends that the believer give up their home whilst adopting the life of a religious mendicant in order to follow the path successfully. It aims at peaceful renunciation into an environment of non-sensuality and non-ill will which is far removed from entering loving kindness away from cruelty into compassion. This will aid the contemplation of impermanence, suffering and non-self.

The third path, "*Right Speech*", involves no lying, no rude speech and no gossip because these lead to discord and harm. The fourth path is "*Right Conduct and Right Action*" which means one needs to refrain from killing, stealing and sexual misconduct. The fifth path is "*Right Livelihood*" whereby one's living should benefit that of others. One should not sell weapons, poisons or intoxicants. "*Right Effort*" is path number six which entails the prevention of the arising of unwholesome states whilst generating wholesome ones.

The seventh path is "*Right Mindfulness*" whereby the retention and mindfulness of the *Dhammas*, which are the Buddhist teachings, is primary. One should never be absent-minded but be conscious of everything you do. It encourages the awareness of the impermanence of body, feelings and mind. The final path, "*Right Samadhi*" means one must find a oneness with meditation, which has a path all of its own.

Obviously, these are the simplest of explanations, but this was sufficient for Bodhi who did not wish to follow Buddhism to the letter, just as he did not want to follow Judaism or Christianity, with their doctrines and dogmas, to their entirety either.

The Acharn was keen to self-enlighten. He was not so conceited or pontifical so as to believe he would become the next Buddha, prophet or messiah. He did not have such vainglory. But just as Buddha did, presumably to suit his own beliefs and requirements, Bodhi wanted his Nirvana, his Ataraxia, to form from his own self enlightenment as Buddha Siddhartha Gautana did. Bodhi wanted to create his own path.

On talking it over with the wonderful Stephanie, Bodhi decided that it was now time to take the plunge and begin job hunting. He updated his CV, calling that past year a "*study year*" which wasn't a complete untruth as he had been writing a dissertation and revising for his final exams.

He wanted to return to work in a school as that was where he felt his skill set lay. Also, he was grateful for the school holidays and a 15 30 hr finish although he often worked overtime but that was his choice. The money wasn't up to much but what was more important to him than financial gain was supporting others, which was reward enough. He did not wish to return to a mainstream school but was mindful of the fact that he did not enjoy working at Hawker School, but that was more to do with the staff than the students. He signed onto various recruitment agencies online in the hope of finding the perfect role. Out of nowhere — there it was! A teaching assistant post at a school for pupils aged between three and nineteen with severe and complex learning difficulties, called Orchard Grove. He had no experience with such children but that wasn't a requirement, but fun and loving laughter was. He could do that! Dedication and willingness to do personal care for the students were also requirements alongside being able to work independently and as part of a team. Yes, he was certainly dedicated to whatever he put his mind to. Okay, he was a depressive but throughout he was able to keep his wry sense of humour and wit. Most were unable to tell he was depressed or anxious as he had the ability, the majority of the time when with other people, to keep it well hidden. He could cope with attending to personal care and he was more than capable of working on his own as well as with others as he was a good team player.

After completing and sending off the lengthy application form, he waited anxiously to see if he had got an interview. A long week later he had the invitation to attend an interview which would have three parts: an assessment within the classroom; a written exercise and the formal interview with the head and deputy headteachers.

The following week, Bodhi sat at his computer researching profound and multiple learning difficulties committing everything he read to memory. He scrutinised the school website with its various policies and read his CV and application form over and over again so that whatever he said matched what he had written. He also thought of answers to every conceivable question they could possibly pose. He could do no more.

Orchard Grove was where Bodhi began to realise that he was and had been taking real steps towards his enlightenment and awakening, for to him they were different ideas. To Bodhi, Enlightenment was to obtain wisdom, edification and knowledge whereas Awakening was vivification, a revival, a stimulation and resurgence.

The school could easily have been a depressing establishment given the nature of the children's most severe disabilities and conditions which were often progressive and life limiting. But every child was celebrated in their own right and in death. Sadly, deaths did occur, but those little lives were exalted. This proved to have a very marked and humbling effect on the Acharn because the individual lives that were celebrated were, on the whole, happy lives. This was all despite the children's pain; despite the obvious frustrations of some; despite having to wear pads at the age of nineteen; despite their varying challenges and difficulties. There was an innocence about these children and young people. Yes, sometimes they were violent, as Bodhi could attest to, but that was born out of frustration not out of hatred. Because of that Bodhi learned the art of patience, non-judgement and forgiveness. He learned humility and the power of unconditional love as that was what was felt within the walls of

Orchard Grove.

At times he felt he was at utter peace with the world when with these magnificent children, especially whilst doing hydrotherapy on a 1:1 basis. He compared this experience to the feelings he gained when he swam with dolphins — magical, peaceful and humbling.

He learned from other members of staff, those he looked up to, such as the forever outwardly calm and patient Siria. One would only be able to tell that her patience was waning when her eyebrows rose up to the very top of her forehead despite her calm speech and posture. This was normally to do with the class teacher, rather than the pupils! If you should need help, of any nature, you went to Siria who was a guiding light. What Doreen lacked in patience she more than made up for in her practicality. She had an ability to get everyone on task, both students and staff. Doreen was a docent.

The staff took a battering from some students, in some form, every single day. They were bitten, kicked, spat at. They had sharp fingernails attack their skin; they had their hair pulled and they were pushed. Most of this was considered low level which is where humility and patience rose to the fore. The students, who shone as bright as diamonds, were mostly innocence personified, even the most violent for they did not realise what they were doing was wrong and they often had no other way of communicating their upset or frustration.

In his final years at Orchard Grove Bodhi worked with the sixteen to nineteen-year-olds in Post-16. He was fortunate to work alongside both Siria and Doreen, who also became his firm friends. During these years he experienced some events which had a profound effect upon him.

First, there was Johnny, an 18-year-old young man with non-verbal autism. He had such a handsome face and an endearing personality, but he easily grew unslaked, thus leading to rather an extreme explosion of violence at which point it often took at least four members of staff to restrain him, within the appropriate guidelines, training and legality, of course. Within a relatively short timeframe, Bodhi was subjected to Johnny's unsated behaviour which flared into wrath. On the first occasion he bit Bodhi's thumb so hard he broke it. On the next he put his hands around Bodhi's throat, semi-strangling him, bringing him to the floor. The aftermath of this incident was whiplash and a torn trapezius muscle (Bodhi's, of course!). The third and final time he repeatedly hit Bodhi's head off a brick wall after which Bodhi began to suffer with extreme dizziness which lasted for up to two weeks at a time and was so debilitating all he could do was lie down. At such times he was unable to work or do anything much at all.

Bodhi learned, via Siria, to have a calm yet firm voice at all times no matter the situation and not to react in a defensive manner which could frighten the student and frustrate them further. Bodhi managed to contain the pain he was being put through. Even whilst Johnny was putting him through a great deal of pain he continued to speak to Johnny with a light, calm and reposeful air whilst inside he felt fearful, roused and in such pain. Calm exterior, unquiet interior. This was when Bodhi learned the strength of forgiveness; the power of unconditional love and the potency of being pacific.

Matthew had a truly beautiful spirit — he was a truly beautiful boy — well, a 6ft 2, sixteen-year-old. He was also a non-verbal autistic lad. He wore pads and a pair of ear defenders as he was extremely sensitive to noise. Matthew was incapable of hurting anyone except himself, which is why, perhaps, the

Acharn had a great affinity with him. Bodhi, well everyone, noticed a severe decline in Matthew's demeanour. He had always been such a happy cheeky lad but all of a sudden in his seventeenth year his distress became palpable, but he was unable to communicate the reason why. His reddened cheeks had scabs all over them due to his constant slapping of them with his big shovel-like hands to go with his tall lanky frame. He cried, he rocked, he became antisocial and hid himself under blankets in quiet corners. Bodhi formed a very strong connection with Matthew spending day after day in a quiet room holding his hand as that's all that the boy wanted to do. Many a tear was shed, not just Matthew's but Bodhi's too and all of the staff that worked with him as they felt so helpless. They hated to see this awesome boy in so much pain. This is where Bodhi learned humility. After nearly one year of this, a place was found for Matthew in a specialised residential placement which upon inspection was wonderful. Bodhi and the Deputy Head drove Matthew there; it was quite some distance away. They had been preparing him for this transition for some time; as a result, he was calm in the car, simply holding Bodhi's hand as they were sat on the back seat. When it was time for Bodhi to leave Matthew in the hands of the lovely staff in his new home, he told Matthew goodbye. The boy then leant forward from his chair and kissed Bodhi on the cheek. An act Bodhi never recalled seeing him do before. Bodhi held back his tears until he turned his back on the way to the door. He could not look back. On the way home, Bodhi thought about how Matthew had this power inside him. The boy "knew" so much. He "knew" a person as his eyes saw through to their inner soul, it seemed. Unconditional love channelled through Bodhi and Matthew in their holding of hands like electricity flowing through power lines. They had such a deep connection. No conversation could ever be verbalised between them as the boy was non-verbal, yet their conversation was deep and continual. He was just the most beautiful, powerful boy with the most pure, powerful and beautiful soul.

Bodhi would never be completely free from his depression, but it still came as a surprise to him when it hit again. It began with paranoia, with certain people being "against" him — mainly strangers in the street and the odd friend or acquaintance. This led to hallucinations which fed the paranoia. But mostly he was lost in the darkest, bleakest forest whose trees blocked out the sunlight so he could never find his way out. He just walked and ran and walked and ran in circles only to find himself back where he started.

One of the teaching assistants, Lou, who Bodhi worked closely with, approached him one day in the smoking shelter to see if he was okay. As no one had asked such a question of him before he was taken aback with tears pricking at his eyes. All he could do was say *"yes, I'm fine"* before the tears broke the dam of his lower eyelids only to come streaming down his cheeks. After a brief conversation, before others made their way to this "den of iniquity" Lou gave him her mobile phone number offering to be an ear and a shoulder. She told him to call her that evening.

It took no little courage for Bodhi to press the numbers on the keypad to his phone, even hoping that the call would go straight to voicemail. It did not. Lou answered. The two were on the phone for several hours that evening sharing their feelings, thoughts, fears and stories. After this they became good friends. Lou was a person Bodhi knew he could trust, so he had no qualms in telling her of his hallucinations and paranoia. Sometimes he would text her these as she had asked him to. Thus, it came as a huge shock and caused Bodhi no little upset and confusion when, in his eyes, Lou betrayed him.

Lou suggested they tell the Headteacher, Mona, that he was unwell and perhaps needed some extra support. Mona was indeed supportive. One day, after Bodhi had not slept one single wink for six consecutive nights, he was certain that he should offer Mona his resignation, which he did. This was obviously out of the blue and out of character. Mona accepted his resignation because, as she told him, he would be able to get help and support if he were not working, which his GP had told him weeks previously, but this was not a motive for his resignation. Indeed, he lacked such a motive. As a result, when Bodhi returned home, he sought out as many medications as he could and some vodka, his suicide drink of choice, and took them to bed.

He woke up in a hospital bed. His mother had found him at home unconscious. The mental health team, thought it best that he go into a psychiatric hospital in order that he recover and be kept safe. However, he was not sectioned as he agreed to go in voluntarily. The ward was stark but as the ward manager had made the ward staff move to a smaller office, too small to have "mothers' meetings" all day, they were actually out on the "floor" interacting with the patients. On the hour, every hour, from 0800 hrs to 2200 hrs, patients were escorted down the iron steps to the garden for a cigarette or as many as they could fit in those ten minutes.

Bodhi was only in there for ten days. Upon his release he made an appointment to see his GP as advised by the doctor on the ward. The GP and Bodhi had a good relationship, so when Bodhi informed him of his resignation the GP stated that Mona should not have accepted it as Bodhi's judgement would have been severely impaired by being mentally unwell. He wrote a letter to that effect to her which was not graciously received! However, a meeting was called, which despite involving occupational health would be very "*a brief informal discussion about their next steps*". It was highlighted that Bodhi need not bring a representative or friend because of its informality. However, he came out of that meeting feeling battered and bruised.

A few weeks later, when he had not received the report from the meeting as requested, he asked for it again. At first, he was given a very brief letter but upon asking for it yet again, what he received was a five-page character assassination. His friend, Lou, had passed over his private text messages he had sent her, hence lay her betrayal, but aside from that the letter was full of lies, conjecture, exaggeration and lacked any context. Fortunately, Bodhi had documentary evidence which proved the lies to be lies, so he wrote his own report refuting these falsehoods including all of the documentary evidence he had. After sending it to everyone he could think of, within two days he received an email from the school informing him that he would be joining the Post-16 team in the new term, after the summer holidays. He also received apologies for every point he raised in his letter and refuted.

When the day came for him to walk through the doors of the school, Bodhi wished he had just left the school quietly as he was extremely nervous as to his reception. As that first week neared its fruition it was as if he had never left. He decided he would stay for that year to prove what courage he had. He also wanted to hold his head high. It wasn't long before Mona went up to him, hugged him, and told him that she had so much respect for him and how she admired his courage! He had little good to say about her, but he accepted this graciously.

The Acharn found himself having to find forgiveness for

both Lou and Mona. Eventually, he found it within himself to do so. This forgiveness enabled Bodhi to keep his head held high and to work aside Lou, as before, with the same banter going back and forth, although Bodhi would never trust her again.

Apart from the practical and theoretical side of his job at Orchard Grove he had to learn how to use a hoist, how to do physiotherapy and hydrotherapy exercises with individual children, have a knowledge of moving and handling, epilepsy, Makaton and such like. But this list was just the bare bones of his "education" there. The Acharn was also learning about himself, spiritually, without even realising it despite changes, no matter how subtle, in his psyche. It was as if the school had "called" him. The job had chosen him. The life lessons and the spiritual lessons he learned had a far greater impact upon him than any lesson he had ever been taught. Bodhi had become a believer of things happening for a reason despite those reasons often being buried so deep it proved hard to unearth them. Bodhi had heretofore been searching for reason upon reason for certain events that had occurred in his life but as yet he lacked the perspicacity. However, finally his mind, body and soul were being awakened and because of that resurgence he was more open to the enlightenment he yearned for. He used the word "resurgence" which is a "revival" because he believed that whilst in the womb all human beings that were due to be born were gifted with awakening and enlightenment but as soon as they left their mother and developed outside the womb this became confused with the world outside the prenatal chamber.

The Acharn never thought that human beings remained static in that they were unchanging. He believed the opposite, that they are constantly changing. As for himself and his soul, the more he worked on himself the more he changed. In so doing it was for his betterment and for the good. Therefore, it could be claimed that his interpretation of the part of the first stage to enlightenment, *Sotapanna,* had, in part, been achieved. He was growing in wisdom and knowledge all the time, therefore changing in the self and the soul. As a result, he was also awakening.

Bodhi had learned the art of forgiveness, although he would concur that some people were easier to forgive than others, but his ill will towards those others had been somewhat attenuated according to *sakadagami.* He realised that in order to move on he had to totally forgive his childhood abuser because he believed him to be unwell, as he figured that no one could be mentally well to commit the heinous acts he had committed. As for his harbouring of ill will towards his mother, this was hard to relinquish as he did not believe her to be unwell, but he considered her to have a cracked moral code and a ruinous mother's love as she did not protect him; indeed, she feigned disbelief. Bodhi postulated that his mother knew only too well about what was happening at the time but as she cared more about *"what the neighbours would say"* she had buried her head deep into quicksand. He had not reached full *Anagami* as far as those two people were concerned but his ill will towards them had abated somewhat. When Johnny first attacked him, he was ashamed to say that he felt some anger towards him, but this anger completely dissolved a short time later. Thus, in terms of Johnny he had achieved full *Anagami.* Bodhi had never been judgemental nor was he the kind of person who elicited ill will against another, apart from those two people just mentioned. As regards sensual desire, it can easily be stated that the Acharn never really possessed any, so he had also achieved *Anagami* there. Thus, he was also close to achieving the second step along the Noble Eightfold Path.

Bodhi was the opposite of conceited; in fact, if anything he was diffident and humble. He had been making great strides in becoming content and at ease with life. As a result, he was growing and learning to live in harmony in his body which was connected somehow to his soul and with the world around him. Ignorant was not a word that could be used of Bodhi either. He was forever attempting and succeeding in bettering himself in mind, body and soul. Bodhi was learning that every action he performed had consequences. He was forming the belief that every action has karmic results even here on earth, such as when he took the overdose which upset and angered those close to him. His action, even if he had been unwell at the time, of resigning caused him untold grief. It may even have led to his suicide attempt. Had he succeeded the karmic results in the next life could have had disastrous consequences. He was aware that "*Right View*" did not just mean this. He had done wrongs to people no matter how small, he was only human, and in so doing karma spun around when others paid him wrongs. So, Bodhi had learned that right actions lead to peace in the mind and soul.

Bodhi was not a liar and he knew that gossiping only led to discord and harm. He believed in supporting others, especially the underdog, whilst attempting to ensure that justice is served. He did not blaspheme — well, not too much. To blaspheme especially when against others meant that he was harbouring resentful, judgemental thoughts and ill will towards others, so he was mindful of this.

He was content that he was along the fourth path of "*Right Conduct/Action*". He knew that right conduct meant favourable karma but that was not the reason that he behaved as he did. He did so because he wanted to help others and live a moral life as that enabled inner peace as opposed to inner turmoil.

Bodhi felt that his livelihood, such as it was, definitely benefitted his students. He also tried to be of some benefit to his colleagues, friends and indeed complete strangers. But he was saddened that he thought that no charitable act was a selfless act, no matter if it was meant that way, because the actor always gained something.

He lived a moral and ethical life. But in no way did he consider himself perfect. Because of those imperfections, which he recognised, the Acharn continually tried to change.

As previously stated, Bodhi did not aspire to become an Arahant, least of all a Buddha, and he was unsure of his beliefs regarding Samsara. His Enlightenment and Awakening would come from within himself combined, admittedly, with some of these Buddhist beliefs. The Acharn aspired to feel unconditional love towards everyone no matter how hard that may be. He wished to offer complete and pure forgiveness.

He became less introspective whilst working at Orchard Grove, developing a stronger compassion and loving kindness towards others.

Through his work he had discovered humility. He found a certain perspective as regards his life and the lives of others. He felt spiritually connected with some of his students, especially Matthew and indeed Johnny. He marvelled at their innocence. These were the true spiritual warriors.

Bodhi felt that although his path would be uneven, rocky even, and he would undoubtedly take a wrong fork from time to time, he was still on the right path to his Enlightenment and Awakening. But was there actually a *wrong* path? He thought not. As long as you found your way back you become the wiser for it. That in itself is an awakening.

"To live, to grow, to grow perhaps to flourish — yes in this growth in life how one flourishes."

xi <u>Petra — The Akran</u>

Petra had found herself *"incarcerated in a lunatic asylum, of all places!"* because Cathryn had left her.

This was to be home for six months, or until they considered her "worthy" of release. As her bipolar had gone through the roof her bipolar medication had been made higher. She had also been put on different antipsychotics and more sedatives. Because of this she had no option but to sleep a lot.

She did not want to sleep, however, because her dreams were only of Cathryn who had still not been in touch. Petra's life had been decimated. She loved Cathryn. She loved the fact that they had been trying to start a family together. That was all she wanted for her life. A family. But now that picture, which had once seemed so possible had since been destroyed.

Whilst she lay in bed, in a drug-induced haze, her thoughts drifted to Cathryn and what might have been but also to the very problematic question as to what would now happen to herself. For example, where would she live? What would happen to Cardi? What about the house? She took the foremost question first. Petra loved the cottage. She did not want to have to leave it but how would she ever afford it and its upkeep on her meagre wages? She didn't want to sell it because it was in negative equity but regardless of that she would not have wanted to part with it. One thing was certain; if she couldn't live in it, then she was not going to allow Cathryn to! But she had no idea how she would ever afford it, so the fear of having to move back into her "parental home" became paramount in her mind which fast led to the questions about her beloved Cardi, who was currently staying with her sister's family whilst she was in hospital. If she should have to move back in with her parents, she would not be able to keep her, plus she knew that Cathryn would want her, despite it being pretty obvious that Cardi "*belonged*" to Petra and that Petra "*belonged*" to Cardi.

After several days, Petra's mobile phone rang — it was Cathryn. Her heart skipped a beat; perhaps she was reneging on her decision to leave; after all she had yet to provide her with a suitable explanation as to why she had left notwithstanding "*The Letter*" which she was unable to recall the detail of apart from the first line:

"*I love you very much but despite that I'm leaving.*"

Sadly, for Petra, Cathryn was sticking to her guns. But what she had to say shredded Petra's heart for she told her that she was now with Jason, who was their next-door neighbour's brother, the one and the same Jason who helped put in their kitchen. Cathryn insisted that nothing had happened between them whilst she was with Petra who did not wish to hear one more word although Cathryn did not appear to have anything more to comment. With that Petra just said: "*Well, I'm keeping the house and I'm keeping Cardi!*" and with that she terminated the call.

Petra was so shocked she had no thoughts for a while. She was just too shocked to think, she merely sat on the edge of her bed shaking her head and wringing her hands. She could not take this information in. It proved impossible for her to process this news, at least for a while. Her immediate thought, as her mind began to thaw, was, "*How did I not see this ?!*" Her second thought was more practical: "*How am I going to afford the house?*" She envisaged Cathryn and Jason both laughing at her as they knew that she did not have the funds.

Slowly, when they finally allowed her to, her thoughts turned more to Cathryn and Jason. What? When? Why? Where? How?

Her mind went to when they had the new kitchen fitted. Nile and Jason had done the work but Cathryn, who made it clear to Petra that she would just get in the way, had helped. So, Petra got supper ready at her "parental home" where they were staying whilst the kitchen was being fitted. She came to the realisation that this was when they must have got together. Had Cathryn forgotten or did she consider Petra that naïve so as to forget that the two of them got together via an affair and that Cathryn had told her then boyfriend that nothing had happened between herself and Petra so as to ease the pain! But that had been a lie!

Petra could only see this as her karma. What goes around comes around. But it did not ease the situation or her feelings which had been completely trampled on and trod deep into the ground.

When Petra's mother came to visit, she found her daughter in the most awful state — one of the worst she could recall having witnessed. The nursing staff eventually injected her with a very heavy sedative but were forced to hold her down in the process because Petra's agitation was well above boiling point. When she had fully calmed, she told her mother about what Cathryn had divulged and for the first time in her life she felt reassured by her mother who simply stated: "*Don't worry, darling.*" She did not know what this meant but decided against asking.

The Akran only "served" half of her "sentence" as she was released after three months having been assessed and considered in sound mind enough to leave hospital. It was only when she returned home to her cottage that Petra discovered what her mother had done for her.

Petra's father had suffered from Alzheimer's disease — well, it was more herself and her mother who were the real sufferers, as whilst her father had never looked so happy in his childish state, it was those two who performed the extremely hard task of caring for him. To be fair, it was more her mother than herself. He died after two long years, but Petra did not shed one single tear. Amidst his illness, Petra's mother had been reunited with an old boyfriend of some forty-five years ago. They ended up getting married shortly after Petra's father had died but sadly her new husband was diagnosed with a terminal illness from which he died eighteen months later. He had left Petra's mother with a substantial amount of money of which she kindly saw fit to put a large amount into the cottage as equity meaning that Petra would be able to afford the monthly mortgage repayments and that Cathryn would not get a look in. Cardi was to remain with Petra without a battle as the new lovers, Cathryn and Jason, did not yet have a permanent home.

So, Petra got her two wishes. The cottage and her dear Cardi. However, this came at a price for from then onwards Petra's mother did not ever let her forget what she had done for her. She made it abundantly clear, at every conceivable opportunity, that she would not be living there had it not been for her money or her goodwill.

Sometimes a price has to be paid — nothing is free.

Petra found living by herself extremely difficult. Although she loved her home and despite having Cardi as her constant companion, there were memories of Cathryn everywhere — in every room. Friends encouraged her to take down photographs of the two of them, but this was not an easy task as Petra was not ready to obliterate Cathryn from her life. However, even with the photos being boxed and stored in the loft, as The Akran could not dispose of them permanently, her mind drew enough pictures of Cathryn even when she least expected it.

She cried most days. Petra missed Cathryn so much. The

343

loneliness was something she found the hardest to tolerate. Cathryn had since ceased any communication since the dissolution and clean break orders had been finalised and signed. However, she was dismayed not to mention angered and deeply hurt when Cathryn cited her for *"unreasonable behaviour"* as a reason for their civil partnership breakdown. Apparently, this was because Petra's initial reaction to Cathryn when she wanted to stop trying for a baby was *"no!"* Petra now suspected the actual reason why Cathryn wished to stop was actually because she was cheating on her with Jason, so therefore, she could not risk becoming pregnant although Petra would have had no legal right over the baby, but Martin would have. The fact that she had been cited for unreasonable behaviour hurt the Akran nearly as much as when Cathryn had left her all those months ago. Even though being told about the affair was a bitter pill to swallow — but *"unreasonable behaviour!"* **NEVER!**

It took a whole three years for Petra to be able to think about Cathryn with ambivalence. During that time every emotion possible from feelings of being bereft, bitter, blue and barren to those emotions of anger, acrimony, animosity, abhorrence and animus. Not only that but The Akran was still dealing with the rapid cycling bipolar whilst using so much energy in keeping herself out of hospital. Despite how it sounds, she was winning, no matter if it did not seem or feel like it but she did not want to live by herself.

As time marched on the days became easier and after three years Petra realised that she was more than capable of living by herself and even found she quite enjoyed her own company. Despite that she still wanted a partner with whom she could share her life with. She knew that the main reason she had survived those awful years was Cardi — the wise wonder dog. However, these three years were complicated somewhat as Cathryn and Jason moved in next door for one whole year which almost killed Petra at first, but she got through it all the same.

She definitely owed some gratitude to surviving the aftermath of Cathryn leaving to two of her dear friends who lived across the road. "Kanga," as she preferred to be known, and her partner Karen. They were a real tonic to Petra as every Friday night as soon as they met, when she and Cathryn first moved into the cottage, was Les Girls night which entailed Petra popping across the road to their house. They put the world to rights whilst drinking wine. This was an open invitation offered by "KnK" to both Cathryn and Petra but when Cathryn decided that Karen's conversation was too heavy and intellectual for her, Petra went on her own. So, after Petra's release from hospital she continued to keep the Les Girls tradition going.

Even though she still felt raw after her split from Cathryn during the second year Petra decided to enter the world of online dating. She virtually met some extremely strange people but out of the mire came Gaby. It was never destined to be a romantic relationship; rather, it was destined to become a very good friendship. Either way, Petra began to find her laugh once more. Slowly but surely, she began to rebuild her friendship base by meeting, in person, one or two more women who also became friends, rather than anything more, but this suited The Akran just fine. As a consequence, Petra's house soon became "The Place to Be" most Friday evenings, which she loved. There was no so-called "lesbian drama" as this group of women were happy being single, apart from KnK; thus, friendship and laughter were their main priorities in this juncture of their lives.

Having said that, Petra did meet Sylvia who not only made her roar with laughter, but so much so she had to clutch her stomach as if hurt through their raucous cachinnation. Sylvia was a glass overflowing kind of person. She was a ball of sunshine in an otherwise relatively dull world. Not only did Petra and Sylvia get along; they also held romantic sparks for one another. Hence a relationship blossomed and bloomed. In hindsight, it was a shame that they met when they did as Petra was still dealing with the remnants of grief after losing Cathryn which was compounded now because her ex-wife had moved in next door with Jason!

Sylvia wore her dark brown hair in a short spiky yet feminine style. She was slightly taller than Petra and sported a slender frame. She shone from the inside out. To this very day, Petra had not met any human being who has a bad word to say about Sylv, not even a tiny one. Anyone who met her, even for the briefest of time, would tell Petra "*what an amazing person*" and they were right. Brilliant not in academia but in her personality. Her rays of light shone out in a crowd whereby she accidently became the centre of attention which she never planned to be. Sylv, who was seven years older than Petra, was living with her parents when they met. They had been dating for a few months when, in true lesbian fashion, because lesbians are notorious for accelerating their relationships at a rate of knots, Petra asked her to move in, which she did.

Petra reminisces upon that time with great fondness as does Sylv. Despite that the fact was that their romantic relationship naturally reached its end two years later. It was not because of arguing or any wrongdoing on either side. Indeed, if you were ever to ask them why their relationship was not destined for greater things, neither would be able to say. There was never a single cross word or even disagreement between them then or when their relationship morphed into the greatest friendship that lasted the test of time. Neither could recall why they broke up, but a friendship organically formed.

Petra had introduced Sylv to the Ship and Anchor, a place dear to her heart but which she had not frequented of late. She had also heard that Susan had moved some distance away so would not be able to go. Apart from having new landladies the pub remained as it had been with a few newer faces. Now back in her singledom, Petra was not afraid to go there on her own as she had met a core of likeminded people who appeared to have taken up residence in the bar area! She attended a New Year's Eve party where she, despite not having anything alcoholic to drink as she was driving, had the very best of times. She even met someone who hadn't been "vetted" via the internet. Somehow this pleased her so much. Petra dated Caz for a short time. This relationship, which ended mutually, boosted her confidence and self-esteem which had taken several knocks.

Petra was certain that everyone she had met in her life she had done so for a reason. Each had taught her valuable lessons in life. For example, she would never have an affair again as it sent her mad! The more recent people she had met had helped her to get over Cathryn although it took almost three years. Finally, all of the upset and anger had been surpassed by joy and calmness; the feelings of resentment and bereavement had dissipated. She now felt nothing towards her ex-wife so could finally move on.

Now, Petra decided it was time to sample the single lifestyle properly and head on. She made a conscious decision to look after herself better, which meant cooking for herself and eating a healthy diet, engaging more in the activities and hobbies she enjoyed such as exercise and writing. Things she could do on her own, but she also needed to make herself go out and be with her friends instead of cancelling which she was prone to do. She did

347

well at this, even to the extent of joining a badminton club. Over time she discovered that she actually enjoyed her own company and did not feel lonely. On the contrary, she felt content — truly so for the first time in years — maybe ever. She remained single for about four years, so when she received a message on a dating app which she had forgotten all about, although ambivalent, she decided to read the message. This was out of pure curiosity as she had no plans whatsoever of dating just yet. When she read the message, it made her laugh out loud as its author certainly had a good sense of humour. Her name was Amy. She was younger than Petra by three years and had super curly ginger locks. Her written profile also made Petra chuckle so much so that she found herself messaging Amy back.

Messaging in this manner on the computer led to exchanging phone numbers and texting. Eventually, Petra took the plunge and called her. The two chatted endlessly about anything and everything. Amy then summoned up the courage to ask to meet her in person which Petra greeted with a definite and certain, "*yes please*". So, a date for one week hence was duly set and their meet up place, Euston train station, was arranged. Sadly, during that week Petra developed a very nasty eczema-looking rash all over her face and neck. It looked so disgusting her friends called her Freddie Kruger from the horror films. There was no way she could meet Amy, for the first time, looking like this, so with a heavy heart she cancelled telling Amy the truth. She even sent her a photograph of her disgusting looking face as she did not want Amy to think she was playing her a merry dance.

Finally, the rain-check day arrived. Petra's face was all clear, so she was good to go. She felt unusually calm for a first date, probably because she had nothing to lose and had no expectations as she was happily single.

Amy had advised Petra that she would be able to recognise her from her *"tiger feet"* and sure enough she did as Amy wore bright orange pumps with black stripes which she noticed when the shoes and their wearer approached her out of the crowd of commuters. Their first date consisted of getting lost whilst finding a bar Amy wanted to go to but when they eventually found it, they had a lovely time sipping on a few cocktails. Whilst sitting outside in the hot August sunshine it was decided that they could do with something to eat. They returned to Euston, finding a table in a restaurant but Amy had a panic attack halfway through their meal, which Petra then wolfed down extremely quickly as she was starving, before they left. When Petra treated Amy to a hot chocolate Amy declared that she had the attack because she really liked Petra but did not know if that feeling was reciprocated. Upon hearing this Petra invited her on a second date. They sat in a comfortable silence as they drank their drinks as the sun was setting.

From then onwards a relationship between them grew.

After Cathryn, Petra believed that her capacity to truly love someone or trust someone again had been blown but now she was realising this not to be the case. She had loved Sylvia but now she understood that this love was the kind reserved for friendship. An enduring platonic love. Her love for Amy was not that of friendship for she loved her in a different sense. Was she *in* love? — of that she was not sure, but what she did know was that she certainly loved Amy and wanted this relationship to work. It was possible that she was desperate for it to work because of her past failures. Maybe she forced that love without realising it. The one thing Petra wanted in life was to settle down and *"be"* with someone. After Cathryn, Petra feared this would not happen. Despite having enjoyed her single life she never wanted it to last forever. At that particular moment in time, she was more than happy to be single but now she had found it she wanted this relationship to work out.

She did not want to go through that immense sense of loss and heartbreak again as she did not consider herself to be strong enough for that to be repeated. Petra admitted to herself that she was withholding her capacity to love in its totality — that all-encompassing embracing love that meant one was "in love". Was she *in* love with Amy? That was a question she was too scared to pose to herself as now she was in this relationship The Akran thought it simply *must* work; this was a subconscious thought, but years later Petra came to realise and understand it.

Petra never actually considered the term "to be in love" as regards Amy. She did not want to go there. She loved her, she could see herself growing old with her and she cared for her deeply. However, Petra realised that if their relationship was to end, she would not completely falter, she would not go into crisis. Naturally, sadness would be an issue because yet another romantic relationship had failed but she would not be inconsolable. Even at that time she realised this, but she was also aware that she would be happy with Amy as they had a strong bond and were undoubtedly good together because friends told them as much.

They did not share the same hobbies or interests but that was not an issue as they considered this to be healthy because they both considered that a couple should be not viewed as "identical twins" which lesbian couples were often confused as. Any major differences could be ironed out. Some might have said that their eyes were blinkered.

One thing that they did have in common was a relatively low sex drive which Petra was secretly relieved about as whilst with

Sarah she mainly had sex because she felt obliged to do so. She did enjoy sex with Cathryn but in hindsight even they did not have sex that often as that well-known trope "*lesbian bed death*" kicked in.

When they decided that Amy move into the cottage it was done so for practical reasons, ones done so out of convenience for Amy rather than any romantic reasons, although this was not realised at the time.

When Petra decided to ask Amy to marry her it was not because she was madly in love with her. It was more because she wanted to share her life, such as it was, with that same person forever. She never thought that she would be able to love anyone as she had loved Cathryn. Did she decide to settle? Possibly, but this was definitely a subconscious thought. What was not subconscious was Petra's aversion to Amy contributing towards the mortgage or even any household bills as she was NEVER going to be put in such an awful situation of having a joint mortgage or a partner having any claim on her house or even herself ever again.

Petra was a romantic at heart despite her two failed marriages. She was a firm believer in the institution of marriage as she did not see any other way to completely commit to another person outside marriage. That piece of paper was important to her — still. So, when she decided to propose to Amy, she did so with love but also because she wanted to commit herself to someone forever. Amy was that someone, it seemed.

She wanted the proposal to be special, so she saved up enough money to buy a lovely ring. They had lived together for over a year now, they got on well even despite Amy's health anxieties, or as Petra viewed, hypochondria. When she bought the ring, Petra became obsessive about it as she took it everywhere lest it should be stolen or lost.

The proposal came about on a trip to Cornwall. Petra decided that they break up the long, tedious drive down. She booked a spa hotel in Bath, organised for a bottle of champagne in their room and arranged massages for them both. On the journey Petra felt anxious as she realised, whilst driving, that they had never discussed marriage, let alone as regards between them. Needless to say, Petra decided against putting her well-made plan on hold. Amy's answer to Petra's proposal was a resounding *"yes"*. However, they both should have foreseen as a bad omen the diamond falling out of the engagement ring only a few hours later. After a frantic fingertip search of their hotel room, Amy miraculously found it in the shower tray but for the rest of the week she had to be content with a cheap *"replacement"* Petra had bought the next day as she was inwardly obsessed that neither should forget their new-found status as an engaged couple. The original ring was fixed upon their return.

Shortly after getting together with Amy, Petra began to look for another job. She found one in the shape of a charity which supported missing people. The job that she saw advertised was that of a support worker role which entailed supporting children and young people who had returned after a missing episode. With Petra's experience of working with and indeed of supporting young people as well as her passion for providing such support and beliefs in justice she believed that she was qualified and zealous enough not only to apply for the job but to get it. She was aware that neither children nor anyone for that matter would run away merely for the sake of it.

Having applied, she had got through to the final interview which was to be held in the charity's head office in London. Whilst there, she was invited to meet the CEO who was in her office. Once inside and having a very interesting conversation with this Chief Executive Officer her eyes were drawn to a photograph on the wall, one amongst many which were all of missing people. Her eyes met those of a young boy who was smiling at her from his place on the wall. She recognised him as a boy who made the news and missing posters from the late 1980s. She remembered his name to be Darren Ball, the one and the same Darren Ball who Evanna, and Course 40, had searched for whilst a cadet. It seemed that his family had been supported by this charity at the time and continued to be all these many years later as he had never been found. She had no doubts that she could do this job and do it extremely well. Which indeed she did!

Leaving the Community Centre, after all these years, did not prove to be such a hard a wrench as she had anticipated. Petra knew she had surpassed her time there and that her enthusiasm had waned after her relationship with Cathryn, who had also worked there, had come to an end. It was time for a change as it had been for some length of time.

Her team at the charity, obviously having got the job, was a small one. It just consisted of herself, one other worker called Tamika and their manager, Dean. The service they were to provide was a brand new one to the county. They, in effect, were the ones to ensure that it was rolled out across the county effectively. Despite the monumental workload, the team surpassed all expectations.

They supported the children and young people whom the police and social services considered to be the most vulnerable and the most at risk from not only going missing but at risk from child and criminal exploitation, drugs, gangs and so forth. It was no easy task as the majority did not believe themselves to be at such risk if any at all. Their clients came from all walks of life: from mansions to children's homes. It was precisely because they were not social workers that most of their clientele trusted them. It must be highlighted that social workers, even the very best, were at a disadvantage simply because of their title: "social worker". No matter how hard they try their young clientele just would not talk to them let alone trust them.

Petra was a remote worker, meaning that she was based at home for her paperwork and so forth but went out to meet the children and young people that she had been given to work with. She could meet them at any safe place they wished. She worked long hours and also "*took*" these young people home with her. She worried about them day and night as they told her such awful things: girls being gang raped or otherwise used by adult males; boys being used as drug mules in the world of gangs and county lines. There were such awful emotional health difficulties among such young people too. It proved to be a dark, dark world she had entered and because she was Petra, having a natural capacity to be trusted by others she seemed to hear everything. Her problem was that she could not let go, which impacted upon her life outside work because she was constantly thinking and worrying about those she supported. The Akran was highly passionate within her working sphere to the point where she became closely involved with those she supported.

Alfie was a fifteen-year-old boy who lived at home with his mother, older brother and five-year-old sister. He had developed a deep hatred for the world and everyone in it. He had been arrested on numerous occasions for violent offences; for carrying offensive weapons and possession of Class A drugs. He was also a user of marijuana. He refused to engage with any professionals including his long-suffering and dedicated social worker. He deeply despised everyone who tried to support him, including Petra at first. His mother was weak, but she was also afraid of her son who had threatened her with a hammer, so in a sense it should have been of no surprise that she did not discipline him. The word "psychopath" concerning Alfie was bandied around the offices of social workers as he showed no or very little emotion and when he did it was often misplaced, such as laughing at others' misfortune that he had caused. He verbally abused people as a matter of course no matter who they were.

The first time Petra saw him he had buried himself deep in his duvet which was on the settee in the living room where he chose to sleep. He had a perfectly comfortable bed upstairs, but he did not like sharing a bedroom with his brother. He always slept fully clothed, he never showered let alone cleaned his teeth. He had been permanently excluded from school, about which he was embittered. He refused to speak to Petra or even show her his face. During that first month, Petra went to his home each and every Wednesday at 1100 hrs. That first month he went from ignoring her to swearing at her, which she considered progress. During the second month he called her "*a fucking lesbian cunt*" at which Petra pointed out that she was indeed a lesbian which she did not consider in the least bit offensive, just factually correct. During the last two weeks of that month, he threatened to attack her to which she replied: "*You try, and I'll put you on the floor in self-defence*" which he must have taken seriously as he did not try. On her fourth visit, that month, something changed. She told him that she would not give up on him no matter what and proceeded to offer him a cigarette, which his desperate mother had allowed. He took one, on the proviso he smoked it outside. Petra told him that when he had finished, she was taking him to McDonalds. From then on, they developed a very close rapport. Bit by bit he began to open up to Petra. They soon established a routine whereby Petra would drive to a McDonalds that was some distance away as the car gave Alfie a safe place to talk. This continued for over a year during which time his constant missing episodes had declined to none at all. That was Petra's job fulfilled but social services requested that she continue working with him for a while longer, which was granted. There was no doubt that he was very depressed and as his violent manner towards his mother had not changed, he was taken into care where he spent his sixteenth birthday.

Zoe was barely fourteen years old when Petra met her, but she looked so much older than those tender years. She also lived at home but went missing a great deal no matter what her mother did. Zoe was being sexually exploited by numerous adult males, aged over thirty, who she was convinced loved her and she, in turn, loved them. Again, it took a while for Zoe to engage with Petra, but when she did a bond and trust developed. She, too, stopped going missing as a result of Petra's hard work, but also Zoe began to confide in her mother with whom Petra also bonded. Zoe and her mother kept in touch with Petra even after Petra had left the charity.

Petra supported innumerable children and young people. Her success rate was high, and she was very highly respected by the charity's partner agencies, the police and social services. She loved her job.

The wedding plans weren't going well simply because Amy could not decide what kind of wedding she wanted. Petra wanted her to choose this as Amy had not been married before.

They were living a happy life which was only enhanced by Cardi and Petra's other dog, a beautiful chocolate Labrador, called Cyril. One Christmas Petra's life came tumbling down when she had to make the worst decision ever as Cardi suddenly became very unwell. Despite Petra's prayers she did not get better although Petra was willing her to. She booked an appointment for her with the vet for later that same evening. As much as her brain was telling her that everything was going to be just fine her heart was telling her something different as her legs were trembling and she had the worst butterflies in her stomach. However, she would not admit that anything bad was going to happen. But it did. As the vet explained that Cardi had a tumour that had recently burst, for which an operation could be performed but one whereby there was no guarantee of success or that Cardi may not even survive, so the kindest option would be to put her to sleep. Petra could do nothing but weep. She knew there was no real choice here. She only had to look into Cardi's imploring eyes that seemed to speak to her saying: "*Please, Mum, I'm tired. Please let me go*" to know that her most faithful companion should be allowed to go to sleep and to pass over the Rainbow Bridge. Cardi had been with and supported her throughout her darkest times. She listened, she "*spoke*", she was oh so very wise. The love between them both was pure and non-judgemental. Petra sat on the floor stroking her best friend whilst staring into Cardi's tired eyes which shone her love straight back. She seemed to be saying:

"*Mum, you have given me the perfect life. You rescued me and I've loved you from that day onwards. I know you have loved me too and that this is so very difficult for you but let me make it easier by telling you that I'm old, in pain and tired. You are doing the best thing for me by allowing me to take that long sleep. I will love you all the more for it and I will never leave you because I will always be in your heart and will be waiting for you from across the Rainbow Bridge when it's your time.*"

Saying goodbye was the worst and hardest thing for Petra. The tears Petra wept as she thanked her most wise, loyal, trustworthy and beautiful companion for the life she had given her. For Cardi had given Petra so very much. They gazed into each other's eyes which mirrored the love each held for the other. Petra held Cardi's paw, as she drifted slowly but gratefully into her deep, deep, sleep. Finally, she closed her eyes for the last time and breathed her final breath. Cardi was never without love nor was she lonely, not even in death, during her fifteen years that she had spent with Petra who now found it impossible to release the paw which she held so lovingly in her hand. The Akran never really got over her grief even over the years that passed. Cyril, who was now three years old, had grown up with Cardi, became visibly depressed with life as he was now without his surrogate mother and best friend. Thus, Petra and Amy decided to get another companion for him. Edward, an adorable black Labrador puppy came into their lives in the February. He was a joy although it took Cyril a few weeks to get to grips with having a boisterous puppy to deal with but after that they became firm friends — brothers in arms. Edward could never be a replacement for Cardi who remained in Petra's heart and soul. Cardi had been right; she had not left her side but was forever with her.

Cardi's death was only one in a line of awful scenarios that was to befall Amy and Petra that year.

Amy suffered from Crohn's which is an inflammatory bowel disease causing pain, severe diarrhoea and fatigue, to name but a few symptoms. So, she assumed that the intense pain she was experiencing was due to that, as did her consultant. However, a routine colonoscopy revealed something different — a tumour which turned out to be cancerous. When they were informed of this news Petra felt the world simply gush down her body and out through her feet, but she knew that she could not falter as she had to be the strong one of the two in such a circumstance.

At work one day, soon after this earth-shattering news, Petra had a couple of young people to visit. Alfie being one. When she attended her first appointment the foster father answered the front door wearing only a pair of shorts. It was not the fact that he was topless that bothered Petra, but it was the fact that her eyes darted to his colostomy bag attached to his stomach. The gentleman apologised and whilst he was putting on a T-shirt explained that he had cancer of the bowel and that the boy she had come to visit was not in. All she could think about was her poor Amy, although no concrete treatment plan had been decided upon. All she wanted to do was go home and hold her fiancée tightly, but she did not want to let Alfie down. It had recently been his birthday and he had not received one single card, let alone a present. He was more depressed than ever as he hated his placement from where she picked him up to take him to McDonald's which was in a retail park. By the time they got there, Petra was experiencing a bipolar high which had been triggered, unwittingly, by the man with the stoma bag. One symptom of such a high, for Petra, was to spend money. Money she did not have, hence she no longer had a credit card and had a limited overdraft facility with her bank. But this did not prevent her from spending. As it happened, upon parking she saw a sports shop where she found herself saying: *"Alfie, let's go in as I want you to choose something for your birthday."* At this, the boy's face lit up immeasurably but as he walked around the shop there was nothing that he particularly liked and would have been happy to have simply left. However, Petra then suggested that they go and look at the trainers, knowing that his had holes in them. He chose a pair which cost Petra, not the charity, £155, but they had made Alfie's day, possibly even his year. He thanked her all the way back to his placement as he stroked them proudly!

As she drove home it occurred to her that the charity forbade its workers to buy any gifts whatsoever. She began to panic but she knew her boss would only really find out if she told him as she did not figure that anyone would complain. She had recently been made upset by her manager as her role, which she had been promoted to, had been made null and void. Petra, in part, blamed herself for this as she constantly fought for an extra worker as their workload was so great. Eventually, this was agreed but no one saw fit to inform her prior to that recruitment that owing to this they could no longer afford her salary, so the team would be restructured, and she would return to her old position as worker as opposed to coordinator. She voiced her upset but was assured by her manager and the director that this was not a demotion, as Petra viewed it, and furthermore they wanted "*to bottle her*" as her skills for this type of work could not be taught. They came to her naturally. However, the need for openness and honesty were never far from Petra's mind, so on the journey home she called her manager, Dean, confessing all. He wasn't exactly pleased but nor did he seem angry. In fact, he told her not to worry, as they had all pushed boundaries at some point, and to go home, have a cup of tea and as it was Friday to enjoy the weekend. He could hear Petra's upset over the phone as she could not contain her tears.

That Monday, Dean phoned to advise her that, for the time being, she was only allowed to do paperwork. She was not allowed to contact let alone see any of her young people. She was not even allowed to speak to social workers et al. In short, she was "grounded" until it had been decided whether to go down the disciplinary route. She was to attend the Head Office in London that Friday for a pre-disciplinary meeting after which it would be decided if any further action would be taken. Now Petra, who prepared for everything she did, went armed to this meeting with a written statement. Afterwards she felt confident that it had gone well and actually presumed this to be the last of this sorry saga. However, to her horror it was not. On the day after Amy had been advised of her treatment plan, which Dean knew, she received an "invitation" to attend a disciplinary. She was given the mandatory 48 hours' notice which was just about time enough to prepare herself. She hurriedly asked a few professionals to write character statements for her, which they readily agreed to do. She then wrote a lengthy statement of her own detailing everything she had done as regards the trainers and what happened just prior which she felt triggered her bipolar, which work had known about from her initial interview. She then printed all of these documents along with the charity MIND's blurb on bipolar and got them bound to look professional. Petra also sought legal advice which stated that she was within her rights to record the meeting, as she declined actual representation. Fortunately, in no doubt because of the folder she presented to the disciplinary panel, she was not disciplined or found in the least bit guilty of anything. On the contrary, they went so far as re-stating how they wanted to "bottle" her and they even paid for the trainers! Despite being a win for Petra she felt bitter towards her bosses for putting her through this, plus the fact that they had made her wait three weeks for them to decide whether she was to have this disciplinary meeting. They knew that all of this coincided with Amy's diagnosis and Petra wouldn't have minded, but it was she who complained about herself — no one else had!

The time had come for Amy's treatment to commence. It was five weeks for five days a week of radiotherapy and oral chemotherapy followed by, sometime later in the year, an extremely large operation which would lead to her having "a bag for life" — that is, a stoma bag. Petra would be taking her to the hospital every day for her treatment, plus she continued to work full time, nurse, cook for Amy and hold her through each night mostly camped out on the bathroom floor as Amy screeched in pain and was being sick. Neither got much sleep. The longer the treatment went on for the worse the side effects became which lasted for several months after the treatment stopped. It was right in the midst of this when Nile, next door, the one whose brother Cathryn went off with, chose to play his music at top volume all night every night because Cyril and Edward happened to bark once that day. It was totally vindictive, plus he knew about Amy. He also sent very abusive text messages to Petra on a daily basis. Petra implored with him to stop but all she got in return was abuse and threats. She thought she was going mad; the music was the final straw.

xii <u>The Oak Tree</u>

Evanna had experienced some wonderful mast years whilst in the police as she had produced hundreds of seeds which had taken root and grown into magnificent oaks. But now it seemed that winter had set in and her branches were now bare. She was devoid of seeds. Those few she did manage to grow were fast eaten by the squirrels and jays but even they were dissatisfied with their taste and texture. Those seeds had to do with her sexual encounters, which some may view as good but despite enjoying the actual sex, The Akerne wanted something more than mere sex. She, like the birds and small mammals, was ennuied.

Her life was once plentiful whilst in the police at any rate. The oak inside her was abundant but now it was left fallow and depleted.

She felt betrayed both by her mother and by Dr Ruth Shearer as the wildlife felt betrayed by her inner oak.

Now she was left with hardly a leaf, unable to work and living in a drug-induced groggy haze caused by the bipolar medication.

Her tree possessed nothing fruitful.

So, to the Akran. Petra's mast years also appeared to be over for now although her internal oak did prove to yield a few good crops as it was able to produce a number of seeds, some of which were eaten but others which were not were found in their buried hideaways and grew into sturdy oak trees. These were grown because of the relationship with Amy and her friendships, especially that of Sylvia. The ones devoured, which were most of them, took on the shape of Petra's feelings for Cathryn and the three years it took to get over her. They were also in the configuration of the more recent times from the death of Cardi onwards.

Her interior oak tree did not have complete mast years, yet it had glimmers of them being fruitful intermingled with the fruitless.

Finally, it was Bodhi who could boast a bumper crop and several consecutive mast years, for he had seen great personal growth. Thus, his seedlings grew into mighty oak trees with plenty of fruit left over for the wildlife to feast upon.

He was on his way to his Awakening and Enlightenment, yet he was realistic about his path so was prepared for some infecund times. However, he was positive that he would learn from them so that they would become more fecund as he had already discovered with his job at Orchard Grove School. He found some fight within himself as the oak battles in winter months to combat the elements. The oak usually wins this contest as Bodhi's intrinsic oak was succeeding too. This took no little courage and moxie.

Chapter 8
The Bark Cracks

Acute Oak Decline (AOD) is a new disease in the world of indigenous British oak trees. It first came into prevalence thirty-five years ago.

The symptoms are rather grave with those affected suffering from weeping vertical cracks in the bark of the tree that ooze a black fluid down the length of the trunk for all to see. In the live tissue beneath these bleeds grows a lesion which is a sign of tissue decay. Some oak trees die between four to six years after the onset of such symptoms which develop rapidly over eighteen months. As the disease progresses the oak's beautiful canopy thins. The tree's death is likely to be caused by multiple agents such as the beetle *Agrilus biguttatus* whose larvae are often found in association with the lesions, as well as various species of bacteria. This disease affects thousands of oak trees in Britain.

Likewise, humans contract conditions and diseases; some fatal, some life altering, some life limiting.

Some such diseases and conditions have been newly diagnosed, but the possibility of their being around for many years prior, is high. With some of these newly diagnosed illnesses research has been limited, a consequence of which is that specialists are few and far between. For example, multiple sclerosis began as a little-researched and misunderstood disease but now is the most common immune-mediated disorder which affects the nervous system.

Like AOD, MS is partly diagnosed by numerous lesions

which develop on the white matter of the brain and spinal cord. This disease is life limiting with the average life expectancy from its onset being thirty years.

Symptoms of a stroke are not defined by such lesions, yet like AOD, an indicator of a haemorrhagic stroke is bleeding. This bleeding comes either directly into the brain or into the space between the brain's membranes.

i Petra -(The Akran)

For a week or so on and off, Petra had been struggling to find the correct words for everyday household objects, but she was not minded by this as she had been struggling on the minimal of sleep.

Although Amy had since finished her radiotherapy and chemotherapy she was still in extreme pain and feeling nauseous. The pain only worsened as the radiotherapy went on and it reached its height in the weeks after the final one as the treatment had burnt the exterior and interior of her bottom, anus and rectum. This combined with Nile's loud dance music, with the occasional outpouring of Boney M, on loop all night every night on full volume, his incessant threatening text messages alongside highly distressing cases at work only added to her sleep deprivation.

Nile's dance music tended to set her bipolar off because of the heavy, repetitive often trance-like tones. Also, with Boney M's song of choice, whose lyrics went "*Mary's boy child, Jesus Christ was born on Christmas Day*" blaring through the walls in July made her question her sanity.

One morning she woke up, after having one and a half hours sleep to discover her speech was slurry, stuttery, high pitched and almost at a whisper, as opposed to her normally excellent elocution. During the course of that day, she lost the power of speech altogether. And so, it continued in this vein day after day.

She was unable to work because of this as speaking was 95% of her job, so her manger told her to go sick.

She was scared and frustrated but convinced it would be righted as the GP advised her it was caused by an intense migraine, the sort without the headache, and it would pass.

However, it did not pass.

ii Bodhi (The Acharn)

Ever since Johnny had bashed Bodhi's head against that brick wall, he had suffered from dizzy spells which lasted some two to three weeks at a time. These rendered him useless as they affected his entire body and were reminiscent of a very fast funfair ride or being so very drunk that the room spun.

The GP put these spells down to labyrinthitis, an inner ear infection without an earache, but Bodhi was not convinced.

One morning midway through his breakfast of porridge, the dizziness returned. It was so bad that he fell to the floor. He was not scared or even worried by this, but he was frustrated that it was happening again. He would have to call in sick once more.

He did not bother calling the doctor because he knew how this went; he would have to spend two or three debilitating weeks in bed and then it would pass, and he would be as right as rain.

However, it did not pass.

iii Evanna (The Akerne)

Evanna's life became yet more focused on physical training. This had been her life for many years. Ever since she was eighteen, she pushed herself through some punishing weight training sessions and hilly long-distance cross-country runs.

One morning she woke up to discover she could not walk properly. She was only able to do so on the outsides of her feet with both arms held up by her chest, elbows pointing outwards with her fingertips of each arm touching the other set. She was very unsteady but try as she might she was unable to place either foot properly down on the floor or keep her arms at her sides. The pains and spasms in all of her limbs were intense. Very soon she resorted to crawling as that was quicker and safer.

She could not run or even weight train as it took every effort to "walk" or even crawl. Not being able to exercise was somehow more perturbing, to Evanna, than not being able to walk!

After a few days her coordination and fine motor skills also departed her. She found she was unable to cut up food with a knife, hold a pen or a fork or a cup properly.

She did not go to the GP as she assumed this strange phenomenon would disappear as quickly as it came to be.

However, it did not pass.

iv The Oak Tree

Once again this shows how closely linked, if you will, humans and oak trees are. They both can suffer from disease and conditions, albeit some being worse than others.

How does this affect The Akran, Acharn, and Akerne (Petra, Bodhi and Evanna)? It merely proves how connected they are to their oak trees, not only mentally but in a sense also physically because, as humans, they can be struck down by illness and disease too.

Book 3
The Way through the Woods

Chapter 1
The Way through the Woods

The Way through the Woods

"_They shut the road through the woods_
Seventy years ago
Weather and rain have undone it again,
And now you would never know
There was a road through the woods
Before they planted the trees.
It is underneath the coppice and heath
And the thin anemones.
Only the keeper sees
That where the ring-dove broods,
And the badgers roll at ease,
There was once a road through the woods.
Yet, if you enter the woods
Of a summer evening late,
When the night air cools on the trout-ringed pools
When the otter whistles his mate,
(They fear not men in the woods,
Because they see so few.)
You will hear the beat of the horse's feet,
And the swish of a skirt in the dew,
Steadily cantering through
The misty solitudes,
As though they perfectly knew
The old lost road through the woods...
But there is no road through the woods." (1)

i A Wood of Oaks

The ceiling of the wood hides the moon, the stars, the sun and the sky. When it's light here, it is not the light from the sun ebbing its way through the canopy. The light is somewhat harsh and artificial in its brightness. It never gets properly dark here. When it tries, the light is but dimmed. There are never any stars. Here, there is never any dawn or dusk. Here there is neither natural light nor shade. Thus, I am unable to predict the time of day or the time of night. There are no lights to guide me home from within this stark and unfamiliar place.

I am lying down, face upwards, in a bed perhaps, for there is something soft underneath my head and something firmer underneath by back. On top of me I can just about make out a white sheet and a blue coloured thin blanket.

Something tugs at certain points in both of my upper limbs. I can see plastic-looking "wires" which seem to have been inserted into tubes that have been fixed into my arms. They wend their way into bags of liquid, one clear and the other white, that are hung upright on a tall stand. On my right finger there has been fixed a grey clip whose wires appear to go into some kind of "television".

I can hear muffled whispers and noise. There are constant annoying sounds of "beep... beep... beep" and the occasional groans and cries. Are they coming from me? Of that I am unsure. Wait, is that Mum speaking? Perhaps even my sister is here too? No, why would they be here in this wood with me?

My vision, when I can muster the energy to lift the weights that are my eyelids, is blurred and out of focus. I can make out shapes but that is all. Do I recognise these two figures seated by my side? One appears to be holding my hand. That I can feel as the hand is clammy with sweat compared to mine that is cold. I can also feel the occasional drip of droplets of liquid and can make out a sniffing sound coming from this figure. Are they tears? Is this person crying?

I can only move my head slightly to the right and left. I cannot move any other part of my body. Nor can I feel any part of my body — it is quite numb. Just like my brain — numb.

As I try to talk all that comes out is a high-pitched garble. It is a voice far removed from my own. It does not belong to me. No one answers, so I stop attempting to communicate, but I am so thirsty.

Am I dying? I am too tired to care but it feels like it. But as I've never experienced death before how can I possibly know what it feels like? Will I float up to the harsh lights above or down into the grey floor below? I can feel myself sinking right down and through whatever I am lying on and whatever is beneath my head. Very soon I will sink through the feather underneath and float into the floor or above my head and through the ceiling. Neither way matters. Nothing matters.

Have I been abducted by aliens? I am too tired to care.

I feel strangely content. I am at peace. I am at ease. I feel no fear. I feel no pain. I feel numb if I feel anything. Nothing of any substance creeps into my mind. I am tranquil. I am ready to be "taken". Am I near Ataraxia? Am I achieving an Awakening and Enlightenment of sorts? This could be my time.

"Hold me down, I'm so tired now
Aim your arrow at the sky
Take me down, I'm too tired
Leave me where I lie
I thought I was flying but maybe I'm dying tonight
I thought I was flying but maybe I'm dying tonight
And I thought I was flying buy maybe I'm dying tonight
I thought I was flying but maybe I'm dying tonight." (2)

ii <u>Withered Boughs</u>

"No boughs have withered because of the wind
The boughs have withered because I have told them my dreams." (1)

Winter is the oak tree's most perilous season. The bare tree needs to stay alive in the extreme cold using almost no energy. The bark acts like a blanket, but if the liquids inside it were to freeze solid, the tree would suffer catastrophic damage. So, it withdraws fluid from the cells, dehydrating itself. The remaining liquid has a high concentration of sugars which act as antifreeze. Most nutrients are stored in the oak's roots during the winter months, but the root system alone is not enough to extract vital minerals from the soil. The tree also needs a vast army of microscopic filaments to survive in order to extract phosphate from the surrounding soil.

It seems that the oak tree mirrors my life, or as the oak came first my life mirrors that of the oak tree, as this feels like the winter of my life as I'm struggling to survive. Yet, this tree is able to draw upon its multifarious mechanisms to fight — in order to stay alive. Where is my Young and Brave Fighter? I know that she is somewhere close by. Where is my Rock upon whom I can always rely? For any awakening and enlightenment will just have to wait a while longer, yet they both seem determined to define themselves to me. Maybe "He" should remain here for a while longer and leave the "Others" to wake up before "Him".

iii <u>How Big How Blue How Beautiful</u> (1)

"What are we gonna do
We've opened the door and now it's all coming through
Tell me if you see it too
We've opened our eyes and it's changing the view

How big
How blue
How beautiful
So much time on the other side
Waiting for you to wake up
So much time on the other side
Maybe I'll see you in another life
If this one isn't enough
So much time on the other side
How big
How blue
How beautiful." (2)

"He" sinks further down through his mattress, as light as a feather, with no thoughts of concern. He wonders whether he may be heading towards Ataraxia. He presumes he must be as before him lies an expanse of the bluest most beautiful sky, or is it the most beautiful clear blue sea?

Despite the pleas of both the Young and Brave Fighter and the Rock to return to them "He" decides to remain on the "other side". He feels desperate to share this view with them. He attempts to entice them to join Him, but they continue to resist.

Suddenly, flashbacks of memories and dreams of the past come flooding through. They are but a jumble and are somewhat distorted. Nothing seems clear let alone definable or in context. The beautiful blue scene is becoming overshadowed by a discombobulation of events, thoughts and feelings that he had since put to bed — or so he thought. A wood of oaks. Yet he still does not want to wake up as he believes he has to pass through this confusion, for the final time, as at its end lies his salvation. So, he continues to swim through this ethereal blue. The Young and Brave Fighter and the Rock try to call him back, imploring him to come through to them, as they wait for him on this other side, for he has spent too long in his. They are ready to make themselves whole once more, but they cannot do so without him.

iv The Way through the Woods

I sink into the blue which is slowly turning into a tangled wood. I slowly begin to make my way through them. Through the dense overgrown oak trees which represent my memories, thoughts, feelings and dreams. I am unable to orientate a way through. I believe that if I successfully navigate my way through to the clear road which has been hidden, I will have reached my Nirvana. My Ataraxia.

At present there are too many tangled oaks; roots, branches and leaves to see that road. But it was there once when my memories and thoughts were clear. When they were not muddied or muddled. I was once an assured and certain thinker but now there is too much surrounding me. Once the road was clear but that was before I began to make memories or develop thoughts and feelings. That was before I planted the trees.

"There was once a road through
The woods before they planted these trees" (1)

I am the keeper of these woods. I am the keeper of the road. I am the keeper of my memories, my dreams; everything they stand for and every thought and feeling that they produce. I am the keeper.

There must be a way through these woods.

v Withered Boughs 2

"No boughs have withered because of the wintry wind
The boughs have withered because I told them my dreams"
(1)

376

I have been dreaming as I lay here unable to move or speak. My mind has been taken over by memories and dreams past. It has been akin to a wet sponge being squeezed of its water. As the sponge's memory returns it to its shape, so the memory of the mind returns all of my thoughts and feelings. Although it is unable to actually "feel" them, it knows how I felt and what I thought during those past events, chimeras and incubus which have flooded to the forefront, at first by piecemeal but then as a flood. They are confused in my brain which is slowly waking up to feel the verity of this past and the corporeality of the now.

It feels as if I am in some form of coma, yet I am awake and am unable to communicate my pain on the outside or the turmoil within. My body and my entire self are akin to the withered bough on the tree. This is because they have endured my meanderings, my imbroglios and torsions. Yet my dreams and memories are not all bad. My subconscious mind has returned these remembrances and reflections. Such an anamnesis was previously blocked.

I am not finished, I need to lie here a while more in order to catalogue and arrange these events, this knowledge, pathos and these sensibilities into some kind of order. I need to recognise who I was then and who I am now in all of my guises.

Chapter 2
The Fight of the Acorns — The Sum of My Parts

i Evanna — The Akerne

Evanna felt scared as her mother drove her to the Accident and Emergency Department at their local hospital, some twelve miles away.

They were both scared, in truth, but neither allowed their fears to be shown to the other, so instead they laughed about the predicament in which the Akerne had found herself. Normally, losing the ability to walk, for no apparent reason, was no laughing matter, but what else was one supposed to do in such a state of adversity?

Since Evanna's walking continued to deteriorate, her mother took her to see the GP who advised them to go straight to the hospital as she feared it could be a neurological problem which might be serious.

As it was a Monday morning, they hoped that the Emergency Department would be empty but, alas, it was full. However, as the GP had called in advance, they were expected and Evanna was sent straight past the hordes of sick people patiently awaiting their turn. The looks they gave the Akerne were ones of not being best pleased, but as she had been given a wheelchair by a hospital porter, she was able to avoid their angry glares as she shut her eyes whilst her mother pushed.

She was shown to a trolley/bed, in a cubicle, which a kind nurse helped her on to. She was then subjected to various tests after which she just lay there waiting. Waiting for what, she did not know but maybe a doctor would be good for starters! Hours passed by despite her mother's protests.

As the Akerne lay there, she thought of her oak tree which she knew was still standing tall, and there it stood in her mind. She had gained strength from this oak on many an occasion, so she knew it would not fail her now. As she dwelled upon it, she began to silently recite a poem which she had learned at school. This poem, too, had built up her defences in times of strife. This was one such time.

The Oak Tree — By Johnny Ray Rhyder
"A mighty wind blew night and day
It stole the oak tree's leaves away,
Then snapped its boughs and pulled its bark
Until the oak tree was tired and stark
But still the oak tree held its ground
While other trees fell all around
The weary wind gave up and spoke
How can you still be standing oak?
The oak tree said, I know that you
Can break each branch of mine in two
Carry every leaf away
Shake my limbs and make me sway
But I have roots stretched in the earth
Growing stronger since my birth
You'll never touch them, for you see,
They are the deepest part of me
Until today I wasn't sure
Of just how much I could endure
But now I've found, with thanks to you
I'm stronger than I ever knew." (1)

ii Petra — The Akran

The GP said it was a migraine, despite Petra not having any form of headache, that had caused her speech to somehow disappear. At times, she stuttered and slurred; sometimes she whispered so quietly; at others it was completely unintelligible; whilst other times no words would proffer from her mouth at all. This was all in spite of words and sentences being properly formed in her head. However, she noticed that there were times when it was becoming increasingly difficult to find words for everyday objects. At such times her speech was slow and laboured whilst she struggled to search for the right word. This all left the Akran feeling so stupid as she was not being able to make herself understood.

The migraine tablets, for her now three-week "migraine", that her GP had prescribed, were not helping, so she decided to make a further appointment but with a different GP. She also decided to take her mother to not only act as an interpreter but also as an antagonist should this be required. The GP was concerned, advising them to attend accident and emergency straight away in case the problem was due to *"some other neurological event"*. The GP told them that she would call the hospital in advance and also armed Petra with a hastily written letter which she was to hand in for the doctor.

Despite it being a Monday morning, the department was packed but as she was expected and owing to the fact that the GP highlighted the urgency of the matter, when she called, Petra bypassed the throngs of sick people in the waiting area and was quickly found a trolley/bed in a cubicle.

The Akran was quite fearful, only because of what the GP had told her. As she lay there, feeling exhausted, she shut her eyes and imagined being sat against her oak tree gathering strength from it. As she did so she silently recited her favourite poem, which she had often read whilst spending time with her tree as her beloved dog ran in circles around its thick trunk.

The Trees — by Philip Larkin
"The trees are coming into leaf,
Like something almost being said;
The recent buds relax and spread,
Their greenness is a kind of grief.
Is it that they are born again,
And we grow old? No, they die too,
Their yearly trick of looking new
Is written down in rings of grain.
Yet still the unresting castles thresh
In full grown thickness every May.
Last year is dead, they seem to say,
Begin afresh, afresh, afresh." (1)

The Akran returned to this poem whenever she was in need of a mental push for survival as she understood the poem to be about just that — survival. It is never too late to bud, bloom and flourish, as the winter only lasts as along as we allow it to. In only a matter of weeks the tree goes from being unrecognisable to being fully alive once more. Petra knew that she had to do the same — fight. She needed to spring back into life somehow. She knew that she possessed this power somewhere within her soul as the tree possesses it within itself but is not afraid to summon it forth. She must believe in herself. She needs to assert herself somehow. She needs to find that power. She needs to survive and to begin _"afresh, afresh, afresh"_.

iii Bodhi — The Acharn

The GP was now uncertain that the Acharn's severe dizziness was due to labyrinthitis. So, he sent Bodhi, accompanied by his mother, to the Accident and Emergency Department, *"just to be on the safe side"*. The doctor rang ahead so the hospital was expecting him. By now, Bodhi's dizziness was so severe he was being continually sick, so along with a sick bag at the ready and now also a wheelchair that his mother had been given by a hospital porter, he went straight past the heaving waiting room and was shown into a cubicle where a trolley/bed awaited him. As he lay, he began to pray. To which god he did not know. Nor did he know for what particular reason. He did not wish to be an alarmist but the mere fact that his mother had heeded the GP's advice, to go straight to hospital, made Bodhi think that he must be at death's door, for his mother did not normally take advice from anyone, let alone a doctor!

His prayer turned into a poem that he had once learned at school. He began to silently recite it. As he did so he envisaged his trusty oak tree which he hoped would give him the strength that he needed.

Trees — by Alfred Joyce Kilmer
"I think that I shall never see
A poem as lovely as a tree
A tree whose hungry mouth is prest
Against the earth's sweet flowing breast
A tree that looks at God all day,
And lifts her leafy arms to pray;
A tree that may in summer wear
A nest of robins in her hair
Upon whose bosom snow has lain
Who intimately lives with rain
Poems are made by fools like me
But only God can make a tree." (1)

Chapter 3
Acorns, Roots, Trunk, Branches and Leaves

i Three Acorns

As I lie here in this waking coma-like state, I think, I reminisce, I try to put a halt to the fear and confusion within. I try to put things in order — in sequence. This poem pops into my mind at random.

The Brave Old Oak
by Henry Fothergill Chorley (1808 — 1872)
"A song to the oak, the brave old oak
Who hath ruled in the greenwood long
Here's health and renown to his broad green crown
And his fifty arms so strong
There's fear in his frown when the sun goes down,
And the fire in the west fades out;
And he showeth his might on a wild midnight
When the storm through his branches shout
Then here's to the oak, the brave old oak,
Who stands in his pride alone;
And still flourish he, a hale green tree,
When a hundred years have gone!
In the days of old, when the spring with cold
Had brightened his branches grey
Through the grass at his feet crept maidens sweet
To gather the dew of May.
And on that to the rebeck gay
They frolicked with lovesome swains;

They are gone, they are dead, in the churchyard lain
But the tree it still remains
There here's to the oak, the brave old oak,
Who stands in his pride alone;
And still flourish he, a hale green tree,
When a hundred years have gone!
He saw the rare times when Christmas chimes
Were a merry sound to hear,
When the squire's wide hall and the cottage small
Were filled with English good cheer.
Now gold hath the sway we all obey,
And a ruthless king is he;
But he never shall send our ancient friend
To be tossed on the stormy sea
Then here's to the oak, the brave old oak,
Who stands in his pride alone;
And still flourish he, a hale green tree,
When a hundred years are gone!" (1)

Within its words, metre, rhyme, verse and chorus I am able to attribute different personas.

Evanna lies within the first verse as she shares the courage and bravery with the "*brave old oak*". Strength sees it through the most mighty of elements as Evanna's strength saw her through some perilous and horrific times. The tree hides its fear of the dark, indeed it "*showeth his might*" against foul weathers. Evanna has had her own storms to weather resulting in her hiding her fears and showing her might against some foul human beings and scary endeavours. Despite the many challenges that are thrown up against them, both the oak and Evanna power on and win through.

The second verse belongs to Bodhi. His passion of history and the ability he has to imagine his oak tree as part of history and within it. This time, the oak stands at the centre of a group of pretty maidens who dance around its roots, to the playful jig of a fiddle, with lovestruck young men. The tree bears witness to this snapshot of time as it has done so to many others in the past and will be witness to in future times. When these "*gay*" folk are no longer, the tree continues to live on — just as Bodhi continues to live on despite the pain of the past. Neither the tree nor Bodhi can predict the future, but the present is now. Bodhi, in a sense, has danced to the fiddle — the fiddle of pain but he has outlived its player.

Petra resides inside the third verse with the perfect Christmas. She shared many a "*perfect*" Christmas, every year, as a child. These are the happiest memories she had of her childhood. The "*ruthless king*" in her life is her father but he has a wife, *the ruthless queen* — her mother. But neither has been the cause of her destruction. She will not be defeated. She has clawed her way back through each and every knock. Nor will they cause her defeat in future times. She will continue to be victorious despite the storms.

"I" lay in each chorus. I am brave. I am proud of who I am and of what I have become. I was born alone and now lie here, in this bed, feeling alone. I don't know what's wrong with me and I can foresee several battles in the midst, but I will not surrender. Somehow, I will survive and flourish, as the oak tree will for many a year to come.

I am the leaves, I am the branches, I am the trunk, I am the roots, I am the oak. I am the three acorns.

Chapter 4
Three Become One

i

This is my second night on AAU, the Acute Assessment Unit. I am awaiting results from an MRI scan on my brain. I am hoping it will prove that I have one! Amy, who is has been sharing visitor shifts with my mother and sister, is by my side. I cannot communicate with her, but I can feel her warmth and love which is vastly reassuring.

It has proved difficult to align all of my experiences that have gone before me in this near half-century. But I have done the best that I can.

My bed is being moved by a hospital porter. It seems that I am on the move, but no one has told me where I am going. Amy accompanies me. As I go through the last set of double doors, I am able to open my eyes just an inch when I read a sign which says, "*Stroke Unit*". I begin to freak out as no one has told me that I have endured a stroke. As I am moved from one bed to another, I try to convey my fears to the ward sister, but she does not understand what I am trying to say. Amy is equally as scared, but the nursing sister will not tell her anything. And there I am left — there it seems I am staying. My waking coma-like state eases over the next few days, but everything else remains the same. I feel useless.

ii

A physiotherapist came to see me today. She wanted to see

me walk. It seems "Evanna's" strange walk remains the same. I fell owing to the impaired gait and a slight tremor. My arms were still positioned in that odd manner. If anything, the walk "belonging" to Evanna had worsened. The physio informed me that I had not suffered a stroke, although they considered that a possibility. I have had no other tests apart from the usual blood tests. She explained that I have something called Functional Neurological Disorder (FND) which will not show up on any scan as it is not an organic problem. Apparently, it's a "*software as opposed to a hardware problem*". My brain is misfiring! She then handed me a leaflet and informed me that she will refer me to a neurological rehabilitation unit but warned me of the long waiting list. In the meantime, I am to remain here. She was unable to tell me any more. Nor was the ward consultant whose sphere of influence was strokes and nothing much else, it appeared. As no other medical professional can tell me anything more, together with Amy and my mother I am doing some research on the internet.

iii

Functional Neurological Disorder is caused by a problem with the functioning of the nervous system. The brain simply does not send the correct signals to the body. There has been only limited research on the condition and there is but a mere spattering of specialists.

A person with the condition can experience different symptoms from another. Each of my symptoms including the new ones, numbness of my hands and feet, temporary paralysis of my legs, bladder weakness, the inability to swallow and non-epileptic seizures can be attributed to the disorder. These symptoms are REAL. They are not imagined.

No one can tell me if I will recover because they simply don't know. Nor can anyone enlighten me as to what caused it. It could be due to the abuse I endured as a child (which I do not agree with). It maybe because of Johnny bashing my head against the brick wall or even to the numerous injuries I suffered when in the police. Or it could be due to the immense stress I had just been through with Amy's cancer, my difficulties at work and those to do with "Vile Nile". It is my belief that it began after the incident with Johnny as that was when the periods of dizziness began. However, I am willing to concede that the more recent stress may have attributed to my brain short circuiting completely!

iv

I call upon the Young and Brave Fighter that is Evanna. I call upon the Rock that is Petra. I call upon Bodhi who continues to search for an awakening and enlightenment. I will need all three to fight this fight. They are within me. They are me. They are the sum of my parts.

Chapter 5
The Sum of Our parts

i

I have lived a life, thus far, that has borne witness to the many faces of the human race. I have experienced it at its very worst — all of my facets lived through, but survived, their childhoods. Evanna also saw the very dark side of humanity in her years in the police. However, I have also seen the very best of humanity. People have entered my life who might have been angels; Marika, Coral and Amelia, to name but a few. Cardi may not have been human but I am convinced that we met because we were destined to meet. She was and still is my guardian angel — of that I am convinced.

ii

Evanna, Petra and Bodhi all came across the very antithesis to humanity. They came across harshness, meanness, hatred, cruelty, hard-heartedness, callousness, flagitiousness, egregiousness — inhumanness — inhumanity. But they continued to fight for their own humanness despite faltering on occasion — but they are only human!

Likewise, the oak tree, who has lived for so many years, has seen goodness but also great badness.

iii

The Akerne, the Akran and the Acharn experienced different things but together they make up one human soul who shares each of these experiences and continues to fight.

We are flawed in so many ways, but we also make one truly humane person. Each facet, Evanna, Petra and Bodhi combine to make the whole. Just as the oak tree's parts, its facets, its leaves, branches, roots and trunk make up the sum of its parts to make the whole. Together they combine to make a mighty force of nature who offers and provides so much to others. Yet it, too, is flawed in its calculated "theft" of sunlight. But without this "treachery" it could be said that many a creature would be denied food and shelter.

iv

The three Acorns experienced different aspects of life with their contra-distinct personalities, accomplishments, adventures, encounters but they share one ordeal which shaped each in such mis-mated ways. But they had mutual causes — that of justice, supporting the underdog and the will to help others. Each succeeded in doing that in small ways.

v

This is the fight that I choose to fight — to fight for myself in order to fight for the justice and the humanity of others.

"Against all the odds we shall fight this fight
We must say: 'we will beat it; using all of our might:
Me
Evanna
Petra
Bodhi
I am'" (1)

The End

BIBLIOGRAPHY

Book 1
Prologue
1. Old Testament — Genesis 1:26 – 27
2. Old Testament — Genesis 35:4
3. Old Testament — Joshua 24:25 – 27

Chapter 3
1. William Shakespeare, Twelfth Night, Act 2 Scene 5, Arden Shakespeare (2008)

Chapter 4
1. William Shakespeare, Hamlet, Act 1 Scene 2, Wordsworth Editions (1992)
2. William Shakespeare, Hamlet, Act 3 Scene 1, Wordsworth Editions (1992)

Chapter 6
1. Walt Disney, "Frozen" (Olaf), Directors Chris Oak and Jennifer Lee, Produced by Peter Del Vecho (2013)
2. https://www.azquotes/quote/411405, Albert Einstein, Wind and Fly Ltd (2020)
3. Anonymous
4. https://www.brainyquote.com/quotes/mauricesaatchi_15 0342, Maurice Saatchi
5. Jane Austin, Northanger Abbey, (1817), Penguin Classics (2003

6. https://www.purelovequotes.com/author/william-shakespeare/afriend-knows-who-are, William Shakespeare

7. Lisa Loeb and Elizabeth Mitchell, "Little Bird" from "Catch The Moon", (2014)

8. Mcfly, "Rockin Robin" From "Memory Lane, The Best of Mcfly"

9. https://www.brainyquote.com/quotes/paul newman_378928, Paul Newman

10.Aston Barrett and Carlton Barratt, "Who the Cap Fits," sung by

Bob Marley, Kobalt Music Publishing LTD (1976)

11.   https://www.brainyquote.com/quotes/Aesop_382936, Aesop

Quotes (N.D.)

12. https://www.brainyquote.com/quotes/Aesop_382936, Miles Franklin Quotes (N.D.)

13.Turkish Proverb

14.Burmese Proverb

15.Sinead Morrisey, The State of Prisons, Carconet Manchester

(2005)

16.Sam Levenson, Everything but Money — A Life of Riches, Open

Road Media, page 124 (2016)

17.https://www.azquotes/quotes/Betsy-Cohen, Betsy Cohen

18.https://www.brainyquote.com/quotes/frederich_nietsche _16049 Frederich Nietsche (N.D.)

19.

https://www.brainyquote.com/quotes/elizabeth_taylor_163355, Elizabeth Taylor (N.D.)

20.CS Lewis

21.https://www.brainyquote.com/quotes/oscar_Wilde_1052
22, Oscar Wilde (N.D.)
   22.Voltaire

Book 2
Chapter 1

Sub-chapter i

1. Geoffrey Chaucer, Troilus and Cressida, Book 2 (1385), rendered into modern English by George Philip, Dover Publications Inc, Dover Thrift Editions, New York, (2006)
2. Geoffrey Chaucer, Troilus and Cressida, Book 2 (1385), rendered into modern English by George Philip, Dover Publications Inc, Dover Thrift Editions, New York, (2006)

Sub-chapter viii

1. English Proverb

Sub-chapter ix

1. New Testament, Revelation 6:1-8

Book 3
Chapter 1

1. Rudyard Kipling, The Way Through the Woods, The Emergency Poet — An Anti-Stress Anthology (Pg. 81), edited by Debora Alma, Michael O'Mara Books LTD (2018)
2. Florence Welch, Usless Magic Lyrics and Poetry, (pg 228), Penguin Fig Tree (2017)

Sub-chapter ii

1. W.B Yeats, The Withering of the Boughs, The Collected

Poems of W.B Yeats, Edited and Introduction by Cedric Watts, Wordsworth Poetry Library (2008)

Sub-chapter iii
1. Florence Welch, Usless Magic Lyrics and Poetry, (pg 146), Penguin Fig Tree (2017)

Sub-chapter iv
1. Rudyard Kipling, The Way through the Woods, The Emergency Poet — An Anti-Stress Anthology (Pg. 81), edited by Debora Alma, Michael O'Mara Books LTD (2018)

Sub-chapter v
1. W.B Yeats, The Withering of the Boughs, The Collected Poems of W.B Yeats, Edited and Introduction by Cedric Watts, Wordsworth Poetry Library (2008)

Chapter 2
Sub-chapter i
1. Johnny Ray Rhyder, The Oak Tree, https://www.ellenbailey.com

Sub-chapter ii
1. Philip Larkin, The Trees, The Poetry Pharmacy For The Heart Soul and Mind (Pg 34), Edited by William Sieghard, Penguin Random Press Book House (2017)

Sub-chapter iii
1. Alfred Joyce Kilmer, Trees, The Light of The Moon, Edited by Gyles Brandreth, Michael Joseph An Imprint of Penguin Books, Penguin Random Book House (2019)

Chapter 3
Sub-chapter i
1. Henry Fothergill Chorley (1808 – 1872), The Brave Old Oak, https://www.Bartleby.comvtrees:flowers:plants

Chapter 4
Sub-chapter v
1. The Author